Carnival

"The de Cats Family," "Uncle Théodore,"
and "The Bear and the Kiss" were translated
for this volume by P. M. Mitchell and W. D. Paden

Carnival

Entertainments and
Posthumous Tales

Isak Dinesen

The University of Chicago Press
Chicago and London

The University of Chicago Press, Chicago 60637
The University of Chicago Press, Ltd., London

Most of these stories first appeared in Danish under the title *Efterladte Fortaellinger*, published by Gyldendal Forlag, © 1975 by Rungstedlundfonden
© 1977 by The University of Chicago
All rights reserved
Published 1977. Printed in
the United States of America

LIBRARY OF CONGRESS CATALOGING IN PUBLICATION DATA

Blixen, Karen, 1885–1962.
  Carnival: entertainments and posthumous tales.

  CONTENTS: The De Cats family.—Uncle Théodore.—Carnival. [etc.]
  I. Title.
PZ3.B62026Car3 [PR6003.L545]   839.8'1'372
ISBN 0–226–15303–7   77–5666

Contents

Foreword

When Karen Blixen died in September 1962, the persons to whom the administration of her literary legacy was transferred decided that, above all, too hasty publication of her remaining stories, finished or unfinished, was to be avoided. Among her papers at Rungstedlund were numerous unpublished manuscripts, but the literary executors had to be satisfied temporarily with cataloging what was found, since they wished to allow a reasonable interval of time between the books that Karen Blixen had brought out herself and the posthumous publication of stories that were felt to belong together in a final volume of narratives designed for a large readership. The remainder of what was in her archives—rough drafts, variations, and the like—could be published in due time in a scholarly edition intended principally for researchers and students of literature.

The short stories in this book either have never been printed or are difficult for the ordinary reader to get hold of. The only criterion for selection has been the demand for quality that one must place upon any volume that is to stand alongside *Last Tales* and *Anecdotes of Destiny.*

"The De Cats Family," with which the collection begins, was originally intended as a comedy in

This foreword is translated and adapted from the Postscript appended to the Danish edition.

—THE PUBLISHER.

two acts, without anything more being written down than the title and a cast of characters. It was first printed as a short story in *Tilskueren* [The spectator] in 1909, and it was reprinted in Gyldendal's Christmas Book for 1962, in a limited edition that largely ended up in the hands of Blixen collectors and friends of the publisher. The fact that Karen Blixen herself considered publishing it in *Anecdotes of Destiny* is even more reason to include it in a final collection, as the only truly original one of those experiments under the general heading of *Sandsynlige Historier* [Likely stories], which she published in the years 1907–9.

"Uncle Théodore," which bears the longer title "Vicomte Vieusac's Uncle Théodore" in a copy in someone else's handwriting but containing Karen Blixen's own corrections, belongs among the juvenilia and was apparently written between 1909 and the author's departure for Africa in 1913. It is here printed for the first time.

"Carnival" is one of Karen Blixen's earliest tales of the fantastic. This too was originally intended to be a puppet comedy. It ended up as a short story, however, and it was Karen Blixen's plan to make it part of a collection of short stories in English, to be called *Nine Tales by Nozdref's Cook*. The number shrank meanwhile to those seven that form the contents of *Seven Gothic Tales*, and "Carnival" was stored away. In her last year of life, while making preparations for a new collection of tales, Karen Blixen asked her secretary to dig out the old manuscript, but she was not able to produce the intended revision. The story, which stems from the late 1920s, is offered here as an interesting supplement to her first master work, even though through the years she borrowed many of its best ideas and themes for other stories of hers, such as "Copenhagen Season."

Several of the stories that Karen Blixen left behind were actually supposed to have been included in various of the collections assembled through the years but were put aside for later use, either because they were not suited to the theme of a particular book or because she didn't feel that they had assumed their final form. This was the case with "The Last Day," which was supposed to have been printed in 1942 in *Winter's Tales*, but which remained lying in a drawer until, the year before her death, she took it out again.

After the publication of *Shadows on the Grass* in 1960, when illness did not stand in the way she worked on a new volume of tales. This was to comprise *Ehrengard* (published posthumously in 1962), another story planned as a sequel to "Copenhagen Season," entitled "Thirty Years Later" but never written down, "The Bear and the Kiss," which was not finished until *Anecdotes of Destiny* was published in 1958, and "Second Meeting," the only one of the many planned Albondocani stories that Karen Blixen succeeded in writing down when she took up the project again after a lapse of several years. The version of "Second Meeting" printed here dates from 1961, and although it is to a certain extent a fragment, it will be for a great many readers the final, moving meeting with Karen Blixen, the story teller.

Lighter in tone than these are the "anecdotes of destiny" she wrote for the *Saturday Evening Post* and the *Ladies' Home Journal.* She herself did not consider it beneath her artistic dignity to write just "for entertainment," and the best of her magazine stories loom large in her life's work.

In December 1949 the *Saturday Evening Post* carried the story about Uncle Seneca under the title "The Uncertain Heiress," but the editor's choice of precisely this story out of the five that had been submitted made Karen Blixen uneasy, so the future anecdotes of destiny were in the coming years offered to the *Ladies' Home Journal.*

At the time of Karen Blixen's death, "Anna," "The Fat Man," and "The Proud Woman" were among the manuscripts in English that had been temporarily laid aside. All three were written with publication in the *Ladies' Home Journal* in mind.

The longest of the stories, "Anna," which had been inspired by Christian Elling's essay "Harlekins Bergamo" in *Breve om Italien,* dates from the early 1950s. With its twenty-three small chapters it can be read as a little novel, even though Karen Blixen never finished it off with the happy ending she had envisaged. Neither was she able to send "The Proud Woman" off to America. As with "Anna," it awaited final revision. "The Fat Man" was written at the same time as "Anna" and appeared for the first time in 1973 in the Christmas number of the magazine *Hjemmet.* The Christmas number of the following year carried the first publication of "The Proud Woman."

Neither *Ehrengard* nor "The Ghost Horses," which exist in generally available individual editions, is included in the present collection, where

Foreword

otherwise they would be completely at home.* In addition, the juvenilia "Eneboerne" [The hermits] and "Pløjeren" [The plowman], published in 1907, as well as the almanac story "Klokkerne" [The bells], published in 1952, have been omitted.

1975

FRANS LASSON

Ehrengard is not included in the present English language edition, but "The Ghost Horses" is, because of its relative inaccessibility in English.—THE PUBLISHER.

The de Cats Family

D ear readers, I should not like to trick you into reading anything which you would later deplore. Here is a story which has no other merit than its excellent moral.

A hundred years ago in Amsterdam there was a family—it may be there yet—which although it was bourgeois, surpassed all others in honesty and righteousness. As this had continued for many years and their great honesty and righteousness seemed to be passed on from father to son, being a member of the de Cats family was equivalent to being a superior person. They held the highest offices in the land, both ecclesiastical and secular, and they did so in accordance with the wishes of the entire populace, for they were known to be not only honest but able—prudent and energetic—and very wealthy.

At the same time there was a misfortune which pursued the de Cats family and which they could never cease to lament, for there was always present among them one member who was as disreputable as the rest were respectable, precisely the sort of person who is called the black sheep of a family, though it was more deplorable and more improbable in this family than in any other. Though all the parents in the family kept this harsh destiny in mind and did all they could to rear their children as true de Cats, they could not circumvent it, for scarcely had a veteran sinner died and they were rid of him and could breathe more easily than it turned out that one of the young members of the family was ready to take up the heritage.

When they reviewed the family history, which they recorded with care and with which all were made familiar, they were forced to observe along with the excellent names of worthy citizens and pious and responsible bishops and mayors and honored wives and mothers, a distressing register of the names of deceased scoundrels. Those who remembered that far back could tell about old Jeremias de Cats who ended as a pirate; Adrian de Cats who, to be sure, was an ornament to the society of Amsterdam but who, it came to be known, had a wife in Utrecht and one in Haarlem in addition to his wife in Amsterdam and two abroad; Cornelius de Cats, who is still mentioned when someone scolds another for miserliness; Petrus, the bishop's son, who could not resist gambling and betting, and played Zeven-Eleffen with Meïr Goldsmet from Lissabon and promised to convert to Judaism if he lost and who, to pay another gambling debt, had in his father's name sold all the stained glass in the Church of Saint Bavo in Haarlem; and Jonas, who in a passion had killed his brother and put out one eye of Admiral Dudok de Wit and so had to flee the country.

While they all did their best, as has been said, to educate their young sons so that similar misfortunes would be avoided, the greatest misfortune hit them where they least expected it, for Amalie de Cats, the loveliest girl in Amsterdam, left town one fine summer morning with her singing teacher and did not return. From that day on they no longer mentioned her name. (She later came into money by marrying a rich slave dealer and lived on Java. When her nephew, the young Petrus de Cats, was being instructed in commerce and went out there on one of his father's ships, she gave a large dinner for him and he scarcely knew how to act on the occasion; he was much embarrassed by the thought of what they would say at home after she had with great pride and emotion drunk a toast to him and the family, just as if there were not and never had been any tension between them, and as a final embarrassment she kissed him.)

When she died they thought they would have peace. Then they grew very anxious, for their most gifted young man, Jeremias, who was studying at The Hague, began to seek bad company and contract debts, and they feared he might follow in her footsteps.

They were not wrong, for the next year he was expelled from the university, and then less than a year passed before he had created so many scandals in Amsterdam that he had to leave the city and the country; and for the next few years they heard with great distress from abroad many bad things about him.

But after matters had gone on in this way for a hundred years, fate seemed to think that they had gone on long enough.

One spring afternoon, while many of the family were gathered in the house of the young Petrus de Cats to celebrate the christening of his first little son, the youngest de Cats of all, and while the ice was melting on the canals and the air hovered over the city like a fine golden fog, in walked Vrouw Emerenze de Cats to consult them.

They were both touched and gladdened by her visit, they offered her the best chair, they offered her chocolate, candied fruits, and honeycake and tried to get the baby to kiss her, but she soon cut short the conversation and said to them, "I have come here to speak with you about something else. I would not have disturbed your happiness today if it were not necessary—though I must admit that to me the news I bring is a joy. My son Jeremias is coming home." They did not know what to say to this, and were silent. At last the old de Cats, Petrus's father, said, "I am glad. I am glad to hear it"; but he was embarrassed. "Thank you," said Vrouw Emerenze. "Still, it was not to force you to show me kindness by saying so that I came here today. I came to ask you a question. You all know that there is in the world a nobility consisting of honest people. By the grace of Heaven we and our relations all belong to it, by birth." (She also had been born a de Cats, being a half-sister to old de Cats and married to her cousin.) "By our blood we have a right to count ourselves among them; we have been called the conscience of the country; let us thank God that it is so. But I know my son has forfeited that right. By his own choice he has withdrawn from among us and no one would think of mentioning his name when speaking of us. I therefore think it fitting for me to ask you—indeed I shall go from one to another and ask you individually—whether you are willing to accept Jeremias in your midst and permit him to return. I bid

you answer honestly and in the way you think you
should answer. If you refuse, I will know it is because you feel justice is thus best served." In reality
it was old Petrus de Cats to whom her words were
addressed, for none of the others would speak here
in his son's house before he had spoken. He was
in no hurry to speak, and while the opinions of the
others as to what he would say had time to shift
back and forth, he sat in silence. They knew that
in his mind he was reviewing Jeremias's entire life,
from the time Jeremias was a neatly combed little
boy who excelled in appearance and intelligence
among the children of the family who came to New
Year's dinner at his house, and through those years
when, on behalf of Jeremias's deceased father, he
gave the youth his first dressings down; to the most
recent years when he knew that every report about
Jeremias would be an omen of misfortune. Old
Petrus de Cats had become more charitable with
the years, and when he finally spoke he said, "Well,
I shall answer according to my feeling. It is simply
yes, we will accept him among us. Let him be welcomed home."

Old Vrouw Emerenze dissolved in tears, for she
knew the value of clemency from a member of her
family and for a moment she could not speak. Old
Petrus de Cats himself was moved. "From none of
us, Emerenze," he said, "will he hear any reference
to the sins of his youth. He belongs among us, and
as a member of the family we will receive him. I
can tell you now, since we are speaking of it: I felt
from time to time that Papa and Mama were too
severe with Amalie." "I know," said Vrouw Emerenze, "that the family has always endeavored to

make justice prevail, but on my son's account I am today in a position from which a mild judgment looks different than it did before. I shall go to my grave filled with gratitude to all of you for this answer." And as this had been a solemn conversation, her brother himself escorted her to her carriage and the others stood silent until the two seniors had passed outside.

No sooner had they left than the young Petrus de Cats said, "That was a mistake." The others were astonished and offended, and turned to him and asked what he meant.

Young Petrus de Cats was in a way their pride, for he was an able businessman and in addition to being well read in philosophy and history, he had studied mathematics and astronomy and even astrology for his own pleasure, and they knew that if he had not been a de Cats he would have been a famous scholar. He had weak eyes and a habit of squinting when he spoke, but to make up for that he had a fine large mouth and smiled frequently.

He said, "It was a mistake for two reasons. The first is that when we speak about justice we should remember that it is equally wrong to decapitate an innocent man and to let a guilty man go free. This is a misstep fate will bring up against us if we ever complain of its injustice. Now, how can we protest when fate ruins honorable men and lets the dishonorable succeed? We should allow justice to be all-powerful," he said; "we will feel the effect of this for twenty years."

"But mercy, my dear Petrus," said his uncle the bishop quite reflectively, "what about mercy?" "And this is the second reason," said Petrus, "—well, Uncle Cornelius, mercy should not set justice aside—one can serve the world in two ways: one can make virtue attractive or vice repulsive. The entire world rests on the principle that virtue is rewarded, but who will believe it if they do not see it? It is for this reason that the country is indebted to us, for we have demonstrated the felicity of virtue. The family has had two reasons to rejoice that we have advanced in the world: virtue has made progress and we also have made progress. But Jeremias—he has given up virtue, so should he make vice repulsive. If he were breaking rocks on the highway or begging in the streets, not even you, Uncle Cornelius, or you, Aunt Carolina, would be a better example for the youth. There would be no one among us whose name would be more frequently mentioned in moral talks to the children. You are destroying for Jeremias, as he is, his only hope of serving the world!" said young Petrus.

This is in a way the end of the first part of the story about the de Cats family.

Now that matters had been settled, Jeremias came back like the prodigal son, and two months later old Emerenze de Cats died and was buried. Jeremias lived in her house; he had little to do with the others, but as they gradually saw more of him they began to like him, and they were of the opinion and said to one another, it was gratifying to see that his reformation was genuine.

It was a year after the death of Vrouw Emerenze de Cats that Petrus de Cats one dead-calm and swelteringly hot day sent a message to his younger brother Coenraad, the most able of the young busi-

nessmen in Amsterdam, asking him to come to him
as soon as he had the opportunity. Coenraad went
to his brother in the evening and as he walked
through the streets he was so deep in thought that
his acquaintances who were also out walking the
streets in the tepid summer dusk greeted him without receiving an answer. He did not know what
his brother Petrus wanted of him and he thought,
"Perhaps it is true, as I have heard, that he is having difficulties with his business and wants me to
help him. We shall see."

When Coenraad had greeted Petrus's wife and
child and the two were alone in the study, Petrus
said, "If what I now shall tell you should surprise
you, please believe me when I say that I have never
been so much in earnest as I am now." Coenraad
thought, "He is very pale, as he always is when he
has worries. It must be serious, whatever is wrong,
and now he is coming to me. But in matters of
business family relationships are not relevant." He
said nothing and continued to sit and to smoke in
silence.

Petrus said, "Ever since I was very young I have
contemplated destiny. Yes, it has been my first and
last object of study; I have observed it everywhere,
in my business, in my studies, in my marriage; at
all junctures its regimen has been most important
to me; even when things went against me, there
has been such a good moral to be drawn that the
last thing has for me balanced the other. I tell you
this in order to ask you to listen to me in silence
until I am through." "Yes, it is easy to put the
blame on destiny," thought Coenraad de Cats.

Petrus said, "A dreadful and strange fate rests
upon us. I do not know if it is a curse, but at the

moment it has turned into a curse. It is a matter of our lives, yes, of more than that.

"We are so much better than other people," said Petrus de Cats, "only because we always have among us one member of the family who takes on the burden of all the family's sins. All the errors that might have been distributed among us all are accumulated in one of us, and by this means the rest of us are freed.

"Nicolaus de Cats bore our sins and once and for all drove untruth out of the family. Petrus bore them and ever since we have been afraid to touch a playing card; Cornelius bore them so that since his time we have given more to the poor than any other family in Holland; Aunt Amalie bore them and now our girls are the most virtuous in the land. But when Jeremias reformed, misfortune really struck us, and if we cannot find a way out, we are done for."

"What do you mean?" asked Coenraad.

"Well, would to God it were only that I am mad," said Petrus, "but that is not the way it is. Our prestige is so great it has not yet occurred to anyone we are slipping. Perhaps it will never occur to anyone, but if that is so then it is the most dreadful aspect of our misfortune, for then there is no limit to the damage we may cause, we who are an example to the entire populace.

"Look about among us," he said to his brother. "Are we still what we were a year and a half ago when Jeremias got the fatal idea to reform and come home?" "Are we not?" said Coenraad.

"It began very soon after Jeremias returned," said Petrus. "One by one we fell; I do not know if there is one among us worthy of bearing the name

9

of de Cats. Look at Uncle Cornelius and recall how all of Amsterdam went home from his church as from an hour of reckoning with Heaven itself. Yesterday in his church he married Prince Moritz morganatically to Antoinette von Waffelbacker. With the power he has, that will be felt in every marriage in Holland. Look at Aunt Carolina, who is a model for all of Holland's wives and mothers—no one can deny that she did the de Smets a great wrong in order to benefit her own children. Consider how Uncle Jonas dropped his wife's impoverished family. Consider Uncle Klaaes, who suppressed his book on the Trinity when the church council's statement on heresy appeared.

"Yes, and I have only mentioned the things that everyone knows," said Petrus. "I have not mentioned a single one of the rumors that are going around. Otherwise I would have had to speak about what circumstance now forces me to mention and which we must pray to Heaven is not true, that Nicolaus has a mistress in Prinsengracht. I should also have alluded to what the entire town is talking about—that Wilhelmina, the young wife of the mayor, has a lover. If you do not believe that is true, then consider our own sister Emerenze, our pride, who has sold herself to the biggest idiot in Holland for a distinguished name—did our girls do that before? There is not one of us who is any longer what he was; not I myself, who am sitting here and talking to you about it, when I should be grieving and tearing the hair from my head—for I must tell you how things are with me: I have felt a kind of satisfaction that we are no better than other people, yes, with each misfortune, a kind of satisfaction that can scarcely be borne."

And when Petrus had made this confession he was quiet for a moment, greatly moved, and Coenraad, who had listened with ever-increasing attention, first blushed deeply and then like a heroine of a novel grew white as a sheet.

When Petrus spoke again he said, "Answer me honestly, are you the same as you were when Jeremias came home?"

Hardly had he said this before Coenraad rose and struck him in the face so that he tumbled backwards, and filled with anger and consternation they stared for a moment at one another. Finally Coenraad said, "Yes, I might have known it. You have not given up the old habits of our childhood, you think you are my judge. But I do not want you meddling in my affairs, you who do not understand business, who all your life have been discontented because you have had to be a merchant and could not study the stars." While he was speaking he felt he was completely in the wrong, and by making a tremendous effort he fell silent, turned about, and went to the window. He looked out in violent agitation, like a person who is unaccustomed to being angry and has no idea what he should do to regain his equilibrium. Petrus said in the middle of the deep and painful silence, "Now the last link in my chain is forged, indeed."

"Oh, my God," said Coenraad suddenly, quite in despair. "It is not to be borne. Since you know about it, let us talk straight from the shoulder. I am being driven mad by the desire to make money; I think of it day and night. What must I do to be free? I cannot escape it, it is far too deeply engrained. Then I think that there is nothing dishonorable in what I have done—can I help it if

Beeverson & Zoon are conducting themselves like lunatics? But I know perfectly well, I know myself, it is not true; in the end I will commit some crime. When I think of what I was and what I am now, I believe I shall go mad." He was silent for a long time and then he said, "Is there any use in talking about it?"

"How could we help ourselves before we knew what the trouble was?" said Petrus.

"Help ourselves?" said Coenraad. "What can we do?" Petrus looked at him, went over to the window and came back and said, "Do you not see that our troubles began when Jeremias reformed and came home? Why can we not get him to revert to what he was before?"

The two brothers looked at each other and were silent for a long time. "Well," said Petrus, "you are thinking that this is something one does not like to do. Perhaps you think it is a crime, but that is not the case. If we prize our own virtue higher than his, can we be reproached for it? To all honorable people their virtue is the thing of the greatest importance. Indeed, all the sacrifices they make, they make only to preserve and strengthen their virtue; that is the reason they are happy to make them. For what we do now, the whole family will thank us in the future." "I was not thinking of that," said Coenraad, "but how will you do it?" "He came home when he had no more money," said Petrus. "Let him grow rich again." "Well, that should not be difficult," said Coenraad. "No one knows yet how much Aunt Emerenze left. Jeremias himself does not know. It should not be difficult to deceive

him. How much will you give?" Without thinking
more than a minute Petrus said, "Fifty thousand
guilders." "And I the same," said Coenraad, and
from this one may see that, although the family
was reputed to be rather careful about its money,
it was of no consequence when honor was at stake.

Some time later Coenraad came to see his brother
again, and was now just as pale as he, and just as
careworn.

"It is not working," he said. "He has taken our
money and all he has done with it is to hire a
French cook and buy a collection of flower bulbs.
And today I heard that young Alexander de Cats
has become engaged to a rich widow of sixty. What
can we do now?" "I can tell you," said Petrus.
"Today I received a letter from Moritz Cannegieter,
and fate is with us, for he spoke of Jeremias in the
letter. He says the person whom Jeremias seems to
have liked best was a Dutch girl named Jacobina,
who was then an actress playing at country fairs.
By chance Moritz has met her again; she is now in
a little town called Saint-Amour, not far from the
Jura Mountains." "Good Lord," said Coenraad, for
Jeremias was after all a de Cats. "We must seek
her out," said Petrus. "Will you do it?" asked Coenraad. "I?" said Petrus, shocked, as if he were exor-
cising the devil with the word. "No. A man with a
wife and a child? No, you must do it, you are still
a bachelor." "All right, of course I can do it," said
Coenraad, when he had reflected a moment. "One
can do anything when it is necessary." Petrus gave
him detailed information about the place, the girl's
name and her appearance, and they parted.

A week later Coenraad told his father and his friends he had to take a business trip into France, but said nothing about the nature of his business. He had never set out on a journey in such uneasiness and with so heavy a heart, but he was a de Cats and forced himself to do what he had planned and indeed to do it right away. When the stagecoach brought him to Saint-Amour on a foggy and moonlit September evening, he changed his clothes and called on Jacobina at once. It must have been a conversation which would be worth hearing, and it took much longer than should have been required, for it was difficult for each of them to understand the other. At the beginning Jacobina's face unsettled Coenraad, for her brown eyes were clearer than wellwater and quite calm, like an infinite depth of innocence, her eyebrows were blackened with charcoal, and her skin was as white as milk. After they had talked for some time he discovered that she and Jeremias had parted in hostility and that this could have been the cause of Jeremias's reformation; in this he felt a sudden satisfaction, as if he had sensed a good piece of business. When he realized she could not guess his motives, he became bolder and suggested unambiguously and in quite a businesslike manner that if she would return to Amsterdam he would arrange to rent a house for her; and he asked her to come as soon as she could.

Though Jacobina was accustomed to dealing with all sorts of people, she could not at first understand what he wanted of her, and she came to the conclusion that Jeremias had come into money and had sent Coenraad to her, and she found it strange

he should send such an ambassador. When she
noticed that Coenraad was very anxious to have
her come to Amsterdam, she immediately sensed
a good bit of business and was inspired to demand
a house on the corner of Heerengracht, a horse and
carriage, and a Negro servant to attend her. Coenraad agreed at once, for with her he had no idea
how to bargain and he was happy to bring the
conversation to a close. She suggested they travel
together as far as the Dutch border, the first place
where he might meet friends, and Coenraad's blood
seemed to freeze at the thought, but he answered
her politely, for the de Cats were polite to everyone, everywhere; he traveled home alone, happy
that he had got off so cheaply and that everything
was now in order.

So Jacobina came to Amsterdam and settled
down on Petrus's and Coenraad's money. She led a
merry life and was much talked about, and it was
an unpleasant time for Coenraad, for his daily path
went by her house and two or three times he met
her in Kalverstraat in her carriage with her black
servant perched up behind. But she did not visit
Jeremias, and his longing for her was not strong
enough to draw him to her house.

As a consequence Coenraad and Petrus met again
to discuss their heavy fate. "Nothing will come of
it, as it is," said Petrus to Coenraad. "You must
talk with her again." "All right, on the condition,"
said Coenraad, "that it is the last time. Why must I
always be the one to talk with her? My reputation
will be ruined. It is dreadful what bad luck we
have had in the matter, and God alone knows
whether she may not think I brought her here for

my own pleasure." "Yes, it is probably of no use," said Petrus. "Have you not heard that the mayor has applied for a divorce from Wilhelmina?" "No," said Coenraad. "That is the way it is," said Petrus.

With a heavy heart Coenraad went to see Jacobina.

It was a December afternoon, one of the first snowy days, and a thin scurf of snow lay on the streets and the roofs of the houses, on the decks of the boats and the barges; in the leafless trees along the canals black crows sat quite still and thoughtful and the sky was a brownish gray, like peat smoke. Far in the west there was already a broad strip of sky colored like a lemon or very old ivory.

Jacobina sat looking out of a window. Incense was burning on the porcelain-tile stove, and she had been reading from time to time in a devotional work; she received him kindly.

"Well, it is an honor," she said, "that Mynheer de Cats comes here. Sit down. Should I send for some Malvasier, or Muscatel?" No matter how intensely Coenraad was concerned with his own affairs, Jacobina's presence seized him and made him feel ill at ease, as if he could see himself with the eyes of others, which was something that otherwise did not happen in the de Cats family. "No, thank you, neither one," he said. "I have come to discuss business." "Very well," said Jacobina and folded her hands in her lap. "Well," said Coenraad, "things cannot go on as they are." "Oh," she said. "When I talked with you in Saint-Amour," said Coenraad, "perhaps I did not explain fully why I asked you to come here, but I thought you understood." "Yes,

I am sure of that," she said. Coenraad looked quickly at her: she now sat with her chin supported by one hand and looked directly at him. "Well, I shall not beat about the bush," he said. "It was for the sake of my cousin Jeremias de Cats that I brought you here and you must make peace with him."

Now it happened that Jacobina was at this time interested in Coenraad de Cats because she had never in her life met a man like him. So she said, after she had thought a moment, "I will not do that unless I know why you wish it." Here was a new difficulty which Coenraad had not foreseen. He thought his problems would multiply forever. "I cannot tell you that," he said. "That does not make any difference." "Does not make any difference?" said Jacobina. "Then it does not make any difference whether I do it or not. I will not do it until I have seen to the bottom of this affair, and that is the truth." Coenraad was so little accustomed to lying that it was completely impossible for him to deceive her. Well, he thought, perhaps it is possible to talk reason with her. "Well, listen, Juffrouw Jacobina," he said, and then he told her the whole story from beginning to end. He did it in despair; he would never have done it if he had not been desperate, that is to say, sunk as far as he could go, and he thought while he spoke: This is something she cannot understand. When he had finished he saw he had been right.

"I have never in all my born days heard the like," she said. "What impudence! Do you think I am so stupid I will believe that? Why, my friend, I can see through the whole affair. There is some old woman in the family who is about to die and Jeremias is to be her heir. So you have concocted a scheme to get poor Jeremias into trouble so she will quarrel with him and disinherit him. That is a pretty picture! and you have tricked me into being a decoy.

"You are a de Cats, you should be ashamed of yourself!" (Jacobina had been born in Amsterdam and knew what the de Cats family was). "Now I shall not mince words, Coenraad de Cats. I liked you because you seemed a true de Cats, and I would rather have had you than Jeremias, but you can be sure that will come to nothing, now. This very hour I shall go to Jeremias and tell him what kind of a family he has. You have given me a horse and carriage to do it in." "For God's sake," said Coenraad, "do not do that." "Oh yes, that is exactly what I shall do," she said, "How can you prevent me? Would you use force?" "You must absolutely not do it!" said Coenraad, with an air of complete authority (though in his heart he was panic-stricken and cursed his fate). "I will tell you why I shall do it," she said. "If you had come to me honestly and told me about it and asked me to help you, I would have done it. But you had me making a fool of myself for three months and you still want to hide the truth from me: How can one treat you like an honorable man?" "I will give you five hundred guilders not to do it," said Coenraad. "Well! So you think you can get away with that!" she said. "What do you think your family will say? Your uncle the bishop and old Joseph de Cats? What's more, I would not think of not doing it for five hundred." "Oh, then, a thousand," said Coenraad, beside himself. "Yes, for a thousand I will not do it," she said. "Give me your word—promise me not to mention my name to Jeremias," said Coenraad. "Very well," she said, "Do you swear it?" he said. "Yes, I swear it," said Jacobina.

Quite in despair Coenraad and Petrus met for a last time; they sat and smoked their pipes in hopeless silence. Finally Coenraad said:

"100,000 guilders we gave Jeremias; my trip (which God knows was unpleasant enough) cost me

500; we have given her

20,000, and

1,000 to be quiet. That is,

121,500 guilders we have paid out and we are no further along than when we began." "There is a worse piece of news," said Petrus. "Aunt Carolina tells me that Dina wants to marry Jeremias. If she does, that is the end of us." (Dina was one of the most promising girls in the family.) "Good God," said Coenraad, "is it true?" He put his hands to his forehead and said, "It is as if everything had turned upside down in the whole world. Never in my life have I been so unhappy."

"Very well," he said after a pause, like a true de Cats, "what shall we do now?" "We can do nothing more," said Petrus. "We have done what we could and it has not helped. Now we must try the last expedient, for we stand on the verge of destruction: we must call a family council."

So they did; they called a family council in Petrus's house on the last evening of the year 1771. No one was admitted except those born de Cats and twenty years of age or older, and it was a lovely sight when they were gathered together and Petrus's brass candlesticks diffused a peaceful light and deep brown shadows over the distinguished white heads with pink cheeks full of vitality and black and heavy eyebrows; starched white caps with fluted ribbons; young dark and blond heads and a single bald pate which shone as if polished. It was a lovely sight when they had all taken their places and quiet and expectation had fallen over the gathering; each was a distinguished type, yet marked as an independent person, completely himself and nothing else, and fitting under no category in the world except, precisely, that of the de Cats family.

A pale Petrus stepped up to his inlaid walnut table, propounded his theory and demonstrated it with the aid of family papers which he had lying before him in a heap, and his audience searched their hearts; he invoked their consciences, which responded so unexpectedly and powerfully that the silent voices horrified each and all. They grew very pale; first one and then another rose and sat down again, but Petrus was not refuted by any of them. They sat as shaken as they could possibly be, the young among them horrified, the old profoundly depressed. If someone had come and told them they had lost their entire fortune, they would have accepted the news with dignity and composure, but when they thought they were no better than other people, it was more than they could bear.

Petrus let Coenraad take up where he had left off and report on his own efforts. Coenraad spoke seriously and with some embarrassment but quite truthfully, for least of all could he lie to his family. When he finished there was a long and dreadful silence which seemed extremely profound, yes unfathomable, because so many were participants and because to all of them it seemed the most horrible experience they had ever had.

Then the bishop of Haarlem arose and drew all their eyes to him. He stroked his white shirtfrill with his fingers, cleared his throat and spoke as follows.

"Yes," he said, "we are horrified at what we have learned, and it is truly horrible. But let us not be confused. We are faced with a new, unperceived, and terrible jeopardy. Very well, we do not know how we may be saved from this jeopardy, but we know we have been saved before. By the help of what? By the help of reason and justice and faith that the course of the world is reasonable and just. Whatever happens is good.

"There are two things I wish to say to you. The first is this: Are we able to envisage the world without sin? No. For how could we who strive for the good prosper in such a world, what could our business be there? How would mercy, forgiveness, yes, even justice, the highest virtues, operate in such a world? Virtue itself is defined by sin. We cannot think of abolishing that principle.

"The second is this, that destiny—life—demands a sacrifice from us today. Yes. Yes, we should ask what it means to sacrifice and to be sacrificed. Is the law harsh? When it is necessary it is not harsh; the laws of the world are just, they are not harsh, only weakness calls them that. Let us ask: What is it that demands our sacrifice? The good, virtue. Is that law harsh which demands sacrifices for the good? On the contrary, the best of us strive to offer up our lives for virtue. Yes, my friends, when we examine it, it is a beautiful and exalted lot to be found worthy to save others through sacrifice. One individual bears the sins of many; their guilt is collected in him; so that they may be exculpated, so that they may live, he is condemned. From the sacrifice of one man proceeds the salvation of many, yes, of an entire people. Let us not be confused. Let us not speak of misfortune or cruelty, it is a bounty and a boon which has been proffered us. Let us act accordingly."

Following the bishop of Haarlem, old Vrouw Carolina Ploos van Amstel spoke. She stood at the end of the table, as erect as a candle, with her strong and restless hands for once at rest, one on the other.

"Yes," she also said, "I will not be silent when I see that we de Cats can be in doubt about our duty. We must speak and we must act, and not in weakness but with strength. When I see the de Cats waver, I know there is a need for forceful speech from an honorable person; I am such a person and therefore I stand here.

"We de Cats are independent people, we will not allow Frenchmen to rule us, we will not allow the nobility to rule the bourgeois or the rich the poor. But there is one thing that has remained constant during my life and which must continue: the best men must rule. We do not desire the privileges of a nobility, but those privileges have been entrusted

to us. We have also been entrusted with the judgment of Jeremias. I pity him; I thank Heaven his
mother is not here today. But if she were here she
would stand up as I have done and remind you of
your duty."

After that a young, beautiful, and pale girl arose
to speak; it was Dina de Cats. A ripple went
through the gathering, for they remembered the
rumor about her and Jeremias and were afraid.
But Dina was a true de Cats; she said, "You know
that Jeremias has asked for my hand. I am standing here to say that after what I have heard this
evening, I want to see no more of him. I do not
wish to contribute to the ruin of the foundation of
my life since my childhood. I will not betray my
father and my mother, I will not betray my family
which has stood firm for a century; as they have
lived I will live. For Jeremias I could sacrifice my
own happiness, yes, but not even for his sake will
I lower myself to the level of the people I look
down on. It is all over."

After Dina de Cats had spoken and sat down,
there was another deep silence in the family gathering. Now that they had answered the question
about what should be done, they did not really
know what they should do next.

They were so unfamiliar with any sort of vice
that they could not suggest any way to seduce
Jeremias; not one of them had an idea to propose.
Not one of them could imagine the next word to
be spoken in the matter. It was a situation in
which the de Cats family had never been before;
they were as inexperienced as children, and as de-

fenseless, and in the course of a few minutes a feeling of dread overtook them all and they felt that they were lost.

They were sitting in the room where a year before they had joyously and happily celebrated little Coenraad de Cats's christening; then the same door opened through which old Vrouw Emerenze had entered to lay the basis for all their misfortune, and her son Jeremias came in and greeted the gathering deferentially.

They all grew quiet. It was as if a mighty blow had struck each one of them, separately, and nevertheless they felt it a relief that fate had taken the matter in hand, though they trembled at the thought.

"Well, if this is a family council," said Jeremias, "it may concern me. Yes, not to waste words," he said, since no one answered (for what could they say?), "I know it concerns me. Jacobina has told me about it. She drove over at once when she had spoken with you," he said to Coenraad, "and told me everything you had told her, because she believed there was something hidden behind it all, but that was because she does not know you. I who know you, I who (so to speak) am one of you, understood at once that there was nothing hidden behind it: you simply meant it. I have meditated upon it ever since. I have come here, not to disturb your council but (with your permission) to take part in it."

"Very well, sit down," said Petrus and offered him a chair.

Jeremias sat down and so became one of them, by virtue of his birth a member of their eminent family gathering and, it seemed, one of the leaders.

"Will you be so kind as to tell me," said Jeremias and looked from one to another, "whether anything was decided before I came in?" None of them answered him; it was completely impossible. As he was a de Cats he could read the answer in their faces, though to everyone outside the family they would be closed books.

"Very well, then, I will advance a suggestion of my own," said Jeremias. "I should like to make an agreement with you which would be satisfactory to both parties. We do not need to go into explanations, for we are all as familiar with the matter as anyone can be.

"For my part, I will promise to leave Amsterdam with Jacobina next week, as she and I have decided today." He looked quickly at Coenraad to indicate that his efforts had not been wasted. "And I will engage during the rest of my life not to come home, not to do anything useful, not to seek acquaintance with respectable people, not to marry, not to save money or to expend it for the benefit of the honest poor, but to spend it in what is called bad company.

"In return, for the rest of my life you will give me"—he thought for a moment—"a salary of fifty thousand guilders a year. I shall not ask for less, for the virtue of all the de Cats family is being purchased; and I do not want any more, either. That is enough.

"Do you wish time to reflect on my suggestion?" said Jeremias. "You can yourselves decide when we will draw up the contract."

When Jeremias had spoken, a great stir went through the de Cats family gathering. It was as if a miracle from heaven (which they did not understand) had saved them when their misfortune was greatest, and as a consequence they felt a profound gratitude to heaven. They almost felt grateful toward heaven's instrument, Jeremias, although it was clear to them that he was demanding a great deal (for all the de Cats understood money). But they could not suppose that Jeremias, as a de Cats, would be modest in his demands, and they gave him what he asked out of ingenuous hearts and willingly.

The greatest difficulty for them was to know how they should respond, and so they were silent a long time after their decision had been taken. It is only just to point out the greatness of the de Cats family, in that they honestly and seriously affirmed their decision even though they did not yet know how it would be carried out. Without looking at one another they were aware through the deep but strong de Cats intuition that they were of one mind. "Very well," said the bishop of Haarlem in a changed voice, "we accept."

"Very well," said Jeremias, "then it is decided. And I am convinced, Uncle Cornelius, that an agreement between two parties within the family will never be broken. I only hope that a young de Cats will grow up among you who in the course of time can succeed me." Involuntarily all of them looked at Jeremias; those who had children thought of them with dread and vowed in their hearts that the successor would not be found among them. The parents' minds withdrew in terror from a man who could speak in such a fashion. For them, one of the strangest aspects of this strange affair was that they owed gratitude to a man whom they could scarcely understand.

Jeremias said to young Petrus, "I am sorry you had such difficulty with this matter. But it was your own fault. You should have come to me at once; we could have talked together and arranged this six months ago, and the family would have been spared many anxieties."

Then he spoke to the whole family council at once, and said, "How wisely and oddly life is arranged, better than I could have imagined it. How pleasant it is that we all of us end in being happy; you have the heavenly satisfaction of being superior human beings, while I who will lack that pleasure will have others in recompense. With all my heart I wish you a happy New Year and hope that your virtue may constantly increase. Good-bye, Aunt Carolina, good-bye, Uncle Cornelius, good-bye Coenraad, Jacobina asked to be remembered to you. I am very pleased that we part in such a fashion that we can all think of one another kindly."

And at this Jeremias de Cats left the room and the story, and those who had conquered fell upon one another's necks.

It is certain that this affair cost the family many sleepless nights. But like all sleepless nights in the de Cats family, these had borne fruit. Amsterdam soon heard that the lovely Emerenze de Cats had broken her engagement, and Alexander his with the rich old widow; in the greatest fright and contrition the mayor's wife sent her lover away. Professor Klaaes de Cats intrepidly published his work on the Trinity. Bishop Cornelius de Cats said in the pulpit that the moral laxity which was spreading throughout Amsterdam was equally reprehensible no matter in whom it was found. Old Petrus de

Cats gave twenty thousand guilders to the new
orphan asylum and young Coenraad de Cats was
soon considered the most serious young man in the
city. And after a while, as time passed, the family
were able to recall with composure the great crisis
they had survived; indeed Vrouw Carolina Ploos
van Amstel discovered a sustaining solace. "Perhaps," she thought, "Jeremias is so true a de Cats
that he derives pleasure from benefiting the world
and the family."

Thus the de Cats family, which had played the
role before, was again the conscience of the land,
as it may perhaps still be today.

Uncle Théodore

One day in May when the chestnuts were in bloom, the old vicomte de Vieusac was walking quite slowly down the Champs Elysées.

In the middle distance stood the Arc de Triomphe, as always in a blue haze; cars and lorries rushed past him in both directions like swallows on a summer day, and as if the vicomte were an old swallow who followed his lonely path among them without being part of the flock. The vicomte de Vieusac meditated upon the strange trick of fate: he who had been so young was now old. "Paris, Paris," he thought, "you saw me young and vigorous rise like a kite intoxicated by you and by my youth; it is only reasonable that you should also observe the sorrow of my old age, and that I should expend my life in your arms. But I do not wish it. I have given you the best of myself: the young handsome vicomte de Vieusac whom women found so captivating. If you are to keep him in your great heart, I should go away. O Paris, for the sake of the young vicomte de Vieusac who was my life I shall leave your boulevards and the Seine and the Abbey. And the Parisiennes. May God be with you, and with me."

A short time later, in the provinces, the vicomte de Vieusac quietly married a very able cook. The next year he stood one day with a little vicomte de Vieusac in his arms and a slightly troubled mind, for this he really had not foreseen. The old vicomte was something of a philosopher. He thought as he admired the child, "My son, if you understood life perhaps you would not thank me for begetting you." Nevertheless he was not without reason proud of having a son. A few months later he grew ill, and one summer evening he left this world to join his forefathers—and suffered several surprises.

Little Jacques was sent to the best schools in France and abroad, like a little postage stamp, forwarded from place to place and receiving all the mandatory postmarks. On the day when he turned sixteen his mother had a serious conversation with him.

"Jacques, my dear," she said, "I love you more than anything in this world, and now you must learn what I expect you to do in return.

"Your father married me for love and I married him from ambition. From the time I was an apprentice I had prayed to God that I might get to sit among those who eat the food. It was a great disappointment. I am too plebeian, too small and fat and pink-cheeked; I cannot make conversation. He who has drawn me for a dinner partner, alas, might as well leave the table. But now my ambitions will finally be satisfied, for, thank God, you do not resemble me in the least. You are a genuine Vieusac —though nevertheless my flesh and blood; yes, in a way, myself. Now learn how we are to live.

"I shall buy a small house in Chantilly and there I shall live quietly with my faithful Victorine, call myself simply Madame Vieusac, and rejoice in being able to think about you. But you, Jacques my dear, shall go to Paris. Though your father's financial affairs were in a sad state when we married, I have saved money: you have some capital, you can live in Paris several years—and you must take a rich wife. Go to Paris, my child, go to the theaters, to the races, become a member of their clubs, take care to have the best horses and automobiles, yes, in every way the best, and send me the newspapers which mention your name. Be happy, Jacques my dear, comport yourself like a genuine nobleman, a nobleman out of the storybooks, and above all else do not bring me into your life: remember your mother's first and final request and do not give me the sorrow of destroying my son's honor. You must keep my photograph in a drawer."

The young vicomte de Vieusac went to Paris at the age of seventeen, with dark eyes and long straight legs, and muscles and teeth and appetite like a young beast of prey. The air of Paris, the wine, the food, the ambiance, the women's glances, gaits, and fragrance intoxicated him at once like a bottle of Moët & Chandon, and in this state of intoxication he remained for two and a half years. Then his head began to clear. When he was twenty-two, he said to himself, "Jacques, you must now make a good match. For otherwise your reputation will go down-hill, or with the best of intentions you will not be able to do anything more than keep it up where it is. People have become accustomed to you. Your friends' faces no longer light up when they see you; workmen in the street no longer smile; women—women, Jacques, will still love you, until your death, but you will seduce no more who will surrender to you because of the pride that fills them and tempts them to cry out to the whole world and even to their husbands, 'It is Vieusac, Jacques de Vieusac who loves me and whom I love.' " Jacques had no desire to marry, but he knew it was useless to controvert fate. He decided to make the best of the matter, and when he began to look about for a wife, since he was an enthusiastic adherent of truth and sincerity, he went to Scheveningen.

There on the broad white sands, where gowns from Redfern and Worth and Paquin went about like small white, rose, and violet motes between an endless blue heaven and an endless blue sea, he spoke—to the accompaniment of booming waves of the Atlantic Ocean—with many beautiful women of all three tints, and steadily deliberated. Finally one stumbles upon one's fate, and finally Jacques met Suzanne Boyer.

She put her head through a wave next to him and, sparkling with saltwater in the sun, wondered whether the water was safe, and whether there was any water in her curls, and frank and uninhibited, when the wave ran back into the sea she stood alone in front of him in the shallow water on her own two feet, with heels as pink as seashells.

Though Jacques loved to love, he had never before known feelings or horses that he could not control. He realized that something within him was taking the bit in its teeth and racing off; he silently commended himself to God. He inquired about her at the hotel, and was told she was the daughter of a wealthy chocolate manufacturer, and was traveling with an aunt who was very ill and lay abed. Further, that she was from Bordeaux, and Jacques was reminded of the song about "une délicieuse Bordelaise, une jambe dont on meurt d'aise." That evening after he had gone to bed he thought, it is true that love sweetens everything, even marriage.

The program for an engagement between two independent young people was now followed, and by
promenading both on horseback and on foot, by
sincerity, and by jealousy—Jacques was also presented to Suzanne's aunt, who could scarcely speak
—and by the intolerable operetta waltzes among the
palms, they worked themselves straightforwardly
toward an evening between ten and eleven when
Jacques stood on the terrace in evening dress and
said to her, "You know I love you. Will you marry
me?" Suzanne looked him straight in the eye; she
thought, "Oh, how lovely." She was so much in
love, her dress was so beautiful, and he was a
vicomte. A minute later they kissed, which was also
in the program. The rest of it they omitted.

When they parted for the night, Suzanne asked
Jacques shyly whether he could not rent a gig the
next day so that they could drive out together; she
had something to tell him. She would not say what
it was, and so Jacques did not know whether it was
the secret of a girl's heart or something frightening:
he did not like it.

Both of them got up early and at half past nine
they were far away in the dunes, where they
alighted and let the horse graze beside a windmill.
Tiny wild pansies grew there in the dry grass. The
sky was vast and the unfettered winds drove white
clouds over it. Suzanne sat in the grass in a black
and white costume with a red toque.

"Dearly beloved Jacques," she said, "I am not
really the daughter of a rich merchant from Bordeaux and my name is not Boyer; my name is Suzon
Pilou. To tell the truth, I do not believe I am much

more respectable than you are, and I am a woman and not a vicomte. I am not worthy of you." Jacques de Vieusac had had his suspicions; he sat very pale, looked out over the ocean and said, "Go on, let me hear about it."

"When I was fifteen," she said, "I sold flowers in front of the hotels in Nice, and in particular I sold small bouquets of orange blossoms to bridal couples on their honeymoons. Baron Salla saw me there one day and said I had possibilities. So he removed me from the business and defrayed the expenses of my education for three years. I can do many things, vicomte de Vieusac." "Go on," said Jacques, who was suffering a good deal. "Well, just think," said Suzon, "at this time he began to speculate in copper stocks, and when he heard he had lost his fortune, he had an apoplectic stroke and could no longer move. You see, Jacques, I have no reason to reproach myself. When he could speak a little he sent for me; I stood and wept when I saw him. 'My dear child,' he said in a weak voice, 'you see I can do nothing at all for you. Nevertheless, I have no apprehensions for you, Suzon. You will always be able to make your way in the world. But I have been lying here and thinking of many things; one never knows, and perhaps it would be best if you married. I still have fifty thousand francs which I put aside in order to fit you out. Take them, see that you assemble a good wardrobe, and set out. I have thought of several places, and I believe that Scheveningen will be the best. You can take the wife of the porter along as a chaperone; she has dignity but you must keep her in the background; in any case, don't let her speak. There are honorable young men in the world; perhaps you may marry. And if you cannot do that and it is not God's will, Suzon, then go to Paris. I shall give you Madame Liane's address near the Theâtre Bouffe.' When he said this I kissed him and went away." Suzon sat silent for a moment, and during the pause she heard Jacques sigh deeply. "You see, Jacques," she said, "the intention was that I should marry, but you must decide. Reflect upon the situation, my boy."

Jacques de Vieusac pushed his hat back from his perspiring forehead, offered her a cigarette, and lighted one himself, and they sat for three-quarters of an hour without speaking. Finally Jacques said, "No, I am a vicomte de Vieusac. I love you, Suzon, will you marry me?" "Oh yes," she said, and crept close to him and they sat pressed to one another. "But, Suzon," said Jacques, "I do not have any money either. What shall we live on?" "You will see, it will work out," said Suzon. "Yes, perhaps it will work out," said Jacques and took off his hat, "but we must invent—" Jacques thought a long time. Driven to a tense and energetic search, he came in his memories upon a conversation between old Madame de Vieusac and Victorine which he had heard one Sunday morning as a little boy. "Uncle Théodore—" he said, "we must invent Uncle Théodore."

"Who?" said Suzon. Jacques said, "My mother's brother, Uncle Théodore. It is of no use on my father's side of the family. My mother had one brother who while she was still unmarried emigrated to America as a cook. There he took over a biscuit company. He could have earned a great deal of money by that." "Yes, he probably could," said Suzon. "He could have earned twenty million—" said Jacques, "dollars. That's a hundred million francs. He could have married an immigrant French girl who was alone in the world and she could have died. So that I am his heir." "You are his heir, heir to a hundred million francs, my Jacques," she said. "Yes. I think I have his picture in a group photograph," he said, "it will be best that you look at it." "Yes. Madame Humbert," said Suzon, "also expected to inherit from an uncle in America." "Having an uncle in America," said Jacques thoughtfully —for he had inherited from his father a tendency to philosophy—"is in reality nothing one should be rewarded for." "With twenty million dollars," said Suzon. "It could very well happen that Uncle Théodore has grown rich," said Jacques; "if it did not turn out that way I do not know whose fault it was, but it was not mine." "I love you," said Suzon. Jacques put his hat on again. "Seriously, I think," he said, "that what mankind needs most is not money. I think it needs most to see something very beautiful." "Yes, such as the way we shall live, Jacques," said she. "Yes," said Jacques.

A few months later the vicomte de Vieusac's marriage took place in Paris. The old vicomte had been the last of his family; people knew he had married beneath him and thought his widow was dead and therefore no one wondered that so few of the bridegroom's family were present. On the other hand, all the best society of Paris, which was much taken with him, came to his wedding. The parents of the bride were also dead; her aunt wore a magnificent dress of black and silver. Baron Salla,

an old friend of the family, though scarcely able
to stand on his feet, was visibly happy to give the
bride away, and the lovely young bride introduced
the jupe-culotte as a bridal gown, under a tremendous train of white brocade decorated with small
bouquets of orange blossoms. In the church Jacques
thought of his mother. He was in a rather serious
mood, and pale.

On their wedding trip there was only one moment when Jacques thought of his Uncle Théodore;
involuntarily he took Suzon's hand. Afterwards
they went home to a little townhouse in the avenue
du Bois, where they lived indescribably happily.
They had a car and a box at the opera and some of
the most beautiful horses on the promenade Aca-
cia, and Suzon's dresses were famous. Their little
circle, like two or three others, considered itself to
be absolutely the best in Paris. And many people
knew they were to inherit from Uncle Théodore.
Jacques put on a little weight with this life; he was
no longer in love with Suzon, but she had become
indispensable to him. Suzon kept herself slender
and supple as the blade of a sword, and was never
tired. Thus a year or two passed, and Jacques con-
scientiously sent newspaper clippings to Chantilly.
There were incredibly many of them.

One summer day Vieusac and his wife sat on a
balcony from which there was a broad view over
Cauteretz and the French Pyrenees. Actually, it was
no fashionable hotel, rather a place where one went
for the treatment of arthritis—but they had been
so fashionable for years that they felt a need to
loosen their spiritual corsets. It was very warm,
and from their balcony, which was in the shade,

they enjoyed watching people and animals walking around in the sun on the white streets, and they drank tea—for they had been well brought up, not by individuals but by good society as a whole—and Suzon also ate a little orange marmalade. Though it was more agreeable not to think of anything, they now had to do so, and they were deliberating together.

The vicomte de Vieusac said, "It cannot go on very much longer." When Suzon did not reply, he continued after a while, "They are beginning to doubt. Everyone doubts, these days. They have doubts about Uncle Théodore." "Not yet," said Suzon. "Even you say not *yet*," said Jacques, "which means they will begin to doubt in time." "Yes, of course they will," said Suzon, "if they are not absolute idiots. He does not exist." "Yes, and then we will be through," said Jacques. "Through," she said. "And they have begun to doubt now," said Jacques.

Suzon sat for a while and looked far into the distance while she licked the spoon. "I think you have got Uncle Théodore on the brain," she said quite meekly. "What did you say?" said Jacques. "I think you have Uncle Théodore on the brain," said Suzon. Jacques was so indignant he almost said something, but it was warm, and of what use was it to scold his wife? He started to drink his tea. "And he was so good, Uncle Théodore," said Suzon after a pause, "he was such a good idea. Nevertheless—then we will be through."

Jacques's head really ached because of Uncle Théodore. Almost the worst part of it was, he could not comprehend the situation. He was facing their ruin as a modern man faces death: he had not the slightest idea what would happen. And Suzon, who usually helped him out of difficulties, did not really take death seriously, or even their ruin; he had a feeling that the first thing he should do was to convince her of it, which he knew to be impossible.

At that moment there was a knock on the door of their salon and when they called, "Come in!" the hotel manager, Aristide, came in.

This manager was to be pitied, for he could see himself that his hotel was not first class, and he found it repugnant to think of it as second class. He had to work for people whom he despised; that he had to work for them was the reason he had to despise them.

"Your Grace, Monsieur le Vicomte," he said, and bowed deeply, "if you will deign to perform it, you can do me a great service. I have received a letter today which is quite illegible. If Monsieur le Vicomte would deign—" "And what makes you think I will be able to read it for you?" said Jacques, who had become alert. "Oh," said the manager, "because Monsieur le Vicomte knows the hand. It is from Monsieur le Vicomte's uncle, Monsieur Théodore Petitsfours, of America."

Jacques thought Suzon had been right, that he had Uncle Théodore on the brain and was seeing visions; he sat motionless. He heard Suzon say, "Oh Lord, yes, his hand is indeed almost illegible!" And the manager actually drew a letter from his pocket and handed it to her. Many thoughts rushed through Jacques's head while he watched her read it, almost with the relaxed joy of a spectator, as if he were watching to see whether an acrobat could perform a difficult feat in a circus; also, he thought that he should be grateful to Salla for having had her so well finished.

Suzon read through the letter. "He wishes three rooms on the fourth floor," she said to the manager, "for himself and his servant, who is a Negro. He is coming this evening. Oh Lord, Jacques," she said to her husband, "our efforts to persuade him have finally borne fruit. What good fortune." "Mon," said the manager at the thought of the rooms on the fourth floor, "Dieu!" and in so saying expressed without knowing it the vicomte's thought.

An outsider serves as a prop for people who have been well brought up, but once the manager had gone away, both of them rose to their feet. Jacques felt he had conjured up a ghost and did not know what he should expect of it. His soul sought madly for a saint's picture; all the ancient piety of the Vieusacs pulsed within him, and his fingers felt the lack of a rosary. Suzon, a child of the proletariat, thought of the police. They stood with pale stiff faces and looked each other in the eye.

Jacques said, "I can die." "No. What stipulations can he make?" said Suzon at the same time. "Who?" said Jacques, aghast. "Uncle Théodore." "Do you think he will make stipulations?" said Jacques. "Yes, he will," said Suzon. "He will say that he has so-and-so much to invest in the business. Then he will want us to do something in return. I can't say what it will be. Perhaps he will want us to introduce him to people—bankers and the like—and he can demand it, because he has capital and we have none." At this juncture Suzon repeated some sallies about capitalists, which she had heard as a child and which Jacques had not the insight to contradict.

Very slowly Jacques same to see that she was right. Uncle Théodore was not the real Uncle Théodore but a swindler like themselves. This comforted him a good deal. "Very well," he said, "let him come."

The Vieusacs did not have the heart to receive Uncle Théodore when he arrived. They said it was unfortunate they could not postpone a little trip to the Pass of Roncesvalles. When they came home at night, their hearts were beating wildly as they went upstairs; they asked the manager whether their beloved uncle had arrived? He had indeed arrived, said the manager, quite wrapped up in blankets; the poor gentleman apparently suffered a great deal from arthritis. The manager had transmitted Monsieur le Vicomte's greeting, to which he had made no reply, and soon afterwards he had gone to bed.

Jacques had the feeling that if he let Suzon out of his sight, Uncle Théodore would loom above him like the justice of heaven; he stayed close to her. Never had his need of her been so strong and so pure; he really loved her.

In the middle of the night they were still lying in bed and talking about Uncle Théodore. "Do you know what provokes me?" said Suzon. "That we ourselves did not think of producing an Uncle Théodore. I know a man in Nice who would have been excellent." Morning was not the time when Jacques was in the best spirits, but since he had struggled with uncertainty through the whole night, he decided at daybreak to take the bull by the horns. Suzon was by then looking on the brighter side of things, and was pleased to have acquired a partner, and proud that Uncle Théodore was such a good idea that some one wished to impersonate him. She hoped only that it might be an intelligent person with whom they had to deal, one who would not damage their arrangements. Being used to casual relatives, she thought of Uncle Théodore with great freedom. Jacques was not so bold, but he soon set out.

Who in the hotel, which was bathed in sunshine, could imagine what a trembling heart went up the stairs to the fourth floor? On the way up he looked out of a window over the city, which had the same appearance as yesterday. Many would have found it heartless, and yielded to bitter thoughts, but Jacques had in his misfortune the one fortunate trait, that he always saw his point of view as the only acceptable one. A month ago—indeed, yesterday—he would have looked with displeasure and pity upon people who did not prosper in the world, but now when he himself was unhappy, it seemed to him that only misfortune was aristocratic.

Uncle Théodore's Negro gave him a slight shock. Even while it was most à la mode, he had not wanted black people in his service, he did not like them. Now it was almost inevitable that he should view Uncle Théodore's black as an unhappy omen. But Suzon's spirit still upheld him, and he spoke quietly to the black, asked for an audience with his master, and very shortly, only a minute or two later, he stood on a balcony over which the awning was pulled down, and from which there was a view better than that from his own, since he had gone up one flight—face to face with Uncle Théodore.

His first impression was that Suzon need not be afraid. This person must be a very great actor. The man must look just like this who had emigrated as a cook from Paris after the collapse of the empire and the commune, and who had taken over a biscuit factory and by it earned a hundred million francs, and who had now returned to the soil of his fatherland, drawn by an emigrant's longing. Completely wrapped in blankets, he sat leaning back in a deck chair; he greeted Jacques with difficulty and offered him a chair, which the Negro brought, but watched him with the arrogance of the lower classes. The verisimilitude was uncomfortable, and from the very first moment Jacques did not like him.

After a while he looked as if he were somewhat surprised that the young nobleman began with such a long pause. Jacques realized he had to talk. "I have the——" he did not know whether he should say honor or pleasure—"honor to speak with M. Théodore Petitsfours?" "That is me," said the manufacturer. "I am Jacques de Vieusac," said Jacques. "Oh," said Uncle Théodore. "It would have been most suitable if you had come first to me," said Jacques, who had just thought of the point. "Oh," said Uncle Théodore. Jacques did not know how he should begin the conversation; he did not even know whether he was right or wrong in considering Uncle Théodore to be insolent. He thought that it was he who should speak and it embarrassed him. "You understand," he said, "that our success depends upon our working together." "Oh," said

Uncle Théodore. "For if people begin to have suspicions," said Jacques, "everything is lost." To this Uncle Théodore said nothing. Jacques felt harassed, but there was nothing to do about it. "Let us be perfectly clear," said he who needed clarity, "how the comedy we are acting in should be played." The word comedy was a great boon to Jacques; it suddenly gave him back his sense of security. A Roman emperor had said on his deathbed that his comedy was ended; if an emperor could look at life that way, so could Jacques, it gave him a point of view. "Our comedy," he said with a slight smile, "here you have it. You have come back from America in order to rediscover your family; your name, I shall ask you to bear in mind, is Théodore Petits-fours. You have previously been a cook in Paris but have earned a fortune by dealing in biscuits in San Francisco. In your absence your only sister married the vicomte de Vieusac, whose son I am. Since you have no other relatives, we shall be your heirs. There has been a slight difference between us but that is over now. After our reconciliation we shall often appear together. I assume you have the money to live in the proper fashion, in any case for a time. What we can offer you," said Jacques, "is, to be sure, worth a good deal more. With our introductions, you will be able to go everywhere. I know you will say to this that at the moment you have the power to compromise us, but we cannot destroy you. Very well, I admit this and await your reply."

When Jacques had said this, Uncle Théodore did not reply at all. Jacques had to take up the conversation again. "Now it is time," he said with a quite Roman face, "that you say to me what you have to say."

This was apparently not easy for Uncle Théodore. During Jacques's speech he had raised himself up with difficulty more and more, and with a last effort he finally stood up, a head lower than Jacques and very red in the face. "Very well," said Jacques.

At that moment Uncle Théodore struck Jacques with his right hand a tremendous blow on his left cheek and then, contrary to Scripture, a second blow on his right cheek. He looked as if he wished to continue, but as if it were too strenuous for him, and after a pause of two or three seconds he suddenly sat down again. What had held Jacques back from jumping on him and killing him was a surprising similarity to old Madame Vieusac, Jacques's mother, which appeared when he grew angry.

"You damned puppy," said Uncle Théodore. Then he lost his voice completely; he sat quite still until the old French blood which had serviced the guillotine in '93 rose within him and started him off again, and indeed with great force. "You damned puppy," he cried. "Cochon! What is it you're telling me? I am a true Frenchman, I am the son of the free French people, the most glorious in the world. My father was a proper laborer for thirty centimes an hour; my mother was an improper one for fifty. I have sought my only sister in vain since I returned. I have advertised in *Le matin*, *Figaro*, *Le petit journal*, *La patrie*, and *L'indépendance belge*, but it has all been in vain. She must be dead now and resting in France's sacred soil. Yes," he cried and beat his breast with a booming sound, "I am a son of the people, and he who insults Théodore Petitsfours insults the French people. One hundred million francs, if you please! Say a hundred and fifty and you will not have said one sou too much. What is it you mean by a little difference, eh? Explain your trickery, explain your introductions, explain your little difference, explain your vicomte de Vieusac, or the French people will kick you off the balcony. Long live the fatherland!"

"Calm yourself," said Jacques de Vieusac, "I shall go voluntarily." And with a firm step he walked from the balcony through Uncle Théodore's salon, but when he came to the other side he walked into the wall and tried to find the doorknob in the middle of a painting which represented Napoleon and the guard at Fontainebleau. He turned around. "I offer my apology, Monsieur Petitsfours," he said with a face pale as death, "and go voluntarily," after which he really found the doorknob and left the room.

He went down the stairs like a stone that had been thrown, he went all the way down, as if Suzon, who was awaiting him on the floor below, did not exist. In his soul there was only one impulse, a desire for solitude.

Something extraordinary had happened to him. In his thoughts he called it a miracle; certainly he was now in an elevated state. To be sure, he had lost his composure after receiving a box on the ear —something that had not happened to him in the last ten years; but, still, it was not that. No, it was as if by a twist of fate Uncle Théodore's blows had been given him with beneficial intent; he accepted them quite humbly. He felt that something very agreeable had happened to him, and he walked past Suzon's apartment indifferently and obliterated her completely from his thoughts as if she did not exist, since she was incapable of comprehending his pleasure, and he had to experience that pleasure.

He walked silently out on the street and began to walk through the town. He stood and looked at some melons stacked in a pile, and at an umbrella, displayed in a shop window, with a handle carved to look like a cockatoo, as if these were wholly novel visions which could not be brought into connection with anything else.

He stood marveling that Uncle Théodore was no swindler but in reality his Uncle Théodore, his mother's brother, who from all the hotels in the world had chosen to come to the one where he would meet Jacques, and when Jacques had suggested they should join forces, had exposed him as a knave and had given him a box on the ear. That was a mishap. But it was of no importance, for as it had really happened, then the world must be different from what one had assumed. Then one ought to try to do what is right, conform to the code of the duel, and persecute the Jews. Then the girl in Lourdes really had had visions, and kings were kings by the grace of God. Then the virtue of the poor would be rewarded and antimilitarists receive their punishment.

As if these comprised the conditions for his true happiness, Jacques felt a great, tranquil harmony permeate his entire being. The heat that day had risen to the unbearable; heaven, earth, and town were equally white, as if all color had been burned out of them, and among the suffering human beings and animals walked poor fat Jacques like a quite ordinary man. Suppertime brought him to his senses and persuaded him to return to the hotel. The elevator boy looked at him, but Jacques looked straight ahead. The elevator boy did not exist for him, nor did Uncle Théodore himself. They had yielded to the overwhelming new sensation which pervaded him.

He found Suzon in an excited state. Later Jacques discovered that when he did not return, she had herself gone up to Uncle Théodore. From her, Uncle Théodore had found out how everything fitted together. Jacques was never really able to imagine how that colloquy ended, since Uncle Théodore had met in her an opponent of equal birth, and when kicked, the French people can kick back. Now she was tired, she demanded to have her dinner brought up to her.

Suzon said they must flee. She had already begun to pack, and in her bedroom her fine clothes lay strewn over the entire floor. She wanted to go to Egypt, because she had a friend who had made her fortune in Egypt. But Jacques did not want to flee. Ever since he had been in school in England, he had thought it intolerable to stand elsewhere than on France's sacred soil. He preferred to stay where he was and take whatever came.

They had scarcely begun to argue about this when there was a knock on their door. Jacques himself went to the door and opened it to fate. There it stood for him in the dignified figure of the sous-préfet of Cauteretz, who was accompanied by the hotel manager; he looked at Jacques, he looked at Suzon, through the door he cast a lingering glance at Suzon's clothes, after which he spoke as if he were another angel in the Book of Revelation.

"Sir," he said to Jacques, "it is my duty to tell you that M. Théodore Petitsfours has formulated an accusation against you, such that the sense of justice of the French people imperatively requires an investigation before you may leave Cauteretz. You are accused of having taken a name which is not your own and of having illegally passed yourself off as the vicomte de Vieusac."

For some time the newspapers played up the affair. In fact the *Worker's Little Friend* of Paris appeared with a large picture of Uncle Théodore on the front page above an exclamation of approval: "Bravo! A True Frenchman! Théodore Petitsfours's Life Story. May the Vicomtes and Swindlers Get It in the Neck!" Among Jacques's friends the news aroused panic. Nobody would believe it really was Jacques. The duc and duchesse d'Argueil drove to Cauteretz in their limousine in order to find out. When they saw it was really Jacques they remained at the hotel in order to follow the trial. By energetic efforts the duchesse obtained permission to visit Jacques and smuggled in to him a bottle of *vinaigre de vin de toilette*, which he had never been able to live without. She attended every single session of the court, but the duc, who had been a very good friend of Jacques, could not stand it and finally drove home. Until then the inhabitants of Cauteretz stood and looked at the limousine and walked about, themselves somewhat restless and oppressed by the fashionable events taking place in their midst—like a bashful young man in his first success.

Suzon was Jacques's weak point, if one may so phrase it. She was unmasked immediately when she spoke about her family in Bordeaux. Baron Salla was dead and could not explain the relations of persons and events, but on close examination it became clear she had not been a Mademoiselle Boyer. When Jacques himself was interrogated, he said nothing. He insisted he was the vicomte de Vieusac but otherwise he would not open his mouth, and treated the court with disdain. In this one could sense the old vicomte de Vieusac, a few of whose former friends were called as witnesses and brought a fragrant elegance of the nineteenth century into the courtroom. One of them thought that Jacques resembled the old vicomte, another that he was very far from the old vicomte's type, but they agreed that the marriage about which they had heard rumors for a short time had been no more than a jest on the part of their friend. Monsieur Petitsfours's sister was advertised for everywhere but could not be found. It seemed that Jacques was not Uncle Théodore's heir at all and that the whole affair would become quite uninteresting.

In the meantime Jacques and Suzon themselves experienced a difficult time, unrelated to the verdict which hung above their heads. Jacques was calm, very quiet, and almost happy. The thought of his promise to his mother, which he was keeping at such great cost to himself, lent his countenance and spirit such a clarity that the jailer himself came under his influence and thought soberly of many things. For Suzon, it was more complicated.

She was willing to wager her head that Jacques was a vicomte. It was a matter of complete indifference to her whether or not he was a vicomte, but she could not understand why he would not prove it, and his refusal hurt her deeply, as much as anything could hurt Suzon. She said to herself that the most reasonable thing to do was to let him take care of himself until he came to her with an explanation; but something had entered his character which annoyed her, and she was not certain he loved her any longer. Consequently she began to bedevil him. Finally there was a great scene, and she took off her wedding ring and threw it in his face. "You can be sure," she said, "you can be sure, vicomte de Vieusac, that I shall have no more to do with you. You can swear to it, my boy, that I will not look your way even if the archbishop of Paris comes and asks me to. I would not touch you for all your Uncle Théodore's moola. Now you know."

During the entire trial the dreadful heat continued. The judge, who was the only one who could not see the clock, because it hung directly over his head, suddenly realized that he was no longer able to think. He was stuck, because he could not think who Jacques was, and Jacques had to be someone or other. The judge assumed a thoughtful expression in order to preserve his composure and said to the advocate Delaisson, "My dear fellow, this is an extraordinary affair."

The same evening Jacques wrote a letter to his mother. It read as follows:

> My dear Mother,
> I am sending you herewith some newspaper clippings from which you will see that I am soon to be condemned for having claimed to be your son. For the law I have no respect whatsoever, and whether I am judged justly or unjustly is of no conse-

quence to me. But your opinion of me I cherish, and I trust you will preserve your kind feelings toward me.

I can write no more, I am weeping, but these tears are a relief.

Your ever devoted son,
Jacques Landry de Vieusac

The jailer quietly went to the post office for him with the letter and had no idea what he was carrying.

The postman in Chantilly, who did not know it either, brought the letter one September morning to the faithful Victorine who stood in the door and with whom he was in love. He was now elderly and had been in love four times in his life, all four times with Victorine, but she would not have him. "Why, Mademoiselle Victorine," he said jokingly, "you are really putting on weight." "Yes; it is not your fault," said Victorine, who considered him a great bore. Old Madame Vieusac read the letter and when she had sat and thought about it for half an hour she sent Victorine out to fetch her father confessor, Father Daniel, right away.

In all the years she had lived in Chantilly he had been her faithful friend. He united the purity of an unbending character with a bland interest in everything human, and he had read all of Jacques's newspaper clippings.

When she had explained the affair to him he had a moral solution ready, as a result of his many years' routine.

"My dear friend," he said, "God is infinitely more ingenious than we are. This is his reward for your love of your son. You have now an opportunity to step forth before the world with éclat as his mother, and to bring him not humiliation but salvation. I bid you to leave at once and in peace."

This she did and as a consequence the court in Cauteretz enjoyed a sensation. On a Thursday when a long interrogation of the hotel manager had been worked through and everybody in the court had dozed off, including the duchesse, although she continuously ate crème de menthe bonbons in order to stay awake, a policeman at the entrance was heard to utter a cry because he had been pushed aside by a small, heavy, red-cheeked woman in black, who, with a little dog under one arm and a small brown briefcase under the other, went straight through the courtroom to the judge.

There she looked the judge in the eye and put the dog on the floor and, while laying the briefcase before the judge, like Jeanne d'Arc laying the captured battle flags before Charles VII, said in a clear and distinct voice so that it could be heard by everyone in the courtroom, "The young man standing there is Vicomte Jacques de Vieusac's and my son. I am Théodore Petitsfours's sister Marceline. In this briefcase you will find my baptismal certificate and the vicomte's, our wedding certificate, the child's baptismal and vaccination certificates, and a certificate of good morals issued by my father confessor. That my son the vicomte has said he is to inherit from his Uncle Théodore is quite reasonable, for I do not know to whom Théodore should bequeath his money other than myself. And as my brother Théodore has asserted here in the court that he possesses more than a hundred and fifty million francs, my son has been conservative in saying he expected to inherit one hundred million. That the French legal system could be preparing to pass a completely unjust judgment does not speak to your advantage, gentlemen." Then she turned to her son and said, "Jacques, embrace your mother."

To describe the joy of the reunion, a reunion wherein the mother had not seen her son for eight years, the sister had not seen her brother for fifty years, nor the brother the sister, the daughter-in-law had never seen the mother-in-law, and the judge had never seen the dog, would be almost impossible. Their great emotion infected the court, sobs were heard throughout the room, and there were some who applauded almost as in a theater in order to express their approval of what had happened.

It might have been quite annoying to the judge to have to take up the whole affair *de nouveau*. But he was also carried away, he was not distressed but proud that the eyes of France rested on Cauteretz, he was imbued with a lively sensation he had never before experienced. Indeed, the arrival of Madame de Vieusac in the courtroom and the reversal of the trial brought with it a change in the judge's marriage which had hitherto been cheerless and childless—but enough of that. That evening and for several days afterwards Cauteretz swirled like a flag in cheerful sunshine and breezes. Many things happened. However, the duchesse had lost interest and returned to Paris.

In truth, Jacques and Suzon had also had enough of Cauteretz. As soon as they could, they traveled with the old vicomtesse and Uncle Théodore to Chantilly, where Victorine made room for them all.

Father Daniel had come almost at once in order to congratulate them; he began a discussion of the story of Lot with Uncle Théodore, who had been for such a long time in America, and during the whole evening they walked back and forth in Madame de Vieusac's little garden and argued with the greatest amicability.

Suzon immediately fell in love with her new family. She had always been able to adapt herself to new situations, and now it was apparent to her that this plain and solid bourgeoisie was her true element; it seemed to her that she was finally among people who understood life and took it seriously. When she had been in Chantilly three days she went to the market in the morning with Victorine in order to buy cauliflower as soon as it arrived, and while Father Daniel and Uncle Théodore argued, she and the old vicomtesse sat and toiled to bring Jacques's affairs into order. In the morning she sat at the kitchen table with curl papers in her hair and drank coffee out of a saucer. The Baron Salla would have been disappointed, but he was dead and a station long ago passed by.

On their first Sunday in Chantilly the old vicomtesse arranged a festive little dinner, for which she and Uncle Théodore themselves prepared all the dishes. For many years the two of them had not had as much pleasure as they did that day, when they went around the kitchen just as in the old time when both of them had been apprentices to Paillard, where the Russian grand dukes ate dinner and the emperor himself sometimes supped. No Russian grand duke ate better that evening than our family in Chantilly. "Do you think there is

enough pepper in the soup?" asked the old vicomtesse anxiously. "Scarcely," said Uncle Théodore,
"scarcely. But with the carp we shall drink Château Yquem, and with this good French wine I
permit myself a toast to the symbol of the unity of
our family, little Théodore de Vieusac, my sole
heir."

The old vicomtesse folded her hands over her
stomach in satisfaction at this thought. In her
mind's eye she already saw a black-eyed little Vieusac preparing sweetmeats in her large pan.

"And what do you have to say, Jacques?" asked
Suzon humbly.

Carnival

U pon the February night of the great Opera Carnival at Copenhagen of 1925, there was gathered shortly after midnight, in a large house a few miles out of town, a supper party of eight, all coming from the ball and intending to return to it.

The party consisted of, to take the ladies first: Watteau Pierrot, Arlecchino, the young Soren Kierkegaard—that brilliant, deep, and desperate Danish philosopher of the forties, a sort of macabre dandy of his day—and Camelia.

They were all four young and pretty, the real beauty being she who was dressed as a camelia in pink satin, which was not in itself more shining or flowerlike than her naked shoulders and back. Her blackened eyelashes were so long that her clear brown eyes looked out at you as from behind an ambuscade, and at whatever place—throat, arm, waist, or knee—you cut her slim body through with a sharp knife, you would have got a perfectly circular transverse incision.

The rare grace of the young Soren Kierkegaard is really familiar to a great part of the highest civilized world, for it is a favorite subject with the young painters of our day. In her own country there was never an exhibition in which it did not figure, and she hangs in the National Gallery as a lady with a fan, and at the Glyptothek in that strange pale-green study: nymph and unicorn drinking at a forest pool. She also wrote what was considered very modern poetry, and it seems likely that in her case the spirit will turn out to be, contrary to what is presumably its normal fate, transient, and the flesh immortal.

Pierrot and Arlecchino were sisters, and showed it in a likeness such as that of the acorn to the oak leaf: not a congenial upheap of heterogeneous atoms, but a heterogeneous upheap of congenial atoms. They were a little more spare of build, and had darker eyes and redder mouths than the others, as if the vitality within them had come out less in plain matter and more in color and brightness, and in a certain finical gracefulness peculiar to them. They also both had creamy skin and that placid and slightly scoffing expression which one finds in the faces of Japanese dolls. Arlecchino was a young girl, and the only one of the party.

Of the four men the Venetian lady was the host, and married to Pierrot. His costume was the costliest within the party, and he wore its heavy luminous silver cloth and brocades, which hung and fell like a great waterfall in moonlight, with as much sense of beauty in the abstract as consciousness of the personal grace of the bearer.

One of his friends also wore the clothes of a Harlequin, and he had put it on because he had promised the young girl to outshine her. But he was a modern or futuristic Harlequin, his clothes being made of soft and metallic materials, in pale shades of jade, mauve, and gray, while she was the genuine classic figure of the old Italian pantomime. Whichever of them did really outshine the other was a matter of taste.

The two remaining men wore a magenta domino and a very beautiful old Chinese costume in yellow. The magenta domino had been put on, reluctantly, by a very fair and very good-looking young man, an Englishman, who came from the legation.

In the Chinese costume was the only elderly person of the party. It did not suit him, because his round face was all of a bright pink, such as the French call *framboise,* which paled into a soft rose toward the top of his bald head, but it was in itself of a rich and glorious hue, which flowed like honey in the lights, and shone and glowed like brass and live coals in the shade of the deep folds. He knew about color, being a great painter, famous all over the world, and he had chosen this because somebody had said that yellow is a color which has no depth. He wanted to prove that they were wrong, as if the statement had been a personal insult, and he could generally be trusted to take up the cause of the oppressed. He was known to have said that all greatness is only a higher form of amiability, and this might be true about his own art, which was inspired by a real delight in everything that he could see, and a great desire to deal the pleasure out again to the world. Since it seemed strange that such a very brilliant person should have a little full-moon face, with no features, hair, or expression to speak of, indeed most of all like the posterior of a baby, the pupils of his painting school, who loved him, had developed a theory that there had been a shifting about in his anatomy, and that he had an eminently radiant and expressive face at the other place. He was at the moment happy to find himself in the company of good wine, of which he wrongly thought himself a judge, and of lovely women, about whom he knew everything, but he would also have enjoyed a coffee party of old women in faded black frocks, within the whitewashed walls of a poorhouse. He felt at home in his costume, which had been that of a high eunuch of the imperial court of China, and he might well have passed as an *intrigant* and brilliant old eunuch, who has taken a shortcut to superiority and equilibrium, and who is watching, from his own serene stall, the gambols of the less simplified human beings with sympathy and without prejudice.

The room in which the party was collected was the large white dining room of one of the dignified villas which are to be found along the seaside north of Copenhagen, and which were built in the early years of the last century, when Danish merchants were making their fortunes out of Napoleon's wars. On this night the small round dinner table was, in honor of the carnival, lighted by candles with shades in many colors: orange, rose, yellow, crimson, turquoise, green. On a sideboard was everything for making up a good supper. The butler was arranging some plates of very pretty fruit, a pensive black figure in the white surroundings, like a fly which has fallen into a pot of cream.

The two sisters appeared first on the stage, having come in Pierrot's car ten minutes before the rest of the party. Outside it was snowing. During the short drive from the hot, deafening, and restless kaleidoscope of the ballroom through that deadly white and silent world, they had not spoken, but the night air had heightened their color.

Young Arlecchino was in the wildly happy mood of a person very fond of dancing. Life appeared to her as it must appear to a daring tightrope dancer, high up, with the greatest confidence in his own skill. She was hot after the dance, so that she felt her thin silk garments cling lightly to her body round the waist, but she felt herself cool as a breeze. Half an hour ago her partner had kissed her below the ear, where her neck rose out of the large ruff, and she ought to have had a sensation of heat and dryness from the kiss, but she was so full of herself that her own feeling was, like his, one of freshness and coolness, as when you touch the petals of a peony.

Pierrot looked over the hyacinths and carnations of the table with the eyes of a hostess and said: "I think there are too many flowers." Arlecchino started singing, to the waltz tune that the orchestra had played when they left the ball: "All the flowers on the tables, of the houses and hotels are reflections, are reflections, of the blue sky of my heart." She let her slim intelligent legs do a few steps, as on their own. "For the law of gravitation has tonight been done away with, and I hate and loathe that law." She put her hand on her sister's white satin shoulder blade, and they danced, both very light, straight and supple, and stopped, just a little out of breath, before one of the long mirrors on the wall.

"Mimi," said Arlecchino, "you are always the loveliest, and you have never been as lovely as tonight." "Moonshine, Polly?" asked Pierrot softly. This was a current password between the two, for it had before happened to them to be rivals, and, incapable of jealousy between themselves, they had invented the expression for the sort of enhanced luster, the gentle reflection of a coveted admiration with which the happy rival would shine in the unhappy rival's eye. When they had been in love with the young pastor who prepared them for their confirmation, Arlecchino had even written a poem upon the theme. "No," said Arlecchino, "but you see, it is like this: we are all dressed up, but I think that you ought to have *been* a Pierrot." "Yes, I think so myself," said Pierrot.

Arlecchino turned all round from the glass. "Quick, quick," she said, "I must speak to you before the others come." "I know what you are going to say," said Pierrot. "Say it then," said Arlecchino. Pierrot took two flowers from the table in her hands, and sang very low: "You will ask me if I still am in love with my friend, with Charlie, for if not, and if it is over—" she made a pause. "And is it over?" asked Arlecchino. "Yes past, past, past," sang Pierrot and let her flowers fall.

Arlecchino picked them up. "Do you pick up my flowers—" asked Pierrot, "and my lover? Are you serious, Arlecchino?" "Yes," said Arlecchino. "God be with you," said Pierrot. "I want him to love me," said Arlecchino. "Yes, he will love you all right," said Pierrot. "I want to love him myself," said Arlecchino very seriously. Pierrot seemed to grow a little paler, and stared at her. "Why should I not have a lover, when you have all got lovers?" asked Arlecchino. "No, there is no reason why you should not have a lover," said Pierrot. "Why should I not be in love when you are all in love?" asked Arlecchino. Pierrot kept on looking at her with her large dark eyes. "Do you want to be in love?" she cried. "You, Polly—coeur de lionne!"—which was the name for the girl used by her circle. "For God's sake, Polly."

She turned one of the large armchairs from the table and sat down, as if overcome by her sister's words. "It is not true," she said after a pause, "that we are all in love. It is only me." Arlecchino thought this over a little. "Is it bad to be in love?" she asked. "I thought," said Pierrot sadly, "that you might have seen that for yourself." "In this house?" asked Arlecchino. "Yes, in this house," said Pierrot. Arlecchino pushed back another chair and sat down opposite her sister, as if ready for a debate. "Do you really believe, Mimi," she said, "that I have been able to stay in this house without catching somehow the spirit of lovemaking which you and Julius radiate?" "God help us," said Pierrot, "is that what I have done to you?" "What did you mean to do then?" asked Arlecchino. "Exactly the opposite," said Pierrot.

"Mimi," said Arlecchino, *"foi de gentilhomme*: Would you change with me tonight?" "Yes," said Pierrot with great energy, "with you and with anybody else who is not in love." "But you are married to the man you are in love with," said Arlecchino. "Yes, what is the good of that?" said Pierrot. "It is always some good," said the young sister. "No," said Pierrot, "it makes it a hundred times worse. If Julius and I were lovers, and met twice a week in his flat, as other people do, I should still have five days in which to be myself a little. Now, in the way in which we are living here together I have no peace in my own house. All my existence becomes nothing but being in love, all my thoughts turn around one single person, there is no sense in it, it is not living." "And your frocks and your hats?" said Arlecchino after a moment. "And my frocks and my hats," said Pierrot, "my parties and theatricals, my music and my brilliant talk—nothing at all has got any meaning to me except for his sake, and for the sake of what he thinks of me. Why, when we both drove in that race," she went on, in deep despair, "I envied you the whole time, Polly, so that my heart ached." "But you won the race," said Polly, "and I was only number nine." "Oh yes, I won it," said Pierrot contemptuously, "but you enjoyed it, you loved your car, you thought that the weather was splendid, you said so. I only went in at all, because I thought that Julius would like it if I won." "God!" said Arlecchino. "It gives me no more pleasure," said Pierrot, "even to be pretty. If I were sure that Julius alone thought me pretty I should not mind knowing for certain, seeing it myself in the glass, that I was looking like Valeria Ollgaard."

"And your Charles?" asked Arlecchino, in a voice low, as with awe. "Did anybody ever think I was in love with Charlie?" said Pierrot. "Alas, my poor Charlie. Do you think that I ever believed that he loved me? No, he loved Julius, just like me—we used to talk about him together."

Arlecchino listened, very still, like a child who is being told a fascinating and gruesome fairy tale. "Do you mean all this, Mimi?" she asked. Pierrot sat in the deep armchair with her legs stretched out, and her hands in the pockets of her coat, the folds of which shone like porcelain in the light. Never had a little ruined and lost Pierrot looked more tragic. "Do you mean that you think I have got *le vin triste?*" she asked. "I have that. But it is lovely to have had so much to drink that you can speak as easily as you can think. Listen, the others will be here quite soon.

"All this that I have told you, that I have lost everything in life—friendship, hats, ambition—that is quite sad in itself, but it is not what makes me unhappy. No, that is this, that if Julius knew how I feel about it he would dislike it so much. I know him well, I make no mistake where he is concerned. He wants me to run parallel with him in life. God, Polly, how sorry one ought to feel for all parallel lines which want to intersect as badly as I do.

"I deceive him very well. I do run parallel with him with all my might, as you all know. I am his ideal friend and comrade, and he believes that it is his car, and his aeroplane, and his collections that I love. But it makes one sad always to deceive.

"All this—that is being in love, Polly, if that is what you want."

"Why do you not go away, Mimi?" asked Polly.

"But you know that I do go away," said Mimi. "I am only just back from those winter sports. I went to England last summer and learned to fly. But it is no good to me, I come back quite empty-handed, like a beggar child who is ashamed to go home.

"Do you know, Polly, what I have thought of?" she went on. "Do you remember those people who were old when we were children—the nuns at the French school, and our maiden aunts—who believed in God? They lived in God, and threw themselves upon the Lord, and rested in him, and all that. Now say that that was the thing which God disliked most of all, and that in the end he would say to them: 'For the love of God' (or whatever words he uses to that effect) 'do think of something to do for yourselves, find some interest of your own in life. I really should not have created you if I had known that you could do nothing but fall back upon me again.' Would that not be dreadful for them?" "Yes," said Arlecchino after having thought it over, "that would be awful for them. But even if it is so, it cannot matter to us, because we do not believe in God." Pierrot nodded. "No," she said.

"When I think," said Arlecchino very slowly, "of all the people who envy you your modern silhouette." "Yes," said Pierrot sadly. "The silhouette of your mind," Arlecchino went on with great force, "might be a Masaccio." "Yes," said Pierrot. She dived into her large pocket for her cigarette case and lighted a cigarette, very carefully. "What you really want," said Arlecchino in the same voice, like Pythia under inspiration, "is to be Julius's shadow." Pierrot sat silent for a moment, then she drew a deep breath, like a child who is being shown its heart's desire. "Yes," she said, "I should love to be his shadow." She thought a little. "But the young men whom we know," she said, "do not care to have shadows, I think. They know nothing about them. They have sold them, perhaps, like Peter Schlemihl, if you remember about him." "To the devil?" asked Arlecchino. "No," said Pierrot thoughtfully, "not to him, I do not think that they know him either. More likely to the world—" "Or the flesh," said Arlecchino. "Change your face now, Mimi, for here comes your husband." She stood up, and looked straight into her sister's face. "Look here, Mimi," she said, very serious, "I shall not fall in love. *Parole d'honneur*. Does that make you feel happier?"

The white headlights of the cars came flashing up the snow-clad drive. Pierrot followed her advice:

her still and empty face took on its slightly surprised and scoffing expression. They put the chairs back to the table very carefully, and ran out to meet their guests in their little heelless shoes.

Hot from wine and dancing, the newcomers felt the adventure of the drive through the snow, and the arrival at the still house, like an hour's armistice within the pandemonium of the carnival. They were all friends—four of them being very much in love with one another—disillusioned, rich, and hungry. The gentle and wild voices of the women reechoed in the long hall, very severely decorated in the Pompeian manner, with four tall vases of marble between the windows.

The young male Arlecchino, whose Christian name was Tido, had come with the Camelia in her car, and was describing to her a happy love affair of his at the ball, and trying to give her an idea of the loveliness of his partner. Great truths had been revealed to him during this last hour, one being the fundamental falsity of the traditional idea of covering up the body and leaving the face bare, when it ought to be exactly the other way round. No woman could ever look her best as much as in a mask only, or actualize to the same extent the combined human ideals of truthfulness and dignity, equally difficult to achieve in clothes, or all uncovered. Your own mask would give you at least that release from self toward which all religions strive. A little piece of night itself, containing all its mystery, depth, and bliss, rightly placed for giving you its freedom without its renunciation. Your center of gravity is moved from the ego to the object; through the true humility of self-denial you arrive at an all-comprehending unity with life, and only thus can great works of art be accomplished. The time had come, in the history of mankind, to obtain freedom by giving up faces. Indeed, now that he had come to meditate upon it, he would be prepared to believe that nearly all the trouble of the human race would disappear simultaneously with the face. And within a utopia so easily reached we should feel like mountains in spring, all verdant and flowering, with sweet fresh streams running and our heads in the clouds.

"She had," he said, "a mole at the small of her back, like"—he quoted an old Danish poet of the last century—"the little shadow of the wick within the alabaster lamp." Looking at Camelia, as she was gently molting her black silk cloak, he exclaimed: "Was it you?" "No," said Camelia.

The slim candles on the table, that had kept themselves, in the empty white room, to themselves, like a party of marriageable young women in their own thoughts, now flashed and beamed at all the intruding colors, it was a meeting, and mating, of light and color, a rhapsody none the less transporting for being entirely silent.

With the light on his painted face, flushed by wine under the powder, in the warm air filled with the scent of hyacinths and carnations, the Venetian lady was holding young Soren Kierkegaard's elbow in his hand. Those two had taken to talking, on an evening, in blank verse, a habit trying to their surroundings—only there are some jokes which gain by being repeated.

"And," he said, "like two masochists, who, married, both, / united in a deadly understanding, / a barren sympathy which holds no comfort, / pant, in homogeneous passion, to unbreech / and feel the sacred smarting of the birch. / So you and I. For could we be in love / with one another hopelessly, how bracing, / like caviar, our tears. But I must always / return to you, for always to my heart / your slim legs are a golden tuning fork, / God's favorite implement, powerfully turning / life's dissonances into harmony. / And you won't break my heart. Bad luck she hath, / who breaks the ceiling mirror of her bath."

The Magenta Domino sat next to Arlecchino. Deeply moved by drink and love, his mind was advancing along a narrow ridge, from which he might fall at any moment, at one side into deep gratitude to God, at the other side into despair. He was kept in balance by being equally drawn to either side. Under his fresh and bored appearance, like that of a milord of the old days, tortured by spleen, he had a capacity for suffering. It fell to him in life to be in love with the Noli me tangeres, wherever such were to be found, and the cheaper goods had no attraction for him. Women's haughtiness and arrogance toward him, and their mysterious high valuation of, and niggardliness about, their own bodies, seemed to him a most excellent state of holiness. It awoke in his heart a desperate tenderness, which was ever likely to bring him into trouble, into the fatal paradoxical melancholy and sentimental cul de sac of those who passionately adore virginity. He had before now felt himself like the troll of the fairy tale, so desperately devoted to little human children that he had to eat them up, and very sorry when he had done it, and there was nothing left. He was telling Arlecchino that he was likely to be moved from the legation of Copenhagen to Egypt, and holding her hand and lifting her little finger to his mouth, he said: "In Egypt Saint Joseph said to the Virgin: Oh, my sweet young dear, could you not just for one moment close your eyes and imagine that I were the Holy Ghost?" The girl turned her somber eyes on him from over the rim of her glass, wincing a little as he bit her rosy finger-tip. "Charlie," she said, "shall we make a shadow theater, you and I, and travel all round the world with it? I am tired of being three-dimensional, it seems to me very vulgar." Julius, who noticed a change in her since he had danced with her, a sort of challenge to the world, as if she would like to kill off everybody in it, or, as a harder punishment upon it, to kill herself, and who understood the working of her mind, said across the table: "Behold the vestal virgin at the banquet, / high priestess she of negativity, / intoxicated by destructiveness. / Thumbs must be down, be down, or all come off." "Do you betray me, Julius?" said Polly with surprise, for those two generally held together. "I beg your pardon, Polly," said Julius, "it was your costume misleading me."

At the other side of the table the old painter, whose name was Rosendaal, was complaining to his hostess of the fact that none of the party was wearing black. He had a high and plaintive little voice, and was in the habit of speaking exceedingly slowly, so that even when describing a thing with enthusiasm he conveyed somehow the impression of piercing suffering manfully born. "You would all have looked so beautiful in it," he said and looked round the table with deep regret. "This is like playing with a pack of cards in which even the ace of spades is pink."

"Black," he said, "I love it." He was the only person in Copenhagen who could make use of the word *love* without his voice trembling with the slightest particle of irony. The lovers of the town used the verb *to adore.* "I know that there is, somewhere, a theory that black will make your coloring heavy. It is a very great mistake. On the contrary, it makes for lightness and does away with greasiness, which is the most deadly danger to a painter. The clay, as you know, before the baking is also greasy, soft, and heavy, but in the burning pottery becomes black, and grows at the same time hard, dry, and light. Thus life. It is necessary to get black into it somehow. You young people know of no black, and what is the result? Alas, that your existence becomes every day more flat and greasy.

"There are only two things," he went on, "which nowadays save a supper party, like ours, from the most disgusting greasiness. Those are the dryness of our wine," he looked at his glass, and here he was honest, he really liked his wine better the dryer it was, "and the starvation of our women. To be, in the midst of abundance, surrounded by people half mad with hunger—and hopelessly hungry, at that, for a poor little girl at a baker's window may have a chance of a kind gentleman, with evil plans, offering her sixpence, but our young mondaines are held in custody by their consciences, and if they let themselves be tempted by a crust, they will have to give up that little quail for supper of which they have dreamed all day, even in the arms of their lovers—

that undoubtedly has got charm, that furnishes us with a little bit of black. If women were as intemperate in regard to food as they are sexually, a supper party would become entirely repulsive.

"In a way," he said thoughtfully, "this fate of theirs is an act of justice, a Nemesis, a clever return upon them. It might procure material for a myth. For what has always been the trouble between us and the women has been their inability to understand that when you have eaten you are no longer hungry. That is, they cannot distinguish between the subjective and the objective point of view. The fact that the connoisseur may value a bottle of wine, or even an omelette, highly, may even be filled with veneration and gratitude in regard to them, and that still his valuation cannot be that of a hungry and thirsty man, is forever incomprehensible to them. Let them then forever rise from their meals burning with desire for food, and flicker—restless little bodies and spirits—in their culinary existence like birds at the pea patch with the scarecrow in it. It is pretty.

"Otherwise," he went on, "you do not believe that I think the fashion pretty, do you? I can imagine nothing more pathetic than you young women who have had to turn your faces all round from your decolletage, because there was nothing but the Desert of Gobi in front of them. But spiritually it has got value, it saves us."

He was so obviously happy to sit there, to eat and drink and look at them, and particularly to talk, that they could not but be happy with him. It was clear to anybody who knew him that his convictions were very loosely founded, it was no good coming back the next day for a continuation, for he would have shed his skin quietly in the mean time, with the ease of an old snake which believes that it has got something better underneath. As a teacher he was capable of contradicting himself without shame, praising a work one day at which he had raged and snarled the day before, but his pupils did not mind, for he gave them, in the midst of any injustice, the invincible ambition to do their utmost.

Julius said: "How dare I love you? Do you know I've eaten / whene'er I wanted to? I have had beef, / and ortolans and beer. I have not known / the faithfulness which turns your clear young eyes / from the full buffet. I have not woke up / at night and cried, and folded my pale hands / over a heart that screamed, and to that heart / said: No, not one ounce more, no not one ounce. / Nor spoken to my flesh and said: Remember. / You wait upon my skeleton. Be still."

Young Soren Kierkgaard said in her low voice, with its slight lisp which still managed to catch, as in a vice, the whole being of Tido on the other side of the table: "O rest that rocking-horse, your Pegasus! / Your own heart moans beneath its canter, like to / an old dead bed from a long shut-up brothel / forgotten in the frippery's attics. Still, / at midnight, going through its ancient paces."

"Do we really manage to shock you, Rosie, by having no dimples in our derrières?" asked Camelia, lifting, with great content, conscious of her own perfection, her shoulders out of her frock, like a partridge basking in the sun. The old painter looked at her across the table, he could not help being struck, as for the first time that he had seen her, by her freshness and gracefulness. "Shocked, Fritze?" he said. "Yes, I am shocked. Aesthetically. How could I be anything but shocked, me, who am an artist, and who have seen, when I was young, ladies who had derrières, to the straight back view, like violoncellos? If you had had dimples in your derrière, I should have seen them long ago through that tutu of yours, and should have felt most honored to sit at a table with you. Alas, I know exactly what you and your friends have got: a little bunch of muscles, just sufficient to hold you in the saddle when you ride, and to act as a rudder when you are dancing. But morally, my dear, your derrière carries a good deal of weight. To my mind you young women of your appalling smart set are, as a class, the only righteous people of our town, the only contemporaries of ours who make it their object to represent an idea. The indolent and gourmande Fritze Rosenkrantz has done duty, has sacrificed many times—in distress too, I take it—to the ideal Fritze Rosenkrantz, the first femme chic of Copenhagen, to produce that derrière, and such as it is, I take off my hat to it."

He did so, with much friendliness, and after the effort leaned back in his chair and drew a deep breath. "Shocked?" he said, "Yes, I am shocked. In all Copenhagen there are only two people who can still be shocked, that is, my friend old Miss von Gersdorff, and myself. We may well be proud. We could dine out every night of the year and gather our *succès fou*, solely on our capacity to be shocked. But we are both old, and what will you do when we have gone? A poor figure you will cut, my children, delivering your daring axioms to one another, like a man holding a *messe noire* for the plumbers' trade union. You are depriving God of one of his colors after the other, until he will have nothing upon his palette but pink and celestial blue, to do little bon-bonnières with."

"But we do not want to be black," said Pierrot on his right, holding a long-stemmed flower to her nose, "we want to be rainbows. I should have come as a rainbow tonight, if I had known what to do with my legs."

"It is so stupid, what you say there, Mimi," said Rosendaal, "that I am ashamed that the others should have heard it. Would you have been a rainbow on the little blue sky of this supper party of yours, then? Or wherever amongst us would you have found either black or brimstone to stand on?"

"That is very charming," said Julius, "the black and brimstone sky, and a ruin to the left, and in the middle distance a Polish horseman in a scarlet cloak, galloping under the ancient curse of his family, who die when they make love."

An expression came upon the old painter's face such as comes upon the face of a little child when you hold a watch to its ear. "Yes, Julius, my child," he said, "I have seen a few little bits of coloring, like that, not very long ago. The municipality, the vandals, as you know, have been pulling down Vognmagergade—a black spot, they considered, upon the fat clean face of the Copenhagen of today—and I have been a good deal with them. There you would get darkness, a black two hundred years old, bottled with fusel and bugs, and oozing out when the cork was withdrawn as the walls fell. We had much trouble in making some of the old inhabitants move away, good decent people, who clung to the right of a man to preserve a little bit of darkness of his own. There was a very nice old woman there, whom I went to see a few times to give her my sympathy and drink a little glass of gin with her, she was seventy-five years old, and blind, and earned her living fairly and honestly by fornication. Glowing little bits of black I had with her, straight in the flat pink faces of the new houses." "When I was in Paris last," said Camelia, "I went with my French aunt to see a rose exhibition at Bagatelle. She is as old as your friend, Rosie, and half blind, too. But in front of the prettiest flowerbeds she held me by the sleeve, and kept on stammering in her little shaky voice: 'Ma chère, c'est un lit d'amour, c'est un lit d'amour!' You will despise me for it, but for the purpose I like her scheme of color better." Old Rosendaal looked at her. "Then why," he asked after a moment, "do you use black sheets yourself? Do not apologize, for you are right. From a colorist's point of view, hell is to be preferred to a modern love affair, and of all the pinks in the world that of the couch of love is most likely to come off on you, thick as grease."

"What black do you want to use for the couch of love then?" asked Tido, who had an acute personal interest in the matter. The painter thought this question over for a little while. "Well," he said after a time, very slowly and somehow bashfully," they had, upon a time, there, a very good black from a terrible bad conscience, a deep guilt, you know. Sin, yes, deadly sin." "Oh, dear, Rosie," lisped Soren Kierkegaard. "Why, yes," said the old man with growing self-confidence, folding his hands over his stomach, "they had it. A fine lovely black. It has gone, you have never seen it, the working secret has been lost. But fine it was." He sat silent again, absorbed in his memories. Then woke up, very happy, to life again. "But jealousy?" he asked them, is that not a good black for you? I know, I know, I too have read modern books, and am aware that it is not allowed with you, the chic thing about it is to provoke its abortion. I have, sometimes, seriously thought of marrying, myself, from the motive of doing some good to the world, of making one woman happy by being the real jealous husband, the jealous husband of the old tales. I feel genuinely sorry for you young women who have to lie down without a word to the fate of being married to cuckolds."

"The time is near," he said, solemnly after a moment, "when we shall have to keep, by government grant, a few Bluebeards, a few Jack the Rippers about to protect Eros from fatty degeneration. Is not man a hunter?" he asked, patting his fat breast in the eunuch's robe.

"No," said Soren Kierkegaard.

"No?" said Rosendaal. "Well, Annelise, no. Is he not a sportsman, still, then? The fashionable sport," he went on quickly, waving away with his hand the risk of a second negative, "of photographing big game—why is it a sport at all? Because the game has, up until today, been killed with poisoned arrows and dumdums. If you stop the killing now, in ten years' time, while you are still, all of you, young women, the photographing of big game will have no more sport in it than a fashionable photographer's job in Copenhagen. The elephant, the rhino and the shy okapi, the unicorn even, will come up and pose for the camera. They will have to keep then, by government grant, a few gangs of poachers about, with deadly weapons, just to make them run from time to time. And shall I, Annelise, be able to decorate the halls of the future with, in lieu of the tearing asunder of the dogs by the black bear or boar, the frieze of the zoologist stalking with the camera? I am afraid when I think of it, I am afraid of the subsequent pictures in the *Fliegende Blaetter*.

"There will still be the Carnivora to photograph," said Soren Kierkegaard.

"Yes," said the painter, "yes. The naked fear of our flesh and blood may be there still, in the end, for our sole inspiration. But beware still, my dears, beware of the *Fliegende Blaetter*."

He held out his glass to have it refilled.

"I, too, have been in France, Fritze," he addressed himself, proudly, to Camelia, "and when I was in Paris last I read in a book about the death of King Francis I. He died, as you have perhaps heard, from the *vérole*—a good black, which they are also managing to do away with now, a strong black, which could run with you, like a long shadow, throwing itself forward and backward, from street lamp to street lamp, on your way to a rendezvous. It had just been imported from America, and had spread like, in our days, the cocktail. A French nobleman of very high birth"—very high birth was one of the weaknesses of the old artist—"had had his wife seduced by the king. He did not go round the world, or go in for collecting old jade, as you do today. He sent his faithful servant to get for him a prostitute of Paris, he passed the gift that he had from her on to his wife, and then watched the king—a charming man, who loved the arts—sicken and die. That was a proud man, who loved his wife, and loved King Francis, his king by the grace of God. That was a fine black night, the last night that he slept with his wife. I thought of that tale all the time, I tried to make a ballad about it, but it would not come off. I believe, though, that I could remember one of the verses if I tried." He took off his glasses, as if he could see his ballad better without them. "No, I cannot remember it after all." He remembered it very well, but, audacious as a painter he was shy as a poet, as some people may be bodily prudish and spiritually shameless, or vice versa. "From there I went to Marseilles," he continued, "and painted a series of still lifes, the best things I have ever done." So were all his pictures, when he recalled them, after a time, the best he had ever done. "If I had not had the jealous husband, the poor lady, the whore, and the king in my head, I could never have painted the dark shells of the lobsters, and the yellow and gray of the oysters, and the fishes' white bellies— no indeed not. All people can see that there are tragedies of high places, jealousy, red love and death in them."

The old painter fell into deep thought, and the tears came into his eyes at the memory of his great performances.

Julius laughed at him in his chair. He thought of the master's last picture, *The Virgin Receives Joan of Arc in Paradise*. There was but little black amongst the crimson and rose pinions, and golden halos of the angels, or the ultramarine of the Virgin's cloak, or in the kneeling maid's armor. Nor was there any in the Queen of Heaven's radiant countenance, as she rushed to welcome her last young saint, or in Joan's deadly serious face, fresh from the stake.

"The whole thing," said the old painter after a pause, "is this: we cannot get any higher than our highest light. It may as well be said: a Chinese white is the greatest glory that we can ever ascend to. Thus we have a scale to work upon, but if you cut off the lower half of it, what melodies can we play? The Marquis Talon of Bologna once gave me a ring, four hundred years old. Under the stone, in a small bezel, there is a deadly poison." He held up his short and broad hand, with the ring on, to show it to them, with the assurance of a person who believes what he is told. "Death and eternity concentrated. Now conditions were, then, such that it would be normally sensible to put it on when you were asked out for supper. Morally speaking, there was more in it than what you take with you, prudently, to a ball. With the torture chamber and the iron cages beneath you, in the vaults, and this small way to salvation upon a finger, you would have, on an evening, a good deal of playing up to the ecstasies of the wine and the beauty of your young naked courtesans and boys. But we, we have amputated the scale of life, we are playing upon a tin trumpet, and courtesans and boys can not possibly give us much pleasure."

Pierrot asked him to let her have a look at the ring, and he took it off and handed it to her.

"But you could perhaps lay in electric light in your pictures," said Arlecchino, who in her spare time was a polytechnical student, thoughtfully.

"Little edges of light, or a little sun, if you wanted to paint a sunset." The old painter looked at her for a few seconds. "When I was in Ingolstadt," he said, "the municipality had many difficulties, Polly, with their electric power plant, which was not strong enough, until they got a lady mayoress. She had proclamations put up, informing the people that little dynamos would be distributed, free of charge, at the municipal office, and summoning all good citizens, when making love, to connect up with these, adjusting them to the main current. For a while the city was brilliantly illuminated. But after a time it was noticed that the illumination, and even the patriotic zeal of the citizens of Ingolstadt, in many ways had slackened off badly, for you should not mix up electric lighting too much with great and noble feelings like patriotism."

Tido, in his soft and glittering Harlequin's uniform, sat with his chin in his hand, looking straight across the table at young Kierkegaard upon their host's right. He had got much to think of. A strange and incredible thing had happened to him, he had fallen in love after he had been quite sure himself that such a thing would never occur again. Now he did not know what to do about it.

He had known about her, and had known her by sight for a long time, as everybody in Copenhagen will know everybody else. Moreover they stood in a sort of romantic relation to one another, inasmuch as her divorced husband had married his divorced wife, and the two were believed to be very happy together. She had looked at him, wondering what this young man was like who had not been able to live with a woman who had shown herself capable of being happy with her husband. He had looked at her with the same sort of thoughts, in other terms, and had admired her too. And then suddenly this new frenzy had come upon him. It was so much like spring that he had all the time in his heart a vision of the sea, breaking the winter's ice, long-forgotten pictures of how with his brother he had used to pole himself about, in the first days of March, upon flakes of broken, salt ice, bareheaded after the long months of furred winter caps, intoxicated by seawater and sand and mild, caressing southerly winds. She was so fresh. Hard too, and cold, and he was in need of cold and hardness, life had been all too hot and soft to him.

She had put on her costume tonight to accentuate the situation. For all students of Soren Kierkegaard will know his deep and graceful work *The Seducer's Diary.* In it the hero Johannes brings into play all his ingeniousness and his great powers of mind, to obtain one single night of love with the heroine, and then leaves her forever. The modern young woman had been at one with the old poet in the fundamental principle—which he himself laments in that exquisite passage: "Why cannot such a night last for ever," etc.—that with one night the cup of love is emptied, the rest is dregs. But she had her own views upon the book, and had maintained, and lectured to him upon, the idea that the triumph of Johannes is not complete as long as he keeps Cordelia in the dark as to his prospects of leaving her forever at daybreak, and that the name of seducer is falsely assumed where you are in any way deceiving your partner. More honest than Kierkegaard's seducer, she had presented her problem straight to him, this night of love was *à prendre ou à laisser*. This ultimatum she had delivered only a few days ago, now her costume as a dandy of the forties brought it home to him. He had spent the evening meditating upon the situation, she would not have liked it, he thought, had she known in what an entirely unselfish spirit.

It had made an impression upon him that she should, at twenty-four, his own age, have it in her to think and behave like a flapper of fifteen. But on reflecting upon her, which was what he now always did, he had come to feel that she would never be more than fifteen: she had the bright metallic enthusiasm of that age, and he remembered having been taught at school that the ancient Persians reckoned upon everybody being fifteen in Paradise. Out of the mouth of babes and sucklings thou hadst ordained strength.

He agreed with her in her views upon love. He did not believe himself capable of making any woman permanently happy, they had never been so with him. He quite understood the words of the old painter as well, he had risen from many beds of love smeared with that pink paint of which he had been talking. He was not at all averse to lying down with her, now, upon the gridiron of Saint Lawrence. He had no faith in marriage, he had been married, so had she. He had also stood, when one of his ships came in, on the wharf with the wives and families of his skippers and supercargoes, he had talked with them and seen them receive their husbands as they landed. Those were the people who knew how to be married, and he admired them as much as the people who know how to play a concertina, for he could not play a concertina himself.

He sympathized with Annelise when she wanted to educate Aphrodite—the old missus needed it by now. And he understood as well as if she had lectured to him upon it—which at times she had also done—the high gamble, the attempt to sail close to the wind, the heroic vow to triumph or die for whatever she was in. He was at the present moment entirely occupied with the thought of assisting her in this enterprise of hers. She was very likely the last love of his life, a precious belonging, he would not for anything on earth let her down. If she were to don this shining armor of an erotic Don Quixote, how was he to save her from falling amongst windmills, of which he would himself be one? Sometimes he was a little tired or shy of her for being so pathetic, so much like a young child or a flower.

He had no confidence in his capacity, as a mere lover, to make his night the center of gravity in her life. Even had he had it, it would not have served him here, for she would walk out of the arms of Casanova as fresh as a lily, with a little ironical smile, were not other forces brought into play. Very loose and casual in most of her modes of living she was, with other young women of her own age, as disciplined as a Prussian soldier in regard to her imagination. She might want an orgy, but a sacred orgy, according to rites as ceremonial as the king of Spain's coronation, and she would turn in disgust from anything which could be had cheaper.

He wished that she had been that lady of the court of King Francis, of whom they had been talking, who threw her glove into the lion court, so that it fell straight between the lion and the tiger, and asked her lover to fetch it up. In the tale the knight went down, took up the glove and brought it back to her, then cast it in her face and turned his back upon her. Be that as it may, those two would not forget one another, not he her in his own castle, near a more peaceful wife, not she him. They would think sometimes of those seconds, of that lion, and the glove. It is, he thought, this dull business of forgetting and ever turning everything in your life into nought which tires one out. The part of the lady would have fitted Annelise, and he himself should have liked to be asked to fetch the glove.

He was no knight errant, he was a very rich young ship owner, with a great love of the sea, who had been born into Copenhagen society and had been chewed up by the women. Still there were these spring winds blowing in his friendship for her, singing of palm groves on far coasts, where he had been as a boy, out for the holiday with his father's ships, the surge of the great breakers— who could tell what throwback to ancient seafaring men, under the brown sails of their boats?

He had drunk much tonight to get an inspiration. Then he had thought that he might kill himself, or kill her, upon the morning, or—over a later bottle —that he might decline her offer altogether, or that he might marry upon the morrow of their one night, a rich and lovely woman who was at the moment in love with him. Would any of these things be likely to be what she wanted, to make her happy?—he thought not. A child he had thought of, and reckoned the idea a stroke of genius, but it would be no good, she would not fall in with it. Or he might hand her over to a gang of drunken sailors, with the geste of the knight in the lion court. That would hardly be fair to her, fairly as she had treated him all through their affair, and he had had experience with Danish sailors, they would see her home in a friendly way, making some very bad jokes about him. He looked at her: her cheekbones and chin, over her white shirt collar and black stock, were as delicately curved and finished as a violin. Under her tattered red hair her fair face, spotted, when May came, like a panther kitten, had tonight a self-luminous pallor.

Under the influence of these various moods and wines he had, on his way to the house, driving across the bridges of the canals of Copenhagen, and talking to Camelia about the advantage of having no face, made a verse, the only one he had ever made in his life:

> Along the ice the snow is driven,
> by the blowing weather.
> In loneliness the wind, the snow, the heart,
> play together.

"Oh Rosie," said Arlecchino, "sweet owl, dear nightingale, dwell in your artificial darkness. But I am all with the mayoress of Ingolstadt, and what will you give me if I find a note on the scale higher than any that has been there before?" "Ah," said Rosendaal, "then I will give you everything that I have, Polly."

"To a hostess," said Pierrot, who had put on the old man's ring, thoughtfully, "it would be a good thing to be able to work up your guests by the presence of dungeons and iron cages under the floor, and poisons upon the table which drive you mad, and bravoes behind the doors, to a success for·your courtesans and boys which otherwise you would never have obtained."

"Come," said Julius, "I will play you a tune upon a tin trumpet. You all know that we would blow in the air, sun, moon, and all the starry legions to give our sweethearts a diverting show, but you also know that we cannot. We must blow what we can, and give them such a show as is possible to us with the instruments we have got. Exiled from the dark, according to Rosie, and shut out from the pit, I will honestly try to take as high a note as the scale will allow me." "We do not want a high note," said Pierrot, "you are all mistaken when you think that we love cocks—we love nightingales. We want a melody, something that has got some sense in it, and repeats itself, and will go on. Alas, that you cannot play us." "How long do you want it to go on, Mimi?" he asked. Mimi thought for a moment. "For a year," she said.

"Can we make a happiness that will last a year?" asked Julius. "Let us try. We are eight people here, all of us—as things are here in Copenhagen—well off. Let us make a fund of all we have in the world, and draw lots for it. The winner will keep it for a year."

"Oh God," said Mimi, "I thought you were talking of a melody."

"What will it include?" asked Camelia thoughtfully. "Only material goods, such as can be handed from one person to the other," said Julius, "there the scale stops to us, and only the lamas of Lhasa who have lived over a hundred years in celibacy can play notes that go higher. Incomes, houses, cars, horses, jewels, objects of art—I cannot promise anybody your equilibrium of heart, not even that sweet-smelling breath of yours, Fritze."

"Yes, I will come in with you, Julius," said Arlecchino. "What will the losers do?" "The losers, walking out of their houses," said Julius, "will make their living somehow. They may even come in for a chance at Rosie's melliferous pitchy darkness of Vognmagergade. They will do what they like." "They will have to promise," said Arlecchino, "to leave the country and stay away for a year. Otherwise the winner will feel it his first duty to ask us all to stay with him, and use his cars." "All right," said Julius.

"And," said Camelia, "they will have to allow the winner to choose from this party one person, whoever he likes, to come with him for that year, and be the Grand Vizier Giafar to his Caliph Harun al-Rashid." "All right," said Julius. They made up the rules of the game, Arlecchino wrote them down upon a menu card.

"Are you coming in with us, Mimi?" asked Julius. "You said on New Year's night that it made you tired to be, at a lot of various times, the same person, and that you would rather be, at the same time, a lot of various persons. You might change, at least, your name, and the color of your hair, twelve times, or more, within this year, and perhaps you would like it." "That is good advice, Julius," said Mimi, "I will go and be a mannequin —for such a job has been offered to me—and I will be twelve different mannequins to twelve different houses, and create twelve different styles. But you must promise me to remember, each time that you see the new moon, to say: 'Mimi est morte! Vive Mimi!' "

"Are you coming in with us, Charlie?" asked Arlecchino. "You are the richest of us." Charlie tried to run his mental eye over the situation, but he had drunk too much for that, and had to let it promenade itself exceedingly slowly. If he had considered that he could say no at all, he would have done it, but could he? Here he was a foreigner amongst them, and had been so very well received —this was a courteous nation. At one time, when the box with his evening clothes had not arrived in time, they had all of them dined in dinner jackets for his sake, and that upon a highly important occasion. If he said no, they would think him a prig. He had liked to play poker as a very young man, and had the game in him still. As long as people did only entirely misjudge your hand, it did not matter whether they overestimated or underestimated it. He knew himself that he was a prig. Then he thought that in case he won, he would take Arlecchino with him for that year. Under the circumstances she would be so totally reckless about his possessions, and particularly about her own, that they would have an amusing time, and there would be no risk that he should eat her up. After all, it did not really matter whether you won or lost in the poker of life. "Yes," he said, "I will come in with you."

"Wake up, Tido," said Arlecchino, "we are arranging a lottery. Will you come in?"

Tido had to have it all explained to him over again. When he had understood it, he came in with them. He began pondering upon what he could do, when he should be, for a year, cut off from his house and comforts in Copenhagen—for in all his life he had never won any sort of gamble, and it did not occur to him that he might win here. In the course of the next few minutes he thought: "I can make old Hansen give me the *Ellen Dahl* to sail for a year. She trades to Lourenço Marques." He saw very clearly again the outline of Table Mountain, smoke-blue on a flower-blue sky, and the long strong breakers of the Cape, also the albatrosses in the air round the ship. That would take him away at least. He would go and see old Hansen about it in the morning. Suddenly the idea came into his head: "Would she come with me?" All his blood took to run so easy as the thought sunk into it, a sweetness, a calm, such as one may sometimes obtain in the sleep of the early morning hours, after a sleepless night, spread through his body and his mind. He would show her the albatrosses. They might sit on deck together, in those warm nights, with the phosphorescence running in the wake. And if it came to that, he might run the *Ellen Dahl* aground some morning, as the sun was coming up—she was a moldering old barge. Already the long waves of the Indian Ocean were, in his thoughts, washing over his head, and hers, in a glass-green darkness and deep rhythm. They would have to marry, because of the principles of the shipping company. But that night, of which she had talked, and at the idea of which he could not help smiling, or stop his smile from broadening, slowly, all over his face—that would not matter at all one way or the other. He might, as she had said herself, take it or leave it.

"Will you come in with us, Rosie?" asked Pierrot. The old painter pushed his little skullcap back, and scratched his bald head. "The capital cannot be touched?" he asked. "It will only be the interest?" He had all his life been a cute business man, and in the course of it had collected a large fortune, of which he took very good care. "Yes, it will only be the interest," Pierrot answered. "You cannot keep it more than a year, the *noir-de-bougie* of indigence." The old man thought it over. "I can keep my painting school—" he said, "I can live on that." "Oh no, Rosie," said Arlecchino, "that is too poorly roared by a Cerberus, a black dog of hell. I had hoped for certain that you would establish yourself, like your old friend, at Vognmagergade, and I would have been your Lysimachus, and have paid double price as your first customer. You must at least paint the misappreciated pictures of a starving young artist, and eat your black bread in an empty garret."

Rosendaal leaned back in his chair, emptied his glass and kept it in his hand, his little paunch gently balanced. His face became strangely rejuvenated as he looked at the girl. It was her words of an empty garret which gave him a deep pleasure. Through all his life he had been a collector, so passionately in love with the things of beauty that he had felt his soul to be in a piece of old glass or precious woven material, and his life dependant upon acquiring it. The friends who loved him had taken pleasure in making him happy in this great passion of his, millionaires, statesmen, princesses, and cocottes had heaped lovely things upon him, his house was filled with treasures. Sometimes, looking at them, he had envied Don Giovanni. Leporello, it is true, had kept lists of his particular hobby as well, but still part of the pleasure to him seemed to have lain in getting rid of them quickly again. It would be a dreadful thing to be a Don Giovanni of so soft or thrifty a nature that you simply could not bear to part with any conquest again, a nightmare to own an indissoluble seraglio. At the mention of an empty garret he seemed to see himself, as of old, high up in a bare studio, which smelt of turpentine and paint, and had a wide view over a town full of priceless things, which belonged to other people. His whole being settled so harmoniously down in the empty garret of his fancy that the flowery dining room, and the gaudy party before him, disappeared to his eyes.

"There need not," he said after a little while, his face still very clear by the glow of his ease of heart, "be any winner at all in your game." He refilled his glass, and drank it down, and explained his meaning, speaking very slowly: "Barum, the pasha of three horsetails—so I was told when I was in Constantinople—had a seraglio of three hundred and sixty-five wives, and used to visit one of them upon each night of the year, though he kept no system of consecutive order. Then he died. But as the question of succession was not settled, and the eunuchs and high functionaries of the seraglio did not want to lose their jobs, they kept his death a secret from his women, and had things going, as far as it was possible without Barum, as usual. In this way the routine, the competitions, and intrigues of the palace went on unchanged. On every evening of the year each lady painted and perfumed herself, on the chance of being the selected of the pasha, and every single one—instead of, as had been the case before, only the three hundred and sixty-four—passed the hour of midnight in an agony of jealousy and disappointment, not knowing herself to be, as in matter of fact she was, the one and only elect and favorite widow of the night." "You will see," he concluded thoughtfully, "that, in this way, a very powerful wheel will go on turning upon a pivot that is no longer there."

"Are you coming in, Annelise?" asked Julius. "Yes," she said. "If you do not win the prize," he said, "you will have to go into a brothel, with my Pegasus—or, otherwise, give up having your poems published. Let us see now how much of an idealist you are." "Yes, you will see that, Julius," said she, "I shall go into a brothel. At Singapore. I have read of them, there."

Tido caught her voice. "All right," he thought, "is that what she means to do? At Singapore." He remembered now a night that he had spent in a brothel at Singapore, sixteen years old. He had come with the sailors of his father's ship, and had sat and talked with an old Chinese woman, who kept a lot of birds in cages and had shown them to him. One of them was a parrot, which she told him had been given her by a very high-born English lover of her early youth. It seemed then to the boy that the bird must be many hundred years old. It could speak various languages, picked up in the cosmopolitan atmosphere of the house. But one phrase it had already been taught by the man who had given it to her, and that she did not understand. Now, on hearing that he came from a far country, she wondered if he might not be able to translate it to her. He had been strangely moved, expecting to hear Danish from that terrible old beak. But it had turned out to be classic Greek. He had been enough of a scholar to recognize it as a line from Sappho. He translated it to her: "The moon has sunk and the Pleiades, and midnight is gone. And the hours are passing, passing, and I lie alone." The old woman had smacked her lips and rolled her slanting eyes as he recited it. "He was drowned," she said. She asked him to repeat it to her, and nodded her head.

As he came out, the sky had been clear green behind the row of oleander bushes, the Chinese lamps in front of the house had hung like large luminous drops in the air, the dust had a strong bitter scent, and the sea, when they came down to their ship, was like molten lead. O Singapore, O great noble earth, O young days and nights of many years ago.

Under the table Julius and Camelia were pressing each other's fingers gently. Those two had a secret between them, which they could not tell the others: They were happy. Were they happy because of some secret? No, their secret was that they were happy. In the democratic world of today people are a little shy of letting out that they have been privileged in any way, even if they run no risk thereby. When their friends talked of their sorrows, the two unpretending young people kept silent, like well-behaved children in a party of grown-up persons, and they were ready to show them their sympathy too, only sometimes they looked at one another. So did they now hold each other's hands under the table only. They had been lovers twice, first when Camelia had still been a girl, second while she had still been married, and they might become so again, but it was not likely. They could hardly be called great friends, as individuals they had got but little to say to one another, they were just brethren in the freemasonry of happiness.

Life was very plain sailing to Julius. He swam away through it, hardly ever flapping his wings, like the albatrosses round the Cape. It was a paradox, significant of the age, that he should have been born a male, and have succeeded in realizing the ages' ideal of a boy and a young man, for by the laws of poetic justice, he ought to have been the heroine of the play. The lady, even the heartless lady—and heartless he was—holds the central place in the fairy tale without ever taking an active part. All happenings take place under her eyes, but she herself can hardly be said to be seen. This was Julius's manner and position within his circle of friends. When he met people he looked at them to see what they were like, but it never occurred to him that they might be looking back at him to find out what he was like, in fact they never did. He had never for a moment, in all his life, given any thought to what other people might think of him. He had, like truly womanly women, or like some phenomena of nature—the sea or the stars—if it comes to that—the capacity of drowning the observer's eye in his own being, and of remaining forever unseen. Within the existence of his friends he held the place of the idol within the temple, all-seeing and invisible. A thing which he liked was lovable to all of them.

As to Camelia, she was happy as a rose or a duck may be supposed to be happy. She did not ask much of life, and had she asked much it would have appeared little in her mouth. Too modest to wish to be an exception, and conscientious in her relation to fashion, she did at times invent conflicts in her life—unhappy love, jealousy, or criminal tastes of some sort—and she carried through her struggles with these monsters of her own conjuring-forth in a sweet and gallant spirit, like a lion tameress in a circus. Pierrot, who was her friend, had been her second in such graceful duels of pure swank, and had got much entertainment out of them. Camelia had even, upon a time, gone in for religious scruples, and had been in the hands of Buddhists, who should have had but little difficulty in teaching her Nirvana.

If she had any trouble it was this, that it was difficult for her to remain in her clothes. The people who had only seen her clothed might blame her for it, to the others it was not possible. And indeed young Aladdin ought to be forgiven for allowing himself, after a long divan with the learned in the law of Bagdad, who probably thought him an uneducated sort of sultan, to rub his ring a little, and call forth a gigantic djinn, just to point out to his court of justice, in a courteous manner, that he himself did also exist. For Camelia did not even dabble in any of the liberal arts, she had no taste for games, and was a bad chauffeur and mechanic. She had seen, at times, her partner in these undertakings summon his patience. And she had only to step out of her last garment to change him into an ecstasy-stricken slave, sobbing at her knees, caught up into the third heaven. To her all the melodies of a love affair were in this particular moment, the rest was silence.

If the fashions of her time had been against her, she would have had to outflank them by some pretty stratagem, like Lady Godiva. But she was now in a gracious harmony with the manner of her day, and there was no woman of Copenhagen who wore fewer clothes, or clothes which looked more as if they might fall off her at any moment. Pierrot had suggested that it would be a pretty coquetry to go to the carnival severely high-necked, she had agreed with the idea theoretically, but in practice it went against her. Her old lover, Julius, was holding one of her slim fingers in friendship and sympathy. Had she called in all her old lovers she would not have had fingers for them, and she would not have needed it either, their friendship and sympathy were at her disposal for the lifting of a little finger.

She was a little thoughtful at this moment, Julius's scheme had given her something to think of. For she had had within her, for some time, a central idea, worthy of any genius: she wanted a child. What a child to have. A cherub, a little star plucked out of the flowerbed of Heaven, she could see him with the corner of the eyes of her heart, but she did not fix her gaze on him—that, according to the best authorities, was not the right thing to do. If she won the prize she would go away, quite out of her own world, somewhere near the sea, where she could pick up the baby in peace, a shell on the beach. She would make Pierrot, her friend, come with her, between them they would manage to keep the trivial things of life at arm's length. It would be a joke that she should be disfigured and heavy, unable to wear fashionable clothes. That she should

Carnival

be sick, and have her fair face spoiled by brown
spots, what a joke. That is, what a joke to her own
heart, for her surroundings would be kept to wor-
ship in the orthodox manner. In Paris her old aunt,
who was frightened to drive in a taxi, had asked
her, when they were out together, to make the
driver go slowly by addressing to him what she
believed to be an all-powerful formula: "Doucement, doucement, je suis enceinte." Camelia had
laughed at the jest, but she had not made use of it,
she had no taste for blasphemy. Like all women
she believed in her heart in immaculate concep-
tion, and did not give the father of her cherub a
thought.

"Are we to go straight out from here to seek our
fortune, if we do not win, Mimi?" she asked. "No,
I do not think so," said Mimi, "we shall have till
tomorrow noon. That will give us time to see the
ball out."

They collected the eight little bits of paper, in
the large three-cornered white felt hat which went
with Pierrot's costume, over her black skullcap. It
was inevitable that a silence should fall over the
party during the following minute, it was the effect
of the gambling in itself. Pierrot, as hostess, prepared herself to take the hat round, to make each
of her guests pick out a little billet. The last one
she would keep herself.

"We will have one glass," said Julius, "before we
draw our lots. Let us clink glasses together, in the
manner of our grandfathers, they may well be looking down at us." At his words the faces changed
and took on a clear and serene look. Like nearly
all their generation, the members of Pierrot's and

Julius's supper party, while they had quarreled with their fathers had been devoted to their grandfathers.

"And give us a little speech, out of kindness," he said to Rosendaal, "you would not withhold it if we were off to the rack and the gallows, do not mind now wasting a word on our bonbonnière coloring."

"No, Julius, my child," said the painter, "it is not that I mind that. But if you were going to the gallows I should be inspired. The present circumstances are very charming, but I do not know what to say within them. An old bachelor may well feel a little shy at addressing a party of embryos, about to enter a world of little pink cradles. I shall be looking, I feel, like an old stork, sadly doubtful whether anybody believes in him at all. I shall have to play my tune upon a rattle." After a moment of meditation he began very slowly:

"My words do not despise, it is wise to be wise —so it follows willy nilly: it is silly to be silly. You are mad to be mad, it is bad to be bad, it is sane to be sane, it is vain to be vain—does my gospel sound alarming? It is charming to be charming, it is sweet to be sweet, it is neat to be neat, it is shocking to be shocking, it is fucking to be fucking, it is bonny to be bonny, it is funny to be funny, it's a bore to be a bore, it is more to be more."

He paused, a little out of breath, and looked round, pleased with himself. They had all been listening very attentively, as if his words were really going to their hearts. The old painter was about to begin again.

"Look here," said Pierrot, "I have just thought of something. We do sometimes, you know, dress

99

up and behave, for an evening, in the manner of some old time, in the Louis XV or Victorian style, for instance. Like my Empress Eugénie party at Christmas, or the Goya party last year.

In a hundred years, I have been thinking, some other people will dress up as a supper party of our period, of a hundred years ago to them. Let us be that tonight, until tomorrow noon, a supper party of 2025, masquerading as people of a hundred years ago. We will be in love with the old-fashioned romantic woman of 1925, and will make love—very, very well—in the manner of the period of King Christian X. For it is a little silly to be a caricature of something of which you know very little, and which means very little to you, but to be your own caricature—that is the true carnival!"

"In those days," said Polly, quickly taking up the line of her sister's thoughts, while the butler solemnly filled the glasses, "came the first incarnation of a female *jeunesse dorée*, those young women who were the most lovable flower of the old romantic civilization—" "And who formed," said young Kierkegaard, "to amuse a fallen world the exclusive Order of the Laughing Sisters, all of whom took the strict vow to renounce for ever poverty, chastity, and obedience—" "And who yet proudly observed," said Pierrot, "according to the prophets of the day, the pure hunger and nakedness of poverty—" "The noble barrenness of chastity—" said Camelia, a little timidly, but laughing herself. "And," said Arlecchino, waving her glass in her hand, "the high ecstatic irresponsibility of obedience, yielding nothing to the dancing dervishes."

"Holy Holbein," said old Rosendaal, in high glee, "what a pas de quatre macabre."

Julius said: "And who, at last, to all men's old dream bending, of love, which holds no secrets and no strife, but openness, equality, and concord, posed sweetly to us as Athenian boys."

The butler had filled the glasses, the wine seemed somehow alive on its own, regardless of the drinkers. They lifted their glasses and joined them, stretching in their arms amongst the flowers. The silence for a moment was so deep that the little ring of the glasses, as they met, echoed, like to the sound of a very distant horn in a long glen.

Just at this moment the attention of the party was suddenly drawn to the lights of a car, coming up the drive and stopping at the front door. After a second it hooted, softly. Julius and Camelia looked quickly at one another.

Petersen, the butler, held open the door to the figure of a Negro, dressed all in black.

He stood for a moment in the doorway, looking at them, as they all looked at him, those who had their backs to the door turning all round. He looked a small dark figure against the white door, very shy, as if put out by the sight of the supper party on their feet, their glasses lifted to receive him. Still he walked, after a second, across the floor with much energy and dignity.

"Good evening," said Pierrot, "you are very welcome. I know who you are. You are Zamor, Madame du Barry's Negro page. I have seen you in a picture of a supper party, in Paris."

At these words, Zamor bowed to her very deeply.

She told Petersen to lay a cover for her new guest on her left, between herself and the painter, and the two moved their chairs to make room for him, the legs of one chair getting entangled in the ample yellow robes of the old man. Zamor stood for a little while as if he did not mean to accept the invitation, then he sat down beside her.

Charlie said across the table: "Is Madame du Barry herself coming with you? There is a tradition in my family that she wanted to marry, at the beginning of her career, an ancestor of mine who was at the embassy in Paris, but he refused, on the ground that it was cheaper to buy milk than to keep a cow, and ran away to England. I should not like to be recognized, here in Denmark, as the descendant of anyone totally ignorant of the economics of dairying."

A sadness, a disturbance, passed over Zamor's face at the name of his mistress. "No," he said, "she is not coming here. Nobody is coming with me. I am alone."

"What will you have, Zamor?" asked Pierrot, looking all over her supper table.

"What can I get?" he answered slowly, either from modesty or fastidiousness, following her gaze along.

Pierrot took his reply to be inspired by the last feeling. "We had nearly finished," she said, apologetically, "we did not know that you were coming. But you could have some oysters—" She went on, suggesting various things from the buffet to him. "And the company of four lovely women, and the conversation, upon life and death, of four men. If you want anything more, let us know." She stopped, quite thoughtful. She had his glass filled for him.

This interruption in their drawing of lots had impressed them all, as a sort of strange omen to it. Tido began to sing, in a low and pleasant voice, the old sailor's song of the girl who suffers from fits and can only be helped by someone making love to her quickly. Arlecchino, from the other side of the table, gently whistled the accompaniment.

The painter kept his eyes on Zamor, taking him in altogether with a sort of hurried gluttony, like an old monkey, nervous about being interrupted, quickly cracking and peeling a coconut.

The costume of Zamor was beyond reproach—it was clear that it had been made, a hundred and fifty years ago, regardless of cost. It was all done in black watered silk, with little bits of point d'Alençon, at the neck and cuffs, and the lace, like the small rose-diamond buttons of the jacket, and the *agrafe* in the tall black turban, the eye of the connoisseur recognized to be priceless. The black of the materials had not faded at all with age. It was so deep that looking at it was really like gazing down into a narrow, bottomless well. The heart of the painter, mature for delight at this stage of his supper, was rocked upon little waves of pleasure at the sight. "No black magic, black horehound, or black homburg, no blackmail, not the black hole of Calcutta," he thought, "could be blacker."

On the other side, Zamor's own color was unmistakably a fake. It was not even well chosen, there is no race with a skin of such an unmixed, sooty darkness, it was a slap in the face of a colorist. But it was laid on carefully, and in the midst of it Zamor's big, grave, gray eyes, with eyelashes blackened as carefully as those of Camelia, produced an effect.

He began to eat very quietly. He had on a pair of black gloves, which seemed to be in his way. "You ought to take off your gloves," said Arlecchino. He looked up at her quickly, and shook his head a little. She thought: "He has not got his hands blackened underneath," and said no more about it.

"Zamor," said Pierrot all at once, "we were arranging a lottery the moment before you came. Will you come in with us? If so," she explained to the others, "I will cut one more paper."

The idea of Zamor coming in with them, quite suddenly gave a new importance to their gamble, although they could not themselves have told why it should be so. In Pierrot herself it produced the sensation which you get in an aeroplane, when you have for some time kept your eyes inside the machine, and then turn and look down—an apprehension of distance, a perspective. Their faces took on a strained, an intent look. Only old Rosendaal drew up his eyebrows.

"You see, Zamor," said Pierrot, "we have thought that it might be a good thing if, instead of all of us having an equal, respectable income, which is unsatisfactory, we did, for a year, make one of us very rich, and the others poor—truly poor, you understand, penniless. My husband even considers that it would be likely to produce a melody. So we have, all of us, put all we have in the world into this hat of mine. There are eight lots in it, one I have marked with a cross. The one who draws that one, gets it all."

Zamor kept his eyes on her over the edge of the glass and said nothing.

"But Mimi," said Rosendaal, making a little face at his hostess, "do we know if your young friend is prepared to put up, in this lottery, his stake with ours? Because," he went on, pushing back his cap, "there would be no sense in it otherwise."

"Yes, there would be sense in it," said Arlecchino. "If he does not win, it will not make the slightest difference."

"No, but if he wins?" said Rosendaal.

"If he wins," said Arlecchino, "we shall be the ladies of Baram Pasha's harem of which you told us, Rosie."

The old painter looked from the one laughing sister to the other. He was not really very keen on their gamble, and thought that it might as well be given up. In any case, he reflected, they should not succeed in taking, at this moment, Zamor away from him. He thought: "These people see in him only a carnival joke. But there is more here. Perhaps a good deal of suffering, despair, a surprise to the whole party. Probably, since he is very young, he is in love—maybe he is in love with one of the insipid women here, poor Zamor. In any case he is the only effective object in the insipid party of tonight."

He waved away the women with his hand, and said: "Monsieur Zamor, there is time enough, and more than enough, for the lottery. But tell me first: Are you the happiest person in the world?"

"No, I am not," said Zamor.

"Then nobody is the happiest person in the world," said the old man, lifting up his hands. "To be the one little light shining in the darkness is held to be a martyrdom. But to be the one central little shadow in a world of artificial rosy lights, that ought to be a treat. You are the little mouche of Versailles, put on by du Barry herself in the most piquant spot, for the old king to find. I envy you, Zamor."

"Give him at least time to drink his wine," said Pierrot, and refilled Zamor's glass.

"Are you, sometimes, jealous of the old king?" said Rosendaal, "do you allow yourself the luxuries of nostalgia, and when you have long enough been sugared for a bonbon à la du Barry, do you let your soul howl for the ways of your own country, and dream that you have the tenderest parts of Madame in the pot?"

Zamor laid down his knife and fork, and looked at the painter gravely. "Zamor," he said, "was a good republican and philosopher. In his old age he kept on the walls of his little room of the rue Perdue the portraits of Robespierre and Marat, and on his shelves the books of Rousseau. He had never liked to be a toy, he had been so only because he could not help it."

"Was it indeed so?" asked Rosendaal. "Very pleasant, Zamor, very pleasant. What a droll little comedy, that in the end an old, gray, and poor Negro should have made the incorruptible his fetish, for having snapped off the head of the woman he loved. But you followed the tumbril which took the lovely countess to the scaffold, Zamor, and heard her shrieks—and what feeling drove you to that? Were you, during that hour, in the streets of Paris, a hyena of the Zambesi, out upon the blood track—or a little, male, somber Stabat Mater, Zamor?"

Zamor did not solve the problem for him, but scowled a little at him, in an unpleasant way.

"Oh God, Rosie," said Camelia, "give us a chance to say something. Was she really so lovely, Zamor?

Were they really lovelier then, when they did never run, or scream? Should we cut a poor figure beside them, if they appeared here, suddenly, carrying their dimples high?"

"Yes, and would the great seducers of the eighteenth century, Zamor," said Charlie, "simply sweep the floor with us, and make the women we have got, and even our vampires and flappers, drop right or left? Or should Valmont, and Don Giovanni, and Lord Byron later on, have to lie down a little until they had picked up the jargon of the movies?"

Zamor, at these words, put his glass down, wiped his mouth on his napkin, not at all unlike a hyena which has drunk at the ford, and rose from his chair. He stood for a moment, the sullen, dark look still on his face. Then he took two long steps backwards, shoving back the chair which slid along the floor. Pushing his right hand quickly down into his pocket he pulled out a pistol, and pointed it straight at the people round the table.

"Put up your hands," he said.

They had to lift their hands, and stared at him.

He stood and looked at them, and slowly a little smile, like that of a sick child, broke through the grimness of his face. "Now you are not so great as you were," he said, and nodded at them.

"I think that you know me," he said. "I know all of you. I am the salesman in Madame Rubinstein's antique shop, and her adopted son. I have sold all of you many things. Now give me five hundred kroner, or else I shoot at you."

They were very surprised, and said nothing.

"I can let you know," said the young man, "that I have killed one person tonight before I came here, an old woman. I am not trying to amuse you only."

He collected his thoughts a moment. "You have read the *Liaisons*, all of you? 'La honte qu'inspire l'amour'? Eh bien, la honte qu'inspire l'assassinat est comme sa douleur, on ne l'éprouve qu'une fois!" —he grinned a little.

Arlecchino was the first of them to find her voice. "Good merciful God," she cried, her voice ringing with all the deepest retained emotions, "Now I have never in my life seen the like of it!"

Old Rosendaal, his hands up, his mouth open, without daring to turn his head, rolled his eyes round at her. He looked like the old man of the sea, when Sindbad the sailor had thrown him off at last, and he was lying helpless on the ground. The little black muzzle of the pistol, pointing, as it seemed, at him, straight at his face only, had in a second done away with him, annihilated him altogether. This was not because he was afraid, anything pointed straight at him would probably have had the same effect. Had Sindbad had the opportunity of pointing anything straight at the old man, he might have got rid of him earlier, and this was why the torturer kept on his shoulders, out of focus. Thus did the old artist sit on the shoulders of life, and of all human beings round him. It was to him only to point at life, with his brush or with his fat forefinger, and a direct personal move, with himself as object, was deadly unnatural to him, he simply could not stand it. Now he looked at Arlecchino, and from her, as far as he dared, at his other *convives*, with their hands up, to find out what they thought of the position. It might be either a joke of the carnival, or again a very serious situation. What was their view? As he looked at them, the truth slowly dawned upon him. "God," he thought, "they do not give the question any consideration at all. Good God in Heaven," he went on thinking, "these people do not know the difference between the two things!"

"Five hundred kroner," said Zamor, "or else I shoot at you."

As he moved back a little to take up a better position, he struck his chair. Not being too steady on his legs, he profited by the chance to sit down in it, still covering the whole party with his pistol.

Pierrot by now had collected herself sufficiently to speak to him, the big dark eyes in her white face opened wide, her hands up by her ears.

"Did you mean to shoot us all the time—when you came in?—when you sat down here at the table?" she asked, the exact emotions of her sister's heart echoing in her voice.

Zamor did not answer at once. "I did not mean to sit down with you at all, when I first came in," he said. "You asked me. Then I was hungry."

This word again stopped their mouths, and made a stronger impression on them than the barrel of the pistol, which swayed slightly in the hand of Zamor, from the face of one of them to another.

"I might not," he said suddenly, "have decided to shoot any of you at all, if you had not begun to talk of the eighteenth century. You do not know yourself, perhaps—though it is your fault—what it is to be dealing in it always. Madame Rubinstein had got nothing outside of it, as you know, it was her speciality, it was all that, just from one end of that rotten period to the other. If I had not broken off the whole business tonight, I should have become, myself, as you have perhaps noticed, a figure of the eighteenth century. And then, when I had done all I could, and came here, you began to talk of it."

"All my life," said Zamor very solemnly, "I shall divide people into those who have knowledge of the eighteenth century and those who have not. If I am told of anybody that he has studied the eighteenth century and knows all about it, I shall know well, at once, what sort of person he is. If I am brought before a court now, over this murder, I shall tell the jury enough about it to make them acquit me. I know all about the mistresses of the regent, and the little Morphée, and the amorous life of Catharine II, and the *Encyclopédie*. I know everything, absolutely everything that you can know, about snuff boxes and clyster pipes. I, I could never make a mistake between a Petitot père and fils—you could do that, you have made it. There has never been anything as damnable as the eighteenth century, and the abbés of it, and the petites maisons, and the women, except the people now, who lick the old mummies on the bottom, and think that you have got le vrai goût de la gourmandise. I have had to live within it, one day after another, all my life. If I had not been careful now, and done something, I should have become Zamor, I should really have become Zamor. And all that for twenty kroner a week, that was what she paid me. She was just like La Goudran."

They did not say anything to this, they could see that he suffered very much.

"Is it Madame Rubinstein whom you have killed?" asked Camelia, in a small voice. She had done much business with the old woman, and stood in some fear of her herself.

"Yes, it is her," said Zamor.

The image of the old woman, in her blood, at these words seemed to be present in the room, and made the moment darker to the listeners than would have done the description of a fair and innocent victim.

"I cannot," said Rosendaal suddenly, "stand with my arms up any longer. Press the bell with your foot, Mimi, and call in Petersen."

"No," said Mimi. Zamor immediately changed the direction of his pistol toward the old painter.

"Or," cried the old man, "give him his five hundred kroner, in God's name."

"No," said Julius. "No. We will not give him five hundred kroner. We will rather die. Let him come into our gamble."

"Now," said Zamor, "I shall count up to eight, one for each of you, and then I shoot."

"Speak to him, Mimi," said Julius, "he is so impatient with me."

Pierrot made a little tiny step forward. "Listen, Zamor," she said, still standing with her arms uplifted, like a Pierrot in a ballet, shining in her white silk. "You cannot ask this of us. None of us knows at this moment if he is very rich, or poorer than you are. I myself, at present, have not got five hundred kroner, nor five even, to give you. I may have to apply for your job, and sell clyster pipes. If Madame Rubinstein has been killed, I may have to reopen her shop. The fate of all of us is in that hat, as I told you."

"One," said Zamor.

"If you come in with us here," said Pierrot, "we shall all be equally situated, we shall have the same chances, and it is just in the hands of fate who of us shall be very rich, and who very poor. Do you not think that that is a good thought? It is not often that a community can manage such absolute equalization. No," she went on, carried away by her own words, "perhaps just once in a hundred years."

"Not that," said Rosendaal.

"If you win," said Pierrot, "it will be more than five hundred kroner to you, you know. And if you do not win—why," she concluded in a sudden inspiration, "you can shoot the winner then."

"But I will not come in with you. Two," said Zamor.

There was a moment of deep silence. Camelia, who had been sitting rigid as a statue and very pale, since she had been made to imagine Madame Rubinstein with her throat cut, and who had, as already said, herself once been given to religious scruples, and was thus acquainted with the language of it, then asked: "Is it because you do not think that it would be right?"

Zamor gave her a short look of contempt. "Keep that for your Sunday school," he said. "I do not think that it would be amusing, that is why."

Again he had stopped their mouths. He himself felt that he was scoring on them, and laughed a little, describing a small figure in the air with the pistol. Camelia looked quickly down herself to find out what it was about her which made him believe that she kept a Sunday school.

"How is it that you think that I would be your equal at all?" he asked. "I would not be like any of you, now that I see you there. There is not one of you, either, who would be like one of the others."

"Wait," said Julius, "a moment. If you have killed Aljona Ivanovna, the police, I take it, may be here after you any moment. If you will come into our gamble we will all of us tell them that you have been with us all night, and it will be obvious to anyone that you must have been so, you join so well in the spirit of the party."

Zamor shrugged his shoulders, in no manner tempted by the offer, and counted: "Three."

"But what do you want to do," asked Tido, "since you do not like to trade in antiques?"

"What right have you to ask me?" said Zamor.

"No, I am sorry," said Tido.

"Oh, and what right have you," cried the old painter in indignation, in a high falsetto, "to point a pistol at us?"

Zamor, in reply, turned the pistol straight at him. "Four," he said.

"I want," he said suddenly, to Tido, his heart so filled with these dreams of his that he could no longer hold them back, "to be a diver. I want to go with the scientific expedition which is to start on Thursday, and goes all over the world to study the breeding of the eel. For five hundred kroner I can get a diver's outfit, and go with them." Then, as if he regretted giving away so much of his soul, he counted: "Five."

"But I can get you a diver's outfit," said Tido, "and I could recommend you to the expedition. They have got one of my ships."

Zamor looked at Tido. The two were a little like one another, except that Zamor was wild, and Tido tame. Also Tido stirred under his gaze, while Zamor kept perfectly still, for no tame animal can be as still as a wild one.

The old painter, the sweat running down his face, had an inspiration, and felt that he might have a finger in this pie still.

"Let me speak to him," he cried, "I understand him better than any of you. Mr. Zamor, I will tell you what you can do. If you win, and lay aside your income for a year, leasing out the houses and whatever else you find available, you may collect, during that year, a capital which will give you—" he made up the calculation with difficulty in his head, his arms still up, though sunk into a sort of arch, as if he was trying to pull the figure out by his old hands, "fifty thousand kroner, or thereabouts, a year, for the rest of your life."

It was clear that the chance did for the first time impress Zamor. He looked steadily at the artist, who thought: "In any case he has given up counting for the moment."

Here Arlecchino, who had not said a word since she gave her first great shout of excitement, but had stood to attention like a soldier, came on the stage again, her voice still filled with much retained emotion.

"There is one thing which you have quite forgotten," she said. "Now I shall tell you, so that you will remember. Last spring, on the fourth of April, I came into your shop, to buy a pink snuffbox with diamonds on it. I said to you that it was my birthday, so that you must let me have it cheap, and at that you yourself told me that it was your birthday as well, so that we had been born on exactly the same day. You went to ask Madame Rubinstein if she would come down in her price, but she would not. I could not buy it. Then, as I was walking away, I took the snuffbox myself. I put it into my pocket. You saw it very well, and you said not a word."

She drew in her breath very deeply. "After that," she said, "I walked round past Madame Rubinstein's shop nearly every day, to see if she were not dead."

The people round the table found a moment's relief in bursting out laughing at Arlecchino's tale. The only absolutely grave faces were those of the two people born on the same day.

"Oh, I am a thief," said Arlecchino, "you knew it. You can inform the police. When they come here for you, they can take us both together."

Zamor opened his mouth, and the old painter jerked back a bit, imagining that he was going to count six, but he shut it again.

"Shoot at me now," said Arlecchino, "for being a thief to Madame Rubinstein. Or else come in with me, and take one of our lots. Take it now."

She lifted the hat from the table, took a step straight up to Zamor's chair, and standing quite close to him, presented him the large soft hat. The barrel of his pistol, in his first surprised movement, knocked against her body, and she pressed herself to it. Zamor lifted it up in the air and backwards, trying to get himself up.

Arlecchino and Zamor stared at one another. Arlecchino thought: "If now there was any God at all,

I should say to him: "You have never done anything whatever for me. Now let him draw the ticket
with a cross on it."

"Do not take it, Zamor," said Tido, "it is the sort
of thing that one regrets."

Tido was too late with his advice. For a moment
the pistol barrel swayed up and down, then, slowly
lowering it, Zamor dipped his left hand down into
the hat, and drew up a small rolled up bit of paper.
Arlecchino, at this moment, dared not look at him,
but lifted her eyes to the ceiling. The people at
the table, afraid still to take their hands down,
stretched their necks to see what was happening.
Zamor, without letting go the pistol, unrolled the
paper with the fingers of his left hand, like a cigarette. It was a blank. He sat and stared at it, and
did not lift his eyes up again.

Arlecchino turned round to the rest of the party.
"No, it was a blank," she said, put the hat again on
the table, and returned to her seat.

"And that," said Pierrot, "is that."

At this, with one great sigh of relief, they all
lowered their arms once more.

"And so," said Julius, "we will go on again, with
your consent, where we left. We shall have to cut
one more piece of paper now. That is all."

In her quality of hostess Pierrot took the hat
round, and each of the party put a hand into it, and
drew out a bit of paper. They stood with them in
their hands, like good children, without looking,
until she herself had taken the last bit as her part,
and flung away the hat. Only old Rosendaal unrolled his bit, scrutinized it, turned it upside down,
and held it up against the light.

"Now," said Pierrot, and smiled, a little pale.

They all unfolded their tickets and looked at them, and from the tickets up at one another. There was a moment's silence.

Very lightly Arlecchino placed one foot on the table, and swung herself on to it, standing up straight, with a still face.

"It is mine," she said, holding up her paper, and turning round for all of them to see it.

The whole party flung down their worthless tickets, and clapped their hands at her.

Young Kierkegaard said: "And ever so was virtue fortune's magnet." Laughing, they thronged round her, and threw their congratulations and good advice up in her grave face.

Julius said: "O fate, O destiny, we are all women before thee, hear thou now our women's prayer! Be the old-fashioned lover, be the ravisher, but not the comrade, the considerate partner. Leave us not ourselves, not to ourselves, but be, like Mozart's hero, all in all. Frivolous and frail, we do not flee from bloodshed, give us a weight, our destiny, any weight! But no, O no more coitus interruptus."

Arlecchino kept her place on the table very calmly, like an exhibited work of art, of high value.

"Now," she said, "I shall choose one of you to follow me."

She looked round from the one face to the other, and gave herself good time to observe every one of them. Her eyes dwelt on Charlie, then on her sister, and, for a long time, on her brother-in-law. At last her eyes and Charlie's met again. "It is curious," she thought, "to get, in each single glance, one whole year, exactly like what it would be."

"I shall take Zamor," she said.

By this time they had all of them quite forgotten Zamor. He sat on his chair still, a little shrunk, he had been following the course of the drawing of lots. The long black barrel of his pistol hung down between his legs, innocuous now, as if slack and empty. At the sound of his name he got up, and went toward the door.

"I shall take Zamor," said Arlecchino again.

He looked up at her, took another step, and stopped.

"You are not going away, Zamor," said Arlecchino, "I want you to stay with me. That was all in the rules of the gamble, and once you have come in, you must submit yourself to them. I want you to come with me for one year."

"But not for an embarkment to Cythère," said Camelia, "for that dates from the eighteenth century, Polly."

"No, I offer you a regular job," said Arlecchino. "I will pay you exactly what Madame Rubinstein did. What did you get from her, now?"

"As much as I said before," said Zamor.

"That is good," said Arlecchino.

There was no more spirit in Zamor, he said neither yes nor no.

"For what job are you engaging him, Polly?" asked Charlie.

Arlecchino thought it over a little. "For a shadow," she said at last. "If Peter Schlemihl could get his shadow sold, they must be marketable goods. Why should I not buy one then?"

"Has that been your ambition: to have a shadow, my dear?" asked Charlie.

"Truly," said Arlecchino, who had acted this part in an amateur theatrical, "I hold ambition of so airy and light a quality that it is but a shadow's shadow. Then are our beggars bodies, and our monarchs and outstretched heroes the beggars' shadows. Shall we to the court? For, by my fay, I cannot reason."

"What do you want with that little drain rat?" asked Rosendaal.

"Is that you asking, Rosie?" said Arlecchino gravely. "May he not well be two hundred years old, bottled with fusel, inebriating you by the fumes alone, when I draw the cork? You carry it so high toward me now, Rosie, you great artist, because you managed, as you ever do, to get more out of the situation than any of us. You had a great fright. But we, who are not so clever, and are not artists, and not great, we must take out of life what we can get."

"Pooh," said the old painter. "I do not think that he ever meant to shoot."

"No, but he pointed a pistol at us," said Arlecchino, "no one else of you has ever done that."

"And I wonder," said Rosendaal, pursuing his own thoughts, "if he ever killed the old woman."

"I knocked her on the head, in any case," said Zamor in a dull voice.

"Well," said the old man, who had all the psychical life of Copenhagen on his five fingers, "and she is so deadly devoted to you that she will forgive you altogether, and come running after you tomorrow, begging you to come back, and raising your wages. You have never run any risk whatever from her."

119

Zamor shuddered, but looked away and said nothing.

"Oh, but she is not going to get him back," said Arlecchino, "do you not understand, any of you, that I am going to make up for what I have done to Zamor? That was his virginity: that he would not be like any of us. I made him sell his soul for a blank in a lottery. It was a bad moment of my life, and Tido was right. I do not know how you, you men, have been able to carry, through all the centuries, the guilt of having seduced virgins. I cannot do it, it is to me a terrible thing to be a seducer, indeed I cannot imagine anything worse. I am giving a year to make good its loss to Zamor. Is it not strange," she went on gravely, "that one should have to live for nineteen years to be taught, in reality, what virginity is?"

"Oh, my dear Polly. Alas, alas," said Charlie.

"Come away, come away," cried Pierrot to her guests, "we must back to the ball. There are still some hours till morning."

Arlecchino turned to old Rosendaal. "Shall I not take Zamor," she said, "to be my conscience for a year? Shall I not be allowed to have a conscience, Rosie? Something black in my life, a little mouche on my soul?"

"And you do not even know his name," said the artist.

"What is your name?" Arlecchino asked Zamor.

"Why, Rubinstein," said he.

"But good God," cried the old man, "he is not even genuinely black, Polly."

"No," said Arlecchino, "he is to be my artificial shadow, my artificial conscience."

"I may inform you, Arlecchino," said the old painter, quoting an ancient Danish comedy. "That everything has got an end, and foolery as well."

"No, on the contrary, Signor Lothario," answered Arlecchino, who was also well versed in her classics. "Everything is infinite, and foolery as well."

The Last Day

Whitsunday morning of the year 1852 was, in Copenhagen, divinely mild and fresh. The air was not quite clear. But it was filled with radiance, as well as with the voices of all the church bells of the town, chiming on overhead, so that it did not seem unlikely that the Holy Ghost, on this his anniversary, might be dwelling up in it. A gay little breeze ran through the streets, dangled the hanging signboards of bakers and barbers, and played with bits of straw on the pavement. All winter the wind had been a bitter enemy to the townsfolk, but today the breath of the air was as sweet as a kiss. It was faintly intoxicating to the young girls of Copenhagen, who this same morning had thrown away their heavy winter garments, and were walking the streets in white cotton stockings and gingham frocks, under summer bonnets. As the caress of the wind ran up their legs, under their starched petticoats, they shivered a little with cold, and had visions of flights. All the people were going to church, and were planning to go out in the woods afterwards. Green dreams of the forests round Copenhagen were, therefore, manifoldly brought into the tall, somber, silent vaults, together with prayer books and folded white handkerchiefs, and the gently wafting leaves of the chestnut trees by the porches to the churchgoers seemed like nature's own first, sweet greeting.

Young Johannes Søeborg, a country parson's son and himself a student of theology, came through

the streets with a black poodle puppy under his
arm. He took the back streets, walked on quickly
and looked neither right nor left, because he was
on his way to a house of ill fame in Pistolstraede.
He would not have been going there, in the full
light of a holy morning, if it had not been for the
puppy. Three days ago he had saved it from being
drowned in the canal outside his window by a
party of drunken sailors—it had broken a paw from
their hard handling. Madam Kraft, Johannes's land-
lady, had refused to let him keep a dog in his room,
and he knew but few people in Copenhagen. The
only person to whom, under the circumstances, he
could turn for help, was a girl named Boline, a
prostitute. She was herself a village girl, who had
come to town and gone wrong there. In Pistolstraede she missed the animals of her childhood,
and one of the few times that Johannes and she
had talked together, she had told him how much
she wanted to have a dog that was her own. She
had added that the fare of the house was so plentiful that they could easily keep more than one dog
there, had they had them.

As he walked, Johannes was kept company by a
misgiving in the heart. For he remembered that,
before he made up his mind to bring Boline the
puppy, he had pondered on means of sending it on
to the island of Funen, to his sweetheart there. Her
name was Lise, she was seventeen years old, and
was the granddaughter of another old country parson. Johannes and Lise had not met for two years,
their engagement was a secret, and perhaps, he reflected, to her it was only child's play, while to him
it was a great thing. He thought of her every morn-

ing and evening. But there was in the idea of the girl's existence—devoid of ambition, all given up to the welfare of others, and in itself innocent and art-less, like the growth of a flower—something from which his thought receded, in reverence or in alarm, as it receded from the idea of eternity. If it had been the other way round, and he had first planned to let Boline have the puppy, he would never have committed the blasphemy of offering it to Lise. And even as it was, the small dog in his arms, which from time to time tried to lick his face, because in his mind it had for a short time been Lise's dog, and was now going to be an inmate of the house in Pistolstraede, weighed down his heart a little, as a symbol of the sin and sadness in the world.

The path of life was not easy to Johannes, nay on the contrary it was strewn with thorns. Two of the thorns went in deeper than the others. One was his disbelief in certain dogmas of the church, on which, nevertheless, he would have to take the oath by the time of his ordination. It was for instance difficult for him to believe in the resurrection of the body, for he distrusted the body. And as this dogma was included in the third article of faith, in the very gospel of the day, his doubt seemed to estrange him and the Holy Ghost, as if the ringing of the bells were not for him. The second thorn in his flesh was no lesser thing than one of the deadly sins themselves: avarice, that panic of losing or spending money, that he had inherited from a long line of peasant forefathers.

He was never for a long time out of the hands of one or the other of his Erinnyes—when in the grip of one he could not recall the other, nor realize that

he had ever thought it equally horrible. His affliction was made heavier by the circumstance that he
was a young man of a desultory imagination. He
could not, in life, foresee or guess, but was under
the necessity of learning by experience, and feeling
his way step by step. In this manner, from former
bitter lessons, he knew that no lost money would
make him suffer such twinges of conscience as that
spent on food. In his childhood he had listened to a
sinister tale of his great-grandfather, a rich peasant
of Jutland. Out on his lonely farm this old man had
stuck to the faith that, by practice, both beasts and
human beings might do away with the need of feed-
ing, and he had seen his cows and pigs die in the
stables before, to the great relief of everybody, he
himself had succumbed to his discipline. In his
heart Johannes felt a kind of sympathy with his
great-grandfather. The incessant upkeep of the body
at times was so loathsome to him that he would altogether give up eating. In the same way, through
experience only, he knew that he was never worried by what money he paid to Boline—indeed it
was gone from his mind the moment it was paid
down. For that reason his acquaintance with the
girl brought him a curious peace of heart.

When Johannes arrived in Pistolstraede, the land-
lady told him that Boline was asleep. He had to
wait for her in a cool room, amongst gilt sofas and
chairs from the last century, that had once stood in
noble houses of Copenhagen, but were now shabby,
and hopelessly out of fashion. Still the salon had
been cleaned up after last night, and there was even
a fresh branch of beechleaves stuck in the tall mirror. He would not sit down, nor set the dog down.

A couple of times he made up his mind to go away, so as to escape facing Boline in the daylight.

At last Boline came into the room, in a petticoat and a dressing jacket. Her face was swollen with sleep, and streaked with the paint of yesterday, and she was in a fierce and quarrelsome mood. In her bed she had been listening to the church bells, and had longed to go to church with decent people. With her nose in her pillow she had recalled to herself the hymns and the timid, solemn steps of the congregation up the aisle. She agreed with the regulations of religion and of the police, that people like herself ought not to come to church. But her rare, deep emotion was turned into a violent moral indignation with Johannes, a parson's son, from her own part of the country, for coming to the house in church hours, on a most holy day. She began the conversation by telling him what she thought of him, in a hoarse voice and plain language. Her speech gave him a curious sharp, grim pleasure, as if she had been in good faith reading the gospel backwards to him.

Boline was a big, golden-haired, handsome girl, and ought to have made a career as a courtesan. But she had a rudimentary soul, to which only the first needs of life signified, and was as devoid of any taste for luxury as a stone-deaf person of the sense of hearing. With better luck Boline might have become a sicknurse and have risked her life for the plague-stricken, while she would have scoffed at all minor ailments. Or she might have been a children's nurse—for many excellent nurses came from her part of the country—and in that capacity have renounced food and sleep for the children in her charge, who all the same would have got no daintiness or finicking from her. In no state of life would she have been anything but the drudge, the slave set to relieve the direst need. Indeed had she been, anywhere, promoted to a higher office and brought into contact with the superfluity of existence, she should have felt ill at ease, and in good earnest wicked. In spite of her dissipate life Boline was in reality faithful to her calling, and so to say monogamous: to her all the men with whom she dealt were the same man, man in the abstract and in dire need of her. A customer asking her for anything above his strict due was fiercely battened and turned off by her, as a person lost to all shame. On this she was well in accord with Johannes, who could not have stood any attempt from her side to give him more. He was a rare bird amongst her clients, and in principle she recognized him as a clergyman's child, and a parson-to-be, but in practice, and in her heart, only as another son of Adam. Still, to mark the scholar out from the sailors, she put on a more sullen face to him than to the others. Both Johannes and Boline would have been surprised had they been told the truth, which was that neither of the two had a better friend in Copenhagen than the other.

At the sight of the puppy Boline stopped her lecture. As Johannes explained that he meant to give it to her, she at once suspected him of making a fool of her, and became very angry. But, when to prove his sincerity and to get off, he handed it to her, and she felt the weight and warmth of the small animal in her arms, her face at once grew perfectly blank. She felt its broken paw and looked up at Johannes, then again stood over the dog, absorbed in the sight. She made the young man wait, much against his wish, while she fetched a plate of milk and bread for it. The dog was bewildered by its strange surroundings and would not eat, not even when Boline held the plate to its nose. She squatted by it on the floor, and began to whisper to it slowly, in the dialect of her province. Her big hands, which had become soft in the town, poked at it and gently pushed it about, till it became so excited that it yapped and turned round and round in the middle of the floor, chasing its own tail. "Why did you not keep it yourself?" Boline whispered to Johannes. "Nay, I must not keep it in my room," said he. In spite of his rancor against her, he avoided naming Madam Kraft, an honest woman, in this place. His words set Boline to thinking, for the second time in one morning, and to Johannes it was like seeing a stone thinking. Her course of thought finished up in a strange, crafty, triumphant light on her broad face. "Boline must not come to the house of God," she thought, "but the small black dog comes to Boline's house." When Johannes took his leave she stared at him, and would have liked to tell him that he might from now come to her free of charge, only she knew that his kind did not accept anything from her kind for nothing. So she put on her usual sullen face, and saw him to the door. As she opened it, the bells chimed out right over their heads, it seemed as if Johannes was walking straight into their embrace. Boline stood and looked after him, with the puppy in her arms, and she suddenly realized that now he would never come back. She wished him well, in this moment of parting, but did not know what to request for him, for the lives of her visitors, from which they came, and back to which they returned, in all directions, for a long time to her had been a matter of no consequence whatever. Still, as his figure grew smaller down the street, and she felt the nose of the dog on her bare shoulder, she slowly collected her mind. "I wish," she thought, "that he may get a good meal" —for he often looked to her haggard and undernourished, and she knew that students and learned people were poor. "And I wish that he may hear a good sermon today, on Whitsunday."

Johannes walked away, his arms and mind unburdened, with a curious feeling of emptiness. It seemed to him as if Boline and the puppy, individually humbler than he, by joining forces had become his superiors, so much so that he doubted whether he would ever return to Pistolstraede. Here again he had not foreseen the effect of his activities, but had had to learn from experience. But as he walked on, and came into broader streets and amongst groups of churchgoers, he forgot the happenings of the morning, and for a while went along, one of the crowd, a young man in his Sunday clothes, and freed of the responsibility of being Johannes Søeborg. For a long time he had lived with books only, now the voices and the movements were new to him, unexpected. His mind took a fresh direction, toward the Holy Ghost.

If now, at this moment, he thought, that heavenly guest of the day were to come down through the air, with whom of all these people would he choose to dwell? Johannes watched one face after another, and rejected both the stout merchant in a tall hat, two young maidens in their confirmation shawls, who tittered over their prayer books, and even the Right Reverend Bishop, who passed him on his way to the pulpit. Lonely, lonely the Holy Ghost would be, amongst his worshipers of Copenhagen. These meditations might have lasted till midday, when he would have begun to ponder on the cost of his dinner, if he had not, just as he was slackening his pace outside the church, in two minds whether to go in or not, been cast out of them by a cheerful voice calling out: "Johannes," and again: "Johannes Søeborg." He turned, and saw a young man in the uniform of a naval officer standing by the other side of the gate, and looking at him with a bright face.

This face brought back to Johannes a faint recollection of his boyhood, yet he could not name it until the young officer came over to him and squeezed his hand. "I am Viggo," he cried out. "Viggo Lacour." Now Johannes remembered him. Viggo Lacour was the youngest son of the squire at Johannes's birthplace, and nine years ago, when they were twelve years old, the two boys had had lessons together at the manor, from Viggo's tutor. Viggo had then been a freckled, clumsy boy, a slow learner, but with an ardent love of poetry and adventure, so that he had made Johannes recite to him all the books he had ever read. Now he had all the look of a gay young dandy. He was still short and square-set, but nimble in his movements, with clear light eyes and, when he spoke, a melodious voice.

"Were you going in?" he asked Johannes. "I was thinking of it myself. But now I have met you, it is much better, indeed nothing luckier could have happened. Look here," he went on. "Do me a service. Come out with me to my ship—she is riding at anchor in the outer roads—and dine with me. We are sailing tomorrow for the West Indies." Johannes could not think of an excuse, he accepted the invitation, and soon the two young men were seated in the barge waiting by the steps of the pier, and were being rowed through the harbor, amongst boats and ships, by six sailors in shining hats. The corvette *Iphigenia*, when they came up to her, rose out of the sea, her sails furled, taller than she had looked from the harbor, with a green shadow round her in the clear, deep water. Johannes thought of Lise, who was also white, anchored, erect. It seemed to him a long ascent by the ladder to the deck. Once up there he found himself in a new world. It was at once martial, with the virile cannon on both sides, and as neat as a lady's parlor. It seemed alive and active too, even in its Sunday calm. Viggo had orders to give, and afterwards called up the cook and with him went through the dishes and drinks of the coming dinner. In the end he had chairs and a table, with a bottle of his own wine—which he had bought at Madeira and valued highly—brought on deck. They would, he said, have a drink while they waited, and the weather was so fine that they might sit up there.

Johannes looked round at the view. The whole world here was pale blue, as if the ship, with them on it, was anchored in the air. Even the red-tiled roofs of Copenhagen were ethereal, absorbed in the atmosphere. Toward the north he had an infinitely wide view and could follow the winding coastline. A month ago the profile of the land had been bare and angular, now it ran in curves and cupolas with the newly unfolded, light beech woods. A party of boys, in a boat, were splashing round the corvette, and talking of her. Johannes again turned his thoughts to the Holy Ghost. He had considered earth and sky as his possible abodes, but maybe the Holy Ghost himself had chosen to dwell in the sea.

Viggo filled the glasses and drank to his guest. He seemed so happy to have met him, that Johannes, who knew within himself that he had given his schoolfellow no thought for nine years, at first felt faintly ashamed. But in the end he decided that his companion was just in himself deeply happy and moved, and in need of an outlet for his emotion, so that anyone would have been equally welcome. What had happened to him?—an inheritance, or some luck in love?—Johannes reflected that it was beyond him to guess at the sources of happiness of a naval officer. Viggo asked him what he was doing, and on learning that he studied theology, declared that it was no more than he had expected, Johannes being so clever. He inquired whether he had a sweetheart, and talked of the pleasures of Copenhagen, the while pouring out his wine freely.

There came a moment when their conversation ceased and they sat in silence. Viggo lifted up his glass, and said: "Now I drink to the town of Copenhagen!" emptied his glass and flung it over the gunwale into the sea. He added: "For I shall never see her again." Johannes was surprised at the gesture, and found nothing to say. After a pause Viggo exclaimed with great vehemence: "You do not know how lucky you are, who may stay here. It is right what I have read: There is no world outside of Copenhagen."

Johannes said: "But your ship is coming back in six months." "Yes," said Viggo. "She is coming back in six months. But I shall not come back. When we come to the West Indies I shall throw up my commission." "What are you going to do then?" Johannes asked. "Oh, I don't know, and it is a matter of no consequence either," said Viggo. "You see, I may get into the American navy. Or I shall find some other place to go to." Johannes wondered, from his host's face and voice, whether he could be drunk at such an early hour of the day.

Viggo leant his elbows on the table, and his head in his hands, like a man overcome with drink. "No, I am not coming back," he said slowly. "I cannot tell the reason to anybody, not even to you, although you are my friend, and I believe that providence made us meet today. If I told it to the town of Copenhagen it would not believe me. I have been favored by the gods, Johannes. You would not think so, would you? For who am I? A dull boy, a sailor. Yet I, I have had such luck, and have been made so happy here in Copenhagen, as no man in a million men."

"Are you dreading the envy of the gods, then?" Johannes asked and smiled. "No," said Viggo, slowly and solemnly as before. "Although you know, they might well envy me, as you say. Jove himself might very well envy me. But they do not envy me. They are pleased. No, but I have to pay the price now, and that is why I must go. And to go away from Copenhagen, now, is like dying. In a way I am going to die, Johannes, this is my last day, and you must bear with me, as with a dying person. It is not difficult to die, only it is strangely enlightening, as if you had got up in the mast of existence. A wisdom comes to you—and when you are not wise in yourself, and have never been wise before, it is a striking thing. People call it an experience, I think.

Johannes listened with some doubt. He reflected that human beings will worry over highly different things, and wondered what it felt like to be worrying over a matter like this.

After a long silence Viggo said: "It is a curious thing, and nobody would guess it before they had tried it themselves, that when you are to pass away, as they say, what you want most of all is to tell someone of your life, so that in a way it may still exist. Of one thing I cannot speak, and it does not matter either, for that I am taking with me. But all the pretty things, which I am leaving, and which are finished today! If I were a poet, and could set them all down, before I went, I should be less heavy at heart.

"That is why, when I met you, I thought it such good luck. For you will remember many things from the time at Sophiendal, so that those, at least, will live on. You will remember how we set fire to the granary, and hanged my grandmother's cat. You will remember Caro, my dog." Johannes did not remember any of these things, but did not like to say so. "Do you remember," Viggo went on, "the tale of the Cyclops, and of him who called himself No One? —you were so much quicker to read it than me. Now I shall be that: no one." "Of what other things are you thinking?" Johannes asked. "Of what others?" Viggo repeated. "Of places, and fights, of services that people have done to me. Of snow in winter, and fishing on summer evenings. To let them all disappear and be forgotten makes you feel ungrateful, Johannes, as if you were letting down something fine and sweet, which had trusted you. Of what other things?" He thought a little, then said: "Above all, you will understand, of women.

"All the time since I knew that I must go," he said, "I have been thinking of the women I have known. It has not been the young pretty women only that I have remembered. No, I have thought of the old maids of this world. When I was a small boy I had an old French governess, a vestal virgin, an old ivory knitting needle. Yes, but she had a way of shaking her finger at me, when she scolded me, that was subtle, a riddle to solve, a promise. It would be worth the while of a man to seduce her still. If now I could make a will, and leave you her picture, it would be a neat little heirloom. And the young girls—" He made a short pause. "When I have been looking at the sea," he said, "or at the starry sky at night, on the dogwatch, I have often thought this: that we may look at them as much as we like, but still they remain, in a way, unseen. Young girls are like that.

"I should like to drink to all the women in there, in Copenhagen—the maids and the married ladies and the whores too—or to set their names on the sky, so that you might count them, and name them, as you name the stars. I should like to tell you of them, you, who are my old friend, and have come on board today."

He was silent again for a time. "I should like, too, to tell you a story about a girl, if you would listen. She has come into my mind these last days, I do not know why. Today, as we were being rowed back to the ship, it seemed to me that she was with us. But I shall have to go back a long way to tell the story rightly.

"Seven years ago," he began, "when I was fifteen, I once walked in the forest of Sophiendal, and there I saw a girl, an elf, a wood nymph. I came out from a thicket, and from deep shade, on to a cleared place, where, in the sunshine, the air danced above the grass. And there she sat on a fence. She had on a pale blue shirt and a purple shift, and she was so fair that it shone from her. She looked straight at me, with wide-open eyes, like a hawk's light eyes, and her glance was not gentle, no, it was severe— wild, you might believe that she was angry with you. But at the same time it was infinitely friendly and encouraging. She knew everything and laughed at danger. She was there only for a minute. Then, in the shine of the midday sun, she was gone, and the place where she had sat was empty. Only a sparrow hawk flew up from a fence rail, straight up, so that its flutter of gray and brown feathers touched my face. I did not forget her. I always wondered if I should see her again.

"Before I met her I had thought little about women. I was a dull, slow boy, as you know. I was happiest alone. But that wood nymph did something to me, her wide-open eyes opened mine. From that day I became aware of the world. Most of all, of the women, who had been there all the time, without my seeing them. I remember, as I walked home that same afternoon, that from the mill bridge of Sophiendal, some way up in the meadow, I saw the miller's two girls, who were older than me, bathing in the river, and the low sun shining on them. I went down and washed my hands in the river—for I had been out shooting pigeons, and had blood on them. Under the big elms where I stood, the shadows were cool and blue, and the river brown, it seemed to me that I was lonely and forgotten by all the world. But up in the meadow the river and the girls in it were all gold, and I felt in my fingers and wrists this golden water running on from them to me.

"Soon after that day—" Viggo interrupted himself and said: "No. I meant to tell you of this girl only.

"But it so happened," he took up his tale, "that last summer I went to Funen, to my old uncle Waldemar. You may have heard them speak of him at Sophiendal. He was a sailor, and was to have been a naval officer, but when he was only a cadet the Englishmen came and took our fleet, and there were no ships for him to sail. So he went into the merchant trade, and traveled all over the world, and he also became, for a time, an officer in the Portuguese navy. He was a fine sailor, and he had that with him that wherever he went the women loved him. He was said to have been married to a Portuguese lady, and to a princess in Java. I cannot say if all the tales about him were true. But one story I know to be so, and although one may laugh at it, it is a sad story. There was a village girl at Funen who had a child by him. She went wrong in life and ended up here in Copenhagen, she drank, and she was ill. But one night a sailor, in the public house where she sat, told her that Uncle Waldemar had been married to a lady in Portugal, and at that she went out and threw herself into the harbor. Now, you see, sometimes Uncle Waldemar's family was pleased with him, and sometimes they were worried about him, so that altogether they liked him better to sail on the Archipelago and the Pacific than on the Baltic. I saw him when I was a boy, and thought highly of him, and he liked me too, so that when he died he left me all that he had. But it was not much.

"But when he grew older a misfortune befell him, he became slowly paralysed and could no more leave his chair. Then he came home to Denmark. He settled in a wing of a farm in Funen, with a servant and an old woman to look after him. I went to see him from time to time. It was not only the sympathy that had always been between him and me which made me go, it was also the curious drawing toward suffering that boys have. It was a melancholy place to come to. The smoke from the chimneys itself, it seemed to me, fell sadly on the white-frozen grass of the lawn. Uncle Waldemar was not glad to see me, and we did not talk much together. Still I believe that a boy of seventeen, a fool, as I was then, with no set ideas about the laws of cause and effect, to him was better company than the grown-up people.

"I had a good deal of time on my hands there, so I sat and read his books. He was keen on poetry, and had got some books that he had been wont to take with him on the ships.

"I suppose that you have read a lot of books, a lot of poetry?" Viggo said. "Do you know the poem of the dying warrior of olden days, who asks his son and his brother to kill him, because he believes, as people did then, that only those killed in battle will go to Odin's place, to Valhalla, while you go down to Hel, a witch in a dark cave, if you happen to die in your bed?—I read it there, many times even. This old earl, then, sends for his son, and begs him to kill him.

> Hela is lurking for me in her lair.
> She means me to go, like a thrall, down there.
> But the swordsman is worth the sword.

But the son will not do it. He asks his brother the same:

> She means me to go, like a thrall, down there.
> But the swordsman is worth the sword.

The brother, you see, declines it as well. Then the poem goes on:

> The earl was wringing his hands in despair.

"It was like that here, as I sat with my uncle. He could not understand that now no one wanted him: before they had all done so. Life would not have him, and death would not take him either. He was not afraid to die, he had faced death many times. He must have thought of putting an end to his life himself, all the same he could not do it. That may have been to him, I thought, like buying the favor of a proud woman.

"I went away again. I had had my fill of suffering. I reflected that if such were the wages of a life of adventure I should try to stay at home. But I did not stay at home. From him I had no news.

"But late last summer, when I was home in Copenhagen on leave, my mother wrote to me that there were rumors of my uncle changing his will, she told me to go and find out. I did not want to go, for two reasons. First I thought it unbecoming to bother a dying man about his will, like a shark following a wreck. And then also, by that time, this thing, of which I cannot speak, had begun to me. Yes, in the month of May last year it began. I knew from the beginning that it could bring me nothing but disaster—that was in the nature of things. Still I did not want the shadow of human misery to fall upon me, or upon the picture which I carried with me in my heart. But my mother was persistent, so in the end I went. It was in the dog days, the weather was very still and hot.

"When I came to my uncle's house his old servant told me that he had been looking forward eagerly to my arrival. And I found the house, and everything in it, changed. It was not that my uncle was any better, it was, on the contrary, clear that he had got only a short time to live. But there was such a strange new hope and faith in the dying man. He looked as I think he must have looked as a young man on the bridge, on his great journeys. It seemed that he was immovable, not by necessity, but in expectation. It was as if an old disused boat had set sail again. And I, you know, I did not wonder at this change. In those days miracles were natural to me. I even believed, I now think, that this mysterious happiness of his, which lighted up his face, must spring from Copenhagen, from the same source as my own.

"He had supper laid for me, and while I ate we talked together. I do not think that any two other men could have agreed so well on the splendor of life as did we two that evening."

Here Viggo stopped, and sat for some time to collect his thoughts. Johannes to begin with had listened without much interest to his friend's tale. All his life he had kept the ideas and moods of his acquaintances out of his own sphere of thought. But here, in the solitude of the sea and the ship, he began to feel that it might be worthwhile to find out what Viggo, and people like him, did really think of the world, of life, and of death. Something in his companion's voice and manner made it unwontedly easy, even pleasing to him to listen. In any case it was like being given a supply of spiritual victuals for nothing.

"In the course of our talk," Viggo went on, "he told me that the old parson of the place had lately come up to see him—he spoke highly of his piety and kindness. I had heard the old man preach in church, and he had sent me to sleep every time. Now I thought: God be with old Pastor Mikkelsen, if he can smooth the last bit of the way for a dying sailor. Only, my uncle said, he was much taken up with parish work. But he and his wife had an adopted daughter, a girl of fifteen, who would then come to his place and read from the Bible. She was quite fair, he said, and held herself so straight. I thought: God be with this fair parson's daughter.

"While I was staying with my uncle this time, he told me many things from his travels, great adventures and remarkable happenings. I shall tell you only one of these, for it has rapport to the tale of the girl. He described to me an earthquake that he had been in, Asia Minor. 'In the interval between the first and the second shock,' he said, 'I realized that it was the earth itself moving under me, and

I was quite suddenly transported into the highest glee. This delight lies in the consciousness that something, which you have believed immovable, has got it in it to move. I felt that the ancient philosopher, of whom you read, had been indemnified for all his misfortune by that certainty: E pur si muove!'

"I was out shooting ducks in the evenings, so that for a few days I did not meet the parson or his daughter. I was a little afraid of both, and content to leave things as they were.

"But one evening, as I came in, I saw a little gray bonnet and cloak in the hall, and understood that the parson's girl was with my uncle. It was a strange, sultry, sulfurous evening, that must needs end in a storm. There was a light in my uncle's room, for the August nights were already dark, the door was ajar, and I heard a woman's gentle, clear voice in there. I sat down by the open window in the drawing room, looked out at the great thunder sky, and listened.

The girl was reading from the Book of Judith. I know that, for afterwards I found the book open on the table, and looked through what she had read. They had come to the end of it, it was Judith's song of triumph, when she has cut off the enemy commander's head, that she recited in her young, frank voice. From time to time she made a pause, as if to give her hearer time to think the reading over. As once she did so, I heard him ask her to move her chair closer to him.

"When she had finished the chapter she sat quite still, and in that deep stillness I heard the old man speak in a low, strong, sweet voice, like the voice of a vigorous young man. 'Give me a kiss,' he said.

"You would think that now I should have laughed, would you not, and have said to myself: So that is the way in which Uncle Waldemar reads the Bible? But I did not laugh, for there had been in my uncle's manner, when he spoke to me of the girl, and there was in his voice itself at this moment, a great gravity and zeal. I felt sure that he had never before asked her for a kiss. The room was as quiet as a grave, until one of the candlesticks fell to the floor with a crash. I went and opened the door.

"Neither of the two saw me. They were close together, the old lame man had raised himself up, he had both his arms round the girl's slim body, and pressed her to him. The girl did not make a sound, her fair ringlets fell down over her face, she held her hands in his long white hair. But the next moment she threw him back in a quick, furious movement, and at that he tumbled down sideways at her feet.

"I ran and turned him over, and lifted him up. He stared at me with clear eyes, and his cheeks were red. We were breast to breast, and he spoke into my face, slowly. 'E pur si muove,' he said.

"I bore him on to his bed, and he was light in my arms. But when I turned to call for his servant, and to send for the doctor, I saw that the room was empty, the girl had fled. I sat with him, and waited, but he did not speak again, nor open his eyes. And during those hours of the night, by his bedside, the last verses of the ballad came back to me:

The earl was wringing his hands in despair,
when the door was flung up wide.
A warrior stood in the sunshine there,
one-eyed was he, but wondrous fair,
with a broad sword by his side.

"The stranger tells him that he has come to revenge his two brothers, whom he has slain, and at that the earl leaps from his bed. The two fight all day, but by evening the earl is wounded to death. The last verse goes like this:

Then spoke the stranger: The fight was fair.
Lay down your bright glaive, my lord.
I am Odin. I saw your despair.
In vain shall Hela lurk in her lair.
The swordsman is worth the sword.

"I went through it many times. And while I thought of it, Uncle Waldemar died, his face solemn and triumphant. I did not know that he had died till I touched him, and felt that he was cold.

"A little while after, I heard that it was raining. There was no thunder that night, as I had hoped, just a mighty downpour of rain, it streamed down the window panes and beat in the gravel below. It turned my mind from the ballad of Odin and the old man's radiant face, toward the parson's girl, and I went down. She had had the sense to put on her cloak and bonnet, they were gone. But I became heavy at heart.

"The little girl, I thought, had never been kissed in her life. She had come up to read the Bible to a dying man, and she had run away from the house alone, in the dark and the rain. The old man's embrace must have been horrible to her. What would she have told her father and mother, I meditated, when she came home, drenched and trembling? My uncle's epitaph was likely to be that of a wicked man, without gratitude, who had tried to ravish his own guardian angel.

The Last Day

"It seemed to me, as I stood in the door and looked out, that the people of the sea and those of the land were a long way from each other. The old parson and his wife were the kind that would sit in judgment on myself, if they knew my state of mind. It was better that I and they should never meet. But in the end I made up my mind to go down to the parsonage the next day to apologize and explain, and to save what I could of my old dead friend's name.

"So I went in the afternoon. It was cool and clear after the rain.

"The old parson must have seen me from his window, for he came himself to open the door to me—a small, round, mild man. There was not a trace of indignation in his face or manner, nay, he took my hand in both his, and gave me his condolences. He led me into the low, sparely furnished drawing room, which was filled with the scent of flowers, for his wife and daughter were binding a wreath, on a table in front of the sofa. The parson's wife, who was small, round, and mild like her husband, greeted me with tears in her eyes, and told me regretfully that her flowers had suffered from last night's rain. The girl, on a narrow chair, in a faded pale-blue frock, rose and made me a little curtsey, then sat down again without speaking, and went on with her work.

"The parson talked for a long time, and when he paused, his wife prompted him from her sofa. They both seemed in a state of beatitude, and after a while the cause of it became clear to me. The honest clergyman had all his life been on the lookout for a real sinner to convert, and had not found any

in the parishes of Funen. My uncle was his great
prize, a fine penitent: he would probably think of
him in his own last hour. While he spoke, the parson broadened and filled out his armchair, he might
have been a bishop. It was, he said, clearly the direction of Providence that his daughter should have
come last night, so that the word of the Lord might
be the last in the ear of the dying man. And was
not, he asked, my uncle's own last word a pious cry
from the heart, a thanksgiving? Yes, I said, it was
so. 'It is a great satisfaction,' said the old parson,
with folded hands. 'But the weather was so bad,' I
said, 'your daughter ought not to have gone home
alone.' The parson's wife smiled to me over the
flowers. 'We know,' she said, 'that you would have
accompanied her, even in your sorrow, but she is
used to going alone.'

"When I had taken my leave, the parson told his
daughter to see me to the door. The girl rose at
once, and walked in front of me through the house.
Her slim back was graceful, and it was true that
she held herself very straight. On our way through
the room I wondered what to say to her. Was she,
I thought, so innocent, that she had not seen the
passion and the tragedy that she herself had
caused? Or had she been too deeply hurt to give
words to her affliction? And ought I, I asked myself, to thank her for her silence?

"But when we came to the door, and she had
opened it, she turned straight to me, put both her
hands on my shoulders, and looked me in the face.
Her own young face was as gravely and triumph-
antly radiant as the old man's had been, when I
held him in my arms last night. And we stood there,

near to one another, like two close friends taking leave. I felt as if I had come back to my own boyhood, to the girl's age of fifteen years. For she looked just like the forest girl of Sophiendal, of the glade in the wood. Her wide-open, light eyes, like a hawk's eyes, were severe, so that I might have believed that she was angry with me, and at the same time they were friendly, encouraging, confident. She knew everything, and laughed at danger.

"I did not thank her then. I think that I held my breath, waiting for that flight of wings, a second time, to touch my face. She was so close to me that in a movement of my head I might have kissed her."

Here Viggo stopped, and sat in thought.

"And did you kiss her?" Johannes asked in a low voice.

"Kiss her?" Viggo cried, and again was silent for a moment. "No," he said slowly. "No. I have not told this story rightly, I see, since you ask me that question. Kiss her? I might as well have bethought myself of kissing Odin. No, except for her two little hands on my shoulders we did not touch one another. When she let them fall I went away.

"I am no poet," he said and laughed. "I can tell you my story but the real meaning of it you will not get.

"But I have kept you too long. Our dinner must be ready. Come! you and I will, at least, drink a glass together to all the fair girls of the land."

Uncle Seneca

Melpomene Mulock, the great actor's daughter, got a letter that upset her peace of mind. It was an invitation from her late mother's sister to stay with her for a fortnight at Westcote Manor, her country house.

Melpomene received the invitation on the twenty-eighth of November, 1906, which happened to be a Wednesday. She was accustomed to bills and summonses, but an invitation was a new thing to her. She said to herself, "I shall keep this letter for three days. On Saturday I will show it to father, and he will know how to answer it. Aunt Eulalia has waited eighteen years before writing to me. Now she can wait three days for my answer."

On Thursday she thought, "How could I possibly go to Westcote Manor? Father and I have been poor as long as I remember, and have been proud to be so. I could not bear to live for a whole fortnight in idleness and luxury, with people who have never thought of anything but their own comfort."

On Friday she thought, "How dares Aunt Eulalia invite me? I should betray father if I accepted her invitation. Her family had no other merit than their wealth, but all the same they despised and rejected

First published under the title "The Uncertain Heiress" in the *Saturday Evening Post*, 10 December 1949, and reprinted by permission. Copyright 1949 by The Curtis Publishing Company.

him. Should I now accept the belated charity of such hard and heartless people?"

On Saturday she reread the letter, and then slowly put it back in her drawer. For a third question had presented itself to her.

"Why," she asked herself, "does Aunt Eulalia invite me? Can it have anything to do with that young man who picked up my portfolio and offered me his umbrella? I have met him three times since that day, and each time his face has stuck in my mind for a very curious reason: because it was exactly like my own."

She got up and gravely faced the glass. She saw a pale, freckled face with a broad forehead and dark blue eyes, surrounded by glorious red hair.

"His hair," she thought, "was more fair than red, and freckles do look different in a sunburnt face. But his eyes, his nose, and his mouth were precisely like mine. If I were as beautifully dressed as he, I should look as handsome. Can it be that I have a cousin like that? I have heard of my wicked aunt almost every day of my life, but I have never heard of him."

On Sunday morning she felt guilty because she had not carried out her first intention. She brought her father Aunt Eulalia's letter with his breakfast in bed.

Felix Mulock read the letter and turned pale; he read it again and turned dark red. He held it out at arm's length.

"So it is time, she thinks," he said with bitter scorn, "that dear Florence's child and her old aunt get to know each other! When I am ill and betrayed by the world, it is time to lure away my child with promises of worldly splendor."

"I shall never leave you, father," said Melpomene, "and I am not accepting her invitation."

Her father was silent for a moment. "Time!" he repeated slowly. "To this scheming woman's eyes it was time once before. Six years ago, when your mother died, she wrote and claimed that I should hand over my daughter to her. She would give you a home and an education. Imagine what you would have been like today, if for six years you had been petted and coddled, if you had never heard the name of our divine William Shakespeare nor of his humble interpreter, your father!"

Melpomene smiled proudly.

Her father again was silent for a moment, then he put down the letter and looked at her. "Go!" he said. "Accept this invitation, and come back to tell me how you have made them feel that we despise their riches and prefer to starve in our own world of great ideals. Yes," he finished in a mighty outburst, "go, and come back to tell me that you have scorned and humiliated them!"

When Melpomene arrived at the country station, on a deadly still December evening, she was met by a fine carriage and pair. At the big house with the tall, lighted windows a dignified butler took her small box from her.

Aunt Eulalia got up from her chair in front of the sitting-room fire to welcome her niece. She had on a rustling black frock, and she had the very same face, although faded and a little flabby, as the young man with the umbrella, and as the girl herself. She stared at Melpomene, then flung her arms around her and burst into tears.

"My lost Florence," she cried, "have I got you back?"

The room was warm, gently lit, and filled with the scent of hothouse plants. Its deep carpets, silk curtains, and large paintings in heavy gilt frames evidently formed a magic circle round an existence of perfect security, difficult for Melpomene to imagine. Into this room no worry or care, no dunning letters or angry landlord would ever have been admitted. What did the people who lived in it find to think about? Did they think at all?

Melpomene at this moment felt proud of her patched shoes and her old frock. They were her credentials. Here it was she who crossed the doorstep as the stern collector, with all the claims of a higher, wronged world in her hand.

Aunt Eulalia's son, Albert, joined them by the fireside, and the girl saw that he was her old acquaintance of the wind and the rain. He was in perfect harmony with the room, and looked so pleasant in his evening clothes that under other circumstances she would have been happy to know that she resembled him. He shook hands with her in a friendly manner, and blushed a little as he acknowledged their previous meetings.

Melpomene at once felt sure that she owed Albert her invitation. But why had he asked his mother to invite her? He had seen her lonely and tired, in wet clothes. He must have been as amazed at the likeness between them as she had been. He must have followed her and inquired about her.

Now he treated her, she thought, as if she were some precious and fragile object which he must be careful not to break.

He made her feel embarrassed, for when she looked at him, it was like looking into a mirror, and when she looked away, she felt his eyes on her face.

Just before dinner an elderly, well-dressed gentleman was introduced to her. They called him Uncle Seneca.

In the evening, before the fire, Aunt Eulalia talked about her dear sister, ten years younger than herself. She had tried to soften the hearts of their angry father and mother when Melpomene's mother had eloped with the actor. When Florence's baby was born, she had wanted to hurry to her bedside, but her husband had forbidden it. Now she did not even remember the exact date of the event.

"I was born," said Melpomene, "on the seventh of August, 1888."

At this, Uncle Seneca turned his bright birdlike eyes at her in a sudden, keen glance.

Melpomene woke up next morning, quite late, under a silk quilt and in a big four-poster, to a day as gray and silent as the last. A maid brought in her dainty breakfast on a silver tray. She had never in her life had breakfast in bed. Now, as she poured out her tea and buttered her hot muffins, she thought of her father, alone in his cold flat, and of the mission on which he had sent her. It might prove more difficult than he had suspected to shock an upholstered and silk-covered world.

During the following week Melpomene often felt as if she had been ordered to strike with a hammer at a featherbed. The whole house folded her in a warm and soft embrace. The old servants did their best to make her as comfortable as possible. And Aunt Eulalia was ever about the rooms, doing her flowers or her needlework, and gazing tenderly at the niece who was so like her dear Florence. Her small flow of chatter ran through all the hours of the day, as if to wash away, quite pleasantly, Melpomene's former existence. She did not question the girl about her father or her home. She dwelt in the past, and described the happy childhood and girlhood which she and her sister had passed in this same house. Or she talked about Albert. No mother had ever had such a good and kind son! Her own sole object in life was to see her dear boy happy.

Albert took his cousin out for drives, to point out views. He told her the names of his horses, and he showed her his dogs, and, to amuse her, every day made them go through the tricks he had taught them.

She smiled ironically at the efforts of her aunt and her cousin. But she began to find it difficult to believe that they were really the schemers and seducers described by her father.

In all the rooms of the house there were portraits of grandparents and great-aunts, and she knew that she had their blood in her veins. She had been amazed to see how much Aunt Eulalia and Albert were like her; now she was panic-stricken to think that she might be like them. She fought down the thought, but it came back. She could not get away from the fact that she had enjoyed flowers in her room and breakfast in bed. She liked Albert's dogs—in particular a little black spaniel.

To strengthen and brace herself she began to talk to her rich relations of her home. She depicted the cold of the rooms, the darkness of the stairs and her late hours of work. She went on in a kind of ecstasy, in the manner of her father himself, as she proudly proclaimed her perfect content in the middle of it all.

Aunt Eulalia listened, her mouth open, and then, all in tears, begged her pardon because she had not come to her rescue before. Albert listened, his lips pressed together, and the next day suggested that she take the black spaniel back with her to London.

Under the circumstances, Melpomene sought refuge with Uncle Seneca. The old gentleman at first had been a little shy with her. Now, whenever she happened to be alone, he peeped out from his own room for a friendly talk. And if he did not speak much, he was a perfect listener.

Melpomene was happier with him than with the others. For he did not feel sorry for her; at times she even thought that he envied her her experiences. He asked her how it felt to be hungry— might the feeling be called a pain? He wanted details of narrow back yards and steep dark stairs, and he took a great interest in rats. He must at some time have bought and studied a map of the poorest quarters of London, for he knew the names of many streets and squares there. Melpomene reflected with dismay that to a rich old bachelor all these things were as fascinating and fantastic as toys in a shop window to a little poor boy in the street.

But she could not be angry with Uncle Seneca himself, for he questioned her and listened to her in the manner of a child. Perhaps, she thought, his eagerness did indeed rise from a nobler motive than curiosity. Sometimes, when she told him about very poor and wretched people, he became restless and his hands trembled a little. "There ought not to be such people," he said.

From Aunt Eulalia, she learned that Uncle Seneca was no blood relation of hers. An old aunt's widower had married again and in his second marriage had had this only son. The boy had been a pretty and talented child, and as a young man had surprised the family by taking up the study of medicine and wanting to become a doctor. But he was a delicate youth, and in the end his family had persuaded him to give up the hard work.

The old man now lived in Aunt Eulalia's house and seldom left it. He did not seem to Melpomene to pay much attention to Albert, but he treated Aunt Eulalia with great respect and consideration. He was, the girl thought, one of those truly chivalrous men with a high ideal of women. "I have had the privilege," he once said, "to be born and brought up, and to have lived my best years, in an epoch when England was ruled by a lady."

He had various small hobbies with which he passed his time: he collected butterflies and was clever at stuffing birds. He also did needlework and would bring his cross-stitch to the fireside. He had a queer little habit of gazing attentively at his own hands. He had inherited a large fortune, which was now increasing year by year, and it was understood that Albert was to be his heir.

But even with Uncle Seneca to support her self-confidence, Melpomene was aware of her false position in the family circle. Within three days she was to return to London. Before that time she must make it clear that she was still a stranger in the house, and still their enemy and their judge.

Two or three times she prepared her speech of denouncement, failed to get it out, and called herself a coward. At last, on Sunday evening, she did her duty.

Aunt Eulalia had dwelt with sadness on the prospect of her departure, and with delight on the prospect of her early return.

"No," said Melpomene suddenly, "no, Aunt Eulalia, I am not coming back. Everything here is sweet and perfect, too sweet and perfect for me. I could not bear to live for my own comfort only."

"Sweet child," said Aunt Eulalia, "you want to live for your father's comfort."

"For his comfort!" Melpomene exclaimed. "Oh, how mistaken you are! It is for his immortality that I want to live!" She was silent for a moment. "I have been suffocating in this house," she went on with heightened color. "To me, it is unnatural and insane to live for the moment, with no thought of futurity."

"Darling Melly," said Aunt Eulalia, "we all have the hope of a better, an everlasting future. And here on earth we wish to live on in our dear children and grandchildren."

"Oh, yes!" Melpomene cried. "You all imagine that better, everlasting future to be exactly like your life here—an easy, carefree existence, one day just like the other, little pleasant talks about nothing, a walk with the dogs. And as to your futurity on earth, I call that a cheap kind of immortality. I myself claim for my father an undying fame! How could I resign myself to the thought that his great creations, as great as any painter's and sculptor's, should all vanish with him?"

"Oh, but we must all," said Aunt Eulalia, "resign ourselves to the idea of mortality."

"No!" cried Melpomene. "No, not at all!" She grew very pale and drew in her breath deeply. "My father," she said very slowly, "has an old friend in London, an Italian and a great sculptor. He has seen father in all his roles, and thinks as highly of them as father himself. They have inspired him with the idea of a memorial which is to preserve father's name for centuries. It is a glorious work of art. On the plinth you see all the figures which father has created, from King Oedipus to the Master Builder. And high above them all stands father himself, in his big cloak, with his splendid hair, and his arm outstretched." There was a long pause. "That," said Melpomene, "is what I live for."

"My poor, precious child," said Aunt Eulalia, "you do not know what you speak about! It is a dream of a person entirely without practical experience! You will never, even if you starve yourself to death, save up enough money for such a thing! Preserve me, the memorial on our family tomb cost three thousand pounds!"

"And what if it cost three thousand pounds?" she cried. "What if it cost six thousand? I am not a person entirely without practical sense, Aunt Eulalia. Father and Signor Benatti have made up a small book with plans and descriptions of the monument; I myself am only to save up the money to get it published. As soon as it is out, everybody in England who has ever seen father on the stage will be happy and proud to contribute. And it is the happiness and pride of my life to work for his undying name."

Again there was a pause.

Melpomene had spoken with her eyes above the heads of her audience; now she looked at them. They all three sat quite still. The faces of Aunt Eulalia and Albert, as often before, expressed mild bewilderment and compassion. But Uncle Seneca listened with profound attention. He looked at his hands.

"A name," he said slowly, "an undying name."

"Uncle Seneca," Melpomene thought, "is the only person here who understands me."

She held her head high as she went up to bed, but she did not sleep well. The sad, concerned faces of Aunt Eulalia and Albert were still before her eyes. She had not succeeded in altering their expression.

Late the next morning when she came down into the hall, she found Albert there.

"Look here," he said, "you talked last night of a memorial for your father. If you had three thousand pounds today, would you spend them on it? And would it make you happy?"

Melpomene looked at him gravely. "Do you mean," she said, "that you would give me three thousand pounds to wipe out your people's guilt toward my father?"

Albert thought her words over. "No," he said, "I cannot honestly say that. I cannot honestly say that I feel called upon to put up a monument for Uncle Felix. But I was wondering whether it would make you happy."

"Make me happy?" said Melpomene slowly. She could not remember that anybody had ever passionately wanted to make her happy.

"Look here," said Albert; "I have wished I could make you happy from that first moment when I met you in the rain. It is a very strange thing. One reads in books about love at first sight, but one never believes that it happens to people in real life. And then it was love at first sight with me myself."

Melpomene felt a great movement of triumph run through her. Albert, young, rich, and handsome, was laying his heart and all his worldly goods at her feet, and within a moment she was going to refuse it all. That would be a finer trophy to carry back to her father than he could ever have dreamed of. The idea stirred her so deeply that she could not find a word to say.

"Look here," said Albert, "I felt at once that you were what people call one's better self. The other girls have all been strangers, somehow, but you were like me. I have had everything and I knew, the instant I saw you, that I should like to give all I have to you, and that only then it might at last be some use to me and give me some fun in life. I should like to see you in pretty clothes, and in a nice room of your own. I should like to see you with a dog of your own. And then I should like you to have your father's monument as well."

As still she did not speak, but only looked at him with clear, bright eyes, he went on.

"As to myself," he said, "I have always been lonely in a way. I have never had a real friend. Now I have got you. I have never believed that I should ever want to marry, and when I told mother that I wanted to marry you, she was so pleased that she wept with joy. I have never believed that I was going to be really happy. It is a very strange thing. Now I should be wonderfully happy if I could make you happy at all."

Melpomene did not speak at once. "No, Albert," she said, "you cannot make me happy. I do not want your pretty clothes; I do not want a room of my own. I am going back to my father tomorrow."

Albert grew very pale; he went to the window and came back again. "I believe," he said, "that you are wrong in going back to your father. I do not believe that you will be happy in London. Look here, Melpomene. I believe that you might come to love me. It is a very strange thing to say—I should never have thought that I would say it to a girl— but I believe that you might come to love me."

Melpomene till now had spoken with self-posses- sion, remembering her program. But when Albert said that she might come to love him, she wavered on her feet, and her throat contracted so that she could not get a word out. To steady herself, in a great effort she called up her father's face. It helped her; after a moment she could speak.

"If I came to love you, Albert," she said very slowly, "I would still not accept a penny from you for father's memorial, for I would know that you did not give it in admiration and repentance. If I loved you at this moment," she went on in a voice that sounded strange to herself, and which indeed seemed to speak all on its own, "I should at this moment vow never to see you again after I have got home tomorrow, and never to open a letter from you until I had in my hand three thousand pounds of my own, for father's monument."

The two young people for a minute remained face to face, both very pale and grave. Then she walked past him and out of the house.

She walked for a long time before she could collect her thoughts sufficiently to realize that she had won her war and fulfilled her mission. That all was well, and that all was over.

At last she stood still; her dizziness had gone; now she felt the cold round her. She had walked so far that she had lost her way, and it was growing dark. She turned and tried to remember the road by which she had come.

She did not recognize it; there were a lot of high fences everywhere, and she had to walk alongside them to find the stiles. Had they all been there on her way out? She suddenly remembered that she had denounced Westcote Manor and all it contained, and wondered if the house had taken her at her word.

At last between the trees of the park she caught sight of lights, and made for them. In the avenue she was surprised to see a figure coming toward her. For a moment it looked very big in the mist, then it grew small. It was Uncle Seneca with a large umbrella in his hand.

He seemed happy to see her. "I was quite worried," he said, "because you did not come back. I thought it was going to snow, so I brought my umbrella."

Melpomene knew how seldom Uncle Seneca went out, and how scared he was of cold weather. She was vaguely touched by his kindness, and at the same time vaguely pained by the memory of how she had once before, long, long ago, been offered an umbrella by a gentleman.

"Eulalia," said Uncle Seneca, "had to go out to see a neighbor. Albert took her in his gig. You and I will have tea by ourselves." They walked up the avenue side by side under the umbrella.

When they came in, tea was ready in front of the fire. The pink-shaded lamps shone on the silver and the china. The gardener must have brought in heliotropes from the hothouse; their scent was strong and sweet in the room.

Uncle Seneca gave two or three little sneezes and looked slightly feverish in the lamplight, as if he might have waited too long in the avenue and have caught a chill on his gallant expedition.

He moved his chair closer to the fire and said, "I forgot to put on my galoshes. Perhaps I really ought to go and change my shoes."

But he did not go. He did not speak for a while either, but gazed at his hands and then smiled at the girl above his teacup. For a long time there was a silence in the room, for Melpomene was too tired and too absorbed in her own thoughts to speak.

"It is an honor and a pleasure," Uncle Seneca began at last, "for an old sedentary person like myself to talk to a young lady who knows the world. People, I suppose, will have been talking to you of almost everything."

"Yes," said Melpomene, who had hardly heard what he said.

"People," he repeated cheerfully, "will have been talking to you of drunkards and opium smokers?"

"Yes," she said again.

"Yes, yes," he said, cheering up more and more. "And of pickpockets and burglars?"

"Yes," she said.

"And of worse than that," he continued, this time a little timidly. "Of creatures sunk still deeper, who really ought not to exist?"

"Yes," said the girl, still in her own thoughts.

"And of murderers?" asked Uncle Seneca.

Something in this queer catechism at last caught Melpomene's attention. She slowly raised her eyes to the old man's face.

"Do you know," he asked, "who Williams was— the man who wiped out two households within a fortnight?"

"Yes, I believe so," said Melpomene.

"Do you know," he inquired again, "who John Lee was—the man who could not be hanged?"

"Yes, I believe so," said Melpomene.

"Do you know," asked Uncle Seneca, "who Jack the Ripper was?"

"Yes," Melpomene answered.

Uncle Seneca gave such a sudden little titter that the girl stared at him. "I beg your pardon," he said. "I did not mean to be rude. It only struck me as a curious thing that you should say that you knew who Jack the Ripper was. For that is the one thing that nobody ever knew."

There was a pause.

"I am Jack the Ripper," said Uncle Seneca. "I was quite struck," he said, "when you told Eulalia that you were born on the seventh of August, 1888. For that was the date of the first of them." He thought the matter over for a moment. "And," he said, "nobody knew. Nobody in all the city of London. Nobody, in fact, in all the world. It is," he continued, "a very strange sensation. You walk down a street full of people. None of them looks

163

at you. And yet every one of them is looking for you." He sneezed again, and blew his nose in a large white handkerchief. "I have never known many people," he went on; "my family was most particular about our circle of acquaintances. But upon that time it might be said that everybody knew me. They gave me a name, 'Jack.' It is a frisky name, a name for a sailor. Friskier than Seneca, do you not think so? And then, 'the Ripper.' Is not that brisk as well . . . smart? I was pleased the first time I heard that this was the name they had given me. I thought it quite bright of them. And nobody knew. . . . You young people nowadays," he remarked thoughtfully, "say 'ripping,' do you not, when something is really pleasant? . . . The second," Uncle Seneca said, after another pause, "was on the last day of the month. The third was a week later. It took a cool hand to come out again to work so quickly, do you not think so? That third one was skillfully done. Some other day, when we have got time, I shall tell you more about that third one.

"There was an odd little circumstance about the matter," he said. "People talked about Jack everywhere, but very few people talked about him to me. My family, I am pretty sure, must have talked a good deal about him, but they never mentioned him to me. They used to put away the papers when they had read them. There were big headlines in the papers those days: Who is Jack the Ripper? Where is Jack the Ripper? I sat and read them by our tea table, which was just like this one here, and I could have answered at any moment, 'Here he is.' In one paper they wrote: "The great skill

points to someone with real anatomical knowledge,' and in another: 'It is possible that after having done the deed Jack put on gloves.' So Jack
did."

He sat for a while in silence.

"It all began," he said, "with my dreams. I have
always had very vivid, lifelike dreams. Now I began
to dream that I did it. I dreamed that I came down
a street at night, and that these persons were there
and that I did it. Night after night I dreamed it,
and I began to walk about in London to find the
street. I bought a map to find it. My dreams grew
more and more vivid, and in the end I understood
that I had to do it."

Again he was silent.

"A name!" Uncle Seneca said, and suddenly
looked straight at Melpomene. "You spoke last
night of a name. Of a person who ought to have
an immortal name to him. Here is an immortal
name which, one might say, ought to have a person
to it. My family had often teased me because I
liked to look into the glass. At that time I looked
more frequently than before into the glass, and at
the person in it, who looked back at me."

He was perfectly still for a long time. Melpomene,
too, sat still; she could not even move her eyes
away from his face.

"Your father," Uncle Seneca said, "was indeed
a great actor. We went to see him in Macbeth. That
was in between the third and the fourth. The bard
is always magnificent, of course. Still, he, too, can
make mistakes. 'All the perfumes of Arabia will
not sweeten this little hand.'" He looked at his
hands. "That is a mistake," he said. "They will. I

understood you last night," he went on, "although
Eulalia and Albert did not. I understand that your
father will want his monument. For with him it has
never been anything but acting. With him it has
never been the real thing. 'As they had seen me
with these hangman's hands.' He must have a monument to have his name remembered. It is a strange
thing," he said, after a pause, "that I should, late
in life, meet a young lady like you, who knows these
places of mine and, just like me, has walked down
Berners Street. I have been happy to meet you,
Miss Melpomene. . . . And nobody knew," he said.

Suddenly his face changed; little nervous twitches
ran over it, and his wide-opened eyes sought Melpomene's. "There they are," he said, "back already.
I had hoped that we might have had half an hour
more to ourselves."

The rumble of wheels was heard on the drive.
The front door was opened and voices sounded in
the hall.

Melpomene got up from her chair; she went out
through the library and slowly mounted the stairs
to her room. She lay down on her bed with her
face in the pillows. She told the maid who brought
the hot water that she had a headache and could
not come down for dinner.

Next day she went back to London. Aunt Eulalia
embraced and kissed her niece even more tenderly
at her departure than she had done at her arrival.

"My darling," she said, "it has been lovely having
you here. Now we are looking forward to your return to Westcote Manor."

Albert shook hands with Melpomene in a friendly
manner, but with a pale face. Uncle Seneca did not
appear. He was in bed with a cold.

In the carriage and in the train, Melpomene kept her mind fixed on her father and her home. When she got back to them, she found the rooms very untidy. The fire had gone out and her father had remained in bed to keep warm.

Felix Mulock had been looking forward to hearing his daughter's report of her visit, and had prepared little biting gibes, in his old manner from Hamlet, with which to accompany it all through. Now he was disappointed that he had to drag the account from her word by word. In the end, he lost patience.

"Well," he cried, "I suppose they have told you they have given me money that you did not know of!"

"No," said Melpomene, "they did not tell me."

"If you had not had all your mother's stubbornness, my girl," he went on with a little bitter laugh, "and of course all those freckles, you might have made Cousin Albert fall in love with you. That would have been a sweet revenge! What a perfect rehabilitation to have the house into which I was never admitted belong to us!"

The idea delighted him. All through the evening he amused himself by depicting in detail his conquest and triumphal occupation of the enemy's camp.

The week that followed on her return seemed very long to Melpomene. The December cold became part of a loneliness that she had never known before. She dared not think of Albert; she dared not think of her father's monument. In fact, she found that she dared not think of anything at all.

One night she woke up with a strange new sensation of happiness and warmth. She sat up in bed, for suddenly she realized that her one place of refuge on earth and her one happiness was in Albert's arms.

The idea overwhelmed her; her whole body ached with it. She did not care for immortal fame. What she longed for, with every drop of her blood, was an easy, carefree existence, one day just like the other, little pleasant talks about nothing, a walk with the dogs.

All through the night she remained sitting up in her small bed in the dark room, her face wet with tears. She felt herself to be a very small figure in all the city of London, in all the world.

"This one little short life," she cried in her heart, "is all that I can be sure of. And I have thrown it away. I have vowed never to see Albert again. I have told him that I would never open a letter from him, so that now he will never, never, write to me."

In this she was wrong. The day before Christmas she received a letter from her cousin.

Albert's letter ran as follows:

> Westcote Manor,
> 22 December, 1906

Dear Cousin Melpomene:

   I am afraid that you will be angry with me for writing to you. But you will receive, one of these days, a letter from our old solicitor, Mr. Petri, and it seems to me that I ought to prepare you for it. So I hope that you will forgive me this one time.

   I first of all have to tell you that Uncle Seneca has died. He got a bad cold, nobody knows how, for he used to take very good care of himself. It turned into pneumonia; for three days he had high fever and was strangely changed, so that he did not seem to be himself at all. But in the end he passed away quite quietly.

You were very kind to him when you were down here. I think you will be glad to feel that at the end of his life you gave him a pleasant time. He was much upset when he heard that you had gone back to London. All through his feverish days he talked of getting up and going after you. But his mind was not clear; he kept on telling us that he would follow you, and be sure to find you, in some street of which nobody has ever heard the name.

Last Thursday, however, as his temperature went down, he lay for a long time without saying a word, just looking very pleased with himself. In the evening he told us to send for Mr. Petri, and when he arrived, Uncle Seneca informed him that he wanted him to draw up a new will for him.

Mr. Petri will come round to see you next week, and you will hear all about the matter from him. I just want to give you here, before Christmas, the good news that Uncle Seneca has left all his money to you. You will now be able to put up the memorial for your father, of which we talked the last day in the hall. Do not believe that I now mean to hold you to your word from that same talk of ours. You may have changed your mind. But I mean to tell you here that I have not changed mine, and shall never change it.

Mr. Petri will inform you that there is a curious stipulation in Uncle Seneca's will. According to that, you must get your father's monument put up, and you must lay the foundation stone with your own hand. And on this stone, which will, of course, never be seen, because the whole monument will be on the top of it, should be cut the following inscription: IN MEMORY OF J.T.R.

I know no more than you what these letters mean, and I can see you smiling quite ironically as you read them here. For one would naturally take them to stand for something romantic, perhaps for the name of a friend or sweetheart. And you will be sure to think Uncle Seneca a lonely old person who cared for nobody, and could never have had a friend, and his whole life too conventional and commonplace for a romance. All the same, since you seemed to like talking with him when you were down here, I suppose you will not mind carrying out what people would call his last wish, nor having his stone to be, so to say, forever part of your father's monument.

Until quite lately—in fact, until the time when I met you—I myself should have laughed at the idea of anything romantic ever having happened to Uncle Seneca. I should, in fact, have been quite sure that it had happened only in his own dreams. For he was always extraordinarily keen on his dreams. These last years he did not talk much about anything, but when I was a small boy, he would talk to me for a long time of his dreams and of the things he had done in them.

But when something really romantic and wonderful happens to oneself, one somehow feels that it may have happened to other dull fellows as well. Their dreams, too, may have come true. So now I think it quite possible that Uncle Seneca has meant something to people he has met in life, perhaps to women long since dead.

It is a curious thing that I shall probably miss old Uncle Seneca a good deal more than I ever expected. In fact, I was quite sad today when I remembered his little habit of looking thoughtfully at his own hands.

I should like to write a great deal more to you. But I shall not do so until I hear from you.

Your cousin,
ALBERT ARBUTHNOT

The Fat Man

On one November evening a horrible crime was committed in Oslo, the capital of Norway. A child was murdered in an uninhabited house on the outskirts of the town.

The newspapers brought long and detailed accounts of the murder. In the short, raw November days people stood in the street outside the house and stared up at it. The victim had been a workman's child, resentment of ancient wrongs stirred in the minds of the crowd.

The police had got but one single clue. A shopkeeper in the street told them that as he was closing up his shop on the evening of the murder he saw the murdered child walk by, her hand in the hand of a fat man.

The police had arrested some tramps and vagabonds and shady persons, but such people as a rule are not fat. So they looked elsewhere, among tradesmen and clerks of the neighborhood. Fat men were stared at in the streets. But the murderer had not been found.

In this same month of November a young student named Kristoffer Lovunden in Oslo was cramming for his examination. He had come down to the town from the north of Norway, where it is day half the year and night the other half and where people are different from other Norwegians. In a world of stone and concrete Kristoffer was sick with longing for the hills and the salt sea.

His people up in Norland were poor and could have no idea of what it cost to live in Oslo, he did not want to worry them for money. To be able to finish his studies he had taken a job as bartender at the Grand Hotel, and worked there every night from eight o'clock till midnight. He was a good-looking boy with gentle and polite manners, conscientious in the performance of his duties, and he did well as a bartender. He was abstinent himself, but took a kind of scientific interest in the composition of other people's drinks.

In this way he managed to keep alive and to go on with his lessons. But he got too little sleep and too little time for ordinary human intercourse. He read no books outside his textbooks, and not even the newspapers, so that he did not know what was happening in the world around him. He was aware himself that this was not a healthy life, but the more he disliked it the harder he worked to get it over.

In the bar he was always tired, and he sometimes fell asleep standing up, with open eyes. The brilliant light and the noises made his head swim. But as he walked home from the Grand Hotel after midnight the cold air revived him so that he entered his small room wide awake. This he knew to be a dangerous hour. If now a thing caught his mind it would stick in it with unnatural vividness and keep him from sleep, and he would be no good for his books the next day. He had promised himself not to read at this time, and while he undressed to go to bed he closed his eyes.

All the same, one night his glance fell on a newspaper wrapped round a sausage that he had brought home with him. Here he read of the murder. The paper was two days old, people would have been talking about the crime around him all the time, but he had not heard what they said. The paper was torn, the ends of the lines were missing, he had to make them up from his own imagination. After that the thing would not leave him. The words "a fat man" set his mind running from one to another of the fat men he had ever known till at last it stopped at one of them.

There was an elegant fat gentleman who often visited the bar. Kristoffer knew him to be a writer, a poet of a particular, refined, half-mystical school. Kristoffer had read a few of his poems and had himself been fascinated by their queer, exquisite choice of words and symbols. They seemed to be filled with the colors of old precious stained glass. He often wrote about medieval legends and mysteries. This winter the theater was doing a play by him named *The Werewolf*, which was in parts macabre, according to its subject, but more remarkable still for its strange beauty and sweetness. The man's appearance too was striking. He was fat, with wavy dark hair, a large white face, a small red mouth, and curiously pale eyes. Kristoffer had been told that he had lived much abroad. It was the habit of this man to sit with his back to the bar, developing his exotic theories to a circle of young admirers. His name was Oswald Senjen.

Now the poet's picture took hold of the student. All night he seemed to see the big face close to his, with all kinds of expressions. He drank much cold water but was as hot as before. This fat man of the Grand Hotel, he thought, was the fat man of the newspaper.

It did not occur to him, in the morning, to play the part of a detective. If he went to the police they would send him away, since he had no facts whatever, no argument or reason even, to put before them. The fat man would have an alibi. He and his friends would laugh, they would think him mad or they would be indignant and complain to the manager of the hotel, and Kristoffer would lose his job.

So for three weeks the odd drama was played between the two actors only: the grave young bartender behind the bar and the smiling poet before it. The one was trying hard all the time to get out of it, the other knew nothing about it. Only once did the parties look each other in the face.

A few nights after Kristoffer had read about the murder, Oswald Senjen came into the bar with a friend. Kristoffer had no wish to spy upon them—it was against his own will that he moved to the side of the bar where they sat.

They were discussing fiction and reality. The friend held that to a poet the two must be one, and that therefore his existence must be mysteriously happy. The poet contradicted him. A poet's mission in life, he said, was to make others confound fiction with reality in order to render them, for an hour, mysteriously happy. But he himself must, more carefully than the crowd, hold the two apart. "Not as far as enjoyment of them is concerned," he added, "I enjoy fiction, I enjoy reality too. But I am happy because I have an unfailing instinct for distinguishing one from the other. I know fiction where I meet it. I know reality where I meet it."

This fragment of conversation stuck in Kristoffer's mind, he went over it many times. He himself had often before pondered on the idea of happiness and tried to find out whether such a thing really existed. He had asked himself if anybody was happy and, if so, who was happy. The two men at the bar had repeated the word more than once—they were probably happy. The fat man, who knew reality when he saw it, had said that he was happy.

Kristoffer remembered the shopkeeper's evidence. The face of the little girl Mattea, he had explained, when she passed him in the rainy street, had looked happy, as if, he said, she had been promised something, or was looking forward to something, and was skipping along toward it. Kristoffer thought: "And the man by her side?" Would his face have had an expression of happiness as well? Would he too have been looking forward to something? The shopkeeper had not had time to look the man in the face, he had seen only his back.

Night after night Kristoffer watched the fat man. At first he felt it to be a grim jest of fate that he must have this man with him wherever he went, while the man himself should hardly be aware of his existence. But after a time he began to believe that his unceasing observation had an effect on the observed, and that he was somehow changing under it. He grew fatter and whiter, his eyes grew paler. At moments he was as absent-minded as Kristoffer himself. His pleasing flow of speech would run slower, with sudden unneeded pauses, as if the skilled talker could not find his words.

If Oswald Senjen stayed in the bar till it closed, Kristoffer would slip out while he was being helped into his furred coat in the hall, and wait for him outside. Most often Oswald Senjen's large car would be there, and he would get into it and glide off. But twice he slowly walked along the street, and Kristoffer followed him. The boy felt himself to be a mean, wild figure in the town and the night, sneaking after a man who had done him no harm, and about whom he knew nothing, and he hated the figure who was dragging him after it. The first time it seemed to him that the fat man turned his head a little to one side and the other as if to make sure that there was nobody close behind him. But the second time he walked on looking straight ahead, and Kristoffer then wondered if that first slight nervous movement had not been a creation of his own imagination.

One evening in the bar the poet turned in his deep chair and looked at the bartender.

Toward the end of November Kristoffer suddenly remembered that his examination was to begin within a week. He was dismayed and seized with pangs of conscience, he thought of his future and of his people up in Norland. The deep fear within him grew stronger. He must shake off his obsession or he would be ruined by it.

At this time an unexpected thing happened. One evening Oswald Senjen got up to leave early, his friends tried to hold him back but he would not stay. "Nay," he said, "I want a rest. I want to rest." When he had gone, one of his friends said: "He was looking bad tonight. He is much changed. Surely he has got something the matter with him." One of the others answered: "It is that old matter from when he was out in China. But he ought to look after himself. Tonight one might think that he would not last till the end of the year."

The Fat Man

As Kristoffer listened to these assertions from an outside and real world he felt a sudden, profound relief. To this world the man himself, at least, was a reality. People talked about him.

"It might be a good thing," he thought, "it might be a way out if I could talk about the whole matter to somebody else."

He did not choose a fellow student for his confidant. He could imagine the kind of discussion this would bring about and his mind shrank from it. He turned for help to a simple soul, a boy two or three years younger than himself, who washed up at the bar and who was named Hjalmar.

Hjalmar was born and bred in Oslo, he knew all that could be known about the town and very little about anything outside it. He and Kristoffer had always been on friendly terms, and Hjalmar enjoyed a short chat with Kristoffer in the scullery, after working hours, because he knew that Kristoffer would not interrupt him. Hjalmar was a revolutionary spirit, and would hold forth on the worthless rich customers of the bar, who rolled home in big cars with gorgeous women with red lips and nails, while underpaid sailors hauled tarred ropes, and tired laborers led their plowhorses to the stable. Kristoffer wished that he would not do so, for at such times his nostalgia for boats and tar, and for the smell of a sweaty horse, grew so strong that it became a physical pain. And the deadly horror that he felt at the idea of driving home with one of the women Hjalmar described proved to him that his nervous system was out of order.

The Fat Man

As soon as Kristoffer mentioned the murder to Hjalmar he found that the scullery boy knew everything about it. Hjalmar had his pockets filled with newspaper cuttings, from which he read reports of the crime and of the arrests, and angry letters about the slowness of the police.

Kristoffer was uncertain how to explain his theory to Hjalmar. In the end he said: "Do you know, Hjalmar, I believe that the fat gentleman in the bar is the murderer." Hjalmar stared at him, his mouth open. The next moment he had caught the idea, and his eyes shone.

After a short while Hjalmar proposed that they should go to the police, or again to a private detective. It took Kristoffer some time to convince his friend, as he had convinced himself, that their case was too weak, and that people would think them mad.

Then Hjalmar, more eager even than before, decided that they must be detectives themselves.

To Kristoffer it was a strange experience, both steadying and alarming, to face his own nightmare in the sharp white light of the scullery, and to hear it discussed by another live person. He felt that he was holding on to the scullery boy like a drowning man to a swimmer; every moment he feared to drag his rescuer down with him, into the dark sea of madness.

The next evening Hjalmar told Kristoffer that they would find some scheme by which to surprise the murderer and make him give himself away.

Kristoffer listened to his various suggestions for some time, then smiled a little. He said: "Hjalmar,

thou art even such a man . . ." He stopped. "Nay,"
he said, "you will not know this piece, Hjalmar.
But let me go on a little, all the same—!

I have heard
that guilty creatures sitting at a play
have by the very cunning of the scene
been struck so to the soul that presently
they have proclaim'd their malefactions.
For murder, though it have no tongue, will speak.

"I understand that very well," said Hjalmar.
"Do you, Hjalmar?" asked Kristoffer. "Then I
shall tell you one thing more:

the play's the thing
wherein we'll catch the conscience of the king.

"Where have you got that from?" asked Hjalmar.
"From a play called *Hamlet*, said Kristoffer. "And
how do you mean to go and do it?" asked Hjalmar
again. Kristoffer was silent for some time.

"Look here, Hjalmar," he said at last, "you told
me that you have got a sister."

"Yes," said Hjalmar, "I have got five of them."

"But you have got one sister of nine," said Kristoffer, "the same age as Mattea?"

"Yes," said Hjalmar.

"And she has got," Kristoffer went on, "a school
mackintosh with a hood to it, like the one Mattea
had on that night?"

"Yes," said Hjalmar.

Kristoffer began to tremble. There was something
blasphemous in the comedy which they meant to
act. He could not have gone on with it if he had
not felt that somehow his reason hung upon it.

The Fat Man

"Listen, Hjalmar," he said, "we will choose an evening when the man is in the bar. Then make your little sister put on her mackintosh, and make one of your big sisters bring her here. Tell her to walk straight from the door, through all the room, up to the bar, to me, and to give me something—a letter or what you will. I shall give her a shilling for doing it, and she will take it from the counter when she has put the letter there. Then tell her to walk back again, through the room."

"Yes," said Hjalmar.

"If the manager complains," Kristoffer added after a while, "we will explain that it was all a misunderstanding."

"Yes," said Hjalmar.

"I myself," said Kristoffer, "must stay at the bar. I shall not see his face, for he generally sits with his back to me, talking to people. But you will leave the washing up for a short time, and go round and keep guard by the door. You will watch his face from there."

"There will be no need to watch his face," said Hjalmar, "he will scream or faint, or jump up and run away, you know."

"You must never tell your sister, Hjalmar," said Kristoffer, "why we made her come here."

"No, no," said Hjalmar.

On the evening decided upon for the experiment, Hjalmar was silent, set on his purpose. But Kristoffer was in two minds. Once or twice he came near to giving up the whole thing. But if he did so, and even if he could make Hjalmar understand and forgive—what would become of himself afterwards?

Oswald Senjen was in his chair in his usual position, with his back to the bar. Kristoffer was behind the bar, Hjalmar was at the swinging door of the hall, to receive his sister.

Through the glass door Kristoffer saw the child arrive in the hall, accompanied by an elder sister with a red feather in her hat, for in these winter months people did not let children walk alone in the streets at night. At the same time he became aware of something in the room that he had not noticed before. "I can never, till tonight," he told himself, "have been quite awake in this place, or I should have noticed it." To each side of the glass door there was a tall looking glass, in which he could see the faces turned away from him. In both of them he now saw Oswald Senjen's face.

The little girl in her mackintosh and hood had some difficulty opening the door, and was assisted by her brother. She walked straight up to the bar, neither fast nor slow, placed the letter on the counter, and collected her shilling. As she did so she lifted her small pale face in the hood slightly, and gave her brother's friend a little pert, gentle grin of acquittal—now that the matter was done with. Then she turned and walked back and out of the door, neither fast nor slow.

"Was it right?" she asked her brother who had been waiting for her by the door. Hjalmar nodded, but the child was puzzled at the expression of his face and looked at her big sister for an explanation. Hjalmar remained in the hall till he had seen the two girls disappear in the rainy street. Then the porter asked him what he was doing there, and he ran round to the back entrance and to his tub and glasses.

The next guest who ordered a drink at the bar looked at the bartender and said: "Hello, are you ill?" The bartender did not answer a word. He did not say a word either when, an hour later, as the bar closed, he joined his friend in the scullery.

"Well, Kristoffer," said Hjalmar, "he did not scream or faint, did he?"

"No," said Kristoffer.

Hjalmar waited a little. "If it is him," he said, "he is tough."

Kristoffer stood quite still for a long time, looking at the glasses. At last he said: "Do you know why he did not scream or faint?"

"No," said Hjalmar, "why was it?"

Kristoffer said: "Because he saw the only thing he expected to see. The only thing he ever sees now. All the other men in the bar gave some sign of surprise at the sight of a little girl in a mackintosh walking in here. I watched the fat man's face in the mirror, and saw that he looked straight at her as she came in, and that his eyes followed her as she walked out, but that his face did not change at all."

"What?" said Hjalmar. After a few moments he repeated very low: "What?"

"Yes, it is so," said Kristoffer. "A little girl in a mackintosh is the only thing he sees wherever he looks. She has been with him here in the bar before. And in the streets. And in his own house. For three weeks."

There was a long silence.

"Are we to go to the police now, Kristoffer?" Hjalmar asked.

"We need not go to the police," said Kristoffer. "We need not do anything in the matter. You and

I are too heavy, or too grown up, for that. Mattea does it as it ought to be done. It is her small light step that has followed close on his own all the time. She looks at him, just as your sister looked at me, an hour ago. He wanted rest, he said. She will get it for him before the end of the year."

Anna

1. A RESOLUTION AND A JOURNEY

Many people know the name of Monsieur Dombasle, the great ballet master of Paris, who died a hundred years ago. But few people know how, toward the end of his magnificent career, a misfortune befell him: he lost his faith in the art of the ballet.

"The ballet of our day," he said, first to himself and then to his friends, "has sold its soul to the devil! May God forgive me, I have myself been middleman to the transaction. It is no longer a rose garden, a live growth, such a thing as God takes pleasure in creating—it has become as barren as a display of fireworks. Our fine feats of skill and dexterity are like a series of notes, the melody of which has been lost.

"According to one school of theology," he went on, "man is saved by faith, according to another by good works. Both are wrong. The whole universe—in which the planets swing so beautifully round the sun, the seasons in their dance form the year, and the years in their march mark out the eras of history—is saved from chaos, and is held in order, by rhythm and melody. So, too, is man. Where the melody is lost, the heart is lost, and out of the heart are the issues of life.

"If I am now," he concluded, "to save the soul of the ballet—and my own soul with it—I must find again the deep wells from which the dance first sprang, I must dig down in the black soil for its moist roots. I must go away from my own frivolous and flat age to those great, dark, and innocent ages in which the muse of the dance first revealed herself to humanity."

So in order to save the soul of the ballet, and his own soul with it, Monsieur Dombasle set out on a pilgrimage to Italy—which is the garden of Eden wherein ballet and pantomime first dwelt—and chose for his goal the small mountain town of Bergamo. For from Bergamo, he was told, had come the figure of Arlecchino, the Adam of pantomime, a man of clay into whose nostrils God breathed life. He took with him his young collaborator and friend Sadoc Silberstein, who limped on one leg, but who knew all that can be known about dancing. The two arrived in Italy in the month of May, which there is the high season of fairs and markets.

And in Italy, near Bergamo, Monsieur Dombasle met with an adventure of which for many years he talked to no one but Sadoc. This narrative tells about it.

2. ABOUT BERGAMO

The ancient city of Bergamo stands upon a rock fifteen hundred feet high and three thousand feet wide. From there, like a hawk with a mouse, it keeps an eye on the Città Bassa, the newer town of trade and crafts which, low on the green plain, runs peacefully along the roads to the outside world.

High up in the Città Alta's maze of broken lanes the dark Middle Ages of Italy are still alive. Other

cities of the Lombardic plain, under the influence
of new times and new ideas, had blossomed as
seats of the arts and sciences, but Bergamo stuck
to its peak, dumb and dangerous, an aging, unem-
ployed condottiere. A famous traveler has said of
the Bergamasque aristocracy that they were all half
mad with malice and lust. They were an insular
race, their minds fossilized like lava, their blood
thick and hot. Their sense of fun has come out in
the figure of the Bergamasque Arlecchino, who is
boorish as a buffalo and agile as a goat, with a
blackened face and a harsh breath, with cat's
whiskers, a coat patched and spotted like a leopard's, and the brush of a fox in his cap.

In a steep, narrow, and sooty street of Bergamo,
and in a steep, narrow, and sooty palace, dwelt the
noble family of Gattamelata.

3. The Gattamelata Family

Once in the good old age of the sword the Gattamelatas had owned and ruled the town.

A family legend reported that five hundred years
ago the founder of the house, a winegrower of the
province, had married a witch of the mountains,
who had opened the caves to her young husband
and bestowed immense riches upon him. Later
these riches had been amply increased by loot and
plunder. But as times grew gentler and as, with
continuous intermarriage, the skulls of the family
grew narrower, their wealth and power had waned
and shrunk, and at the time of this story they were
pitiably poor. They kept but one old lackey, with
trembling knees and holes in his livery, and one

old woman-of-all-work swept their stairs, carried their water, and cooked their thin soup. Even the rats had left the empty larders of the palazzo.

The ups and down of the province, the alternating governments of French and Austrians, had passed unnoticed over the heads of a doomed race, striving to keep alive. But the Gattamelatas still held these heads high above their empty stomachs, sat up stiff in their bare rooms, and silently swallowed the deadly ennui of a bird of prey in a cage.

In the heroic heyday of the family few of its men had lived to grow old. Their women—widows, mothers, and daughters of condottieri, with their own raging red blood in their veins—had kept one another company behind the thick black walls of the palazzo. And as if still holding on to this noble tradition, the Gattamelata household was even now predominantly female.

In the top rooms of the house resided the grandmother, herself by birth a Gattamelata. She had grown perfectly bald, but she still possessed two proud black eyebrows, like a pair of scimitars, which she had managed to pass on to all her descendants. She spoke but little, but was aware of all that went on in the palazzo.

A flight of stairs down lived the widowed Countess Giulia and her children.

Countess Giulia had first mounted these stone steps twenty-five years ago as a little bride of fifteen, straight from the convent school. She had then been much admired for her golden hair, and had been acquainted with very few facts of life. Since then her golden hair had faded and her slim figure grown fat and flabby, and a good deal of the facts of life had come tumbling down on her head, in a haphazard way, most of them incomprehensible and all of them dismaying. She had shut her eyes to them as far as possible and clung to the good nuns' teachings, like a woman in a thunderstorm closing her eyes and counting the beads of her rosary. In the depth of her heart she still preserved a number of her childhood dreams and fancies. She never contradicted any member of her family, but she wept easily, and sometimes managed to get her own way by a kind of soft, passive obstinacy. Her comforter and adviser in life was her old confessor, Father Bonifacio.

She had five young daughters with long necks and shining eyes, and with only two black silk frocks among them for going to Mass, and at the end of the pretty row, one son, Alessandro, the hope and pride of the Gattamelata house.

The five sisters were fully aware of the fact that their individual existence might with reason be disputed or denied, since they had come into this world as failures in the attempt to acquire a Gattamelata heir, and were—so to say—but blanks drawn by their ancient house in its lottery of life and death. Their family arrogance was fierce enough to make them bear this sad lot with a high hand, as a privilege out of reach of the common people. But within the daily life of the palazzo they by no means consented to accept any kind of nonexistence, but one and all passionately and pitilessly impressed their reality upon their young brother.

Alessandro, in that same daily life, felt himself theoretically prized beyond rubies, but in practice

seven times henpecked, and had become somewhat
sullen and abrupt in manner, a lonely, hardened
young misogynist. He stuttered a little when he
spoke, and because his sisters mocked this defect,
he hardly ever opened his mouth in the house.

4. FATHER BONIFACIO GIVES ADVICE

Countess Giulia passed many a sleepless night worrying about the future of her dowerless daughters.
One morning she sent for Father Bonifacio, poured
out all her troubles to him, and when she had finished, sat immovable with her wide-open, pale, and
melancholy eyes on his face.

Father Bonifacio was of humble birth, but had
ministered to the aristocracy of Bergamo for thirty
years, and was by now familiar with its view of
life, its ambitions, and griefs. He found the women
of the palazzi, in their quality of penitence, prefer-
able to the men. The haughty Bergamasque noblemen, even when amply provided with material for
confession, were slow to unburden their souls, and
scowled in the task. But the ladies, within an un-
eventful existence, welcomed their hour in the con-
fessional as a weekly spiritual bath or beauty treatment. The old priest had come to feel at home in
the world of woman, and to be an expert on household matters and matrimonial affairs.

Now Father Bonifacio, after having scratched his
head and picked his nose, suggested that the countess should take on a lady's maid for her daughters,
in order that these young noblewomen might appear in society in a manner suitable to their estate.
The countess thought the matter over and replied
that she would reinstate the old maid-of-all-work,

brought with her from her own home, in her former dignity as lady's maid, if on his side Father Bonifacio would provide her with a young female for the rough work of the household. Upon this the priest informed her that he had at hand the very person wanted, a village girl of fifteen, hardworking and modest. Her name was Anna.

Could the countess be sure of Anna's honesty and diligence? Indeed she could, for Father Bonifacio happened to have known the little girl from childhood, and her mother had been brought up in the small nunnery of his own native village. But the girl, the countess inquired, somewhat alarmed, was born in wedlock? In wedlock, the old man confirmed, although her father had not been a native of the province but had come from far away. Some faint uneasiness in the priest's manner and a slight hesitation in his speech made the countess scent a tale. She was always keen to hear a tale of adventure or romance, and she questioned Father Bonifacio about this. In the end the good father folded his hands upon his greasy cassock and began his narrative.

5. Pia's Story

Anna's mother was named Pia, and had had a sorry and bitter childhood, for she had been the seventeenth child of poor and unenlightened parents and, sadder still, she was born deaf and dumb. The other children in the village mocked her, chased her away from their games and dances, and told the grown-up people that she was possessed by the devil, so that in the end the child's own father and mother at times believed the same thing.

Anna

Now in the village there was a small nunnery, holding only eight nuns. These eight good sisters never themselves went outside their house, but at the same time the work of their hands traveled far and wide, for they cut and sewed little frocks, cloaks, and caps for our Virgins, saints, and Bambinos, and they were so inventive and so clever with their needles that great cathedrals in Spain and Paris were their customers, and no Magi in any nativity were as elegantly or tastefully dressed as theirs. The mother superior of this convent was a holy woman, untiring in prayer and fast; moreover, she was the daughter of a potter renowned in the province for his bold experiments with colors and tints, and through him had much knowledge of coloring and dyeing. The good saints, she said, in her dreams would show her new patterns and combinations of colors, and in accordance with their instruction she would send the village children up in the mountains, there to collect the herbs and roots from which she extracted rare dyes for her cottons and silks.

Mother Agape took pity on little Pia, initiated her into her science, and found that the lonely mute child would go to pick herbs on such steep slopes and tall peaks as the other children were afraid to climb.

After a while, Mother Agape, she told her sisters, in a dream was informed of how she might teach the little deaf-and-dumb creature to read people's speech from the movements of their lips. She took Pia in hand and worked with her every day, and although the villagers smiled a little at her extravagance, she persisted in her work and became quite pleased with the progress of her pupil.

Now again, Father Bonifacio recounted, it happened that a fabulously rich Englishwoman, traveling all over the world, came to the village and stayed there for three days. This woman's name was Lady Helena, and her Italian servants informed the people of the village that she had now for many years gone from one country to another in search of a particular, very rare sort of blue china, which till now she had never found. To pass the time she entered the little convent chapel, and five minutes later she sent for the nun who had made the Virgin's blue mantle. In this way she became acquainted with Mother Agape and with her strange ambition in regard to the deaf-and-dumb child. She gazed for a long time at the old nun and the little girl.

"I myself," she said, "have given much time to the study of color. I can never rest or settle, for I must look everywhere for a blue color, the which I know to exist, but which till now I have not succeeded in finding. The blue in your Virgin's mantle comes nearer to it than anything I have yet seen. And although I myself mean to find that blue in a different material, in a china jar, I feel a sympathy for you as for a woman of more than ordinary insight. You will, good Mother, without doubt, have made more than one attempt before you obtained your result?"

Mother Agape answered that she had made fifty-five attempts before obtaining her result. But she had, she added, been shown the colour in a dream and therefore had known it to exist.

"The process of staining china," said Lady Helena thoughtfully, "is highly intricate, because, before the burning, the lump of kaolin and felspar in the potter's hand is dull and colorless. Great cleverness is needed in the task. You have now, I see, taken in hand a bit of dull and colorless clay"—here she looked at the child—"and I wonder whether you feel that you have the cleverness necessary to turn it into a piece of blue china?"

"Signora," Mother Agape answered, "my dear father was a potter renowned in the province for his bold experiments with colors and tints, and through him I have some knowledge of the process of which you speak. I am well aware that it takes more than one burning to produce a fine piece of china. In the potter's art, my father told his apprentices, two things are needed: a fire, and patience. Indeed, 'Patience, patience!' was his motto. With the aid of that good gift, patience, I have after many experiments managed to turn out the blue of our Lady's mantle, at which you have been gazing. With its help, too, I may manage to produce, if not in the first burning then in a second, out of a dull and colorless material, a thing with a color and shine."

"Patience?" Lady Helena said after a silence. "A donkey in Italy has got more patience than a horse in England, but I am not aware that they get any further with it. Still I am aware that the donkey is allowed into your Nativity, where no horse is to be found. And when I look at your Virgin's mantle, I feel that I shall be happy to lend a hand to the patient person's work. If I cannot pray, good Mother, I can pay. Some people can stay peacefully in a whitewashed room, others must travel from place to place. But when in the future you think of me as a restless and impatient woman, remember that I may well at the same moment be thinking of the donkey by the crib."

And so when she left the village, Lady Helena placed in the hands of Mother Agape a big sum of money for Pia's education.

6. PIA'S STORY CONTINUED

"And what then?" asked Countess Giulia.

"Then," Father Bonifacio answered, "then we naturally all imagined that Mother Agape would receive Pia, with her pretty dowry, into the sisterhood. But here the good woman with her patience and her scruples undoubtedly made a mistake. For she kept on praying the saints for guidance, watching the girl, and asking herself if Pia had the real vocation to become a nun. And in the meantime she let Pia assist the nuns in the house, and sent her out to pick herbs for her. It is true that Pia remained a queer, reserved, and sulky person. She never made any friends, and although she could now both speak and understand other people's speech, she was hardly ever seen in the company of the other village girls. The only thing in which she took any real interest was when people danced in the marketplace—naturally, as she could not hear the music, she could not dance, and probably the movements and figures of a dance seemed to her extraordinary things, but she would stand stock still for hours gaping at the dances. Perhaps in the end her sad lot came from this queer passion of hers. I myself spoke to Mother Agape many times and admonished her to hurry up and have Pia become a nun. But she kept me off one way or another, and one time mysteriously begged me to remember that she had a great responsibility toward the English lady. The good Mother was growing old.

"She was growing old," Father Bonifacio continued, drawing from a fold in his cassock a small horn box and taking a pinch of snuff, sneezing gently. "And Pia herself was no longer young and was still working as a kind of lay sister and was growing with each year more stiff and stubborn. Mother Agape was keeping a careful account of the English lady's money and was even making it yield a little interest. Possibly she imagined that some day the girl would marry.

"One spring a troupe of jugglers came to the village. Amongst them was a tightrope dancer, a nimble boy some six or seven years younger than Pia. The deaf-and-dumb girl attended every performance. She must have caught the juggler's attention —probably he made inquiries about her and learned that she was, in our village way, an heiress. He was a lazy boy, fond of fine clothes—very likely he thought that by marrying the woman, who evidently adored him, he could secure his leisure and get his vanity satisfied for the rest of his life. One day he and Pia presented themselves before Mother Agape and announced their decision to marry. At this time it was not easy to follow the way of the good Mother's thoughts. She begged them to wait until she had brought the matter before her saints. In the end she consented. I myself was absent from the village, otherwise I might have stopped her.

This queer couple got married, and the Mother paid out part of the money left to her for the bride to start a small pawnbroker's shop in another village. They lived there for some time, and Pia, it must be said, worked hard for her young husband, who never did anything but drift around. Nine months after the wedding he suddenly got tired of his wife and his life, and when his old troupe passed close by he ran away and joined it. But Pia was a woman with a strong mind, her husband was the only person she had ever cared for, she would not let him go. She sold her shop and although far gone with child she began to journey on the track of the troupe from village to village in the province. It was really rather a sad thing, Signora, this deaf-and-dumb woman so deeply in love pursuing the silly boy, and it ended in a real catastrophe. For when one evening Pia caught up with her husband, and he from his rope high up caught sight of her, he had such a shock that he fell down and in the fall broke his neck. His poor widow saw him buried, then walked straight back to her native village, and there gave birth to a daughter, the girl Anna, of whom I have spoken. Mother Agape by this time was ill, but she asked to see the child and gave her her blessing, and shortly after she died. Pia demanded to have the rest of her money paid out, and she went away with it and started a small pawnbroker's shop in Caprino.

"You see," said the old priest, "I have a kind of sympathy for this child through the good Mother."

"It is a very strange story," said Countess Giulia, "and with the exception of Mother Agape I find the people in it unattractive. But if the girl is as hardworking and modest as you told me, and if she will take on the work for the wages you have mentioned, I will give her a try."

In reality the lady was so interested by the story that she could not miss seeing one of the chief characters in it, and even felt quite excited by the idea of having Anna under her roof.

7. ANNA BRINGS LUCK TO THE GATTAMELATA HOUSE

Anna walked through the lofty dark gate of the Palazzo with a modest bundle in her hand, bare-footed and clear-skinned, with quiet eyes like a heifer's and a mouth like a rose, a strong, patient beast of burden.

The two old town-bred servants of the house turned up their noses at her, and from their higher steps in the household dropped a good many heavy pieces of work, like a whole load of firewood, upon the head of the little newcomer at the bottom step. They were somewhat surprised to see her catch and carry the logs as if they had been toy balls. All through a working day that began before sunrise and lasted till after the stars had come out, the peasant girl displayed a quality of her own, a calm, gentle equipoise, which made her lift up a burden as lightly as she laid it down. One might imagine her to be the very young child of a giant race, who would some day balance the Gattamelata Palazzo, with all that it contained, upon the palm of her hand.

The five young ladies of the house—who were now busy with prying into chests and cupboards for bits of ancient velvet or brocade, and with making old Fima modernize their frocks or dress their long hair according to the latest fashion—hardly noticed the new servant, or if they happened to notice her, casually remarked to each other that she was quite pretty in a rustic way. The old grandmother, who never came downstairs, two or three times when Anna was sent to the top of the house gave the maiden a long, deep, and fierce glance.

But Countess Giulia, who was ever easily moved, at the very first sight of her new maid, sat down and, with both pleasure and fright, felt half-forgotten rose-colored dreams of the past stir in her bosom.

For on her wedding day her godmother had given her a wooden image of Saint Anna, the patron saint of married women, in a blue frock, with rosy cheeks and dark eyes, to bring her luck in her married life. Young Giulia had confided the first problems of her new state to Saint Anna, and had more than once been helped by her. But shortly before the birth of her eldest daughter the image had been lost, nobody knew how. The Countess had grieved over the loss, and for many years had secretly felt it to be at the bottom of all misfortunes that befell her family and herself. Now Anna in her blue frock was so strikingly like the lost image that the lady for a moment believed she saw her patron saint alive and breathing, now younger than herself, reenter the house. Hope warmed her chilled and benumbed soul. Experience had taught her that all hopes are likely to wither and die, leaving nothing behind them. All the same, she felt, they were sweet while they lasted.

She told nobody, not even Father Bonifacio, of her vision. But as, slowly and wonderfully, it took shape before her eyes and consolidated, she triumphed in her heart. After all, she reflected, she saw clearer, and knew more, than either her daughters or her mother-in-law. Then in the end she almost forgot her dream in the whirl of actual, happy events.

Not more than a month after Anna's arrival at the palazzo, a widower of Bergamo, of a certain age, but of fair birth and wealth, applied for the hand of Claudia, the eldest daughter. The wedding was quiet, since the gentleman's first wife had died recently, but the old moldy and creaky coach with the Gattamelata crest on its door was once more drawn from the carriage shed and was seen in the streets of Bergamo, with the old lackey in a pair of new white cotton gloves at the back of it, driving the bride to her new home.

A fortnight later the seventh son of the Marquese Malipiero began to pay his attentions to Maria Grazia, the second in the row. Under these favorable aspects the long faces of the three younger sisters rounded. At times they suddenly blushed, slowly and deeply. A new wind, a soft, fragrant breeze of spring, wafted through the gloomy rooms of the old house.

8. ALESSANDRO'S GOOD LUCK

A big, shining coach stopped before the gate of the palazzo, and an old, gouty, but distinguished gentleman stepped out from it. He presented himself as Baron Alfani of Genoa, and begged for an audience with the Countess Faustina Gattamelata.

At first his name, brought up to the top of the house by Anna, puzzled the old lady. She had never, she declared, known any Baron Alfani. Then she remembered and came to life. Before the old gentleman had climbed the last step of the stairs she was in the most vivid agitation, a high color in her old face, a smile on her lips.

Fifty years ago young Baron Alfani had been in love with Contessina Gattamelata, but had been rejected by her parents as a youth of inadequate descent. In despair he had left Bergamo and gone to Genoa, there to make a fortune with which to win his beloved. In Genoa he had learnt first that it is a difficult thing to make a fortune and then, secondly, that his lady in Bergamo had been married to her cousin. He considered suicide, but thought better of it and in the end married into a pretty Genoese fortune. By the time of this story he was a very wealthy man and a widower. But he had never forgotten Bergamo. When, three months ago, he had had a stroke, young Faustina's face had appeared before him, and he decided to go and see her once more before he died. He was now partly recovered, and had laid out his journey to the baths at Monte Catini by way of Bergamo.

Up in the top room of the palazzo the old lovers talked of old times. Countess Faustina once more smelt almond blossoms and walked on moonlit and dewy garden paths, and her skinny hand trembled a little as in the course of the conversation Baron Alfani pressed it to his old lips.

How far away, she sighed, were the days of youth. But in a way, he sighed back, they might be made to return again. During his illness he had conceived the plan of marrying his granddaughter, and only heiress, to the grandson of his first love. The young lady was but thirteen years old, the marriage would have to wait for two years, but then Alessandro too was young. The future Countess Gattamelata had a slight squint, but would outgrow the defect. Countess Faustina listened in silence while the baron developed his project. The memory of herself as a sweet young girl melted into sweet hopes for Alessandro, the person she loved most in the world. When her old lover had finished his speech, two tears, like two drops of resin, slowly trickled down her cheeks, from eyes that had not wept for half a century.

Before the baron left, an agreement was made up between the pair. When in a fortnight the old gentleman's water cure was finished, he should once more pass through Bergamo, and should then take young Count Alessandro with him to Genoa, in order that the boy might make the acquaintance of his future consort.

Baron Alfani descended the stairs, got into his coach and drove on to Monte Catini. Countess Faustina, still strangely moved and animated, did not wait to inform her daughter-in-law or Father Bonifacio of the event. She at once sent for her grandson to notify him of his luck.

9. A MEETING ON THE STAIRS

Alessandro came down the stairs from his grandmother's room, and halfway down met Anna, who was on her way up with two buckets of water on the yoke across her shoulders. She stepped aside to let her young master pass, but was not quite quick enough. He knocked against the bucket, and a little water splashed over his trouser leg.

Young Alessandro after the interview with his grandmother was in a black mood and more than ordinarily inclined to revolt against all women in the world. He spun round toward the maid, seized the bucket, and emptied it over her head.

Anna neither shrieked nor giggled. When afterwards he thought the scene over, he was not even sure that she had given him a glance through her long eyelashes. For a moment she stood quite still on the stone step, drenched and dripping like a flowering tree in a shower of rain. Then she set down her buckets, poured water from the one into the other to obtain equilibrium, again lifted them on to her shoulders and continued her way upstairs.

Alessandro kept standing where she had left him, and followed her with his eyes.

10. ALESSANDRO AND ANNA

In one of the rooms of the palazzo there was a big dark picture which represented Jacob's dream at Bethel. Alessandro as a small boy had often stood still before it, gazing at the light figures of the angels and wondering at the celestial coquetry of winged beings who would still deign to make use of a ladder. As now he looked at the girl's ascending figure he felt that it was being carried upwards as by a reversed law of gravitation, with all the mild majesty of one of Jacob's angels.

Alessandro is the hero of our tale, this is the place to say a few words about him.

In appearance he was like his sisters, although somehow the best-looking of the Gattamelata brood —possibly because the family type came out better in a young male than in a female. In most other ways he was unlike his kinswomen.

The Gattamelatas, during the five hundred years in which they themselves had been hardened and sharpened on the rock of Bergamo, had yet, out of reverence for that peasant ancestor of theirs who had married the mountain witch, preserved his land and his vineyards a few miles out of town. In his childhood Alessandro had often visited the farms, and even now would sometimes in his dreams wander through them. Indeed one might have imagined that the love of the country, together with all the gentler tastes and inclinations in life, the liking for trees, animals, and music, had latently accumulated for fifteen generations, to come out dimly in the last scion of the house. Alessandro was aware of a nostalgia in his nature more fit for a shepherd than for a nobleman. He felt that it was a shameful weakness, and that it must be hidden behind a dark frown and an arrogant manner. In defense against it he had become the best fencer and wrestler of Bergamo. He was pleased to find that with every year his body was becoming harder and more like his forefathers' coats of mail, and his reputation amongst other young noblemen of Bergamo more formidable. His distrust of women made him a somewhat solitary figure in their circle, but if he was known as an ascetic, or even a stylite, he was also known as a desperado. "Oderint," he thought, "dum metuant."

It is difficult to explain why, in the short meeting with the wet village girl, the hard and sulky boy for a moment saw heaven and earth smiling upon him. Showers swept over a wide landscape, leaving rainbows in the sky, radiant days mellowed into clear evenings, and stars sprang out upon the vaults of night. The fields and the forests welcomed all in a sweet spirit of consent unknown to the fierce world of Bergamo. All the elements of life combined here as in a melody.

Our story does not relate any words spoken between Alessandro and Anna during the fortnight after their collision on the stairs. Neither of the young people was much given to talk—very likely the actual remarks exchanged between the two were of an entirely commonplace and impersonal nature, and if written down would hardly fill up a page.

All the same the moment came when the boy felt compelled by all forces around him and within him to press the girl's soft body to his own steely frame, and to bury his hot hard face in the cool petals of her cheeks and her lips. The experience was completely new to Alessandro, who in wrestling had pressed other boys' lean bodies against his own, but had never felt a young woman's form filling his arms, and had only reluctantly kissed his mother and his grandmother. So it was strange that he should feel it as a homecoming, the one natural and reasonable thing in the world.

11. THE MASTER OF THE HOUSE

Within this same hour Father Bonifacio in the red drawing room was compiling a list to the dictation of Countess Giulia. In her gratitude to Saint Anna the good lady had decided to offer her priest a gift of cheese, eggs, and wine for his poor. When the list was finished the two went downstairs to the pantry together in order to select the goods. As the countess opened the door she saw the live image of Saint Anna, with the bodice of her blue frock unbuttoned and torn back over her shoulders, in the arms of her son.

Anna ran out of the room, the countess sat down on a barrel of olives, the old and the young man, both blushing scarlet, faced one another.

It is difficult to describe Countess Giulia's state of mind at this fatal moment, for the lady's emotions were always somewhat diffused and chaotic.

No mother will really, in her heart, resent a son giving proof of his young manhood, and indeed Alessandro's mama had at times worried about his indifference toward her own sex. She might have seen him kiss any other pretty girl of Bergamo with a slight feeling of relief and pride. But he had kissed Anna, and thereby might have challenged the heavenly powers themselves. She at once had a terrible presentiment that if Anna should be deprived of her innocence by the son of her house, according to a kind of mysterious divine justice the daughters of the same house would be left with theirs for ever. She began to tremble on her barrel.

Father Bonifacio on his side was genuinely shocked and grieved.

He was himself a man of unblemished chastity. For thirty years he had listened to confessions of immorality with deep dismay: what would these forces be, which made people risk their temporal and eternal welfare for the sake of brief and frivolous pleasure? He had at time succeeded in making his noble penitents renounce the sins of anger or avarice, but experience had taught him that he was powerless against that other deadly sin of lust.

The Gattamelata Palazzo to the priest had been the last stronghold of righteousness. The old count had been dead these fifteen years. The Lady Faustina was past her days of escapades, Countess Giulia, his favourite penitent, was pious and timid by nature, and had at an early age been frightened out of her wits by violent passion. Nobody in Bergamo would for a moment dare to doubt the lofty virginity of the five proud sisters, and the confessor of the house had been happy to know that this noble quality did, exceptionally, exist even in the young son of the house.

In his sudden, sad disappointment Father Bonifacio remained without a word to say, till in the dead silence of the room he became aware of Countess Giulia trembling. Then he realized that it was his duty to depict to her erring son the sorry consequences of seducing an innocent girl in one's own house. But in his distress and perplexity he automatically fell back, word for word, on the sermon which in such cases he was wont to deliver to his peasant penitents.

Here he made a mistake. For Alessandro at once caught the tone of the lecture, and felt that he was being treated like a peasant boy. The young nobleman's blood was stirred and swept him away. With every second his face grew a darker red, he raised himself to his full height, and when Father Bonifacio had finished his speech he looked him straight in the face, and delivered his retort without a stutter.

"I am not," he said, "seducing any servant girl. I am going to make Anna my wife before all the world."

He paused, drew his breath twice, and went on slowly:

"I am the master of this house. Shall I not marry Anna in the Duomo of Bergamo, and have five hundred wax candles burn at my wedding—I, a Gattamelata and a Bergamasco?"

12. ALESSANDRO GOES AWAY

Now what could Countess Giulia or Father Bonifacio say or do?

Father Bonifacio's mind never worked quickly. He realized that against his own will he had conjured up catastrophe and disaster. But he was totally unable to perform the volte-face demanded by the situation. Besides, Alessandro at this moment was so much like his father that the old priest felt himself growing very much smaller. He stood before the young man as he had stood before Count Ottavio Gattamelata, a timid village priest. He opened his mouth twice, but no word came from it.

Countess Giulia rose from her seat, then sat down again. She felt, as so many times before, that she was the innocent victim of hostile and irresistible powers. Once more a hope had failed, had turned into doom. After a few seconds her despair passed into a flaming, choking indignation against Anna. How vilely had that girl deceived her! She had sneaked into the house in a sacred and beloved disguise, pretending to raise it up—now she was causing it to tumble down upon the heads of a noble and pious family. Countess Giulia, like Father Bonifacio, said not a word.

At this moment there was a knock at the door. It

was the old lackey who, having looked for his mistress all over the palazzo, announced to her through
an inch-wide opening of the pantry door that Baron
Alfani's coach was outside the gate and the gentleman himself waiting in the red room. The baron
had been delayed on the road and was in a great
hurry. He offered a thousand apologies to the ladies
of the house, and begged the young Count Alessandro to step into the coach and come with him to
Genoa at once.

Alessandro might have answered the baron that
since he had no longer any intention whatever of
marrying his granddaughter he would by no means
come with him to Genoa. But the boy lacked the
presence of mind for such an answer, and the experience of the world as well, for he had never before received an invitation. Possibly in his heart he
was grateful to be offered a natural quick exit from
the stage of the drama. All the same he was not
going to leave it without a final assertion of his
newly won, glorious authority.

"Anna," he said in a deep voice, "is mine. I am
leaving her in your care. I will not have a hair of
her head hurt while I am in Genoa."

He paused, clenching his right hand till the
knuckles whitened, as if he had been squeezing the
hilt of a sword.

"Anna," he repeated—and what sweet triumph
there was in the very pronunciation of the name—
"is, I have told you, to be honorably married, she
is, from this moment, to be treated with esteem
and respect by everybody in my house." He remembered the sensation of the girl's body in his em-

brace, his young face grew very pale, and he finished solemnly and severely: "She is to be revered as a goddess. Do you swear that it shall be so?"

Even if the boy's mien had not been so threatening, his mother would not have had the nerve to keep Baron Alfani waiting any longer. She answered her son in a terrified whisper: "Yes, Alessandro. Yes, I swear."

Alessandro turned to Father Bonifacio, his hand still upon his sword hilt. "And you?" he asked. "Yes," said Father Bonifacio.

The old lackey brought Alessandro's cloak and traveling case, the etiquette of normal life swept him away. Within a quarter of an hour compliments had been exchanged, leave taken—Baron Alfani gently jesting with the countess upon her tears at this first parting with a beloved son—and Alessandro's luggage stowed in the baron's coach. The boy drove off by the smiling old gentleman's side, passion-tossed like a ship in a high sea.

His mother and Father Bonifacio from the balcony of the palazzo watched the coach disappear and reappear in the steep downhill-winding streets of Bergamo.

13. Cauldron Bubble

Both Countess Giulia and Father Bonifacio would much have preferred to keep the matter from Countess Faustina.

For Alessandro was the apple of his grandmother's eye. She saw the boy's shortcomings with unbribable sharpness: he was weak, obstinate, and a fool. It made no difference, he was still the glorious past of the Gattamelata house, its conquistadori and politicians all in one. And he was still its future, triumph, and power to come. The mother and the priest turned pale at the thought of the terrible wrath with which the old woman would receive their report of Alessandro's new folly.

But it would be impossible to keep her in ignorance. She had lived behind the walls of the palazzo for fifty-five years, and sounds, smells, and currents of air told her what was going on in it. Besides, the two felt incompetent to act on their own in the matter. They dared not even, as they thought of the penetrating black old eyes, allow Anna to leave the house.

So the Lady Faustina was told, received the news without moving a muscle in her face, and turned to Father Bonifacio.

"You brought the girl here," she said. "You will know about her. Has she got a father and mother?"

"She has got a mother," said Father Bonifacio.

"Then bring the mother to me," said she. "I shall speak to the woman."

Father Bonifacio explained that it was somewhat difficult to speak to Anna's mother since she was deaf and dumb.

"Deaf and dumb," said the old countess. "I might have known. That girl has learnt from childhood to speak without words. She walks, she turns her head, she lifts her arms—you fools, I have seen it all coming."

Anna's mother lived in a village at some distance from Bergamo. Alessandro was staying away only for a fortnight. There was no time to waste, Father Bonifacio set off at once to fetch her. Countess Giulia went through three days of feverish anguish and did not leave her rooms. Anna was forbidden to show herself upstairs. The household felt that the girl had done something terribly wicked, old Fima and the lackey did not speak to her or look at her. Only Alessandro's mother could not help peeping through the shutters as Anna walked across the courtyard, and each time she was frightened afresh because the fatal figure did still bear an incredible likeness to her sainted namesake. She looked forward to the talk with the girl's mother, which would end the unbearable state of things.

Once more she was sadly disappointed.

The appearance of the pawnbrokeress gave her a last, sickening shock.

The deaf-and-dumb woman was a short, heavyset person, but moved almost without a sound. Within the frame of her black shawl her round face was colorless as wax. She kept her pale clear eyes fixed on the lips of the person who spoke to her in order to read each word. When, always after a pause, she made her answers, her voice was flat and raucous, but she was able to make herself understood. It was, Giulia thought, like speaking to a stone, like being answered by a stone.

Countess Faustina spoke first. She had thought her speech over before, and shortly and haughtily informed Anna's mother that she had found her daughter foolish and wanton, that she disliked the thought of a maiden being ruined under her roof, and that she ordered Pia to take the girl away at once.

She advised her, she finished, to have Anna married off as soon as possible.

After a short silence the deaf-and-dumb woman answered. She thanked the noble lady a thousand times for concerning herself about a poor peasant girl. But how, good lady, would she marry Anna off without a dowry?

And how, good woman, came it—Faustina asked —that she had been so improvident as not to save up for her daughter's dowry?

Times were hard, very hard, Contessa, and Anna was but fourteen.

A silence. This time the peasant woman broke it on her own.

Luckily, Contessa, she said, she was not without prospects for her daughter. Madama Melita, of the "Giardino delle Rose," had made her a pretty offer in cash if she would let Anna enter her service.

Here followed a pause of several minutes, during which Countess Faustina took in the facts of the matter and mentally licked her lips.

Probably in the course of five hundred years, within this same room, long-dead Gattamelatas in the same way had plotted the fall of a foe and in the same way had licked their lips. The dire degradation and ruin which awaited a maiden in the Giardino delle Rose was but a just reward for one who had threatened the honor of the Gattamelata house.

But Father Bonifacio stirred in his chair. He read the thoughts of the Bergamasque noblewoman. But he himself was country-bred, from childhood used to looking after young things—lambs, calves, and chickens. It was he who broke the silence.

"No," he said. "It would not be quite a satisfactory arrangement. Anna ought not to remain in Bergamo, and it was of marriage that the kind lady had spoken. Could not, at some distance from town, a suitor for Anna's hand be found? If so, he finished, with unwonted and unexpected firmness, the countess might graciously consent to dower her servant girl with the same amount that Madama Melita had offered.

14. How the Vows Were Kept

Pia thought the matter over. Yes, she said, Anna had a suitor. When questioned upon the matter, she explained it.

The nuns of the small convent in which she herself had been brought up made little frocks for sacred images. But the images themselves were made for them by a youth named Angelo Masi. When Anna was three years old, Pia had taken her with her on a visit to the nunnery, Angelo had made her pose for a statue of the Virgin as a child. Some time later the young artist had gone away to Naples to study under a great master, and from Naples he had come back ill with a disease which was slowly depriving him of his eyesight. Under this misfortune, my noble ladies, he had lost his faith, he would make no more saints.

Within the darkness slowly creeping upon him his only thought was to make a statue of a pagan goddess, the name of which Pia had forgotten. This work of art, he told Pia, was to surpass any statue of the Virgin ever made, and by the time he himself was blind, it would make his name shine all over the world.

He would have nobody but Anna for a model, and had sent for her many times. He knew that he had but a short time left, and if his eyes were dim, his hands were very sensitive, he would let them run over the girl and carve out a perfect likeness. But Anna would not pose for him. The gentle girl, who was generally obliging to other people's wishes, had obstinately refused to go.

Now—Pia finished and suddenly fixed her eyes on Faustina's face—Angelo Masi, who was a man of some means and owned a farm and a vineyard, had offered to marry the girl. In this way he would have her to himself day and night. Only, Contessa, he would naturally expect a decent dowry with his wife. If such a dowry could be produced, she would herself bring her daughter to him, and would set off within this same hour.

The pawnbrokeress had been silent upon the name of the future husband's abode, as if she guessed that the noble ladies would prefer to have Anna disappear in the dark, leaving no trace.

At this point of the meeting the actual negotiations began.

They went on for some time, but in the end through the mediation of Father Bonifacio, Anna's dowry was fixed. A small ironbound chest was sent for and unlocked. Each piece of silver was put down on the table slowly by the countess, but the pawnbrokeress did not so much as look at the coins till they were all counted out in a row of small piles. The agreement was then confirmed in a long look from woman to woman, more binding than any signature or seal.

On the same afternoon Pia and her daughter, on two little gray donkeys, left the palazzo.

This time Alessandro's mother did not follow the travelers with her eyes. She remained in her

deep chair, her hands folded. Her lips were closed,
but her mind spoke out loudly:

She is to be honorably married—do you swear
that it shall be so? Yes, Alessandro.

She is to be revered as a goddess—do you swear
that it shall be so? Yes, Alessandro.

15. A VISITOR

Alessandro had been away for a week, and Anna for
two days. Old Fima had once more been set to carry
water and peel onions, and the four sisters were
once more fretfully darning their own stockings.

On Thursday morning the ancient black palazzo,
for so many years silent and quiet, as if sunk in its
own thoughts, was once more stirred up by a call
from the outside world. A foreign gentleman, after
having for some time looked up and down the
house, knocked at the gate and asked the old lackey
for an interview with the lady of the house. He
handed the old man a white, shining card which
was to precede and announce him, and declared
that he would wait in the porter's lodge until he
could be received by the countess. The old countess, asked the lackey, or the younger? The gentleman was silent for a moment. If there be more
than one, he answered—both. The lackey looked at
the card, he could read and was proud of the fact.
Upon the card was printed:

SIDNEY HARDING

Avvocato

"Avvocato," the stranger explained, letting his
finger run along the printed word.

The avvocato was a young man, but never had
such a sedate young man been seen in Bergamo.
He had red hair and eyebrows and was dressed in

black clothes of a fashion not known to the town, but of excellent cut and material. He spoke Italian with a strong accent, but seemed to feel that it was his Italian which was correct while that of the natives lacked distinctness. Under his arm he carried a big black portfolio.

When brought before the two Gattamelata ladies in the old countess's room on the top floor, he saluted them both, placed his top hat and portfolio on the table, for a minute looked from one lady to the other, and addressed himself to the elder.

"Madam," he said, "I apologize for taking your time. But I am here, in my person, representing the firm of Grey, Sterne, & Black." He paused, with as much assurance as if having stated that he had come on behalf of the Father, the Son, & the Holy Ghost. The countesses did not grasp the foreign names, but all the same the gentleman's mien and manner from this first moment of the conversation made them sit up.

"I come from London," said the gentleman. "I have had to give some time to tracing a person, the presence of whom is demanded by my firm."

Here he suddenly opened the portfolio on the table and selected a paper from it.

"The name of this person," he went on, "is Anna Segati. Age: fifteen years. Sex: female. After careful investigation I have concluded her to be in service in this house."

As the ladies found nothing to answer he went on.

"The mission with which Messrs. Grey, Sterne, & Black have entrusted me is to convey to the spinster Anna Segati the legacy bequeathed her by a client of the firm."

"A legacy?" asked Countess Faustina.

"A legacy, madam," said the young man.

"Whoever," Countess Faustina asked after a moment, "whoever, in London, from where you say you come, is bequeathing a legacy upon Anna Segati?"

"I shall inform you, madam," said he. "My firm has given me a free hand to speak and act in the matter as I think expedient, and I shall inform you."

16. The Lady Helena's Will

The Englishman carefully put the paper back in the portfolio and carefully singled out from it another paper.

"On the twenty-first of January this year, madam," he said, "the will of the Lady Helena Selborne was opened and read out by Mr. Grey himself. It was found that Lady Helena, after having disposed of half her fortune in favor of various relations, servants, and tenants, had stipulated: 'The other half of my property I leave to the girl Anna Segati in the village of San Rocco in Italy.' This, madam, was the reason why the head of my firm sent me off to find for him the girl in question."

"How—" Countess Faustina asked, "how in all the world did it occur to the Lady Helena to leave half her property to Anna Segati?"

The avvocato put back the paper and took out another.

"In a letter," he said, "an appendix to her will, dated ten years back, the Lady Helena writes: 'I make the girl Anna Segati my heir because from a letter sent me by the old nun Mother Agape of San Rocco I understand that this little girl, while still in her mother's womb, has managed to kill off her papa, and because I myself have always disliked papas.' "

He let his eyes rest on the paper in his hand.

Countess Giulia spoke for the first time, in a trembling voice.

"Did the Lady Helena," she asked, "hate her father very much?"

"Lady Helena and my old lord," he answered, "had somehow become estranged, to the best of my knowledge, on account of a shipwreck."

Countess Giulia recalled what she had heard about the immensely rich milords who traveled through the country, their trouser pockets filled with gold coins which they never counted, and with peacocks in cages dangling beneath their coaches. She realized that all Englishmen were mad, and said no more.

"However," said the avvocato, "in a letter dated ten years later, just before her death, Lady Helena writes: 'I make Anna Segati my heir, because Mother Agape was right in preaching patience, because the true blue color may come out in the second burning, and because very surprisingly God is merciful.' "

There was a pause.

"This," said Countess Faustina, "is a very extraordinary will."

"Madam," said the Englishman, "it is far from being the most extraordinary will with which my firm has had to deal."

There was a longer pause, in which the avvocato collected his papers.

"What," asked Countess Faustina, very slowly, "what was the amount bequeathed by Lady Helena to Anna Segati?"

"Fifty thousand pounds," he answered.

"What," she again asked, "would it come to in real money?"

The young man once more changed the papers, and from a new sheet read out: "Two million, six hundred eighty-five lire, twenty-five centesimi."

The two ladies for a minute said nothing. Then Countess Faustina repeated the figure: "Two million, six hundred eighty-five lire, twenty-five centesimi." But she made no remark of her own.

"And now," said the young lawyer, "I should be obliged if you would send for Anna Segati."

"Anna Segati," said Countess Faustina, "is not here. She is not in the house."

"If it be so," said he, "will you, madam, kindly inform me of her present abode?"

Countess Faustina made a movement in her chair. Twice she opened her lips and shut them again without speaking.

"I cannot tell you at all," she said.

The young man rose, collected his portfolio, and made a bow. He drew a little short sigh. "In that case," he said, "I must continue my investigation."

Upon the threshold he made a second bow, then walked away, his portfolio under his arm.

17. THE TWO WIDOWS

The room which he left might have been empty— there was no word, sound, or movement in it. But if thoughts had been audible he would have had to stop his ears to a row of long, terrible shrieks and laments following him down the stairs and across the courtyard.

For an hour the two black-clad women sat in silence.

At first their sad courses of thought ran parallel. What have we done! What have we done to our house!—to the sons and daughters of it! We held the salvation of them all in our hands, and we have thrown it away deliberately!

They turned their minds to the possibility of a miracle in the eleventh hour. Their thoughts, like trapped rats, jumped against the walls of the prison, searching madly for a way out. But they found none. In all probability Anna at this moment was already married, and her millions were in the hands of the blind sculptor. Or if, by some wonderful stroke of luck—by the girl refusing to marry or Angelo Masi suddenly dying—she was still free, her mother would be in control of her and her fortune, and from Pia they could expect no mercy. And even if, by direct intervention from the saints, both the man and the mother should have been done away with—how, in what words, would two great ladies of Bergamo explain the changed position to their turned-out servant girl, and how implore her to return to their house?

Nay, there was no exit. They turned their faces to the wall, like the prisoners, who in the old days, had been lowered down into the palazzo's subterranean dungeons to die there from hunger and thirst. Their dry throats contracted, had they wanted to speak they could not have got out a word.

Here the thoughts of the elder and the younger woman parted company.

This time it was the grandmother who gave herself over to dreams and fancies. Her mind began to play with the fortune which two days ago had been within her reach. Its fantastic, its inconceivable size fitted in with the ambitions of the old woman. The mountain witch, wife of the founder of the Gattamelata house, was reappearing in its chronicle! The old black palazzo began to beam and glow with her fairy gold. Faustina saw Alessandro dominating Bergamo, buying back his ancestors' lost possessions, magnificently dowering his sisters, outshining the rival houses of the town. She looked up and realized that all was lost. Her tortured breast let out a deep groan like a death rattle.

Countess Giulia's mind took no such high flight but remained with her son. Her thoughts fluttered round him like trembling hands, passionately longing to touch a beloved form, and held back by fear. So she had been right about him all the time. Alessandro had proved himself to be the one clearsighted person in the house, wise and wonderful. When he had spoken as master of the house he had indeed been securing its honor and prosperity in a masterly way. She might triumph, now, over a world which had failed to appreciate him, but it was a sad triumph. Alessandro himself would turn against her and would tell his mother that she had forfeited his greatness and glory, as she had broken his heart. Alessandro! Alessandro would never forgive her.

The sun went down while the widows of the Palazzo Gattamelata sat, immovable as if turned to stone, in their two chairs, and they did not ring for Fima to light the candles. Darkness became them.

Soon it grew and swallowed them up—their white faces and hands held out for a while, then the two black-clad women became one with the Bergamasque night.

18. ANNA ON THE ROAD

While these things were happening in Bergamo, Pia and Anna on their donkeys were slowly proceeding along the highroad. Pia let her daughter ride a little in front of her, as if she were driving a goose before her and fearing that she might at any moment turn off the track and run away. The while she was thinking hard, going through the figures of her bargain.

Anna swayed gently on her donkey and thought of Alessandro. Her pity for her lover was intense, for hard and heartless people had torn from him the girl that he had held in his arms and had wanted to carry off to his bed. All the same she sat straight in her saddle, holding her two young breasts high as if carrying them before her with care and pride, for Alessandro's hands had fondled them, Alessandro's burning lips had pressed against them, and they were the nest upon which in the end his hard and lonely head should find a rest. In the midst of her sadness she was still confident. Alessandro would save her, he would know how to defeat his enemies. It was impossible that the body which he had clasped to his own should be touched by profane hands.

In the village of Urgnano there was an osteria by the road. Outside it two ostlers were unharnessing the four horses of a big coach, and a peasant with a cart was watching them. As the women passed the group, Pia's donkey kicked the peasant's mule. It shied and upset its cart, and oranges and pumpkins rolled to all sides.

Anna in her tender mood could not stand the sight of an unhappy person. She reined in her donkey and slid off to help the peasant pick up his goods. Pia shrieked a few shrill words at her, then, observing that the sun was sinking, declared that they would sup and sleep at the inn. She too got off her mount, and the ostlers led the donkeys into the stable.

It was a mild and lovely evening in the month of May, the month of the great fairs and markets in the province of Lombardy. The dew was falling, the air was filled with the sweet smell of orange flowers.

In the yard of the osteria a troupe of traveling players had erected a small stage for their great performance later in the evening. Chinese lamps in all colors were hung up at the corners of it, so light that they looked fantastic and almost unreal. Still they gave a faint shine to boards polished with use.

Half a dozen small boys from the village, who had watched the lively gaudy strangers putting up their theater, had taken possession of it while the players themselves were supping, and were endeavoring to perform a classical ballet five feet above the ground. One of them was playing a flute and another beating a tiny drum. They had felt the lack of a prima ballerina to their performance. As Anna lingered a few moments in the courtyard to gaze at them they caught sight of her and stopped dancing. They first held a short counsel, then one of them politely approached her and begged her to come to their help. The whole company joined him, surrounding the girl and trying to persuade her.

Anna, as a true child of Lombardy, had a deep love and a kind of religious feeling for the art of the dance. As a small child she had often escaped from the bleakness of her daily life by performing a short solo in the pawnbrokeress's backyard or garden. Later on she had keenly watched the steps of the ballet dancers. While working for her mother, carrying water from the well to the house on her head or sweeping the stone steps she had felt happier if she could imitate them and move as if to a tune. When the little girl became a maiden, the blood of the rope dancer, her father, suddenly ran quick in all the veins of her body. When other girls longed to love and to be loved, she had longed to dance.

In the dusk of the osteria courtyard her yearning for Alessandro had for a moment become so overwhelming that she had feared she would die from it. Now, with the sweetly pleading faces round her, and with the sweet notes of the flute in her ears, she felt that she might express the sentiments of her heart, and might even send a message to her distant lover, by taking part in the dance. Her mother, she knew, would be expecting her in the osteria—but she could not possibly forgo the short minutes of release and happiness.

She smiled at the children, and as she nodded her head to them they all clapped their hands. The flute struck up a new pretty tune, and the smallest urchin, a lovely child, gave her his hand to lead her up the steps. She mounted the stage like a person stepping from a storm-tossed raft to a rescuing boat.

Soon the little pantomime took shape round her. The drum fell in with the flute, and the choir of dancers into rhythmic movements. The Chinese lamps floated in the clear air above their heads like new gay and gentle fairy globes.

The while, the two foreign gentlemen who had arrived by the coach were having their supper at a small table in the neighbouring osteria garden.

19. A MEETING IN THE OSTERIA

"Sadoc, my friend," said Monsieur Dombasle. "We will go back to Paris tomorrow. We will not even proceed to Bergamo, for it will only be a waste of our time. I have seen a hundred Arlecchinos by now—they may have some life in them, but they are all boorish as buffalos, and their smell gives offense to a Parisian nose. I have been the dupe of an illusion. For the muses are all dead, and Terpsichore died first of all. But what does it matter? I myself am old, with one foot in the grave, I belong to the past, my ideas are ridiculous—antiques fit for the lumber room. And what does it matter? No, do not fill my glass, wine without the muses is distasteful to a civilized person. What does it matter? *A la fin des fins*, what does it matter that nothing matters?"

Sadoc kept his eye on Monsieur Dombasle's face. He knew that when his old friend said that nothing mattered, he was in his most fatal mood, and as dangerous as a leopard crouching to spring. Nobody, at such times, could foresee the consequences of either a contradictory or a sympathetic reply, and silence itself might be perilous. As a rule, a casual indifferent remark would be the safest thing.

So he said: "There is a girl picking up oranges on the road."

Monsieur Dombasle turned his head a little, then again stared in front of him with a face of stone and exclaimed: "Fill my glass, all the same. I will drink a toast in the words of Andrea del Sarto: "Death to the arts in Italy and France!"

In spite of this mortal resolution the old artist left his glass untouched.

After a while Sadoc lightly remarked: "They are going to perform a ballet on that stage now."

"Who?" asked Monsieur Dombasle.

"Seven small boys," Sadoc answered, "and a girl. The girl of the oranges."

The idea of a ballet or pantomime being performed so close to him perturbed Monsieur Dombasle. He stirred in his seat and stole a scowling glance at the show.

"Absurd," he said. "Ridiculous. That big girl amongst those tiny male dancers!"

"At what time are we starting tomorrow?" asked Sadoc.

"Unless," Monsieur Dombasle after a moment remarked, "unless it be a representation of Snow White and the seven dwarfs. Not a bad plot for a ballet after all, that old tale of Herr Grimm's."

The little pantomime went on, Arlecchino and Colombina gracefully going through their classic row of troubles.

The identity of the plot with her own situation deeply moved Anna and carried her away. It was

sadly sweet to express her love and misery in amorous and tragic poses to the harmonious tune of
the flute. It so happened that the part of Arlecchino
was acted by the smallest boy. Possibly she could
not have gone through her own part as amorosa
so passionately with any of the others, but now
she embraced the Cupid as if he had been a minia-
ture Alessandro. Her abandon animated the whole
small troupe, Pantalone raged and threatened, and
the clown gamboled and fell on his behind in the
true grand style.

Before long Monsieur Dombasle had turned his
chair so that it faced the stage. Twice Sadoc
rose as if to go out and give his order for the departure, both times Monsieur Dombasle kept him
back with a movement of his hand.

At a short pause in the performance he folded
his hands.

When in the final scene Arlecchino knelt to Colombina and she raised him to her bosom, Monsieur
Dombasle too was drawn upwards from his chair,
his full glass in his hand. He took a step forward,
and as he passed Sadoc he gave him a short deep
glance, in itself almost hostile, but at the same
time so luminous that Sadoc knew the danger to
be over and his old friend saved.

For a moment Monsieur Dombasle stood immovable. Then he lifted his glass and solemnly proclaimed: "The muses are not dead."

He emptied the glass in one draught, then sent
it flying back over his shoulder to break into a
hundred pieces.

"Vivat!" he cried. "Vivat Terpsichore."

He sat down, and for a while was sunk in deep

thought, lost to the world. Then very slowly he filled another glass and looked up at his companion with shining soft eyes.

"Sadoc," he said. "Sadoc, my friend. I am taking that girl back with me to Paris, I shall have to make sure of her at once. Tonight."

20. ANNA IS SOLD A SECOND TIME

"She has never been taught to dance!" said Monsieur Dombasle. "*Eh bien*, what does that matter! She does not know an entrechat from a pirouette? *Eh bien*, pedants of all the world, *eh bien*, what does it matter?"

"May I remind you," said Sadoc, "that according to your own thesis a ballerina must be taken in hand at the age of three, or she will never be worth looking at."

"And a butterfly, Sadoc, a butterfly," said the old man reproachfully. "Does it not dance on its own from the moment it leaves the cocoon? This girl has danced on her own, on a morning, in the dewy grass, before her mother knew that she could walk. Her first kick was an entrechat! Sadoc, my friend, the fact that she has not been taught to dance is her greatest quality. She has not been taught because she was predestined by God himself to teach us.

"But we two are chatting here," he went on, "discussing abstractions and wasting minutes which may be priceless. Go and find out with whom she has come here. If she has got a father or mother or a grandmother, bring the person here and we will settle the matter. For we are going back to Paris tomorrow, in a beeline, Sadoc, as I told you. Only she will be sitting by my side in the coach."

So Sadoc went, made his inquiries, found out that Anna was traveling with her mother and brought Pia back with him.

When the old ballet master discovered that the mother of the future prima ballerina was deaf and dumb, he was delighted. Indeed, he confided in French to his companion, he had already guessed the circumstance before he ever set eyes on the woman. This child had learnt to express herself in movement as other children learn to express themselves in trite and trivial speech. The fact of Pia being deaf and dumb also facilitated the negotiations, for now he could carry them on not in Italian, of which he knew little, but in pantomime, of which he knew everything.

This second sale of the pretty village girl was from the beginning a livelier affair than the first. But just as in the first, great passions were at play.

Monsieur Dombasle put forward his proposal with a solemn and radiant face, picturing to the mother the glorious career he was offering her daughter. When he realized that the prospects made no impression whatever on the peasant woman, he was at first stupefied, then indignant, then furious. Before the matter was settled, Sadoc more than once had to put a quieting hand on his master's arm or knee to prevent his great gestures from shaking him to pieces.

Monsieur Dombasle learnt that the peasant woman was accompanying her daughter to the home of her future husband, and that the wedding was to take place within a few days. The news in itself alarmed him, and his horror increased when he was told that the bridegroom was blind. He trembled at the idea of this girl of all girls being given to a sightless man, the mere thought of such a crime broke his heart. Pia must give up her monstrous plan at once.

Pia remained as immovable as in the top room of the Gattamelata Palace, her round eyes fixed on the old man's face. But the noble gentleman must understand, she explained, that it was impossible for her to give up her plan. A great and powerful family in Bergamo wished this marriage to take place, and had dowered her daughter for the purpose. If she did not carry out their wish, she would have to return the dowry.

The heartlessness and lack of understanding in the mother of a great artist for a moment crushed Monsieur Dombasle. Sadoc came to his assistance, and brought the negotiations down to a business plane.

And what, the young man inquired, was the actual figure of the young woman's dowry? Pia after a moment's hesitation named it. Very well, said Sadoc, and if the gentleman from Paris was prepared to indemnify her in ready money, could the matter be settled? Pia after another pause shook her head. No. For the good will of this noble family in Bergamo, the gentleman from Paris must understand, was essential to both mother and daughter. They would be offended, and would not easily forgive them, and the welfare of two poor women was all in their hands. Very well, Sadoc repeated, and what would this good will be worth in cash? A very faint flush rose in Pia's pale face.

Monsieur Dombasle, inspired by his zeal, managed to follow this part of the conversation, and his hope rose.

"Anything," he cried to Sadoc in French. "Offer this old harridan whatever amount she wants."

Sadoc was ready to oblige his old master, but it went against him to waste money. He took a few minutes to bargain with the woman, and the while Monsieur Dombasle grew as impatient with his friend as with his opponent.

Did not Sadoc know, he cried out, that he was a rich man? One of the richest men in France. Did he not know that through a lifetime he had denied himself comfort and pleasure and saved up money in the bank? And did he not realize that now he had found the one thing worth having in the world? Must a Jew always, in any situation, and even when a friend's happiness was at stake, indulge in the pleasure of haggling? He waved Sadoc aside and annihilated him, while he hurled fantastic figures in French at the face of the stony woman before him.

The faint blush in Pia's pale face deepened a little. In her head she summed up the situation.

The Gattamelata family, she reflected, might never learn of this deviation from the agreement made in Bergamo. Or if they did learn of it they might not mind. What they wanted was to have Anna disappear. And here, the mother understood, her daughter was to be taken out of the province, into an unknown country. Very likely nobody would ever hear of her again. She herself, in accepting the foreign gentleman's money, would be running no risk. Half an hour later the bargain was closed. Sadoc fetched the money and counted it up on the table.

Monsieur Dombasle, exhausted but transported, found himself in the position of having bought a young girl of fifteen, cash down, on a highroad of Lombardy.

Pia, taking no risk, collected her money and her donkeys, took leave of her daughter and proceeded, dumb and rigid, toward the next osteria on the road, and out of this story.

21. THE PERFECT IDYLL

Many years later, in Paris, Monsieur Dombasle told Sadoc that he had, from the moment when Anna had become his property, felt the envy of the gods upon him. He had known, with a terrible dead certainty, that she would again be torn from him.

But here his memory played him a trick. For a period of twenty-four hours he had been happy as a bridegroom and unsuspicious as a child. Perfect and divine happiness filled his heart, ran over, and turned the osteria into a perfect and divine idyll, Arcadia itself.

He first of all bethought himself that Anna must be hungry, and ordered a meal for her, all composed of sweets and dainties. He had devoured the girl with his eyes and been ready to eat her up every bit. Now he hardly dared to steal a glance at her, and was as afraid to touch her as he would have been to touch the wings of a rare butterfly. He surrounded her with an atmosphere of tender and romantic courtesy, he led her to table, holding

Anna

the tips of her fingers with his lifted hand, and while she dined on his sweetmeats he carried on in a low soft voice a conversation with Sadoc about poetry, flowers, and birds, as if he felt that he had purchased a young angel who must at all costs be kept in ignorance of the facts of life.

He might have spared himself his trouble. In the midst of an angelic innocence Anna was aware of most of the facts of life, and at the present moment realized, as clearly as seller and buyer, that she had been sold and bought a second time.

The last sale differed from the first inasmuch as in Bergamo somebody had passionately wanted to get rid of her, while in the osteria somebody had passionately wanted to acquire her. She was a young girl, she must needs feel the circumstance as an improvement of her situation.

It was all, she felt, the work of Alessandro. She herself had only to hold on to him in thought, and the lord of the Gattamelata house would have it in his power to save her from danger and trouble. Like her father, the tightrope dancer, she was during these days proceeding spiritually along a narrow line, gently and firmly keeping her balance. The line of her existence might pretend to turn and twist, she herself knew that it was perfectly straight, and that at the end of it lay the moment when she was to give herself back, body and soul, to the poor unhappy and misunderstood boy who needed her.

22. MONSIEUR DOMBASLE'S FLIGHT
The next morning the weather had changed, the air was heavy and sultry, a thunderstorm was gathering.

Monsieur Dombasle, ever sensitive to atmosphere, began to shiver a little, realized that he was in a foreign country, and longed to be back in Paris with Anna. All the same, in the afternoon he set Anna before him in the garden and showed her a few elementary steps and attitudes. He made her lift her skirts un poco, un poco, he warmed to his task, and for a few minutes himself took part in a classical pas de deux. "My God, my God," he afterwards said to Sadoc. "What feet! Like a pair of swallows—winged, gay, naive, cunning, at home in the air!" He did not want to tire out the girl, and only repeated the lesson for a short time in the late afternoon. As he escorted her back to the house for a meal and a rest, a long, low murmur of thunder ran along the horizon. Monsieur Dombasle felt a corresponding, long vibration run through his whole body.

A carriage, he noticed, had stopped outside the osteria, and in the hall he discovered a stranger, lean, grave, and dignified, all dressed in black and with a portfolio under his arm, talking to the padrone. At the very sight of this gentleman Monsieur Dombasle had a sickening presentiment of disaster.

He collected his courage, and with Anna walked past the black figure. In doing so he caught a phrase of the conversation, and understood that the stranger, who seemed to speak Italian with some difficulty, was making enquiries about a young girl traveling with her mother, whose track he had followed from Bergamo. Monsieur Dombasle's heart gave two great thumps, then stood still.

He seized Anna, like a cat bringing her kitten into safety, dragged her up the stairs and pushed her into a room. He locked the door from outside, and in the whitewashed corridor, feeling like a man carried away by a raging stream, his mouth already filled with water, called out for Sadoc.

In a whispering voice he informed his young friend of what was going on beneath them.

Why, why, he wailed, further enraged by the necessity of whispering, had they remained in the osteria, exposed to, defenseless against, any attack from an unscrupulous and merciless world? Why had not Sadoc, who had got nothing else to do, warned him in time? Here, now, was the first delegate from that hateful universe, following on his track, determined to tear Anna from him and in doing so drive him to madness and suicide. If, in this eleventh hour, Sadoc still cared for his master's life and reason, he would go down at once and, employing all the shrewdness of his race, turn the demon off the track. The stranger spoke Italian so badly that the padrone might not yet have understood what he meant. And in any case Sadoc must manage to bribe the old Italian to swear that Anna was no longer in the house.

Sadoc went down to negotiate. Monsieur Dombasle, outside Anna's door, was able to catch a little of the conversation below, but could not stand listening for long. He went to the end of the corridor and there conceived a new plan. If Sadoc failed to drive off the terrible man in black, he would explain to him that Anna was his daughter, and that she was very ill and must not be disturbed. He took out the key, unlocked the door, and having entered the room on tiptoe again locked the door from the inside. In a low voice he ordered the girl to undress and go to bed at once. He dragged a chair to the door and placed himself upon it, with his back to the girl and his ear to the keyhole.

After half an hour, which to the old man seemed like an eternity, he heard the rumbling of carriage wheels, and realized that Sadoc must have sent off the enemy.

A minute later Sadoc himself came up the stairs. He first knocked at Monsieur Dombasle's own door. When he got no reply, he tried Anna's, and finding it locked, communicated through it with Monsieur Dombasle, who still dared not move or turn the key. He and the padrone, he reported, between them had succeeded in making the stranger, an Englishman, go on to a village at some distance, in a direction which Anna's mother was not likely to have taken.

Monsieur Dombasle was wonderfully relieved, as if the four legs of his chair had been lifted a few inches up in the air. A situation parallel to this, of fifty years ago, suddenly and vividly came back to him. Young Ambrose Dombasle was sitting in a dark room—for the sun was down now—with his ear to the keyhole in breathless suspense, waiting for the danger outside to pass by. It was a sweet and unforgettable moment. And there had been a young lady in the bed behind him just like now. The thought of the young lady now in the bed behind him again brought him down to earth, and for a few seconds very much lower down, into an abyss of shame. In what light must he, the most gallant and chivalrous man of Paris, now appear to Anna? What did she think of him, and how would she account for his behavior to her? For some time he dared not even rise and turn round to apologize.

When in the end he did so the room behind him was dark and without a sound. Hesitating and very nervous he struck a match, lighted a little candle on a table and approached the bed. He found that the girl had obediently carried out his instructions. Her clothes lay on the chair beside the bed, neatly folded. In the large old fourposter itself Anna was asleep, breathing softly and regularly, her long eyelashes on her fresh cheeks.

23. BACK TO BERGAMO

The old artist went down to have supper with his young friend, and during the whole meal, in spite of the danger being over, he hardly spoke a word.

"Sadoc," he said at last, "I have thought the matter over. I feel convinced that there is only one thing for me to do. To make sure of Anna I must marry her. The problem is now to find, as quickly as possible, a place where she and I can be made one in holy matrimony."

"Dear Master," Sadoc remarked after a pause. "Do you remember how many times you have congratulated yourself on not being married?—and have vowed that whatever happened you would never marry?"

Monsieur Dombasle looked hard at him. "Ah," he replied at last. "That was before I met Anna." And after another pause: "What else is there to do? There are moments in life when one must resort to any expedient."

Again he sat for a long time in his own thoughts, then resolutely declared: "As this dreadful Englishman came from Bergamo, it seems to me that

that will be the last place in which we are likely to meet him again. And at Bergamo, surely, there will be somebody who knows how to marry people. Therefore, Sadoc, we will go to Bergamo tomorrow."

Sadoc had known his master for many years and said no word in objection. Only after a while he observed: "All the same I should like to know why the Englishman has traveled from his own country to look up a girl whom he has never seen." And again after a while he added: "There is something in this matter that intrigues me. There is, somehow, a smell in it, that pleases my nose. I wonder if somehow there is not gold in it."

24. ALESSANDRO IN GENOA

Alessandro was in Genoa.

He had left Bergamo in a state of wild fury and triumph. For he had held his own against the women and the priest, and had at last asserted his own existence. If the whole world were against him, at this hour he felt capable of defying the whole world.

Under the circumstances it was almost unbearable to him to be borne away upon soft springs and silk cushions, in the company of the most urbane and benevolent of gentlemen. It was strange and highly disquieting to be lodged in luxury and elegance at the villa in Genoa, it was queer to be welcomed and surrounded by smiling and amiable people. He was paid pretty compliments, and he had never in his life been paid a compliment.

Baron Alfani in his young days in Bergamo had lived in awe of the house of Gattamelata, particularly as personified in old Count Alessandro, Faus-

tina's father, who had shown him the door with so
much arrogance. Alessandro's surprising likeness
to that imposing figure, and the idea that this un-
tamable bird of prey was to give his name to his
granddaughter and his blood to his great-grand-
children, fascinated and charmed him. He prome-
naded the boy among his rich and polite friends
in Genoa, took him to receptions and conversazioni
and on board fine merchant ships in the harbor.
He endeavored to give him a taste for art, music,
and the theater.

When he learnt that Alessandro was a skillful
swordsman, he arranged a fencing match at the
villa, wherein a row of handsome Genoese fencers
competed for handsome prizes, and Alessandro
carried the honors of the day. His future bride had
been brought from her convent school in order
that the young people might make one another's
acquaintance, and witnessed his victory.

The boy of Bergamo was desperately shy. His
mien and manner till now had been a deadly challenge to the world. But within the world in which
he was now moving, that attitude was untenable,
it began to feel childish and somehow cowardly.
For a while he felt lost, even betrayed.

Then slowly it began to dawn upon him that the
change in the atmosphere round him had mysteriously been brought about by Anna and was, mysteriously, a natural consequence of the kiss in the
pantry. The music was Anna, the soft silks and
sweet smells were Anna, the blue sea even was
Anna, and in the shady rose garden he for a moment met Anna face to face.

His young fiancée, small for her age and frail, with enormous dark eyes, observed him vigilantly, with great childish dignity. Alessandro till now had known few females younger than himself, and it gave him an unexperienced pleasure to be able to protect a person of Anna's sex. And on the terrace before the villa or in the avenues of the garden, two or three times an idea brushed his mind—he might bring Anna to this flowering peaceful world which evidently belonged to her, or he might live with her on his farm outside Bergamo, in the shade of big trees, with lambs gamboling in the glades.

But after a while Alessandro was overtaken by the unescapable fate of the Bergamasques—a devouring nostalgia for Bergamo.

His ancestors, wherever they had set eyes on a treasure belonging to the world outside their own town, had immediately laid claim to it and carried it back to their eagle's nest on the peak. Now the young Gattamelata, too, as he began to understand and value the treasures round him, longed to bring them back to his native town. Why should the Genoese boast of them and the Bergamasques have to do without them?

In Bergamo, he knew, in the black and steep palace, his grandmother resided, and with her his mother and the priest, the people who had opposed him and whom he had defeated. It made no difference, it was to this hard world that he belonged, as it belonged to him, and out of it he could not live. In particular he felt that the bond between him and his grandmother could never be broken. It must be possible, and it must fall to him, to reconcile and unite the two worlds, the old dark world which was in his blood and the new bright world which, through Anna, had been revealed to him.

With this conflict and problem he became uneasy and melancholy. He tried hard to conceal his feelings toward his surroundings, and succeeded, not because it came easy to him to conceal his feelings but because it came hard for him to show them.

At times he would steal from the villa to stray in the streets, a lonely young figure.

25. THE DANCING VIRGIN

On an evening he came to a small church in a narrow, crooked street. Something about it reminded him of Bergamo, and half against his will, he lifted the heavy curtain, went in, and looked round him.

Here and there in the half-light of the silent, empty space candles gleamed before the altars. The boy slowly walked up to the high altar, and from that to the side altar on the left. Before it he dwelt a long time. He was sunk in his own thoughts, but all the same, while his eyes remained upon it, a strange peace came over him.

An old friar came trudging through the church. On seeing the young man's immobile figure he went up and spoke to him, happy at the chance of a chat.

"This holy image, my son," he began, going through his often repeated rigmarole in a monotonous tone, "illustrates the great and lovely, but too little read, Gospel of Saint James."

At the sound of his voice Alessandro turned a little toward him, uncertain about the speaker and about himself.

"Which tells us," the old man went on, "that when the Blessed Virgin was three years old she was carried to the temple and delivered into the hands of the high priest. And the high priest received her, and kissed her, and blessed her, and said: 'The Lord has exalted your name amongst all generations.' And he set her on the third step of the altar, and the grace of the Lord came over her, and she danced upon her feet. And all the house of Israel loved her."

Here the eyes of the old man and the young man met.

"Our image," said the friar, inspired by the urgency of the other's glance, "was made, twelve years ago, by a pious young artist of great promise. We have since been told that his eyesight is failing, which seems a sad thing. But it will be a most wonderful consolation to him in his blindness to have created this lovely blessed child, who has worked and will work great things." He waited a moment to watch the effect of his words, and proceeded on his way round the church. The boy from Bergamo was left alone in a state of deep, turbulent emotion, a piece of hard metal in the melting pot.

A faint ray came toward him from far away, slowly, to lighten up the darkness of his mind. It might indeed be possible to unite the glory of his new world, the sweetness of Anna's world, to his own old world of Bergamo, out of which he could not live. All things were possible, there was an unexpected, overwhelming grace in the world. He had known it, in a way, from the moment of the kiss, and had he dared to trust in it, it would have spoken to him before now. Now, at length, it spoke and answered him.

He did not kneel down. He had been made to kneel down when taken to Mass by his mother and grandmother, and he had never liked the attitude. He was, he felt, paying truer reverence to the little Virgin by standing up before her image, like one of her own tall thin candles.

He wanted to lay his heart and his case open to her. But it was difficult, difficult, to set the whirlpool of his feelings into words. Dumb and bewildered, he crossed himself three times. In the end he found his voice.

"If," he said, "if you will make it possible to me to remain, at the same time, loyal and faithful to Anna, to my grandmother, and to my name, I promise you to remain, all my life, a loyal and faithful husband and grandson, and a true Gattamelata."

He realized that he was setting the Blessed Virgin a hard and difficult task. It was as if he had been asking her to allow—in his particular case and just for once—two and two to make five. But then, he reflected after a time, if anybody on earth or in Heaven would be powerful and gracious enough to allow—in his particular case and just for once—two and two to make five, it would be the dancing child upon the altar. After a while he left the church.

The Ghost Horses

A child lay ill in a big house. She got better and then had a sudden relapse, and from this she seemed to refuse to recover. The famous doctor who had been called from town pronounced that she was over her illness and ought to get up. But the little girl lay in her bed listless and limp as a rag doll. When the people round her spoke to her she kept her eyes closed, but when she thought that nobody looked at her she opened them to stare sadly at nothing, and sometimes big tears trickled down from under her long eyelashes. She would not eat and she would not speak, and when her nurses tried to coax her into standing on her legs she cried out that they were hurting her.

The child was six years old and was christened Oenone, but in daily life called Nonny. She was a beautiful little girl with a mass of dark cloudy hair and blue eyes. She was an only child and had been spoiled all her life; her small sickbed was surrounded with splendid toys.

The house in which she lay ill was two hundred years old, a stately gray building in a large park. It had belonged to the same family for many generations, and strange, romantic tales were told about it. In the parlor a father had gambled away his only daughter in a game of faro. A fatal duel

First published in the *Ladies' Home Journal*, October 1951, and reprinted by permission. Copyright 1951 by The Curtis Publishing Company.

had taken place in the hall. A century ago the young mistress of the house had run away from her husband with her good-looking groom, and had taken the family jewels away with her.

Nonny's mother had inherited the house from an old aunt, and she and her husband had taken great pleasure in modernizing it. There was now a radio in each room, and the old stables had been turned into magnificent garages.

The doctor said to Nonny's mother, "We are dealing with an unusual case, my dear lady. A deliberate choice between life and death is being made before us, and the person about to make the choice is six years old! And, mind you, Nonny is a child of remarkable will power."

"Doctor, what do you mean?" asked the mother.

"An infant's world," said the doctor, "generally turns upon one single, magnetic personality. It is natural that it should be an admired young mother. For three weeks Nonny has had you all to herself, now she will not allow this happy state of things to cease. She insists on being ill, in order that you shall be anxious about her; she may insist on dying, in order that you shall miss her."

"What am I to do?" cried the pretty young woman. "And must one," she added after a moment, with tears in her eyes, "be a curse to the people one loves?"

"You are to go away," said the doctor. "And Nonny is to realize that only when she is perfectly well will you come back to her, and you and she will be together again, for good. Your husband has been talking about a fortnight's motoring tour in France. My advice is that you should start on it tomorrow."

Nonny's mother looked at the doctor, then looked out the window.

"You are leaving your child in excellent hands," the doctor went on. "Miss Anderson is a trustworthy, serious-minded person, Miss Brown a fully trained nurse, and your little Swedish nursery maid devoted to her charge. I myself will call every day."

"Perhaps," said the mother slowly, "it would be a good thing to go away."

"The four of us," said the doctor, "will agree to talk about you to Nonny every day, and to tell her that the quicker she gets well, the sooner will you return to her. Then our headstrong young lady will concentrate not on dying but on recovering."

"My brother is arriving from Paris tomorrow," said Nonny's mother. "I have wired for him."

"Your artist brother?" asked the doctor. "The young man who draws such amusing pictures for Nonny? The very person we want. He will describe your journey to your daughter from day to day, and illustrate it too."

So Nonny's mother set out for France with her husband, in her new big car.

It so happened that she met her brother in the seaport. They lunched at a hotel and when after lunch Peter, the husband, went out to take a look at the car, the two others had a long talk over their coffee.

The brother and sister were twins and much alike, so that their friends named them Sebastian and Viola. They had always been great friends. Cedric had surprised his family first by wanting to become a painter and later by making a kind of name for himself as one. He lived in Paris in a circle of artists of whom he thought highly, while he was modest about his own work. He was a pleasant-looking young man with gentle manners and the kind of equilibrium found in boys whose people have lived for generations in unaltered economic circumstances, either very good or very bad.

Annabelle told her brother that a child's world centers upon one single magnetic personality, and that she was going to France to save Nonny's life. He must now talk about her every day and hour, tell Nonny that she would come back to her as soon as the child was perfectly well, and send reports of the progress to various addresses in France. Cedric promised to do all she asked him.

"But that was not why you wired for me," he said.

"No," said Annabelle, "it was not." She paused, then said, "I wanted your advice." She had often before wanted his advice.

"At your service," he said.

"Yes, that is easy to say," said Annabelle, "but the thing is that Peter and I have been spending more money than we have got. Living beyond one's means, people call it."

"What, you?" Cedric asked in surprise.

"For heaven's sake do not begin to bully me," said Annabelle. "It is terribly unpleasant to live beyond one's means. I can't stand it—and you couldn't either, could you?"

"No," said Cedric, who lived very soberly in Paris.

"There, you see," said the sister. "Just lately we have got a wonderful chance. Peter has always wanted to do some work. Now Sir Maurice Mendoza has offered to take him into his firm as a partner. It will be the very thing for Peter. So don't you think it is wonderful?"

"Yes, I do," said the brother.

"You do, do you?" said the sister. "And what about me?"

"Yes, what about you?" he asked.

"Oh, Cedric," she said, "try not to be so terribly dense. The thing is that Sir Maurice admires me."

"Like everybody," said he.

"No," she said. "No, not like everybody, Cedric."

"And Peter always likes to see you admired," said he.

"No," said she. "No, he might not like it, if he knew about it at all."

"And how do you yourself like it, my dear?" he asked.

"Well, Cedric," she said, "it is like this. I love Peter. And I have loved him for seven years, so that I feel that I know him by heart. Sir Maurice I do not know at all. He is a mysterious person, as you will be aware from his reputation. He is not rich in the ordinary way, he is like somebody in a fairy tale. It is Aladdin's cave: rubies like cherries, sapphires like grapes! I come to think of that old fairy tale of ours because Sir Maurice has got such wonderful knowledge of precious stones. How I wish that Great-great-great-grandmother Annabelle had not taken the family jewels with her when she ran away with her groom!"

"Yes," said Cedric slowly, "there generally is some kind of trouble about those romantic love affairs."

"The night before Nonny got ill," said Annabelle, "we dined with him, and he showed us a big ruby that he had got in Holland. He asked us if, when Peter and he had settled the matter, he might give it to me in a bracelet. As a red seal to our agreement, he said. Then Nonny got ill and I have not seen him since, and we have got this fortnight in France to make up our minds, and there it is, and what do you advise me to do?"

"Do you give me, too, the fortnight to think it over in?" asked the brother.

"Yes," answered the sister.

Here they saw Peter coming up to their table, and changed their conversation.

"It is very queer," said Annabelle, "that during all her illness she has been talking about horses, about nothing but horses, and racing and hunting and grooming. Why, she has hardly ever seen a horse! When she went on about them Peter bought her a beautiful mechanical toy just like a horse. But she did not care for it."

Upon this they parted.

Cedric was looking forward to his holiday, for he had a big new picture to think over, and wanted to be alone.

He had never been in his sister's house when she was not there. Now that he had time and peace to walk about and take it all in, it seemed to him a new and fascinating place.

"If this house had been mine," he thought, "I should have left it as it was. If I had then lived in it I should have been able to paint like Zoffany."

He went up to Nonny's room. She was even prettier than he remembered her. But what did the severe, haggard, and hopeless expression do in the flowerlike face?

In obedience to his instructions, he talked to Nonny about her mother, described her journey and illustrated it with paper and pencil. She listened without the slightest sign of interest and hardly looked at the drawings. The mechanical horse stood by her bed; he admired it, and her face became still more tragic.

"If I am worth anything as an artist," he told himself, "I must be able to put this pretty *Portrait of a Child* right."

He asked, "What are we going to play, Nonny, when you get up?"

For the first time he got an answer. After a silence Nonny said, "We can't play. Not you and I."

He thought the thing over, then said, "No, not you and I. Who can play?"

Nonny answered, "Billy."

He did not want to force the matter, so left it at that.

The doctor came, examined the child, and inquired if she had been up. When the nurse shook her head he told her that it was becoming a serious thing and that they must needs have the little baggage on her feet by the time of his next visit, then he drove away.

Cedric said to Nonny, "You would get up, wouldn't you, if you could go and play with Billy?"

"Yes," said Nonny.

"And why is it now," he again asked, "that you can't do so?"

The child's face grew dark with indignation. "You know!" she said.

"I have been away in Paris so long, my dear," he said. "Many things, I find, have happened in the meantime. Do you mind telling me?"

"Because Billy is dead," said Nonny.

By this time Cedric found that he was occupying himself as much with Nonny as with his new picture. He felt that he would get no assistance from either Miss Anderson or Miss Brown, so he turned to the little Swedish nursery maid, Ingrid. She appealed to his painter's heart, for in her white cap she looked like a Dutch picture. He took pains to find her alone and sat down with her. They discussed Nonny's illness, and agreed that they must get her well for her mother's return.

"And by the way, my dear," said Cedric, "who is Billy?"

Ingrid grew pale, stared at him and said, "Oh, sir."

"You see," said he, "I can't help you about Nonny till I know."

"I had hoped," said Ingrid, "that nobody should ever know."

"And why must they never know?" he asked.

"Because Billy is dead," answered Ingrid.

"I have understood that much," said Cedric, "and I am very sorry indeed. But there must be something more to Billy than just that. If you will be kind enough to tell me, I shan't let it get any farther."

Ingrid drew her breath deeply. "I shall be glad to tell you," she said. "I have been unhappy about it, sir."

Gravely, from time to time pausing and looking him in the face, as if to hold him to his promise, she told him.

Billy was old Mrs. Peavey's grandson. And who was old Mrs. Peavey? Old Mrs. Peavey was the old coachman's widow. The old coachman had lived in the small flat above those stables which were turned into garages; after his death his widow had been allowed to stay on in the flat.

The gentleman would probably never have seen old Mrs. Peavey? Nay, that was because her legs were poor and it was difficult for her to climb the stairs. She and Ingrid first had become friends because Mrs. Peavey came from the real country, her father had been a farmer and had bred horses, as the Swedish girl's father had done, and the two had many interests in common.

"It must have been very nice for both you and her," said Cedric.

"So it was, sir," said Ingrid.

Mrs. Peavey had an only son, who worked in a big racing stable, was married and had seven children. When his wife died and he married again, his new wife could not be bothered with the youngest child, so old Mrs. Peavey had taken him on. The little boy's eldest brother had brought him here, a groom at the racing stable himself, a nice young man. Cedric wondered whether the groom was not the interest which the old and the young woman had had in common. The small boy had then lived with Mrs. Peavey, above the old stables.

"That was Billy, sir," said Ingrid.

Billy was three months younger than Nonny, a very pretty and clever little boy. But he was deaf and dumb.

Sometimes when Miss Anderson told Ingrid to take Nonny out for a walk, the two would instead go up the stable stairs to visit Mrs. Peavey. Ingrid would sit with her and do a little darning for her, but Nonny and Billy went into the big harness room next to Mrs. Peavey's own rooms, to play.

"But there was no harm in that," said Cedric.

"Yes, sir, there was," said Ingrid, "for it was from Billy that Nonny caught the measles." She wrung her hands in her lap. "And just when Nonny was recovering," she continued, "Billy died. It was when Nonny heard about it that she got so very bad again."

"How did she hear of it?" Cedric asked.

She had heard of it from Ingrid. Ingrid had gone to see Mrs. Peavey, and had wept with her over Billy, and when she came back Nonny asked her why she had been crying. They sent for the doctor in the middle of the night. When Nonny had been delirious, Ingrid feared that she would speak about Billy, that it would all come out and old Mrs. Peavey be sent away. But Nonny had been loyal, and had said nothing then either.

"My sister told me," said Cedric, "that she talked about horses."

Yes, she would talk about horses. There were a great many pictures of horses up in the harness room, and Billy had told her the names of them all.

"How could he tell her," Cedric asked, "when he was deaf and dumb?"

The thing evidently had not struck Ingrid as particularly strange, but she could not quite explain it either. Nonny and Billy had always insisted on being left alone to play in the harness room, they had even locked the door of it, and they had been playing almost without a sound in there. Billy had been taught, or had taught himself, to read from people's lips; she believed that he had taught Nonny too.

For Nonny would say to Ingrid, "Now I am going to tell you a wonderful thing," and then just move her lips, and pull a face when Ingrid did not understand her. Sometimes, too, when Ingrid had put her to bed, she would laugh to herself for a while, and then tell her, in a low voice, that she and Billy had got beautiful horses to play with.

"I think," said Cedric after a silence, "that I shall speak to Nonny about Billy."

"Will that be right, sir?" asked Ingrid.

"I believe that it will be right," said Cedric. "The doctor told my sister that to a child there will always be one outstanding, fascinating personality who will hold its attention before anybody else. He thought that to Nonny it was her mother. But I now see that it was Billy."

Cedric had been sending a post card to his sister every day. Now he himself received a post card from her. France, she wrote, was lovely. It was lovely traveling with Peter. It would be lovely to get back to Nonny. Sometimes she wished that she had not got to go back. Love to Cedric.

Cedric said to Nonny, "If I were you I should get rid of that horse."

Both looked with contempt at the mechanical horse by the bedside.

"Things," said Cedric, "which are exactly like other things are a great nuisance."

Nonny looked at him, but was still suspicious and did not speak.

"The only *really* real things, you know," he said, "are those which one makes up oneself, and which are not *like* other things. In my house in Paris I make up a great many *really* real things: flowers and birds, and a lady who throws herself into the river, because she is unhappy. They smell and sing and jump into the river very well, very sweetly indeed."

After a silence Nonny asked, "What do you make them from?"

"I generally," he said, "find something to make them from. Don't you?"

A pale little smile, the first he had yet seen, lit up her face. "Yes," she said.

He waited a moment. "Now as to horses," he said, "*really* real horses. I suppose that Billy could *really* make them do everything."

Nonny looked him in the face, another thing she had not yet done. Her own face was grave and proud, but not unfriendly. "Billy could explain everything they did to me," she said.

"I know," said he, "because he was not able to speak the way other boys do."

She seemed to be gong to say more, but again closed her lips tightly.

"Well, Nonny," he said, "so long. I have got to go for a drive in the car your mummie left here for me. It is a bore, really, because a car becomes so slow when you begin to think about Billy's horses."

"You will come back, Uncle Cedric?" asked Nonny.

He went away and thought, "The change is coming. It is difficult, difficult to get it right, but it is coming. May God help me, now, to choose the proper brushes and the proper tubes of paint!"

The next day he succeeded in making Nonny play a kind of board game with him on the counterpane. While he was pondering on a move she asked him:

"Where do you keep your flowers and your birds, and the lady?"

"I put them up against the wall," he answered, "then nobody can see them. But they are there all the time, of course."

If this time Nonny did not speak it was not, he felt, from lack of sympathy but, quite simply, from lack of words wherewith to express their new, happy understanding. At last she said, "Our horses are in their boxes. And in their stable."

"Like most really fine horses," said he.

When she had won the game, and as he was putting the pieces back in the box, Nonny suddenly asked, "Shall I show you my horses, Uncle Cedric?"

"Please," he said. "I have been thinking about them. It isn't right that they are not watered or groomed, now that Billy is not there and your own legs are too weak for you to go."

"They are not," said Nonny, and stood up in her bed.

"One ought to have fine strong legs to work in a stable," said Cedric. "Perhaps you can go tomorrow."

"No," said Nonny, "today. After lunch." She looked round her and said, "Miss Anderson and Miss Brown must not know."

"No," said he.

"Ingrid can dress me," said the child.

"Ingrid can dress you," he agreed, "and I shall tell Miss Anderson and Miss Brown that you are taking me for a ride in the car."

257

As she stood up, in her small flannel nightgown, her face was on a level with his. What lovely eyes and delicately arched eyebrows, what rich hair. And what a sudden, strange power in the whole frail figure.

"Because," she said slowly and solemnly, "you will never, never, never tell!"

"Because," he repeated slowly and solemnly, "I shall never, never, never tell!"

Her clear eyes looked into his, gravely, searchingly. Her short life had held disappointments and catastrophes; in this matter she could take no risk. He scanned his mind for an oath which would bind him unconditionally.

"If ever," he said, "I speak a word about the horses, or the boxes, or the stables, to any live soul, may I never paint a decent picture in my life. So help me God."

He talked the matter over with his fellow conspirator. It was arranged that Miss Anderson should have her day off, and that Ingrid should keep Miss Brown occupied.

It was a lovely afternoon of late summer. The air was drowsy with sweetness above the box hedges and the long beds of roses and stock, the big trees' shadows rested lightly and peacefully on the lawns. Nonny, on Cedric's arm, gazed round and up. He wondered whether a child could have any idea of time, and whether she realized that time had passed, and things happened, since she was last in the garden.

"I have sent away Parker," he told her on their way to the garages. "We will go straight up the stair to Mrs. Peavey."

She looked at him as if to ask him how he had come to know the way so well, but said nothing.

On the stair he thought, "I am going back ten years on each of these worn old steps." He had reached the days of Zoffany when he crossed Mrs. Peavey's doorstep.

A very small old woman, by the geraniums on the window sill, at the sight of her visitors tried to rise from a big chair, gave it up, grew smaller still, and began to cry. Nonny gave her a kind glance, but had no time for speech.

"It is all right, Mrs. Peavey," said Cedric. "Nonny is well again. How are you yourself? And we should like to go into the harness room."

"Oh, I am afraid, sir," said Mrs. Peavey, "that there will be a terrible lot of dust in there. I have not been in the harness room since my little grandson passed away. I had a little grandson, sir."

"I know, Mrs. Peavey," said Cedric. "I am very sorry indeed about him. And it does not matter about the dust."

"Billy put the key on the inside of the door," said Nonny "He could turn it too. You will put me down in there, Uncle Cedric."

"Yes, Nonny," said Cedric.

He opened the door to the harness room. The smell in there met him even before the light, then the two melted together into a quiet welcome, both humble and dignified.

The room was large and low, it went all through the house and had two windows to the east and two to the west. Everything in it was covered with dust. The old woman's statement that she had not been in here since Billy's death was probably more than true: this delicate layer must date from the old coachman's time.

It was so lovely in here that for a moment he forgot his task and stood quite still. The mellow golden light of the afternoon filled the empty room and turned its bareness and poverty into splendor. The whitewashed walls had the luster of alabaster and the old wooden ceiling the deep gloss of metal.

All along the two walls there were pegs and stands hung with harness and saddlery. There were hames and neckstraps, breastbands and bellybands, bridles, girths, and stirrups. There were sets of single and double harness, and harness for tandems and four-in-hand, brass-mounted and plated, with crests on the blinkers. There were hunting saddles, racing saddles, and sidesaddles.

Cedric knew very little about saddlery, he did not remember ever to have ridden in a vehicle drawn by a horse. He looked at the things and saw that they were moldy and cracked, but that they had been beautifully made, from fine leather and metal. Skilled, careful, patient hands had worked at them.

On the other two walls were pictures of horses, single or in groups, and in magnificent attitudes: galloping, jumping fences, gamboling before phaetons, pacing before coaches, carrying ladies with sweeping trains. They were old prints, neatly made like the other objects in the room, and like them faded and flyspecked, some of them with their glass cracked or gone.

He was, he felt, in Billy's kingdom.

In this room people had lived who thought and talked about horses, who knew everything about them, and whose deepest satisfactions and highest ideals in life were in some way connected with horses. Billy himself—the trainer's son and the coachman's grandson, very likely the last descendant of a line of horsemen and horse breeders reaching back into the dark ages—had been the lawful heir to this old and gone horse world of England. A small, silent keeper and custodian of its last, forgotten province or reserve, he had made it rise and come to life gloriously, before the eyes of his friend, the child of the motor age.

Nonny had demanded to be set down on the floor, and had stood still there like Cedric himself, gazing round the room with passionate, tender pride. Now she demanded to be lifted up again, in order to show the guest her pictures. They agreed that she was feeling strong enough to ride on his shoulders, and in this way they slowly made the tour of the place.

"This one, Uncle Cedric," she said, "is The Ranger, who won the Longchamps. This is Boiard, who won the Ascot. This is the queen's favorite horse, and this is Prince Albert's. This is Robert the Devil, who won the Saint-Leger—and doesn't he look a real devil too? And this one is Gladiateur, who won the Derby! It is all written underneath them."

"But you cannot read, Nonny," said Cedric. "How have you come to know so much about them?"

"Billy could read," said Nonny. "He explained it all to me. . . . And look!" she cried in a sudden burst of delight. "There is the Queen's coronation on the twenty-eighth of June, 1838!" She became grave and silent for a moment. "I shall get down," she said. "We will do the coronation procession today, you and me."

Cedric looked all round the room. There was no cupboard or chest anywhere, only, in a corner, a basket with clothespins and some empty bottles. He had believed that he was near his goal; now he stood on the bare floor feeling sadly clumsy and grown-up. What objects up here, he wondered, had been animated and exalted by Billy's magic wand, so as to make up a royal procession?

There was a grandfather's chair in the room, with its stuffing coming out through the ragged horsehair covering.

"Look, Nonny," he said. "I shall set you in the chair. Then you just order me about."

"No," said Nonny, "I won't sit in a chair."

"And why not?" he said. "If we are to have a race, it will be the judge's chair, and you will be the judge. And if we are to have the coronation cortege——" He stopped, not quite certain just what Nonny would then be.

"I shall be God," said Nonny in a clear voice, "looking down at it. God looks down at all horses, Billy said."

She seemed very small in the big chair, but she sat in it as upon a throne.

"Open the stable door," she said, "and let out the horses on the floor!"

"Yes, my dear," he said. At random, afraid of doing anything wrong, he took down a picture, and set it against the wall.

"No," said Nonny, "not Ormond, Uncle Cedric. That one: Zeodone, who won the Grand National!"

Upon the wall was Zeodone, on her hind legs and hung onto by a valiant groom.

The Ghost Horses

Nonny said, "You would never have found the stable on your own, would you, Uncle Cedric? Billy found it all on his own. And he had got to stand on the sidesaddle on the saddle horse to reach it."

As the picture was taken down, a square hole appeared in the wall. It looked dark and deep.

"They are in there," said Nonny.

In the niche there was a pile of large and small boxes. He took them down one by one, and when he had taken down three or four he began to guess what it was he was handling.

The boxes were all prettily made in morocco or velvet, with golden clasps to them, but they were moldy and cracked. He was told to place them all on the floor and then to open them. They were lined with faded satin. But the jewelry on the decaying fabric shone, clean and radiant, in a hundred dazzling smiles.

"Have you ever seen such shiny horses, Uncle Cedric?" asked Nonny joyfully. "Billy and I washed them with a small sponge, and groomed them with a wash leather that had been Billy's grandfather's. When you put them out one by one, in a row, they go from that wall to that."

There were rings set with diamonds, emeralds, rubies, and sapphires. There were brooches made like bouquets or flower baskets, arabesques, or stars. There were bracelets, pendants, and clasps. Five boxes contained necklaces or big ornaments, the stones of which for some purpose had been taken out of their settings and were lying scattered or in heaps. The strings of two pearl collars, one very long and one shorter and made from incredibly large and even, roseate pearls, had both been broken or had rotted away—the pearls rolled gently against one another as the box was moved. There were pearl earrings and long diamond eardrops. There were three tiaras, the biggest of them all in diamonds, and very regal.

The radiance of the cut stones, and the soft gleam of the pearls, filled the artist's heart with deep and humble adoration, with simple gratitude for the beautiful things of this world. He stood immovable for a while, gazing at the display, picking out first one, then another object as the loveliest.

Then he thought, "So that is it. And God only knows what has happened here. Did the lovers, after having prepared their flight so carefully, at the last moment have to hurry away to escape the husband's revenge? Or did Great-great-great-grandpapa George come upon them before they got off, and am I likely to find skeletons under the floor if I look for them?

Nonny in her chair was content with the impression which her stables were making on her young uncle's mind. She gave him a minute for dumb admiration, then she told him to set to work.

Obedient to her orders, he went down on hands and knees and arranged the cortege. The long procession was to wind from the wall to her chair, and he was to begin by the head of it. While it took shape under his hands it grew more and more glorious, for the queen's own coach made its appearance almost at the end.

First of all and before anybody else came Mr. Lee, high constable of Westminster. Mr. Lee was a tall seal carved in agate, cut with the family crest.

He could stand up, and bore himself with great dignity.

Then came a squadron of the Life Guards, in fine rows of smaller rubies from the necklace.

Then followed the carriages of the royal family, sparkling bracelets with teams of two or four rings to each; the last of them was the coach of the queen's mother, which was made from a tiara, and had a team of six rings. The queen's mother herself, a very large pearl made as a pendant, leaned back gracefully against the inner curve of the tiara.

Next came the mounted band of a regiment of the Household Brigade, all brooches.

The round, roseate pearls of the shorter necklace followed; they were the queen's forty-eight Watermen.

Then came a superior squadron of the Life Guards, the bigger rubies of the necklace, and after them the Royal Huntsmen, in green, from the emerald necklace and ornaments. The Yeomen of the Guards, on white horses, were all of them diamonds.

And then, at last, came Her Majesty's coach, the big, luminous tiara, drawn by six pairs of eardrops, the smallest in front, the very long and heavy pair nearest to the coach.

"Now," said Nonny, "put the queen in her coach. Isn't she beautiful, all in white? It is really me, you know. Billy said that it was really me!"

With great care Cedric placed the one huge diamond in the center of the half circle formed by the tiara. He remembered that he had heard about this diamond, bought a hundred years ago from a maharaja.

Behind the coach marched a regiment of pearls from the long necklace.

"Get up, Uncle Cedric," said Nonny, "and look at the procession!"

He rose, tried to dust his trousers, gave it up, and looked at the procession. Nonny's gaze followed his; her face was calm and rosy with happiness.

"Say something about it now, Uncle Cedric," she said, her voice soft with delight.

"It is like Aladdin's cave, Nonny," he said.

At the sound of his own words he remembered his sister, and their talk at the hotel, and became thoughtful. "One big ruby from Holland," he said to himself, "to be set in a bracelet. And then all this. All this in her own harness room. Alas, Annabelle!"

"Nay, Uncle Cedric," said Nonny, "you should not say that it is like Aladdin's cave. When it is really exactly like a coronation."

"My dear," said he, "that is what I did say. It is *really* a coronation. That is what makes it so valuable, and so fascinating. But some people might say that it was a little like Aladdin's cave."

"Oh, yes," said Nonny. After a while she added. "When we have finished, you will put them all back, and put Zeodone up to be the stable door, won't you, Uncle Cedric? So that nobody can find them."

"Yes, Nonny," he said. "And won't it be, then," he added after a moment, "quite as if Billy was still here?"

She was silent for a while. "No," she said at last, "not quite. But in a little while—" She stopped for a second or two. "In a little while," she said in a steady, sonorous voice, "I shall be perfectly well. Then Billy will come, and he and I shall be together again. For good."

The Proud Lady

In the year II of the revolutionary calendar—to Christendom, A.D. 1794—Citizen Samson, the executioner of Paris, was a well-known figure in the town.

At a time of brilliant speeches, and of brilliant and indefatigable speakers, the lady named La Guillotine held her own by virtue of silent efficiency. Like the lady herself her servant Samson was deeply feared and widely popular, like her he had many pet names but few personal friends.

Citizen Samson was finishing his supper in his rooms in the rue du Bac when his concierge informed him that two citizenesses begged to see him. The executioner was in a kindly mood, he granted the citizenesses their request and received them at his supper table.

One of his visitors was a middle-aged woman with a white cap round a rosy face, the other a slim, pale girl of fifteen. Both were dressed as plainly as possible and both looked as unworldly and ignorant of the world as the nuns whom Samson remembered to have met in the streets, in the old times before the revolution.

"And what can I do for you, Citizenesses?" he asked, leaning back in his chair.

It was the middle-aged woman who answered him, and who during the fifteen minutes of their conversation acted as spokesman. The girl until the last moment of the interview kept her lips and indeed all her young face firmly closed. As Samson threw a second glance at this pretty still face, it seemed to him that he had seen it before, only a day or two ago.

"Citizen Samson," said the woman. "We come from the town of Avignon. There our neighbor, the good Citizen Dubosc, has told us that you have a kind heart. We are both poor and honest women and faithful to the republic."

"As Baptiste Dubosc has sent you," said Samson, "you are not likely to be anything else."

"And faithful to the republic," repeated the woman, "which is to make all people in France happy. Our prayer to you is innocent. To us it means much, but to you it will be of small moment."

"It is my own habit, as you will know," said Samson and laughed, "to cut things short. You do the same now."

"Nay, good Citizen Samson," said the woman with a little gentle smile which showed her fine teeth, "let me go about my story in my own way. You should know, I am sure, who the women are who come to trouble you so late in the evening.

"As to myself," she went on, "my name is Marie-Marthe Lemoine. I was born in the province of Anjou, and all my life I have been in the service of Madame la Marquise de Perrenot de Lionne. You will forgive me," she added, her round ruddy face suddenly flushing deeper, "for using the old words, I have used them so long. But I mean no harm."

"Hello!" Samson exclaimed. "The woman Perrenot de Lionne! You know, do you, that she is having her head cut off tomorrow?"

"We know that, Citizen," said the woman.

"It is about time, too," said Samson, "there never was a harder, a more cruel or miserly old hag in

France. She was known in London and Saint Petersburg as a gambler always in luck at the card tables, but she grudged her own servants and serfs the food in their mouths. Why, that was the woman who knocked out the eye of a peasant with her horsewhip because he did not take off his cap quickly enough to her."

"That is so," said Marie-Marthe, "and the poor old man was my father."

"And who," said Samson, "shut up one of her maids in a tower room for three years because she had displeased her."

"That is so," said Marie-Marthe. "I myself was that maid."

Samson looked at her. "Who left her only daughter to starve," he went on, "because, against her designs, the girl married an honest man, a friend of the people."

"Yes, that is so, Citizen," said Marie-Marthe.

"And if I remember right, now," said Samson, "she made an aristocrat and duelist kill her son-in-law in a duel."

"No, good Citizen, there you have been misinformed," said the woman. "Madame knew nothing of that duelist. It is true that some people believed once that by her mere wish and will she brought about the poor young captain's death. But the priest—you will forgive me again, Citizen, but there were still priests at that time—blamed me for thinking so, and told me that such things did not happen in our days. All the same the captain was killed, and his wife took her death over it. And this girl, who has come with me tonight, is the child of those two, and Madame's granddaughter."

Samson once more gave the young girl a long searching look.

"So now I know," he said slowly, "why I thought that I had seen you before, little Citizeness. I happened to attend your grandam's trial. When they asked her her name she condescended to give it— and a good long rigmarole it was—but after that she spoke not a word, whatever questions they put to her. You are like her, a sad thing in such a pretty little republican. I wish we could drain the Perrenot blood out of you, then you might make a pleasant wife for any good sansculotte."

"Do not say that, Citizen," said Marie-Marthe. "Do not say that."

"And why not?" asked Samson.

"I shall tell you later," said she.

"Well, in any case," said Samson, "your story begins somehow to amuse me. I see that you two have got a pretty long bill to present to the old hag. If what you want from me is a seat from which to see her pay it, your prayer is already granted. Have you ever seen your grandmother?" he asked the **girl**.

Her face was so still that he did not know if she had heard his question, and it was the elder woman who answered.

"Yes, Citizen, yes, she has seen her," she said, "but not this last year."

"I shall tell you," said Samson, slowly filling his pipe, "why I took the trouble to go and hear that trial. I do not often go there these days. But she will be, I think, my last aristocrat. We have rid ourselves fairly thoroughly of them by now. It was only by hiding away in a corner of her old château

270

all alone that the woman Perrenot escaped the
sharp eye of the republic for such a long time. She
is to drive in the cart with rougher company than
she would have mixed in ten years ago. And her old
legs must tread her last minuet all by themselves,
for she will find no noble partner to offer her his
arm. But go on, Citizeness."

Marie-Marthe was silent for a moment. "I was
then," she said, "for many years maid to Madame's
daughter, Mademoiselle Angélique, who was five
years younger than myself, and I was her best
friend as well."

"What?" said Samson. "Would the proud lady
allow her daughter to be friends with a peasant
girl?"

"How would she mind her daughter being friends
with a girl from her own land?" said she. "It lasted
until Mademoiselle Angélique was sixteen years old.
When her daughter was two years old Madame had
already arranged a splendid marriage for her with
the eldest son of the comte de Germont. But what
will you? Man disposes, and someone else—the
Supreme Being—disposes."

"Much the Supreme Being bothers about arranging marriages for the aristocrats," said Samson.

"That is what I tell you, Citizen," said Marie-
Marthe. "The brilliant marriage never came off. For
in the same year in which the old king died, Captain Louis de Kerjean came to the province of
Anjou on recruiting business. My young mistress
eloped with him, and they were married by a poor
village priest. Even I myself knew nothing about it.
Mademoiselle Angélique, who till now had told me
everything, did not tell me this, for she would not

271

expose me to Madame's anger, and she only wrote to Madame herself after the marriage.

"Madame," she went on, "did not say a word when she read the letter. Afterwards she said that her daughter had gone mad, and that I must have gone mad too, or I would have known about it and informed her. She told my father and mother the same thing, and that was the time, Citizen, when she shut me up in the tower room of the château. For three years, Citizen. Nobody was allowed to speak to me.

"Not that she did not have me looked after. I was well fed, and in winter I had a fire in the room. I was not cursed with idleness either, for Madame had a loom put up for me, she had a bag full of different wools sent to me with the words: 'Let me see what kind of things a mad girl can think out.' And indeed, Citizen, during those three long years I invented a new kind of carpet that became famous in the province. This was a good and lucky thing for me, for since then I have been able to support my demoiselles by my skill.

"During these years Madame was but rarely at home, for it was then that she traveled all over the world and that she did, as you say, become famous as a gambler who would always be in luck. Some people believed that she thought of marrying for a second time so that she could have another heir instead of the daughter who was dead to her."

"Why the deuce, if she was never there, did not her other servants let you out?"

"They did so, Citizen," said Marie-Marthe, "three times. Three times in the course of those three years, I walked again in the open, below God's blessed sky, on the grass, such as I had been used to since I was a child. For I was a peasant's daughter."

"But why did you go back again?" asked Samson.

"Oh, Madame had decided it so," she said, "and I would not bring distress upon my fellow servants. And in a way it was sadder to be out than to be in, for although nobody was allowed to speak to me I learned that my friend, the young man to whom I was to have been married, had taken another wife. What will you? Nobody could expect him to wait for me forever.

"All this time," she went on, "I could hear nothing of my demoiselle, but I always thought of her. Later on I learned that in these three years she had had two sons, but that they had died. The housekeeper said that she thought Madame had been pleased about it, for she did not want her own blood to live on under the name of Kerjean. And when I had been shut up for three years the poor young captain was killed in a duel."

"I remember the story," said Samson, "although it is a long time ago."

"Fifteen years," said Marie-Marthe.

"I was told," said Samson, "that Captain Kerjean in those days, ten years before the revolution, was a revolutionary at heart. A soldier was hanged for stealing half a bottle of wine left in the officers' mess. Captain Kerjean spoke his mind. This caused a duel, and his opponent was the better swordsman."

"When the news of his death was brought to his young wife she gave birth three weeks too early to her daughter.

"Madame herself, three days later, came to my door, unbolted it, and told me to go to Namur to her daughter, for by now, she said, I must be cured of my madness, and Mademoiselle should have somebody from her own land with her. She equipped me and made a lackey travel with me to Namur. It was a good thing, for I was quite confused by seeing people's faces round me again and by hearing them talk. Mademoiselle Angélique lived with her child in a small house in Namur and on a poor pension. So you see, Citizen, what a good thing it was for me that up in my tower room I had learned to weave my carpets, for I kept up the small household on them.

"I was happy in Namur. Sometimes it went to my heart to think of the dancing masters and riding masters and music masters that my own demoiselle had had as a child, and to see her daughter grow up without anybody to teach her but her poor young mother. But I generally was too busy to think of such things.

"Later on my aunt told me that a great change had come over Madame with the death of her son-in-law. In some way or other, she thought, after he had gone, Madame reconciled herself to the situation. She was no longer quite without hope. She bethought herself, my aunt believed, that after all her granddaughter was half her own blood. She then conceived a plan.

"The young comte de Germont, when his intended bride ran away with her lover, had himself married a very noble young lady. And they had had a son in the first year of their marriage. Now Madame began to imagine that the marriage which she had once arranged for her daughter might still be brought about on behalf of her granddaughter.

Only to make up for the lack of nobility in the girl's father a much bigger dowry than her daughter's would be needed. It was from this moment that she gave up traveling and gambling and instead set herself to hoard up money. She did, my aunt said, become an old woman almost from one day to the other, she no longer cared about her own looks, she had no more frocks made and hardly left her own land. It is from this time, Citizen, that all those stories of her greed and avarice date. It was then that she grudged her servants the food in their mouths, and she herself sat down in her big dining room to plain meals. All this, my aunt said, she did for the sake of the child whom she had never seen and at whose father's death she had rejoiced. From the time of Mademoiselle Angélique's marriage till her husband's death she had never once mentioned her daughter. She corresponded with the comte de Germont about the matter. She would talk of the little boy, her granddaughter's bridegroom, too, speculating whether the dowry would soon be big enough to satisfy him. All this my aunt told me when we met again.

"In our little house in Namur I could not know about any of these things. But it was a very strange thing, Citizen, that my young mistress, although she was so far away from her mother and never did write to her or hear from her, seemed nonetheless to be aware of them. She would not mention her mother's name any more than Madame mentioned hers, but she would sometimes sigh deeply and say to me: 'Marie-Marthe, my good Marie-Marthe, somebody is thinking of us. Somebody is thinking of my child.' Once she said: 'For three

275

hundred years, until my first little boy was born, no child of my name has been brought into the world by love. And they both died.' At another time she sighed: 'Good Marie-Marthe, look, she is growing so pale and frail, as if somebody would want to drain the Kerjean blood out of my girl's veins.' And that, Citizen, was why I begged you not to say that you wanted to drain the Perrenot blood out of her. For what would there be left of the poor girl?

"All the same, while her two little boys had been named after their father and his family, Mademoiselle Angélique had given her daughter her own mother's names: Jocelynde Jeanne.

"My young mistress was so pretty that people turned in the street when she passed. She could have married again many times, great and rich people too, but she told me that the thought of such a thing to her was more horrible than anything else. Therefore she wore hats that almost hid her face, and she would only go out when it was almost dark. She could make lace, and most of her time she would sit with her lace pillow opposite to her husband's portrait. In this way we also gathered in a little money.

"I stayed with my young mistress for eleven years in the good little house in Namur. Then she died. While she was ill she worried about what was to become of little Jeanne. But before she died she said to me: 'Marie-Marthe, let it be so. I left Montfaucon and the house and the land and the forests and the people who were mine, for the sake of my happiness in life. From the first moment I saw him I belonged to my husband, I belong to him altogether now. Our two little boys too belong to him and me. Then let the account be settled and let me not grudge Montfaucon this daughter of mine.'

"A short time after Mademoiselle Angélique's death, Madame sent for my little Jocelynde Jeanne and for me.

"When the grandmother and the granddaughter met they looked at one another for a while without a word. Later on Madame once said to me: 'It was like looking into a glass of thirty years ago, when Jocelynde Jeanne was innocent and light at heart and had faith in human beings, and not a wrinkle in her face.' And my little Jeanne said to me: 'Marie-Marthe, when I looked at Grandmama I thought I was looking into a glass, an awful glass where something had twisted and blackened me— I cannot tell you how wickedly.'

"Things were much changed at Montfaucon. Food was scanty even at Madame's own table. There were only two or three old horses in the stables, the coachmen and grooms and lackeys wore old faded liveries which we had to darn and patch all the time. But Madame took care that little Jeanne had dainty food and plenty of it, for when we arrived she had scolded me because the child was too thin. She also gave much of her time to teaching her granddaughter to play the spinet and sing and to dance the minuet, for she had once been famous at the great balls at Versailles. Madame's own old groom taught her to ride, and this the girl liked very much.

"Already, at this time, Citizen, people were beginning to talk of great changes to come. I remember the first time I heard the word *revolution*. But Madame did not heed it in the least. Even when, as I was told, the old privileges of our nobility were lost, she only laughed. 'When all this nonsense is over again—' she said at every message from Paris, or, 'When things are back in the good old way—'

"At this time Madame saw few of her neighbors, so there were many things she did not hear, but when she was first told that many of the great people in France had left their land and their houses to go to foreign countries, she was angry, and said they ought to have their heads cut off.

"From time to time she wrote to, or heard from, the comte de Germont. And two years ago, Citizen, the count himself, his lady and that boy whom Madame meant to be Jeanne's husband, who was then thirteen years old, came to Montfaucon, for they had resolved to leave France and go to England. They stayed for two nights, and all the time Madame and they talked together about how to arrange things. They said that they were surprised to find that Madame knew so little about what was going on. That I heard myself as I went through the room. And again I heard that they talked about the dowry and said that it would be safer in England than in France, and that Madame answered that she would have had it all paid down, and that she would even have consented to let the marriage take place there and then by our own good village priest if they would stay in France, but in dealing with emigrants she could not make up her mind. But when all this nonsense was over, she repeated, they would have a fine marriage and all that she had saved would go with the bride.

The Proud Lady

"While the grown-up people talked, the two children were left to themselves, and they walked and
played in the garden. Madame had been very careful about Jeanne, for she would not run any risk of
losing her as she had lost her mother, and she had
hardly ever had any other children to play with.
The lad, too, had been much alone. But they got on
well together, and for the two days the Germonts
stayed at Montfaucon they did not like to part even
for an hour."

"Aha," said Samson, "so in spite of all your
father's virtue you liked to have an aristocrat for
your cavalier, little Citizeness, did you?"

"Oh, you should not grudge the child that one
playmate of all her life," said Marie-Marthe. "And
in any case he has gone, together with his father,
and he is in England now.

"It was only a short time after this that they
burned down a castle near Montfaucon. You saw
the sky all red from our big terrace. Then I believe
for the very first time Madame began to believe in
the revolution. She said to me: 'I shall stay here,
but my granddaughter will be safer with you, away
from Montfaucon.' Three times she told me so, but
each time gave up the plan of our leaving. By that
time she had only two servants left. She drove us
herself through the forests and across the fields to
the end of her land. We went back to Namur, for
there I had my best customers. Our small house
had been sold, but we got rooms with a baker's
widow, and we lived there just as we had done before, Mademoiselle Jeanne and myself.

"We had no news of Madame until quite lately,
when my aunt, who is now old, came to join me,

279

all trembling and exhausted with the long journey. She told me how Madame had lived on at Montfaucon after we had gone. My aunt had been the last of her old servants to stay with her, but Madame did not mind, my aunt said, neither did she much appreciate the faithfulness of that last one. She always thought, said my aunt, that it must be a great honor to wait on the marquise de Perrenot. She herself, however, had sent my aunt away from her when things began to look dangerous for her, and even then she would still be talking of the time when all the nonsense of the revolution would be a thing of the past. My aunt did not want to leave her, for how, she said, would Madame carry her own firewood and water? But Madame answered her that it would always be an honor and a pleasure to carry firewood and water for a Perrenot.

"When Madame was arrested, she was living all by herself in the old castle, just as you said, Citizen. Down in Namur we heard about all this. We heard, too, what you told us, Citizen, that she would be the last of the nobility to be beheaded, and that she would drive to the guillotine with not a single person of her own rank. Then after a while Jeanne said that we would go to Paris to see you, Citizen Samson, and to bring this prayer of ours before you.

"I have," she said, "one single possession of value, a ring that Mademoiselle Angélique gave me when we were girls together. Perhaps, Citizen, your good wife might care to have it."

With these words she loosened a string round her neck and placed a ring on the supper table.

Citizen Samson laughed.

"You are so innocent, Citizeness," he said, "that to the eyes of a man of less experience than me you would look suspicious. It is a grave offense to try to buy any servant of the republic. What then the husband of the lady La Guillotine? But I happen to have been in close contact with men and women of all sorts. I know my people when I see them. You are, as you told me when you came in here, poor and honest women, and you have gone through much in life, and all by the pride of the woman Perrenot.

"I told you that I was in the mood for a tale tonight. Now I will add that I am in the mood for something more.

"While you have been telling your tale I have been looking at the little citizeness who has come with you. The pavement of Paris does not today produce many slim white lilies like that. There is a kiss owing me—I should like to get it tonight. If you will give it to me, granddaughter of Jocelynde Jeanne de Perrenot de Lionne, in return I promise to grant you your prayer unheard."

For a few seconds silence reigned in the room, and he got no answer at all. Samson once more leaned back in his chair, and a grim smile spread over his face.

"Wait a moment, little Citizeness, wait a moment," he said. "Do you know what you are going to do now? You are going to kiss Samson, the man who cut off the heads of the king and queen of France. You may still become the wife of a sansculotte, but no aristocrat will ever kiss those lips which have kissed Samson. Even if all this nonsense of the revolution comes to an end, and even if you should happen to find your grandmother's treasure, after you have kissed Samson there would be no reason for you to go to England to join your friend of the garden of Montfaucon."

The girl listened to him gravely without a word, slowly she came up to his chair and stood still there.

"Perhaps," Samson laughed, looking up into her face, "perhaps living with your friend Marie-Marthe and in the château of a great lady, you have never been told about a kiss? Still, in the minuets at Versailles at the end of a dance the cavalier kissed the lady. Shall I have the first kiss you ever give, then? Well, I am an unsociable man, it is some time since I kissed a woman. It may be my last kiss."

He drew the girl down on his knee, pressed her face close to his and kissed her lips. He felt a long movement run through the slim body so light on his knee. The executioners of old, he thought, would have experienced that in the thieves and harlots on to whose seething flesh they pressed their white-hot branding iron. He let her go.

She seemed to waver on her feet for a moment before she stood up straight as before, her young face for a moment was dark red. Then very slowly the blood sank from it.

She had been silent all the time while Samson and the other woman had been talking. Now she spoke. If her face and figure were those of a child, her voice was very clear and sonorous, and although it was low and slow it was controlled and authoritative.

"Your prayer has been granted," said Samson. "Name it."

The Proud Lady

"I beg you, Citizen Samson," she said, "at the moment when my grandmother has mounted the scaffold, to lay away your hat and to say to her: 'At your service, Madame la Marquise.'"

The Bear and the Kiss

I n the year 1883, when the railway between Narvik and the mines at Gellevare was being built, three young engineers who were to work on the project sailed north from Christiania on the steamer *Fulda*.

They sailed between the skerries and the shore, and the days on the little ship passed slowly.

Two of them were old school chums, and all three soon became friends, and on the deck and in the narrow salon they discussed politics, philosophy, and railway building—and their own future in the unknown land to which they were sailing. At Bodø the last of the other passengers had gone ashore: the three were the only passengers left aboard.

It was September and the days were shortening over the entire northern hemisphere, but they regularly lasted a little longer in the north than they did farther to the south, so that the *Fulda* could just about keep up with the process and see the sun go down at the same time every evening. The three young men talked a good deal about this, for they knew that at the equinox there would be a change, and then every day the northern night would encroach upon the day from both ends. Finally, in December, the night would have completely swallowed the day and all fieldwork would have to stop for a time. It was as if they were sailing slowly and with open eyes into a trap of darkness which nature had set for them.

The darkness was not empty; it pulsed with life. Legends and stories which had been exiled from their native cities had taken up their abode there, and lived in caves and mountain ravines or followed the blowing snow over the plateau. Up north anything could happen.

The long talks of the three young men usually ended on one of two subjects: hunting and women.

They had been told that grouse were plentiful around Gellevare; the two friends had brought along brand-new shotguns and game bags, and fired rounds at the sea birds from time to time for practice. They knew that up north there is nobler and more dangerous game. In the great pine forests there are lynxes and wolverines. Packs of wolves follow the tracks of the Lapps' reindeer herds or sit in circles in the snow and howl at the winter moon; the most feared among these are the small dark wolves called *fjeldskridere*—that is, mountain climbers. They are just as shrewd as they are ferocious. They can find a footing down the steepest stone cliff, and on the way down each wolf of the pack places his paws in the prints of his predecessor—the second, the ninth, the fortieth in the prints of the leader—so that people cannot determine from the snow how many wild bloodthirsty guests they must deal with. But the real monarch of the Nordmark is the mighty, solitary bear, who remains silent until the height of his rage, who can fell an ox with one blow of his paw, and who can suddenly stand upright toward heaven, take a hunter in his embrace and tear his face off. An old bear sometimes turns into a hunter of men and is not good for a lonely traveler to meet on a narrow path over the reindeer moss.

There are legends which tell of Finnish and Lapp girls with black eyes and red lips, with soft limbs and soft voices, who are adept in witchcraft. A young Lapp girl with bashful eyes like two black-fringed slits in her flat fresh face may come to a house in the daytime to sell reindeer cheese, embroidered leather belts, and buttons made from reindeer antlers. At night in the winter, under the northern lights, with rolling eyes she drives her long wild wolf team at a furious pace over the snow. And in the bright summer nights she sits quite naked, dreamily, on a heavy, clumsy mount, a bear, and slaps him on the flank with a birch twig of which the leaves have just begun to spread from the buds, so that the old flatfoot willingly scrambles with her on his back over trees which have been felled in the woods by the winds. These girls can be disastrous to men. Gundhild, a Finnish girl, was the ruin of King Erik Bloodaxe, whom she taught ruthlessness and the magic by which he got rid of his four brothers. The Finnish girl Snefrid was the undoing of great King Harald, who could not be persuaded she was dead and brooded over her corpse while his good ships and his perplexed and sorrowing men waited outside in the spring breezes. These dark-eyed, soft-spoken women can be costly acquisitions; they may cost a man his life or his reason.

"We can only hope they have become less expensive," said one of the three friends, whose name was Carl, "and can be got at a reduced rate."

"We will see how things go," said his schoolmate Carsten.

The third young man, who had been reading, sat up and laughed. They asked him what he was laughing at. "Well, I am laughing," he said in a low pleasant voice, "because what you were saying matched what I was reading." They asked him what he was reading. He closed the book, keeping a finger in it as a bookmark, and read off the title like a schoolboy: "Johann Friedrich von Schiller, *Ballads in Translation.*" He added, "The one I was reading is called *The Glove.*"

"Oh yes, that old story," said Carsten, "I had to read it in school. I think there's a tiger in it. But we were through talking about wild animals; we were talking about girls."

"There is a girl in it, too," said the reader.

He was the youngest and the slightest of the three, a poor lad who had been dependent on scholarships to gain an education. He was bashful because he was not used to speaking about such matters as the other two discussed, and because he could never get rid of his dialect. He had been baptized Bjørn—that is, Bear—and on the voyage that had been something to smile about, for he was such a thin little bear, with large joints from childhood rickets—and was it not perhaps, the others had asked, in order to make up for his scrawniness he had let his thick hair grow into an unruly piece of fur? During the years when he was growing up he had had to work so hard on his schoolbooks that he had not had time to read for pleasure. On the voyage he had discovered the ship's small library and had dived into it with such passion and so deeply he could scarcely be extricated, and his companions understood that for him anything which was written in verse was a remarkable, novel adventure and experience. They were amused at this, without malice, for Bjørn himself was much given to laughter.

He said, "I shall tell you the story."

"King Franz," he began, "sits with his whole entourage on the balcony of his court of lions; they are to watch a fight between a lion and a tiger. The ballad describes how the animals are released from their cages under the balcony; first the lion walks majestically into the arena, looks about him with a long booming roar, and then stretches himself out on the sand; then the tiger rushes in, circles the lion, and finally lies down motionless opposite him. And then," he said and looked down at the book,

> There drops from the balcony's edge
> A glove from a lovely hand
> And comes to rest on the central sand
> Between the tiger and lion.

"Ugh," said Carsten.

"Yes, ugh. But listen," said Bjørn. "For the Lady Kunigund turns to Sir Delorges"—he pronounced the name in Norwegian—"and says to him that if his love for her is as great as he has sworn, he will go down and fetch her glove."

"Ugh again," said Carsten.

"Yes, ugh again. But listen," said Bjørn. "You understand that everything becomes deathly still as he walks down the stairs from the balcony and across the arena and," he looked again into the book,

> from the dread sand
> Deftly picks up the glove.

And when he has turned about and walked up the stairs and is safe," Bjørn continued happily, "loud applause bursts forth. And the Lady Kunigund herself walks beaming toward him. He throws her glove into her face and says, 'Do not mention it, my lady,' and walks away and leaves her forever."

"That is what she deserved," said Carsten.

Bjørn closed the book and laid it down. "Well, I wonder," he said slowly. "Was it what she deserved? You see, I had never read anything about knights before I came here on the *Fulda*. As far as I can make out, that is what knights are for, just that sort of thing—to do great deeds so that one can write songs and ballads about them. How else can songs and ballads be written? And it probably is not always those who can perform great and remarkable deeds who can think them up. The ladies are supposed to think of deeds for the knights to do. The ladies are not to be won for a low price, but for a great deed."

"And the singers," said Carl, whose fiancée had forsaken him for a poet, "were there to sing ballads for the lady and win her sweetest smiles behind her knight's back."

"Yes," said Bjørn, happy to have his theory rounded out. "So the Lady Kunigund found a deed for the knight Delorges. He braved a lion and a tiger at once and before the eyes of the king. He can never have a comparable deed offered him again; this will remain the only lion in his life. He will never meet a comparable lady, either."

"While the incomparable one herself sat comfortably on the balcony," said Carl.

"Yes, on the balcony," said Bjørn happily, as before. "She must sit on the balcony so the glove can fall down from the balcony. There she sits in a lovely and fashionable gown, and cannot be won for less than the glove, but by the glove she can be won. Then he throws the glove in her face. After that, what will become of them?"

The two others laughed because he spoke as if the event were real and had just happened, and they realized how little he understood about literature.

"Let us take it easy," said Carsten. "You will see, it will work out."

"And a ballad was the result," said Carl, "if that is the important thing."

"A ballad," said Bjørn slowly, as before. "Yes, for us. Not for him. One can imagine the Lady Kunigund as an old woman who sometimes hears the ballad sung and smiles with real satisfaction. I met an old woman in Christiania—we were two students from my home district who ate dinner with her once a week—who might very well have heard such a ballad sung about her own youth and would have smiled with satisfaction to hear it. For the Lady Kunigund, you see, was a true lady and there in the lion court had thought of both him and his honor, while he thought only of himself. As an old knight he will sit quietly in his castle where he has sat his whole life through—for one cannot suppose he will undertake any other deed after this one of the glove—and a singer will come and sing the ballad about the great heroic deed in the lion court. And the knight will order the doors to be closed. Would that not be the saddest thing for a knight—-almost the very saddest thing that can happen to him—that when the ballad about his great deed is sung, he must order the doors to be closed?"

"You should have fetched the glove yourself," said Carsten.

"I?" said Bjørn and nothing more. A good deal lay behind the single word. He had again been put in his place, the small thin young man who had been supported by scholarships during his studies, to which he had kept himself so rigorously he had not had time to read about knights.

"Or you should have composed the ballad yourself," said Carsten. "Then it would have ended with a marriage and champagne, Bjørn." Carsten had bought a bottle of champagne on the evening the *Fulda* weighed anchor and it had had a tremendous effect on his young comrade.

Bjørn thought for a bit. "No," he said very loudly, "I could not do that." He thought of some of the marriages he had known in his childhood and youth. "No," he said as before, "A real legal marriage to last an entire lifetime, to be determined by a moment in a lion court—that we shall never see. No, he had escaped alive, and it was proper and reasonable for him to let that suffice. But he might well," he added still more slowly, as if he were filled with a deep pleasure because he had been permitted to return to his knights, "he might well have given her a kiss."

While they talked there had been some peculiar movements of the ship and a peculiar growling and pounding in its bilge. They had been but partially aware of these things, and became conscious of something unusual only when the *Fulda*, groaning heavily, swung around in a semicircle and lay still. They broke off their conversation to go up on deck.

As they came up, the sun was setting.

The open sea lay farther out; on all sides were long darkening islands and skerries. Just where the sun was sinking into the sea was a clear view between two skerries of the noble straight line of the horizon: light within light. It was as if two lovers at the last moment—during a dance or during a game—had flung away everything which separated them and blissfully sunk into each other's arms. So powerful was this open meeting of immortal forces that it forged a ring, an eddy of dark and light spots, between them and the eyes of the mortal spectators. The three young men stood still until the uppermost edge of the sun's disk was immersed and the light about them grew cool, like a memory. A day was past—that is always something.

There was no one else on the deck and they walked around to the port side and saw that they were quite near the shore, and that the mountains ranged both high into the clear evening air and, upside down, deep into the clear, bottle-green water. The feeling of a great distance up and down made the little ship on the dividing line seem weightless and suspended in space.

There was a great noise aft; the anchor was being lowered. Shortly afterward the captain of the ship came up, dirty and perspiring and in a bad humor, and gave them an expert's explanation: the *Fulda* had engine trouble, a bolt had broken in a coupling and it was necessary to let the fire go out under the boiler. The little bay which was otherwise unimportant had seemed a good spot to anchor; the *Fulda* had run in by the lead and would lie there the next day and the next night. He summarized the situation with the brief remark that he would be damned.

In the lives of the young passengers this unexpected event was an experience, and full of possibilities. To console their skipper they invited him to have a drink of rum, and fetched a bottle from their cabin. It was a new experience to lie quietly near the land, and the evening was so dead calm that they brought out their greatcoats and sat on coils of rope on the deck for a time, with the bottle of rum, while they drank to the repair of the damage and a good trip the day after next.

Bjørn, who had been standing up against the gunwale and looking over toward the land, said, "A light was just lit in there. Some people must live here."

No, no people live here, said the captain. For the last few days they had been sailing along uninhabited shores. "There is a light, anyway," said Bjørn.

The others also got up, looked toward the coast and exchanged guesses. Suddenly the captain exclaimed in a low voice, "Maybe it is Joshua!" and fell silent.

They wanted to know who Joshua was, but the captain was reluctant to explain and protested it was not easy to say who Joshua was. He did not have an equal, he said several times. Finally he explained as well as he could. One summer, he said, there was an artist up from Christiania who had painted a picture of Joshua. He called the picture *Olav Tryggvason*, and had reminded people how King Olav could walk about a ship on the oars while the men were rowing, could use a sword equally well with either hand, and could throw two spears at once, and then those who knew Joshua considered they also knew Olav Tryggvason well. In a wild mood Joshua had sworn never to let his hair be cut again; it was very fair and had since hung down over his shoulders. If he had a picture to show them, the captain said, it would be easier to explain who Joshua was.

During his voyages to the north the skipper had met Joshua fairly regularly during the course of nine years. But it was now seven years since he had seen him. Despite such digressions, the young men managed to elicit Joshua's story. Actually it was a sad story. It could be divided roughly into three parts.

A remarkably large and strong boy had been slow and dull of mind during his adolescence, as sometimes is the case with unusually large, strong children, who seem to be hampered by their own strength. But fourteen years ago, when the boy was nineteen, and half a head taller than his fellows, he went into the woods one day without a word to anyone and shot a bear which experienced bear hunters would not have tackled, for the animal had done away with three of them. And from that day on he seemed to be able to do everything, so that what for others was impossible was for him a game, and people thought that with the first bearskin he had brought home the strength of twelve men, which a bear proverbially possesses.

As for the account of Joshua's deeds during his nine great years—it was long, and the narrator began by saying that it probably did not seem credible but should be believed. The deeds seemed to be legendary; fragments of an old epic about a folk hero and a devil of a fellow, and it was strange to hear them told about someone who was still alive. The mountains and the sea were the settings, and the air too, for there were tales of strange mountain climbs and a story about how the hero once had fetched a baby eagle from an eagle's nest on a rock which projected high over the valley. Whales and bears came into the story. Of the latter there were seven in all, of which one had been conquered in a hand-to-hand struggle, breast to breast, with only a sheath knife as weapon. There were fantastic voyages, swimming races, and ski runs, and there were also tremendous fights in which two or more antagonists had united against the lone giant—but there was no mention of anger or resentment in the constant victor. On the contrary, it was as if the entire epic had a background of laughter.

The story could not be told without mention of deeds on the dance floor or among girls. Girls, yes, said the captain. Joshua left them behind here and there, and some of them drowned themselves in the fjords and others lost their minds, but none of them would look at another man. It might seem strange, added the narrator, that Joshua had not been slain for one of these affairs; there was something about him which kept it from happening that way.

Though the young listeners would have liked to hear more, there was no more. They thought the skipper might perhaps have himself been among the rival suitors in the past, and therefore might prefer to leave some things untold.

The heroic poem ended like many others, with the arrogance and defeat of the hero. Since Joshua succeeded at everything, he had no ability to judge what was dangerous. During a storm he forced three other men to accompany him in his boat to save some people from a wreck. When they had come back to land, the skipper from the wreck complained about some fine English binoculars he had not been able to save, and Joshua offered to go out once more after them. This time no one would accompany him. And on this last trip, when he was alone in his boat, it smashed on the shore and Joshua had one leg crushed, and later he wore a wooden leg.

Even after this, the second canto of his epic, Joshua was a man of great deeds; but he changed, grew wild, became a fighter and a braggart. The last thing which happened to him was that he got into a brawl with three Finnish seamen who were down at the harbor and who had wagered with other seamen they could defeat Joshua, and who attacked him all at once, with knives. In this, his last fight, big Joshua growled like one of his own bears and when a fallen antagonist rose again to attack him from behind, he performed his final deed—which sounds strangely grotesque when it is told. He tore off his wooden leg and, standing on one leg, struck out with the other until the three Finns tumbled down like bowling pins; but then he himself fell. This was reported to the authorities and the matter was brought before the chief of police. Joshua was released, not exactly because the others had begun the fight, but because they had been three against one and had used knives, and these were serious offenses in the little town. Nevertheless, either because he had struck too hard or because he had taken the life of another strong young man or because he had hurt himself badly when he fell, Joshua began to reflect for the first time in twenty years. Some time later he sold his house, collected his nets and shotgun and other possessions in his boat, and sailed away. It was early in the morning and clear; only some women who had gone out to milk their cows had stood watching him until his sail grew smaller in the distance and finally disappeared. Since then, no one had seen Joshua, and that was seven years ago.

When he had seen the light on shore that evening, the captain said, it occurred to him that this could be Joshua.

The story made an impression on the three young travelers because while it was being told the darkness deepened about them. The deeds which were told them were the kind they themselves had once dreamed of performing—and now it seemed they would have to be satisfied with less. The air grew colder and when they looked toward the land and saw that the light there had been extinguished, they felt closing in upon them that defeat in life and great loneliness which young men fear above everything else, and they suggested to the captain that the four of them should go down into the salon and play cards.

While Carsten dealt the cards, Carl said, "So for seven years he has not said a word."

"Yes, one word," said the captain, and after a pause, "He has his wife along."

This thought—and the lamp over the table in the little salon—was reassuring and encouraging. One of the seduced girls had evinced loyalty to the crippled man—here was the loving woman who anointed Alcibiades' body and provided the obol for his transport across the Styx. They asked the captain about Joshua's wife.

The narrator changed his tone. He had been willing to tell about Joshua's deeds, he had made an effort to dig them out of his memory, and he had spoken about them in an agreeably sympathetic fashion: a free man's sorrow over another free man's misfortune. But about the wife he would have preferred to be silent; the story about her came out rather against his will.

He knew something of her family. She was a Finnish girl; her grandfather was Anfin, who was called Ganfin after the last great Finnish wizard up north, who could sing songs of sorcery and dance dances of enchantment and who sold seamen wind in a sack, the string of which they cautiously loosened when they were becalmed, and the mouth of the sack provided three suitable tacks. Anfin himself believed he was descended from one of the sorcerers who had wanted to envelop King Olaf in darkness at Øgvaldness and for that reason had been tied down by the king on a skerry over which the water rose at floodtide. In his old age Anfin had, inexplicably, lost his power over the winds, just like the sorcerers who can no longer perform their sorcery, for in the big snowstorm fifteen years back he had died in the mountains with all his reindeer and it was then his granddaughter, who in some strange way had survived, sought out people on the coast. To be on the safe side the clergyman had baptized her; her own people called her Lahula, but at the baptism she was given the name of Mary Magdalen.

Could she also sing and dance, asked the listeners. Yes, dance, yes, that she could, said the captain.

They asked whether she was pretty. In any case she is not now, said the captain, almost pleased. Finnish women grow old quickly and they are either as fat as sows or as emaciated as sick cats. As the story again grew sad, they preferred to drop it and Carsten dismissed it with the remark that it was Joshua's own business if he did not leave the lonely peninsula and his wife.

The captain pushed back his hat and scratched his head a bit.

Well, it was uncertain, he said, whether the decision was Joshua's.

That required an explanation, but he only put a new question: whether they knew anything about what people call jealousy.

Carl knew something about it, but he would not talk about it.

Or perhaps he should say, continued the captain, about what people call jealous persons.

Oh yes, both Carl and Carsten knew about them.

Very well, said the captain, he did too. His own wife back in Stangereid was just such a jealous person. It was not only girls she looked askance at, but ships and even the ship's dog. If she had her way, he figured he would end up in her living room without permission to look at a square-rigger through the window. And it was strange with these jealous people, he went on, as if there were thoughts he had repressed but which suddenly burst forth, when they are sitting and guarding someone that way like a cat in front of a mousehole, they take one's breath away so that it is difficult to move— and they themselves shrink until there is life only in their eyes. When he had been at home for any length of time, his wife became no bigger than a thumb. Incidentally, he cheerfully admitted, his wife was good enough, and after a moment he added, to give her her just due, that he had himself once been deranged by jealousy and at that time had thought of killing a man, but nothing had come of it.

But, he said in conclusion, it was not certain that it was Joshua's own decision whether or not to leave the peninsula.

He looked at his cards and said "Pass."

Carl said "Pass."

Carsten now laid down his cards and declared that since the *Fulda* was to lie in the bay all the next day, and since people lived on the shore who could act as guides, he and Carl might as well row in and see whether there was anything to hunt there.

By this time the group had shaken off Joshua's story. Carsten and Carl brought out their shotguns and examined them and discussed bird hunting for a long time. The result was that the hunters were to be rowed to land early in the morning and fetched back to the *Fulda* in the evening, and that they should talk to the cook about some provisions. Bjørn had no shotgun, but he brought out a large sheath knife, which he had inherited from his maternal grandfather, and looked at it while the others laughed at him. He would go along, he said, and watch his two friends shoot.

At first the captain talked of going ashore with them in order to greet his old acquaintances, but then he remembered he had too much to do on board. He gave them a pound of coffee for the wife, since Finnish women—he said—grow gentle and sweet of speech over coffee. They should also say some nice things to her; she would like that. They thought it wouldn't be easy to say nice things to an old witch. Oh yes, said the captain, a witch; he had called her that himself, but there was a difference whether one called a woman a little witch or an old witch. "Although the devil knows," he added, unexpectedly.

The next morning as the hunters were rowed away from the ship there was a fine rain. It was so early the gulls were still asleep on the water and a small waning moon rode high in the heavens. Gradually their surroundings began to take on shape, and while they steered between islands and came closer to the land, Bjørn, who was sitting in the stern of the boat, thought he caught a glimpse through the dark water of the shifting forms of dark stones at the bottom of the sea. Then the land began to make itself known by the odors of heather, bog myrtle, birch, and mountain ash—a silent evanescent greeting which met the boat and was most moving after many days spent among the odors of saltwater and tar.

The entrance to the settlement was so well hidden that they missed it several times and would have given up looking for it if they had not seen the light on land the evening before. They called out a few times toward the mountain and got no answer except an echo. When they finally found it they were surprised to come to an attractive, impressive landing place. A large flat stone which stretched out into the water had been made into a fine wharf by blasting and erecting a wall. This was first-hand evidence of what they had heard about Joshua's unusual strength, for it was difficult to believe this wharf was the work of one man. Two boats, one large and one small, were moored to the wharf.

The three hunters stepped ashore and lifted their things out of the boat. They had a lantern with them to light their way, and the men who had rowed the boat in for them wished them good hunting and rowed back to the ship; the strokes of the oars died away in the quiet morning.

It was gradually growing lighter and their eyes had become adjusted to the semidarkness, but the wavering water all about them and the rain from above made them feel as if they were moving on the bottom of the sea. There were tall seaweeds reaching upward on both right and left, and rock formations in this sea on which no human eye had ever rested, and the path which stretched dimly before them was that of some sea beast in the depths.

While they were looking about with the lantern, its light suddenly hit a pair of green eyes, and the first living creature to receive them was a gray cat which sat on the path and meowed quite dreadfully. Soon afterwards, a bit further on, they caught sight of a large figure which, though presumably alive, closely approximated the stones and plants and held itself motionless among them as if it had struck root. In the morning dusk things look larger; it could have been a whale or a sea cow lying in the seaweed and awaiting them. The figure extricated itself and came toward them, and it was a man with a wooden leg.

The tale they heard the evening before had quickened their fantasy, and the surroundings gave it force; they were silent during the first moment of the meeting as they stood opposite an unreasonably large human figure, and while their hands were gripped by a large fist. They returned to reality sufficiently to say who they were and to explain their errand on shore, and then they learned that the whale or sea cow on the path really was Joshua.

He asked them no questions and did not seem to wish to establish any relation with his guests, even after he had been told about the *Fulda* and heard the captain's name. This made it more difficult to ask him to show them the way further inland and to give them instructions and good advice regarding grouse hunting. After they had introduced themselves, he seemed to inspect them one by one, and finally he began to move.

He let them go past and ahead of him on the path as if he disliked displaying his disability.

At a turn in the path they caught sight of Joshua's dwelling and were greatly surprised, for what seemed a village lay around a large clearing. Three or four roomy dark houses lay further back in the brush, and closest to them stood a small round house, the only one with a light. They stopped in amazement, looked around and asked their guide, "Who lives here?" "I live here," he answered.

The gray cat had followed them along the path and had rubbed up against their legs; it hurried toward the round hut and disappeared and at the same moment the door of the house opened and the light from within came—so it seemed—straight toward them, and the woman of the house stood in the middle of the doorway.

Her appearance was in itself an invitation, and she nodded to them. They accepted and went inside, having to duck under the lintel—thinking what must Joshua do? From the darkness and moisture and endlessness on all sides they came into a very small room where the air was dry and warm and almost stifling, filled with the odors of hides and smoke and other smells of various kinds. The light sparkled—a hurricane lantern hung above the table, and there were live coals in the fireplace —and the shadows in the room seemed to be even more alive. In the corners of the room strange colors flashed and glowed; it might be that the witch who lived there had a supply of amber and jewels.

In this lighting they observed their hosts, the people who lived there.

The Bear and the Kiss

Joshua, having come in last, stepped into the middle of the room and they could see him well for the first time. Though to be sure they had the captain's story to prepare them, it was strange and ominous to see him move, and they were uncertain whether he would stand still or keep moving.

In the low-ceilinged room the man was really half a head taller than any of them, and broad-shouldered compared to his height, beautifully built: a vision of manly strength. In his years as a hermit, in his renunciation of the world, Joshua had kept his extravagant youthful vow—his hair and beard were neither cut nor trimmed, and flowed over his head, shoulders, and chest—a crown and cope of pure gold. By this the large figure's torso acquired improbable volume and weight, while farther down it narrowed and in meeting the earth ended as a column of wood: the whole figure could be said to resemble a tree with a slim trunk and a spreading crown.

They saw now that despite the wooden leg and something irregular that it caused in his gait, Joshua moved easily and soundlessly, almost airily, like a man who stays well within the limits of his strength. They were in the presence of a superior force, perhaps a god. But in the man's entire image and in his impassivity there was something not only painful but ugly, as if it were unnatural—it might be called a kind of affectation. The superior force might be a giant, and they could not be sure how friendly he really was.

While they were still under the influence of the fantastic, their attention turned from the man of the house to the woman, Calypso, the warder of the radiant Laertides, and a mood of horror, something tragic and hostile, was suddenly released; it stuck in their throats like a primitive coarse laugh.

The woman was as extremely and unreasonably small as the man was large. Clad entirely in Lapp costume, with a leather jacket, a leather cap, and Lapp shoes, she was as erect as a cork in a bottle and seemed to lack the midsection of the usual or accepted figure of a woman, so the captain's comparison with a thumb recurred to them. However, in her thumblike being there was nothing of what one ordinarily associates with being all thumbs, for her shortness was a concentration; she was the thumb which cocks a shotgun. She was wrinkled like an old apple and did not have a tooth in her mouth, but her lips covered the naked gums like strong supple bands, a pair of leeches which could grasp and suck more than the short clay pipe which she had put aside when she received her guests. As she spoke to them the young men became uneasy, for her strangely modulated voice was not that of a human being: the old woman mewed, gurgled in her throat, cackled, twittered, and whined—until suddenly from deep down in her breast arose a couple of pure golden notes, clear as spring water, like the nightingale's first trials on a summer night.

All in all the Finnish woman gave an impression of the heartiest satisfaction and contentment, absolutely sincere and unalloyed, like the joy of a little child or an adult slightly mad. She twitched and wriggled about somewhat, soundlessly, as she stood and spoke with them; the two housemates, the bear and the little old cat, were equally silent in their movements. The hostess gave her guests her hand, a collection of tiny bones. And soon afterwards, on receiving the coffee, she hallooed through an entire scale with happiness and gratitude. Coffee must be made at once and her guests must join in drinking it. Oh, now they would be happy, so happy.

Before they knew it they were sitting on benches around the table in the hut. Lahula fetched pewter cups down from a rafter in the ceiling and loaf sugar and cream from a shelf, while the strong, stimulating smell of coffee, overcoming a raw morning, flowed into the room's aromatic air. They were being entertained in the underwater cave or palace of the witch herself. They were met by colors and sounds quite as fascinating as the odors, and they knew there was more here than met the eye. When they looked at Joshua they understood he was a prize no woman would give up willingly, but what were the means his dark little wife used to keep him captive? They remembered from their childhood: the fenris wolf which no bonds could hold was fettered by a chain made of cat's stealth, woman's beard, and bird's saliva. Having themselves entered the magic circle, they were unable to accept the idea, even though they wished to, that Joshua some day might end his long captivity and leave.

Since Joshua himself said nothing and there was neither a beginning nor an end to his wife's chatter, they had to create a reasonable conversation themselves. They asked about game and about roads and paths into the mountains, and their questions seemed to reassure Joshua, as if he feared something else from them. Once started, he was fairly accommodating about telling them what he knew

—yes, there were lots of grouse a bit further inland; he had been up there recently with his horse,
for wood, and had come upon many of them in the
heather. They exhibited their shotguns, which he
inspected closely; he evinced considerable expert
knowledge, smiled a bit because the guns were so
little used, and began to encourage them; perhaps
they would have a fine hunt.

During this discussion Mary Magdalen had sat
quite still, like a little girl on a school bench—for
her feet did not touch the floor—and seemed slowly
to concentrate her attention on the youngest guest;
she suddenly asked him his name, while the others
were talking. Her face lit up when she heard his
name was Bjørn—that is, bear. He had no shotgun,
she said. No, said Bjørn, he was only going along
to watch the others shoot.

Joshua paused in his explanations, and the two
young men became aware of the conversation between the wife and Bjørn. He had a knife, they said
smiling, and they got Bjørn to show his big sheath
knife. When Joshua had looked at it and put it
down, his wife took it up surreptitiously, pulled it
out of its sheath and replaced it, and moved closer
to its owner. The cat also went over to Bjørn and
began to slither about his legs.

Though the hot coffee had tended to fuse the
group together, the hunters now had to bestir themselves, for the sun was up and they must get on.
The man of the house, who was now in good humor,
continued for a time to tell about his own grouse
hunting; in contrast to the assertion of the captain,
who had said he was a braggart, Joshua seemed to
be eager to keep close to the facts.

The Bear and the Kiss

Bjørn lifted the cat from the floor and at once it began that mad mawkishness peculiar to cats, purring loudly and kneading his shoulders and neck with all four of its paws. He fondled it and noticed the small teats on its belly and asked Mary Magdalen whether her cat had had kittens. Yes, kittens, she mewed softly and confidentially in reply, she had indeed had kittens but the tomcat had eaten them all; he did not want to have other cats on the peninsula, no, he did not. "Poor kitty," said Bjørn, and the woman smiled at him. "Do you say that?" she asked. "Do you say, poor kitty? And you, why do you not have a shotgun?" "Well, I have never had money to buy a shotgun," said Bjørn. "Oh, money," she said and was silent. A little later she took hold of his hair and shook him. "Now there's something for a girl to pull at, in bed," she said, and her leech-like lips moved, stretched, and contracted. "Oh, but you have a beautiful large knife," she said. "You might get to use it if there were something other than gamebirds, something that you could capture with a knife." "Yes, then I would be able to use it," said Bjørn.

This peaceful conversation, carried on in very low voices while Joshua, Carsten, and Carl continued to examine the beautiful shotguns, visibly disturbed the man of the house at this point.

Joshua looked up and said curtly, "There is no other game."

"No, no," agreed his wife placidly, "it is just that, there is no other game."

But when the others had resumed their conversation, she whispered hoarsely to the young man next to her, "There is a bear, too." He realized that

309

this was a secret communication, a confidence, and asked softly in reply, "Where?" "Well, I could easily show it to you," said the woman. "I could easily go along and show you the uphill path where it walks. It is an old bear, an evil bear. It was not so long ago he took our cow—we had two, now we have only one left—he has been shot once and limps and that is why he is ferocious in his old age and sometimes comes all the way down here, near the house. He is dangerous and to take him one should have a good new rifle. But I will tell you," she added, "there are those who have gone hunting for bears with a knife."

At this point Joshua interrupted his conversation with the other guests again. He quickly laid the shotgun he held in his hand on the table and said angrily or fearfully, "There is no bear here at all."

"No, no," said the wife as compliant and friendly as before.

When he turned away from her she again began to whisper, "I was a long way up after some herbs yesterday; I usually gather herbs around here, you see. Then I saw its track, yesterday. A fresh track. A large track."

"Why are you saying that?" said Joshua to her, dully. "If there were a bear, I would not send a puppy like him after it. He cannot even shoot."

"No, that is just it; he cannot even shoot."

Here Bjørn interrupted. "Oh yes, I can shoot well enough," he said. "When I was a soldier that was not what I was poorest at."

"No, that probably was not what you were poorest at," she said.

"Be quiet over there," said Joshua. "If there were a bear here and if he could shoot, he would not have anything to shoot with. Even if the others were to sacrifice their hunt and lend him a shotgun he would still have nothing to shoot with. These," he said and put his large hand on the shotguns, "these are only for shooting birds."

"No, then he would have nothing to shoot with," said the wife. Then she looked straight at her husband and added, "Unless you would lend him your old rifle."

Bjørn also looked at Joshua. "Do you have a rifle?" he asked.

Joshua sat silent for a long time and took the measure of the young man. "Yes," he said, "I have the rifle with which I shot six bears. It was good enough for the largest bear. But it has not been fired for seven years and it has not been cleaned or oiled for seven years and it is too heavy for a child like you."

"Oh yes," said Lahula, "it has been cleaned. I cleaned it and oiled it and put shells into it."

"When?" asked Joshua.

"Yesterday," said Lahula.

Joshua was silent for a long time. Then he stood up without a word and went over to a big chest, took out a heavy old rifle and examined it for a long time. He laid it on the table in front of Bjørn.

Carl and Carsten were silent, for it was as if the affair had become a matter shared among the three others and for each of them had a private significance incomprehensible to the other two guests. Lahula sat and smiled pleasantly at her husband and at Bjørn.

"It is colder up there than you think," she said to the latter. "It will be better if I give you my scarf to wear." She loosened a red scarf from about her shoulders, tied it around the neck of the young man and caressed him under the scarf with her small fingers as softly as the cat had recently caressed him. "It looks nice on you," she said.

"At home," she began suddenly, and as she spoke her chatter began to acquire coherence, "there was a young man, a boy, who was stupid and wild and thoughtless, and he had a red scarf just like the one you have now. One day he decided he wanted to shoot a bear which had taken his mother's cow and he went up after it when the sun rose. When his mother and his brothers and sisters were having their evening meal, he came back. He said nothing about the bear and did not want to eat, but he talked pleasantly and calmly with all of them and more seriously than he ever had before. He also talked about our Lord and about baptism. The whole time he kept his left hand in his pocket. Just when the sun went down he said to his mother, "Well, I have to go now, there is someone who is waiting for me." His mother said, "You tore the red scarf I gave you in two." "Yes, it got torn on something sharp up there," said the boy and left. Scarcely an hour later a couple of men came running to the house who had found the boy dead far up the mountain. The bear had killed him but went away when people approached. It had bitten off only his left hand. And the bear had got a piece of the scarf between his claws: they found it some distance away."

While she was talking it had grown lighter and the colors in the room had faded and grown pale as the ship's lantern over the table lost its strength and became a drowsy red blob. The wife went over and pushed open a small round window, and the smoke and darkness in the room undulated over the sill for several seconds toward the light and the.fresh air of the early morning outside, equably, until the light conquered and all the darkness vanished; the sun had really risen. Joshua remained sitting at the table for a time as if he were reflecting on a difficult matter, and he scowled briefly at each person in the room individually. Then he stood up, took a cap down from a nail and his heavy cane. "Come with me, the three of you," he said. The two bird hunters took their shotguns and game bags; Bjørn stood still by the table and looked at Joshua's rifle.

"Look at him," said Joshua to Lahula, "If he meets the bear, you will never see him alive again."

"No, if he meets the bear," said Lahula with a sweet, gentle ring in her voice, "I shall never see him alive again."

"Take it then," said Joshua, and Bjørn tossed the rifle over his shoulder in a military fashion and put two extra shells in his pocket.

When they came out of the hut and looked about, they were surprised once more. There was a large area neatly cleared and graded and covered with heavy flat stones, and around it there had been built what looked like an entire set of farm buildings, three wooden houses and a storehouse, all well built and cleverly and carefully decorated with carvings.

"Who built these houses?" asked Carsten.

"I did," said Joshua.

"Who lives in them?" asked Carsten again.

"Nobody does," said Joshua.

Carl, who was interested in old houses and old carvings, left the path in order to look at the buildings more closely. "This is very well carved," he said.

When they had reflected a bit, they grew silent. If Joshua really had executed this work alone, he must indeed have brought the bear's strength of twelve men with him from the mountains, as had been said. They found the thought depressing. A captive beaver in his forced inactivity will continue to drag logs with all his might and to build according to his ingenuity. Nobody lived in these houses and nobody was ever to live in them, but the giant prisoner had been forced by his very nature to work strenuously, as if he would keep himself alive through his diligence.

Joshua's wife stood a little way behind them and heard, happy as always, the praise which was given to her husband's work. "You are keeping a great artist captive here, you little bitch," thought Carsten.

"I will show you the way," said Joshua to Carsten and Carl. "We have to walk north a bit here. And I will point out the path to you when it gets so steep that I cannot go on with you. For I have a wooden leg, as you see."

The colors on the mountain had begun to come forth, the rain had stopped, the early morning light was mixed with a fine sheen of gold.

Mary Magdalen stood quietly next to Bjørn. "For you, little one," she said, "it is a matter of going higher up. Let me see that you are able to do it. When you are so high that you can see all the ocean, it grows very steep and there are many loose stones; from there you can send your friends north or south, whichever they wish, but you must continue to go straight up, for the bear does not come down there. When you have come up to where it flattens out again look around you carefully. Go straight inland and look around you carefully."

Carsten stopped. In the room it had annoyed him that the old witch and the boy had, so to speak, sucked the marrow out of his own enterprise. But now that they really were under way, he wondered whether he as the oldest and most intelligent did not have some responsibility.

"You are not going up there?" he said to Bjørn.

"Why, yes," said Bjørn, quite surprised, "why yes, I am going up there."

"There are no bears up there at all," said Carsten.

With this, they left. Lahula sat down on a stone and remained sitting there for a long time.

In the course of the day, some shots could be heard from above, two, then one, and then two or three more, here and there on the mountain.

Having started the hunters off, Joshua came back and began working with his horse to transport timber some distance to the settlement. After a while he had another thought, unhitched the horse and put it in the enclosure and began to break rocks and carry them to the area between the houses, just as he had done when they first came to the place. He worked very hard, struggling with stones so large that scarcely any other man would have tried to manage them and tossing them against the cobblestones so that the sparks flew. When his wooden leg got in the way, he kicked like an angry horse. He dripped with perspiration, he groaned during his work. From time to time when he was dizzy he stopped, stood still, and looked straight ahead without looking up.

When it began to grow dark he put down his heavy iron crowbar and went inside.

Shortly after that Lahula left the house and walked uphill a way, and the cat followed her. After she had stood there for a while, she heard people coming down, and voices. She listened and recognized the voices, nodded to herself, and went inside again.

Carsten and Carl came down together as the first ones of the party to return. They had been together most of the day, had parted for a time, but had called to one another so that they met and could walk together on the last part of the way back.

They came in, making more noise than they actually needed to, put down their shotguns and gamebags on the table, and collapsed on the benches without saying anything.

"Did you get anything?" asked Joshua after a short pause.

"No, we did not get anything," they said.

"Did you see something?" asked Joshua and smiled slightly.

"No, we did not see anything," they said.

"But you shot, nevertheless," said Lahula almost apologetically.

"Yes, a couple of crows," they said.

"Oh," said Lahula, "and now you are very tired."

"Yes, as if our legs were broken," said Carsten. "It is not hard to think of something more pleasant than running up and down among the stones and having nothing to show for it."

"Oh yes, one can indeed," said Lahula. "One can imagine something more pleasant. Wait a bit. You are going to have a glass of brandy first and then porridge and fine flatbread and smoked ocean salmon which my husband caught and I smoked."

While she was speaking, she set out these viands and the sight of them alone cheered up the tired hunters. The wife sat down and looked pleased that they ate and drank.

"Oh, you will see," she said. "Your tiredness and the soreness in your legs will pass, and while you are mourning the fact that you did not get anything, that will pass too. This day—you will forget it soon, you soon will not think any more about it at all."

After a little while they asked, "Has Bjørn come back?"

"No," said the woman and smiled pleasantly at them. "No, he really has not come back."

This troubled them and made them uncomfortable even though their physical well-being was returning. How had things gone with the third hunter? They had not taken the talk about his bear hunting seriously, but on the mountain everything is possible. He could really have met a bear, he could, even thought it did not seem reasonable, have shot a bear, he could also have been killed by a bear.

While these disquieting thoughts passed through the minds of the two guests, the woman of the house received no answers to her friendly chatter.

A little while later they heard some one coming down toward the house. The sound stopped, then continued. It was very irregular, pushing and pulling, as if the person who was coming stumbled and fell and got on his feet again. From the sound one might well suppose he was dragging something, a very heavy burden. He staggered and fumbled outside the door, missed it, and crashed against the house so that those who were inside got up to help him. Lahula herself sat perfectly still. Then the door burst open and Bjørn fell in over the threshold.

He looked miserable and could scarcely keep on his legs. One of the sleeves of his jacket was torn all the way up, he had a gash on his forehead and his clothes were covered with mud as if he had fallen many times. His gashed face was white and completely expressionless.

No sooner had he fallen over the threshold than he vomited, which embarrassed him very much. When he finally had collected himself, he walked very unsteadily to the table, took the old carbine down from his shoulder, and placed it with as great care as he could manage in front of Joshua. He seemed to want to say something while he was doing this but he could not get a sound out of his chest.

"Well, did you get something?" his friends asked him in order to get him started, but with more tension in their voices than they intended.

He looked briefly at them and turned to the man and wife of the house.

"Well, did you get something?" they repeated.

"What?" he said, "No," he said, "no, I got nothing."

The other two hunters immediately felt relieved and told themselves they could have clear consciences, for it was great good fortune that the inexperienced hunter had come back unscathed.

"Did you see anything?" they asked.

"What?" he said again. "No, I saw nothing."

"You did not meet the bear?" they continued in a more relaxed tone.

"No, I did not meet the bear," he said.

As a result of the brandy and the food and the warmth of the room his two friends were in a merry mood, and they burst out laughing. Their young friend was safe and that was good. And he came empty-handed from his great hunt and that was something to laugh at. He himself, so little and thin with a mop of hair—and now so profoundly solemn—was something to laugh at.

"What *did* you meet up with?" they cried to him.

He was unable to answer because he started to vomit again, was again much embarrassed, and tried to get up and leave. But Lahula laid her dreadful little paw softly upon him, pulled him down on the bench and wiped off his mouth.

"Now you're going to have some brandy," she said. "And coffee. Women always give that to bear hunters when they come home." At this Bjørn looked up at her.

"You fell even if you were not felled," said Carsten.

With one hand Bjørn felt himself all over and drew his mouth into a smile. "Yes," he said and added with difficulty, "there were loose stones in many places."

"And you shed blood," said Carsten.

Bjørn felt his forehead. "Yes," he said.

He emptied his brandy glass a second time and groaned. Lahula brought him a large cup of boiling-hot coffee which she later refilled a couple of times.

In the meantime she sat opposite him and nodded to him many times, although not as before, frivolously like a little child, but seriously and solemnly to match his mood.

"No, not the steepness, not the sharp stones. But the danger of death. That's the way it is when death is just at one's heels."

The two other young men laughed, but she remained serious and nodded again. "You must have heard the bear several times?" she said.

"Yes," said Bjørn. "When I got up stones tumbled down from some distance away."

"Yes, and you saw it too," she said. "Many times?"

"There were some large stones," said Bjørn, "which resembled one."

"And then, fear," she said, "then you were really afraid."

Bjørn was gulping down coffee and could not answer. She said, "This is a day you will not forget. When every time you drew a breath you thought you would never draw another." And after a pause she added, "You will not be afraid any more, the way you were before. The bear is something more than your little scarecrows."

Joshua had been sitting, inspecting his rifle; he turned it one way and the other and took it apart.

And suddenly the silent man began to speak, like a person who is not used to saying anything, and continued like a person who, once he has begun to speak, does not know how to stop.

He spoke slowly and in a strange new voice; he told about his bear hunts; he spoke of seven bears. It all came out like a lesson which the man had learned by heart and had often repeated to himself. His audience was puzzled while they listened, for if he spoke truth he had done extraordinary deeds, the like of which they would not hear told about again.

"I got him with a sheath knife," he said. "The sheath knife was all I had. I have lost it since, but it was the same kind—almost identical with the one"—he turned to Bjørn—"you have there. Blood poured from his throat over my head, hot, so I could not see. Then he fell and I just managed to spring aside, otherwise he would have fallen on me. In those days," he added, "I could jump."

He was interrupted by long cries some distance away. It was the people from the *Fulda* who had come to fetch the hunters back and had run along-side the landing place with their boat. The day in the mountains was over.

They had to help Bjørn up from the bench. On top of his exhaustion, the brandy had given him a new dizziness; he moved heavily though without any more noise than Joshua himself. Having man-aged to stand up, he did not seem to know what direction he should take. When the others had bid-den their hosts farewell, he was left standing, as if completely perplexed. He walked toward Joshua and held out his hand to say thanks for the day. "And thanks for the loan of the rifle," he said. Joshua's mouth and his beard twisted into a grin, a pleasant one.

Lahula had stepped back completely into the shadow and Bjørn looked about a bit before he saw her. He walked toward her as he had toward Joshua and took her hand in his, but he was unable to get away from her so quickly, for they stood for a time and looked at each other. He put both of his arms about her neck and pressed her face to his and gave her a kiss.

Then they heard the Finnish woman laugh with a laughter which came from a world different from their own, the kind of girl's laugh which is never heard except in mawkishness and wildness. Laugh she did, so that she gurgled, and in the middle of the laughter she returned the young man's kiss with a big smack.

Neither the man nor the wife of the house accompanied the guests farther than the door; from there the guests provided their own light down to the wharf and got their own baggage on board as they greeted the men in the boat. The cat had run along with them, and at the moment when the boat pushed off it landed in the boat with a large jump. They had to row back to put it ashore again and hold it off with an oar and they left it on the wharf meowing loudly, as it had done when they arrived.

The people on the ship asked the hunters jovially about the results of their hunt. "Well, did you get something?" "No," said Carsten and Carl, and their tone of voice put a stop to further inquiries.

"Well, did you get something, you with the sheath knife?" they asked Bjørn.

Bjørn drew a deep breath. "No," he said.

"No, the fact of the matter is," said Carsten, "as all reasonable people know, nothing happens here in the world. At every new opportunity, we imagine it is going to be the time something happens. But nothing happens."

"However," he added, "he got a kiss from the old woman."

"He got a kiss?" asked the captain, strangely moved.

"Yes, a kiss," said Carsten.

"Did he get a kiss from Lahula?" the captain asked again.

"Yes," said Carsten and laughed.

The captain went to the railing, looked at the land, and came back again.

It had taken the brandy a long time to have its effect on Bjørn. Now it had its full effect and he suddenly burst into tears like a child. The two others, on whom Lahula's brew had had an enlivening effect so that they in part had got over the disappointments of the day, were surprised and uncomfortable, smiled indulgently, and decided to help him to bed. Bjørn tore himself away from them with astonishing force. "No," he said, "no, I will not go down as long as one can see a light in there."

To this Carsten replied that it was really a melancholy light.

"Yes, melancholy," said Bjørn. "Yes, the saddest in the world. A light from a prison. And what sort of bunglers we were. What sort of a bungler was I, that I was not able to free her."

"Free her?" said Carsten.

"Yes, she must have expected that of me," continued Bjørn, still greatly moved. "I should have brought her along. She wanted to leave with us. She wanted to jump into the boat with us."

"No, that was the cat," they said.

"All right, then, the cat," said Bjørn. "You heard it yourselves," he said suddenly, and turned toward them. "The tomcat had eaten all the kittens; he did not want to have any other cat there on the peninsula."

"There they sit now," he said, and turned completely around, with his eyes to the land. "The strong man whom Lahula once had so aroused that he stepped forth with all his strength. We heard about it ourselves this morning: it was fourteen years ago when she came down to the village and he who had been half-asleep went up the mountain and shot his first bear. For she has such a voice, she knows such a song which can get all men to shoot bears. And to dance. And to save shipwrecked victims from a wreck, and now he has a wooden leg, now he cannot kill any more bears. And nobody else must do it. There he sits silently and guards the great witch who has become almost as silent as he, as if he had cut her vocal cords."

"Is it he who is guarding her?" said Carsten and laughed. "Could it be he who is jealous and not the witch?"

"No, it is not the witch," said Bjørn. "Jealous, that word scarcely is to be found in the witch's dictionary. She has the devil's own word that she is almighty. There he sits now and looks at her and concentrates his entire body into his eyes until he is no bigger than a thumb."

"He is no bigger than a thumb?" repeated Carsten as before.

"No, in reality he is no larger: he is an unhappy man," said Bjørn.

"Well, so perhaps she is big?"

"Big?" said Bjørn and thought for a moment. He again had control of his voice and was struggling to be collected and calm. "I will tell you, in my grandfather's storeroom there used to be many bats hanging under the ceiling. And they looked very small. But when they unfolded their wings, then they grew large. In other countries there are also very large bats. That is the way witches are. And there is nothing in the world so innocent as a witch."

The others asked him how he knew so much about witches.

"Well, I do," he said, "for, I shall tell you, things have gone downhill for my father's family. His great-grandfather was a clergyman and eager to prosecute witches and he once had a witch burned. And they told me," he added slowly, "that he made sure the witch's small children should be standing at her pyre so they should learn a lesson."

"Oh, so that is the way it was. Well, I thought," said Carsten, "she was very attentive when we said your name. She can scarcely harbor gentle feelings toward anybody in your family and it was not strange that she wanted to have you eaten by a bear."

"No, that is not the way it was," said Bjørn. "I must tell you that my mother's family has come up in the world and my mother's father was the best broom maker in Bergen. He made brooms that were known all over Norway. There were many old women among his customers."

"And now," cried Bjørn, "now she has no broom. I should have taken one along and given it to her."

The others had had enough of this.

"And nevertheless," said Bjørn suddenly, "nevertheless, the two of them in there are better off than other people. For the bear, the only bear of my life, they have it in there. They are the ones who have it."

"The bear you did not get?" said Carsten.

"Yes, that one," said Bjørn.

"Well, but the ballad," asked Carl, "Who is going to write it?"

"Well, that is just it," said Bjørn.

Second Meeting

Lord Byron was heading for Greece. His ship, the *Hercules*, rode at anchor in the harbor of Genoa. Twice, in the belief that he was shaking the dust of Italy off his feet for good, he had gone on board, and twice a fierce wind or a dead calm had made him turn ashore again. He had sent away his companions, he was alone in the empty Casa Saluzzo.

On the table before him was a bundle of accounts and bills concerning the Greek expedition. He felt as if those convolutions of his brain which had to deal with them were worn out and raw; endeavoring to give them a rest by emptying them of their contents, he turned his mind from one thing to another, and in the end settled down with animals which he had known in his life. He sat in the palatial Italian room in the company of dogs in England dead twenty years ago.

His old majordomo, who had remained in the house but had got out of his sumptuous livery in order to deal with the furniture to be sold or sent away, came in to tell him that there was a man in the hall who wanted to see him. Lord Byron did not want to see anyone, and with that message sent the old man away, but after a while he made a second appearance and informed his master that the visitor was still standing in that place in the hall from which a statue of Apollo had recently been moved.

"What does he look like there?" Lord Byron asked.

"Milord," the majordomo answered, "indeed he looks like yourself! So much so that if he were standing in the door at the end of this room, and you were walking down toward it, you would believe that I had put up your cheval glass there."

"It has never, Luigi," said Lord Byron, "been held to be a good omen to meet your double. Neither, to the best of my knowledge, has it ever been good luck to anybody to meet me. Still, since he has looked me up at this hour of my departure, he may have something to tell me, and I shall see him."

The visitor let in by the servant made a bow in the doorway and walked up the long room almost noiselessly in his large cloak to repeat the bow twice near the chair of the master of the house. He looked at Lord Byron with clear, keenly observing eyes, but did not speak.

"Does it give you satisfaction," Lord Byron asked after a short pause, "now to be able to tell people that you have seen me?"

"Your Excellency," said the stranger, "do you not call to mind that you and I have met before now?"

"You and I?" Lord Byron asked. "And where?"

"At Malta," said the man.

"That will be a long time ago," said Lord Byron.

"It is fourteen years ago," said the man, "in the sweet summer days and full-moon nights of Malta."

"If you be not a ruminant by nature," said the poet, "which I do not happen to be, the cud becomes an offensive thing: a belch, and bitter at that. Why must I be brought back fourteen years to a full-moon night of Malta?"

"Speak not so disparagingly, Milord," said the man, "of that sacred thing: a second meeting. On a full-moon night of Malta I had the honor and the good luck of saving Your Excellency's life."

"My life!" said Lord Byron. "What a thing to save. But I must have my mind somewhere today —in God's name let us go back to that long-past summer at Malta. And since the relation between you and me seems to be somewhat out of the usual, tell me your name and your role in life. Take a seat. When a man begins to talk about himself he generally wants his time."

The stranger did as he was bid and sat down with dignity and grace.

"My name," he said, "is Giuseppino Pizzuti. But the people of Italy, amongst whom I am well known, have given me the name of Pipistrello. By métier I am the director of a marionette theater.

"I am a native of Malta and have got many different kinds of blood in my veins. My grandmother held that hers was Arab and of the noblest quality, since she was descended from the Sultana Scheherazade, who sweetened the sultan's nights by her eyes and lips and by her tales. But in the course of the years a maiden of my blood let herself be seduced by a Norman chevalier, whose name may well have been Biron, so that it be to this love affair that I owe this honor and good luck of mine to be like Your Excellency in looks.

"My mother had wanted to become a nun, but her father married her off to a wealthy neighbor, and I was the last of her thirteen children, born to her late in life. I myself had wished to be a priest, but after my father's death I could not be spared from the farm work. Still the love of God was ever the chief idea of both my mother and myself. We kept our eyes on him, our chief occupation was the observation of his will. At times we found our task difficult, but we stuck to it."

"I am familiar with your position," said Lord Byron. "During the War of the Peninsula the crew of a small ship were taken prisoners by an old corsair, about whom they knew that his name was Lambro, that he was very mighty, almost, it was said, almighty, and that he sided with one belligerent or the other, only they did not know with which one. As this to them might be a matter of life or death, they set themselves to find out. 'Let us,' they said, 'on one day talk with great devotion of one section, sing its anthem and wear its colors, then on the next show the same feelings about the other party. By so doing, from the way in which we are rewarded or punished we shall in the end find out with whom old Lambro himself sides.' It is like that, Giuseppino, with us poor mortals on the small island of our earth. We shall have to experiment in order to find out with what party of the universe he sides whom we call Providence and hold to be all-powerful. It is an interesting undertaking, although I myself doubt it will ever result in a certainty. But do go on with your tale."

"You came to Malta," said Giuseppino, "on board the *Townshend*, a great gentleman of England, to whom, as I was told, I had some likeness in looks. Your valet in Malta became my friend, from him I heard about your wealth, your castle in your own country and the brilliant prospects of your future there. I felt that I had met one of the favorites of God my Father, so richly equipped, with good luck in every way, that you must certainly be the child whom he sets on his knee. It was up to other people, and to me who was like you, to see that his plan with you was carried out in every way. I took trouble to be near you, although maybe you did never see me. And when I learned that your life was in danger, I told myself: this must not be, our Father might take it to heart. Better that I should die, whom he has somehow cast in the same form, but for whom obviously he has no special predilection."

"That," said Lord Byron, "was nobly thought, and far from the spirit in which I myself have nursed a grievance. For this feeling alone, Pipistrello, I should be in your debt. But how could it come to be tested? Why did you hold my life to be in danger?"

"It came about in this way, Milord," said Pipistrello. "From where I herded our goats on the mountain I had come to know three brothers, proud and vindictive people, who had taken refuge there because in the past they had committed grave breaches of the law. They had got a sister younger than they who was named Marianna, a pretty girl, who at times stayed with their mother in the village and at times came out to bring them provisions and news. I do not know, Milord, if you will remember setting eyes on this maiden and making arrangements with her that you should find her one night out in the forest."

"Now that you speak about it," said Lord Byron, "I seem to remember a gentle child with big black eyes, whom once or twice I met near the harbor of Valetta."

"I learned about the matter through your valet," said the director of the marionette theater, "and made up my mind that it must not be, since the young maiden's brothers might well either cut your throat or press your people for a big ransom. I resolved to go in your place. I made your valet give you a message that the girl could not come till a later day, and from him I borrowed your clothes and the horse on which you had gone about in the neighborhood. Few people, I think, while fixed upon carrying out the will of God, have got only that in mind, and I shall not deny that as I rode out to your rendezvous, together with my submission to this divine will I also in my heart held some pride and delight in being, even with my life in danger, for a few hours Lord Byron himself.

"I fell into the hands of the three brothers all right, but the young sister gave me away by screaming out that I was not the great English nobleman but just Giuseppino of their own village. At that one of them wanted to kill me, but the others laughed and decided to claim a modest ransom from you, at what you might think the life of your impersonator might be worth. Do you remember, Your Excellency, such a claim being presented to you?"

"It seems to me now that I do so," said Lord Byron, "and that I had the ransom paid through my servant to robbers in the mountains. But do enlighten me now as to whether you did find out through this adventure and by the way in which you were rewarded or punished for it, on what side our almighty old Lambro stands, and what be his character and his tastes."

"It is I, Milord Byron," said Pipistrello, "who have got to be enlightened. It is for this purpose that I have come here tonight. What indeed did I save when I saved your life?"

"Up till now," said Lord Byron, "you have presented me with fourteen years, whether that is to be taken as a blessing or a curse. Say that, if I had died at Malta in the comparative innocence of my youth, I should have gone to Paradise, while now, owing to my behavior in these fourteen years, I shall go to the other place, will you feel any responsibility toward me? In any case you have presented me today with a fine story, of which the spirit of your ancestral grandmother may approve."

Pipistrello shook his head. "Nay, she will not approve of it yet," he said, "but she will do so before I leave you. And that is the reason why I have come back. After that, you and I shall not meet again."

"Let me offer you a glass of wine," said Lord Byron.

"But now when I think the matter over," he went on when they had drunk together, "I may be said to have bought yours. That sovereign which your friends the bandits accepted from me, what did it buy?"

"My friends the bandits," said Pipistrello, "laughingly made me a present of that sovereign of yours. With that I started my marionette theater, which has since flourished, has supported my mother and me, and has made me famous in Italy. If you had come to see my theater, you would have found out there what you had bought, for everything that has happened to me since I have turned into a story. That has been my life.

"For I shall tell you," he went on, "in accepting my life then, and the sovereign, I forfeited my claim to a real human life. The harmony of it from then on was the harmony of the story. Certainly it is a great happiness to be able to turn the things which happen to you into stories. It is perhaps the one perfect happiness that a human being will find in life. But it is at the same time, inexplicably to the uninitiated, a loss, a curse even. What I have gained through these fourteen years is then a knowledge of the story and everything concerning it.

"But tell you me, Your Honor," said Pipistrello, "what I came here to learn. When I saved your life, what did I save?"

"What," Lord Byron repeated slowly, "when you saved my life, my dear Bat, did you save? Fourteen years, you told me just a short while ago."

"I may see fourteen bottles of wine on a shelf," said Giuseppino, "and still ask the owner of the cellar what he has got there."

"You will know something about my fourteen years already," said Lord Byron. "For your humble servant has been a good deal more talked about than he deserved, or than was to his liking. There has been really fine wine in some of my bottles, poison in some and wormword in a few, tears in one. Have you come to make an inventory of the cellar of my experience? I shall give it to you. Some really honest good wine drunk down in the company of not too honest friends—kisses, talks and discussions, base slander, and all too cheap triumphs. Gray hair on my head, sad distrust of man, and compassion with womankind. With what more can I oblige you?"

"I have indeed come to make an inventory," said Giuseppino, "to round off your stock and collect it into a unity—as you say, a cellar. I am going to turn it into a story. That is what a second meeting does. It is the story's touchstone, the last curve of the parenthesis, which joins up with the first curve and makes a unity of its contents."

"There are few persons," said Lord Byron, "whom I long to meet a second time, a good deal more of whom I think with fear and trembling, and others that I should much dislike to see again. I did not realize that it was you who were to make a tale of me."

"You know," said Pipistrello, "the story of Ali Baba, a fine story, the very model and precept of a tale. I shall repeat it to you in case you have forgotten it.

"Ali Baba, who is just a plain innocent man of Baghdad, unaware that his name is going to be the title of a tale, comes out in the forest with his small donkey in all innocence to cut wood there, and with no idea of a story. The forty thieves and their captain there come upon him without seeing him or knowing of him. Ali would much like to prevent the meeting and makes as little of it as possible, for he chases his donkey into the thicket and himself climbs a tall tree, so that the robbers see him not. When now the story is all collected and ready to be finished, the forty thieves and their captain come to Ali's house. They do not want to be seen, the forty robbers are hidden each in his sack. But between this first and second meeting the story lies, and if the second meeting had not been there, there would have been no story. I have turned the tale of Ali Baba into a very perfect play.

"There is," he went on, "another story of a second meeting, which I should much like to make into a play. But it is a very great story, Your Honour, and up till now my courage has failed me. I shall picture it to you today as I see it myself.

"You will have read about the first Christian congregation of Jerusalem, and how they were all staying together in peace and brotherly love, with the Blessed Virgin as a mother to them all. You will have read further about the day of Pentecost, when they were all assembled, and there came from Heaven a sound as of a rushing mighty wind, which filled the house—for which wind one might very well have the machine in the wings—together with tongues as of fire which sat upon each of the apostles, and for which one would have to make special arrangements in the lighting system. Here each of the apostles begins to speak with other tongues, as the spirit gave them utterance, and men of every nation dwelling in Jerusalem came together, all my puppets in a crowd, and are confounded because every man hears them speak in his own language. Parthians and Medes, Cretans and Arabians are all amazed and in doubt, crying to one another, 'What meaneth this?'

"There twelve strong men, Milord, who are about to alter the whole world, under the might of the Spirit tumble to their knees on the floor, and some of them even beat their brows against its stone. One slim and graceful figure only, Milord, in this hour of the hurricane remains serene. The Virgin stands unmoving, her face turned upwards, her hands crossed upon her breast. As you will know from the paintings, upon Good Friday all blood had sunk from her face. Now once more it mounts to her cheeks in one sweet roseate wave, and she again looks like a maiden of fifteen. In a low voice

—and for this I shall have to use my loveliest so-
prano—she cries out: 'Oh, is it you, sir? After these
thirty-four years, is it you?'

"Between the distant first meeting of those two
and the present meeting lies the story."

"I see," said Lord Byron. "It might make a fine
scene—so, after thirty-four years you've come back,
the same divine wind once swept o'er my threshold
—a great scene, Pipistrello."

"Milord," said Pipistrello, "what applause should
I not, upon it, get from my audience!"

"But," said Lord Byron, "what story have you
come here today to make?"

"It is like this," said the other. "You have been
to me the cause of many speculations. For the Lord
our Father has given you all: birth, wealth, great
beauty—forgive me saying so, who have been told
that I am like you—genius, fame. And what have
these fourteen years given you?"

"What have they given me?" Lord Byron repeated slowly.

"A series," said Giuseppino, "of small self-in-
flicted defeats, each of which will make the observer wonder. You could choose freely between
all the women of England. How did it come that
you chose a mistress without sweetness? Why did
your marriage fail in every way? Any man would
have been proud to be your friend, but you have
today no one for whose company you really long.
It is high time for our second meeting."

"And how," said Lord Byron, "are you going to
make one story of all this?"

"I have felt it in my own bones, which are like
yours," said Pipistrello. "What you need now to
round off all these sad details of fourteen years,

is one great and deadly defeat, brought on by no fault of your own. That is going to make a unity of the disintegrating elements."

Lord Byron was beginning to tire of the talk of his visitor and to want to go back to his dogs.

"It is rare, I think," he said, "that the birds of ill omen flap their wings straight in your face. Tyrants might have had you hanged for your audacity. I at least might have you thrown out of my house."

"Do not take such a dark view of my prophecy, Milord," said Pipistrello. "You will in the future have compensations for the defeat."

"I know," said Lord Byron. "You are going to tell me that in a hundred years the readers of the whole world will have my books standing on their shelves to take them down with reverence and delight. I have had it said to me before."

"But wrongly said, Milord, wrongly said," said Pipistrello. "In a hundred years your works will be read much less than today. They will collect dust on the shelves."

"I do not much mind," said Lord Byron.

"But one book," said Pipistrello, "will be rewritten and reread, and will each year in a new edition be set upon the shelf."

"Which book is that?" Lord Byron asked.

"*The Life of Lord Byron*," said Pipistrello.